A Haunt for Jackals

Jackals

Land of Exile Book 2

J. L. Odom

Azimuth

Cover Art by Jeremy Adams

Cover Design by Rafael Andres

Map by Rhys Davies

ISBN: 979-8-9900244-3-4 (Paperback)

ISBN: 979-8-9900244-4-1 (Hardcover)

ISBN: 979-8-9900244-5-8 (ebook)

To Laura. Without you this book could not be what it is. The pages herein are suffused with your friendship and your wisdom and your kindness.

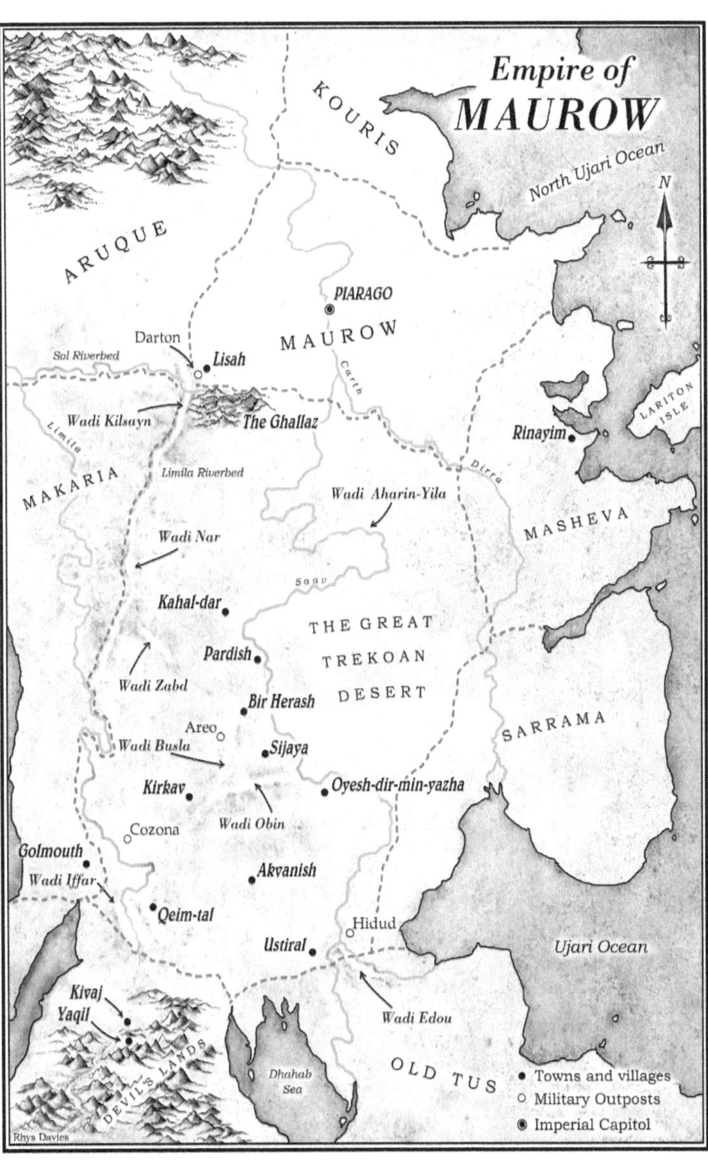

Empire of
MAUROW
KOURIS
North Ujari Ocean
N
ARUQUE
PIARAGO
MAUROW
Darton
Sol Riverbed
Lisah
Carth
LARITON ISLE
Wadi Kilsayn
The Ghallaz
Rinayim
Limila
Dirra
MAKARIA
Limila Riverbed
Wadi Aharin-Yila
MASHEVA
Wadi Nar
Saav
Kahal-dar
THE GREAT
Pardish
TREKOAN
Wadi Zabd
Bir Herash
DESERT
Areo
SARRAMA
Wadi Busla
Sijaya
Kirkav
Oyesh-dir-min-yazha
Cozona
Wadi Obin
Golmouth
Akvanish
Wadi Iffar
Qeim-tal
Hidud
Ustiral
Ujari Ocean
Kivaj
Yaqil
Wadi Edou
DEVIL'S LANDS
Dhahab Sea
OLD TUS
Rhys Davies
Towns and villages
Military Outposts
Imperial Capitol

1

The terror of that day always came to him unbidden. Then the heat and color would seep in, darkening his mind sudden and storm-like.

He had barely been five years old, so the memories were scattershot, with hazy gaps between images.

First, he remembered his raspy breaths and aching legs. Then he could feel the wind and dust, twisting around him, pushing him along, coating his mouth, filling his nostrils. As the dust rose higher and thicker, and the sun began to set, the whole day—the whole world—turned the deep red of a glowing ember. He felt for all the world like he was suffocating inside a great clay oven, its mouth sealed. No way out.

He was warned not to speak a word in his native tongue. Only Makarish.

Somehow they found a lowland village, and received hospitality in their tents. Somehow it was discovered that his mother, Birai, had deceived their father about when the child in her womb was to be born. "Many weeks yet," she had said, but she had been in labor for hours. A midwife was found, a birthing tent secured, and Aadin's little sister Sereya settled to sleep. Aadin, for some reason, remained with his mother.

He remembered none of that. It was later told to him.

What he did recall was the soothing voice of the young midwife, saying soft words he couldn't understand in Shayali Trekoan. He remembered lamplight and warmth. Perhaps his mother screamed in pain, perhaps she did not. He felt strangely secure.

But more stark and clear and irrefutable than any of that, he remembered the ear-splitting CRACK in the air, like a stone shattered. Then came a rumble Aadin felt deep in his chest. He thought the Gods had come to battle. He thought the world was breaking to pieces; dry lightning was a very rare omen, even in the lowlands, and a very bad one.

"Here is your daughter!" the young midwife sang out in mangled Makarish, while the rumble lingered. "Your daughter. Praise God, your daughter!"

Aadin knew all that followed only from what his mother and father told him. He knew that Birai was exhausted and needed much rest. He knew that the midwife worked quickly and deftly to tend to both mother and infant. He knew the child was rubbed over with salt and spoken over with prayers. Those accursed prayers. Then braided, scarlet threads of the desert god's blessing were tied onto the child's wrist. That damning blessing.

He knew also that the midwife was killed for her mistake not two days later. He knew that the child had been born under too many omens, in foreign tents, under an enemy god, and should have been killed that day. For its own sake. For everyone's sake.

But before he knew any such thing, it so happened that the little girl was handed to him straight from the womb, not yet washed of blood and viscera and white resin. Strong and wakeful with a dark, wet shock of hair.

It is not often one holds a curse in their arms, smiles at it, and touches its ear in a furtive burst of affection.

A hand reached out to grasp his shoulder, but Azetla sat up before it touched him. The watchman's arm withdrew into a casual field salute as he turned and left the tent. It was strange how the body knew when it was supposed to rise. And how conscientious to always do so several minutes too early. Azetla could hear the steady breaths of the other sleepers. Beyond that, warm silence.

These short, star-flecked minutes before daybreak had become so precious to him. He learned early on that the only way to make the slog of the days tolerable was to make them just that much longer. Breathe in silence. Say prayers in solitude. Read little scraps of the poets and prophets by firelight.

Well, not read *exactly*. The two partial scrolls of holy writ came as a gift from Rokh Imal of Saqiran. They were inked in Mashevi script, but the words were an old, formal dialect of East Trekoan. Azetla could understand only a little of it. If Tzal came in the early hour—that was an unpredictable matter—he would read, fumbling through unfamiliar words, and she would translate for him. He learned some Trekoan that way, though she extracted a heavy price in Mashevi from him each time. She picked up every word he laid down, fiddled with it till she was certain she had it right, and pocketed it.

But Tzal did not come by the watch fire this morning and it was just as well. He was accustomed to her presence, but there was no reason he ought to be glad of it. He read over a passage that Tzal had already translated for him, a traditional chiastic song of praise and lament. It was one he had memorized when he was a small boy, so he could mouth the Mashevi words while his eyes passed over the Trekoan ones, using the few words he recognized as checkpoints. And he could hear his mother's voice, singing it over each newborn child. Singing it in the West Mashevi dialect of her childhood, where the blood of both tongues had mingled and touched and made exchanges. Surely she had sung it over him too.

But the light began to rise. The day would turn harsh, burning, and wind-whipped. He folded soft thoughts and solitude away, tucked safely under a firm, careful, curated demeanor.

Even after three arduous months at Areo outpost, he was no more certain of being allowed to live than he had been the day he arrived. Six thousand men were under his charge, most of whom were loath to answer to him. In fact, some of them found a marvelous camaraderie in their hatred. And above him stood two Maurowan colonels who dangled an Imperial execution order over his head at the slightest provocation, but who had precious little to say when their officers called Azetla a "filthy jackal" to his face.

"Hate him if you must," Colonel Everson would say quietly to his senior officers. "But do as he says."

They gave him little more than that to rule by.

They wanted to squeeze such blood from this stone. They wanted organization and training and respect. They wanted a shining symbol. Something to stand still and look mighty behind them while they enacted a silk-soft coup.

Well Azetla was going to hand them the real thing. A sword where they expected a training stick, and they would scarcely know what to do with it.

That, too, was just as well.

Azetla took his breakfast with the officers of Areo. They did not like it when he did this, so he only did it one or two mornings of the week, hoping to outlast their irritation. It seemed important to do it today, especially. Their contempt for his presence was palpable and—as yet—not much diminished. He knew what it was like to feel forced to behave just so when a commander strode through the room with a critical eye. Jokes ceased. Posture stiffened. Words were guarded.

His aim was to cultivate the opposite effect, as Captain Hodge had done. Captain Hodge used to go to the lower fires some nights and eat with the young, common men. He would tease Dersha about the girl he would not stop talking about, and he would speak with Baze about the craftsmanship of his knife. If ever the men grew quiet and nervous, he calmed and warmed them. He had stories. He had ballads. And they adored his every word.

But even if Azetla were not Mashevi, and his shoulder not empty of rank, he had none of the natural ways about him that might draw the officers out of their hatred. He did not have the loud, easy humor—"barely any humor at all," Joseph often chided. He could never be so warm and casual as Hodge had been. He didn't have that kind of freedom. That kind of surety.

Cold and condescending.

How many times had Joseph used those words?

And how could he overcome them?

He knew all the soldiers' names and clans, as well as those of their most immediate subordinates. He had asked about their families and battle experience. He knew of their long-standing shoulder injuries, their sensitive digestion, which ones could read and which ones could not. He watched them all closely during training and knew who would make good on their rank and who certainly would not.

Some grew less monosyllabic. A few warmed. It took courage too, for it displeased their peers.

But the barrier remained. He was Mashevi.

He asked them how they slept.

"Well."

He asked them if they were ready.

"Yes."

He encouraged them to ask him questions about today. For their own sakes. But only three did, and the heavy atmosphere of social pressure kept them from following up on those questions. The good officers in the Black Wren always asked Azetla and Captain Hodge questions freely. But then, Captain Hodge had been easy to approach and Azetla had been under that comfortable shadow, approachable by proxy.

He finished his coffee quietly and left the officers' mess.

The heavy din of preparation faded as Azetla jogged up the steep stone staircase. The steps coiled round and round and he had to bend his head to keep it from scraping the rough rock above. The last turning brought him out onto the rampart walkway, fifty feet above the ground. He was struck in the face with fierce wind and hot light. Captain Istamo, both colonels, and several other officers awaited him.

"I don't like the look of this," Lord Colonel Verris said as he peered over the stone and saw the long fall. "I've never seen the new regiments do this sort of thing."

"Forgive me, my lord, but when was the last time a Maurowan regiment took an enemy fortress?"

They ought to know the answer. It was a point of Maurowan pride.

"It was the final bastion of North Culliton," Lord Colonel Everson offered with a smile. "Seventy-four years ago. Makes a pretty story."

"Certainly," Azetla said. "When only nineteen men are left out of four thousand, and they take the graveyard and rubble that was once Ulghan-dyr. Then they rule mightily over the three dozen people—mostly children—who survived the slaughter. Very pretty. The commander was lauded and rewarded, his name etched in gold. And he killed himself a year later."

Lord Verris and Captain Istamo looked at Azetla with muted horror, though it seemed impossible they did not know that part of the story. The footnote that, in Azetla's opinion, changed the whole tale.

"You cannot expect to use a muscle you have never trained. And while the Black Wren has never taken a fortress like Ulghan-dyr, we did take back the towers of Qameda when the tribes overran them in protest. And the Black Wren secured the citadel of Suul during the last uprising."

"Come now, Suul was a mite before your time," Lord Everson said with a tisk.

"Nearly. I was fifteen, new to the battalion. I did not acquit myself well. But I was there. And so were nearly half of the men still in the Black Wren. Instead of chafing and worrying, my lords, just watch," Azetla said. "Be displeased after. Not before."

He briefed them on what his soldiers would do—or fail to do—and explained to them their own assignments. He was careful not to word it so that it seemed he was giving orders. But he was. They grew ever more tense as he spoke. Lord Verris kept touching the hilt of his sword, pulsing his grip over it, and Everson's jocular manner flickered.

Azetla bowed in departure with one last glance at Captain Istamo.

"Don't forget to tally the dead. Every single one."

He felt their silence at his back as he walked away, and he could not deny that it gave him some grim satisfaction.

The Sahr stood in the shaded corner where he turned, arms crossed.

"What?" Azetla said with a slight shrug.

"Nothing. Just curious how you would go about it."

"You said you thought it would be more effective to alarm them than to reason with them. I did both."

Tzal raised an eyebrow. "Right. Anyhow, they're ready for you at the north gate. I can stay here and interpret it for them, if you like."

Azetla hesitated. She could paint the picture with a deft hand, there was no question about that. They would see what she told them to see, feel what she told them to feel. But who knew what angle she would cut, what *she* wished to be understood, what benefit she took from it all.

It would work, though.

He nodded and walked past her, taking the stairs at a fast clip, shaking off the faint concern that ran through his mind. He would only meet the same old questions and they would only have either the same old answers, or none at all. This was the pattern he had allowed to form. A choice he had made and continued to make. The Sahr would offer some advice or thought or useful action, and leave it to him with disinterest. Azetla would stand back, scrutinize, hesitate—and that in an increasingly perfunctory way—then, often as not, pick up that which she had set down and use it.

The Sahr laid low the first few weeks at Areo. Azetla had thought it was because Colonel Everson meant to take custody of her; apparently she had often been his tool on loan from Rokh Imal. But Colonel Everson denied any responsibility.

"The Shihrayan? You intend *me* to throw on the leash?" Everson had said when Azetla asked what was to be done with her. He laughed. "No, no, no. That devil was never quite at heel even when I did have charge of her. She's the sort of animal that will never break the rope, but might drag you with it. You understand."

Colonel Everson's tone and knowing smiles—as if Azetla was being let in on some derisive joke—grated against the nerves.

"In any case, Mashevi, you're best off not trying too hard. Rokh Imal used a heavy hand, and I don't know that it served him well in the end. If a sufficiently intriguing task is left to her by the wayside, you might draw her in a given direction. She can't be fooled, exactly, but she sometimes can be baited."

Colonel Everson always spoke of Tzal like this, as though she was a horse he broke, or a game he mastered. Azetla had his doubts about that. But he listened to the Colonel with an impassive face and gave calm, neutral responses.

In the end, her silence and inactivity proved to be mere convalescence; six weeks of captivity, wounds, prison rations, and poor conditions had taken their toll. When she finally came to the training fields—quiet, observant, keeping to the edges—Azetla realized he had never once seen her hale. His first clear sight of her had been as a limp body, ground into the dust, bleeding under his knife.

He didn't for one moment imagine Tzal was on his "side" because he didn't think she cared about sides, or remained with them long. And he didn't think she helped him out of some sense of generosity, but rather out of a survival instinct; those who wished her dead had to face the barrier that his use of her provided. Most of his men still waited in hopes that he would give the word, and they could slit her throat.

As for why she was willing to remain at Areo at all...he had no clear answer for that. He had only suspicions. Troubling ones which helped him none at all.

Azetla did not justify himself. He felt less guilt than he probably should. And he had no plan to alter course. He would suffer the threat, hold it carefully, and reap the consequences. The Sahr was not exactly the greatest risk he was taking just now.

⚔

Tzal looked straight down to the ground to grasp at the dizzying effect of the drop. No such luck. The sturdy stone, chest-high, blunted the sensation. Out on the mesas, you could stand on a jut of rock and know with all your blood that a sudden rush of wind could take you. It was a dreadful and livening feeling. Tzal often sought it as she suspected men sought drunkenness or whorehouses; staggering into a short-lived, increasingly unsatisfactory experience in an effort to solve a problem that would never thus be solved.

She had attacked a battalion she could not possibly defeat for the same reason. She provoked Gods against whom she could never

9

prevail, Gods who would never listen. She kept doing it, even though she knew it was useless.

Nothing solved. Nothing known. Nothing gained. She felt as though, despite being renounced by every hand that had gripped her, and despite each choice being entirely her own, she had been yanked in the mouth by a bit, and made to return by the way she came.

A shadow fell across her shoulder.

"I haven't come up here since that time you goaded me into sitting on the wall. Dared me to dangle my legs over," Rahummi Bin-Deghan said. "I was sure I was going to die."

"I'd forgotten about that." She had not forgotten about it. "But I didn't goad you—"

"*Yes*, you did—"

"I just climbed up. Youth and pride did the rest. Why are you up here now?"

"Uncle Imal is watching from the wadi's edge, but he wanted me to describe it from this vantage point. I'll stay out of the way."

Rahummi kept away from the lip of the wall. Tzal had known him since he stood just below her height, until he grew well past it, and she had never been able to rid him of his fear of high places. She'd probably made it worse, coaxing him up to her favorite haunts against his will.

To a Shihrayan, heights were home.

"Stand over there," she said quietly, tilting her head toward the alcove. "Then you can see without getting too close."

The Maurowan officers began to mutter as they saw the dark sea of soldiers on the ground heave like a wave and rise toward Areo. Tzal leaned her shoulder against the stone, glancing back and forth between the thunder of men below and the expressions of the men on the wall. She would wait for the worry and confusion. People tended to listen to her better when they felt that she was being forced to answer, rather than volunteering the information freely.

Rahummi did not ask questions. But as the roar came closer and closer, he grew tight-lipped and wide-eyed. He inched closer to the stone edge, in spite of himself.

Amid the onslaught, flag-signals waved between companies. The response to the flags was not as fast as it should be—Tzal said nothing about that—and the observers did not seem to understand the shift in movement right away, but were merely confused. Colonel Everson had a deeply knitted brow as he struggled to comprehend what he saw; now the watchtowers were being swarmed. He glanced at Tzal.

"To prevent us from sending for help?" he said.

Tzal nodded. "If the assault fails—"

"Then a siege."

Everson stared off in thought for half a moment, but was quick to correct himself. He sniffed, smiled, and brushed the silk on his shoulder. He did his best to watch with amusement and indifference after that, but it was for the benefit of the other lords, not Tzal.

The watchtowers were taken very quickly, or so it felt.

Azetla's army was pitching at the walls soon after.

The siege ladders landed with deep thuds you could feel inside your skin. The Maurowan high-bloods flinched and stepped back. Real, lusty shouts from soldiers' throats rose up to the rampart. They were caught up in the moment. Playing the part.

The assault spoke for itself.

She had watched Azetla drill this and map it with his men over and over and over, so she knew what was supposed to happen. But at key points, she translated for the Maurowan officers, adding a few words to draw the high-bloods' attention to something they did not know enough to see. She lured them toward the crucial observations, but refrained from saying them out loud. It worked better that way.

They must see their present vulnerability. Then, they must see who it was that would make them strong. They must see the wide, deep river of all they did not understand because most of them had purchased or were gifted their commissions, and had never fought like this. Some had never fought at all. Everson, in particular, needed to see the changes wrought in his men; they may hate Azetla, but they had learned from him.

So had she. By experience, she knew trap, ambush, information, silence, deception, skirmish. But Azetla knew the tactics and maneuvers of open warfare—all that bled into it, all that bled out of it. This was new to her. She listened to everything he said. Like his Mashevi language, she could usually turn his words over in her mouth till they sounded as if they had always been hers, as if she had always known what he knew.

The assault was now well-advanced; the rampart soldiers were called upon to defend. Tzal spoke quickly then—back and forth between Maurowan and Trekoan—narrating their bloodshed in detail, omitting only that which she herself did not understand.

A kill was counted by a tap on the shoulder, given by Captain Istamo, Tzal, or one of the observers down below. At first the Areo soldiers felt the strength and security of the defensive position. They "killed" dozens and dozens of their comrades as they climbed. They "toppled" two of the Sojj Pine ladders, which were marked with red banners so they could no longer be used.

But the tide turned. The wall was overwhelmed.

Tzal began to tap the defenders on the rampart.

Dead.

Dead.

She tapped Rahummi. "Bystanders will get killed too, you know. Dead."

"What about you?" Rahummi said wryly.

"I'm not a defender. I'm an infiltrator," she said with a smile.

Another tap. Dead.

She touched Colonel Verris' shoulder.

A young captain's.

Colonel Everson gave a strange smirk as Tzal lifted her hand toward him.

"Well I wouldn't be all the way up here in real life, would I?"

"No," Tzal said. "But from now it's only a matter of time. They would have you."

"I think it's amusing how you pretend to know about all these things, little devil."

She shrugged, enjoying Everson's irritation.

"I'm only telling you what I see." She rapped his shoulder with her knuckle. "*Dead*. Tally it, Captain."

The bell rang out, as if struck with a wild, desperate hand. The gate watch was defeated.

The game was over.

Azetla had taken Areo.

2

Joseph hurried through the lower camp toward Azetla's headquarters, head low, a bit of cloth tied firmly over his nose and mouth. The dust grew thicker, and the wind more gutting by the minute. It was a miracle they had finished the exercise at all; within an hour the air all around was pinkish haze. The further the sun sank, the more the sky above looked like hellfire. The Sahr devil called such weather "red-days," when nearly all living and doing and being halted until the wind calmed and the dust could find its way back to the earth.

Joseph dodged into the mess tent and, almost instantly, he heard the words dart past his ear. Words he never would have been allowed to hear if not for the cloth covering his face.

"I swear by Serivash, I will slit that jackal's throat the first chance I get."

"Bloody son-of-a-whore has no right to be in this position. No right to put us on a wall, pretend to slaughter us by these arbitrary rules, as if it were his own personal tourney."

Joseph paused and glanced furtively to the side. The two speakers were sitting on the ground, close enough that he could have kicked them. A Corporal and a Tackman. Both North Maurowan by the sound of it. Neither took notice of Joseph, for the mess tent was over-crowded with soldiers seeking shelter from the choking dust, and they didn't seem to realize how loudly they spoke. The tone of voice was casual and calm. Like those who claim they would win a race they are absolutely sure they will never, ever have to run.

"I can't see that the Colonel lets this go on much longer. Too much of a scandal. An insult."

The Tackman frowned and muttered, "Colonel's odd about things sometimes."

The Corporal shook his head. "In the beginning or middle, maybe he is, but never in the end. He's practical, underneath it all. Does what makes sense. He'll have that jackal up by a rope when the time comes. We'll go back to how it was."

Again, the Tackman seemed uneasy. "I dunno, Pertus. Lieutenant Bulman says he likes the way the jackal does the books. And the drills."

Joseph smiled as other soldiers shouldered their way around him. That was something. *Everyone* liked Bulman. One good, honest word heard out in the wild outweighed a hundred idle "I'll-kill-that-jackal-I-will!" threats.

Oh, he really shouldn't have done it, but Joseph was feeling too spry and vengeful. He turned and crouched till he was at their level. He pulled the cloth from his face to show them a smile as wide as the day is long.

"A good fight today, ah boys?" he said.

They both went stiff as stone. Joseph smiled on, giving the Corporal a playful jab in the shoulder. Good and hard.

"Cheer up! The Commander is leading your skirmish drills next week, and you'll be able to try for victory again...Ah, it's tough to win if you insist on taking blood from your own side, though. Let me know how it goes, I'll be very interested!"

He stood and gave them a nod.

By Serivash, that felt good. He left the mess tent with a cool gait, bracing again for the wind, but noticing it less now.

Azetla *never* let them retaliate. He had far stricter rules for the Black Wren than for anyone else; no brawls, no taunts, no revenge, and *no* harassing the Areo soldiers on his behalf. There were, of course, strict punishments for direct insubordination, or any improper thing done to his face. But nothing—he was so bloody insistent on this—*nothing* for what was said behind his back. The Black Wren chafed under the imposition.

So Joseph startled them a little. If some outsiders had talked about Captain Hodge the way these men so thoughtlessly spoke about Azetla, there would have been blood soaking the ground.

Joseph wanted to shout in Azetla's face, knock some sense into him with a fist.

No other officer would tolerate this!

But it was no use. He did have to tolerate it. And more. He'd always had to deal with a whip at the neck, or spurs digging in the ribs.

And yet. Somehow he always ended up with the reins in his own hands, damned jackal.

Joseph finally reached what was called Azetla's "headquarters"—two small rooms on the side of the field storage house. Much like the mess tent, the thin doors and heavy canvas windows could not really keep the dust out, and the room looked strange and smoky by the light of a pit-fire and two lamps.

Azetla was kneeling next to the rectangular clay flat that lay in the center of the small room. He had a large map rolled out across the flat, with stone weights holding it down. He acknowledged Joseph with a glance, but his eyes turned quickly back to the map and fixed on it. The parchment was an enormous one, adjusted so that central Trekoa was featured under the rings of lamplight, with a few hand-width's hanging off the far edge.

"It could have been a lot worse," Joseph said cheerfully.

"True," Azetla said.

"Lieutenant Bulman may be coming around."

Azetla raised his eyebrows slightly, but did not look up from the map.

"That *would* make a difference," he said. "The notes?"

Joseph handed Azetla his morning's work. Assessments of all the upper and middle officers who had been assigned to him during the exercise. Azetla held the parchment in his hand a few moments before he finally tore his attention away from the dotted villages and river lines of Trekoa.

"I wouldn't say any of them did a *brilliant* job—and I didn't expect them to—but the Juniper battalion Captain took initiative, used signals, made sensible assessments. His men were the most responsive too." Joseph sighed. "There's no way around it."

The Juniper commander, Captain Ishelor, was proving one of the best leaders at Areo, and was even more of a lynchpin than junior lieutenants like Bulman or Mavoz. Ishelor was an experienced, genial, sharp-witted officer, whose wife and children resided at Areo with him. He had been at Areo for five years, and hailed from a high-blood family of both Kourisad and Maurowan background. Ishelor was the sort of man that Joseph usually liked and befriended. His men loved him.

And Ishelor *despised* Azetla. Even in obedience to orders, that contempt was palpable. And infectious.

Azetla rubbed his hand across his face and turned back to the map again. "I don't know what to do about him."

Joseph sat down against the wall, feeling similar frustration, and wondering why Azetla—commander of five thousand eight hundred and ninety-three men—could not have a damned sheepskin rug or field chair in his dusty, barren little room.

"I don't know, Azetla. You need to give them a bawdy joke every now and then. Pretend to laugh with them about their exploits. Utilize some workaday vulgarisms," Joseph said.

"Oh, you think that would do the trick, do you?" Azetla said irritably.

"No. But I'd enjoy it plenty."

The door opened suddenly and the cloth hanging billowed inward. The Sahr devil stepped in, clapped some dust off itself, and uncovered its mouth. Joseph inadvertently curled his fingers into fists against his knees, and his smile pinched down to a taut line.

"What do *you* want?"

The Sahr gave him an inscrutable look, holding him with it for longer than liked, then turned to Azetla, handing him two short vellum coils.

"These maps are smaller and less detailed." It knelt down. "This is the best one, actually. And it's not very good."

The Sahr touched the map gently with the tips of two fingers and clicked its tongue as if in reproach. "It has the larger towns and the old roads, but none of the tribal routes, almost no indication of terrain, and no *wells*."

Azetla grabbed his satchel, pulled out his ledger, some ink, a reed pen, and a bit of charcoal.

"Go ahead," he said quietly, sliding the ledger to Joseph and gesturing with the charcoal.

The Sahr spoke the land.

Azetla drew it.

Begrudgingly, Joseph wrote it.

He held his tongue as the map took shape, transforming from confused sketch to meticulous guide. Joseph detailed in his ledger all that the map could not contain: alliances, water feuds, grudges, and the contested boundaries that made up the whole delicate edifice that was Trekoa. The Sahr seemed to enjoy excoriating the Maurowan-made maps: "that valley is a lie...that hilltop is not here but there...that well has run dry. This is the better path. That is a sharp drop to a canyon that cannot be seen until almost the moment your feet reach the edge."

It was becoming harder for Joseph to protest. Since the day they arrived at Areo, he had set his shoulder hard against Azetla regarding the Sahr, loathing every instance of its usefulness. He did not care if it had slaughtered Qatlani attackers. Probably it would slaughter anything, if given the chance.

The argument remained, but Joseph had a sneaking suspicion that he was beginning to lose. Not just because of Azetla's quiet, infuriating obstinance, but because Joseph could no longer ignore how much marrow there was yet to be scraped out of this bone. Let it pay in knowledge what it owed in blood.

And then, when the knowledge was well used up, it could pay the blood too.

After nearly an hour's work, Azetla decided it was enough. Joseph left to receive the rest of the reports from Brody. Tzal spent some time after that silently perusing the smaller maps, but soon she tied a covering over her face and left without a word. As usual. She gave what she felt like giving, gleaned what she wanted, and the latter was probably far more than Azetla realized or intended.

He leaned back against the wall and allowed himself to be still. His eyes burned from dust and smoke and strain. His voice was half gone. Hands black with charcoal. Shoulders ached. He had worked too long, forgone the mess, and was hungry. The wind made a wild racket, beating the canvas, scraping across the stones. Azetla listened to it, but did not think about it.

For some time, he did not think about anything at all. The air was warm and oppressive. It lay heavy upon him and he dozed lightly. Not long, though, for the lamps and pit-fire were mostly unchanged in their flickers when he forced his eyes open again. But the sun had nearly set. Slowly, with a grunt more like a man of sixty than a man of twenty-eight, he came to his feet. He tried to rinse the charcoal off his hands but only managed to smear it around. He turned to put the maps in the proper order, but found that the Sahr had already done so, tying the most recent addition with twine and placing it—correctly—at the top left corner.

With a strange compulsion, he picked up the last map, adjusted it slightly, and put it back. He sighed at his own absurdity. Controlling insignificant things when the significant ones were beyond him.

It was curious, though. Tzal was never so considerate with anything as she was with maps. She could not read, but she pored over these the way Azetla pored over the histories, prophets, and prayers of his people. He sought comfort and firm ground. He had no idea what she sought. Flaws, it seemed. But he knew it was sometimes soothing simply to run your gaze over that which was even faintly familiar, or to say words that you had said a hundred times.

Resisting the temptation to read back through Joseph's notes, Azetla kicked down the fire and put away his ledgers. He recited the prayer to greet the week's day of rest, and hummed the song his mother always sang when the sun set, her face glowing yet blurred through the candlefire. Or was it blurred through his memory? He did forget things sometimes. But surely not that.

Some of the Areo officers had begun to realize that their patterns of work and rest were dictated by the Mashevi rhythm, though no word was spoken about it. It was hard for them to complain. The Maurowan calendar had many holidays, but no mandates, and the army was both stingy and arbitrary when it came to offering reprieves. Weekly rest was unheard of.

With how ruthlessly Azetla was pushing, pushing, pushing these men, they *needed* rest and regularity.

And he did as well.

He was about to put out the lamps when Sarrez came through the door, carrying with him a cloud of dust, and a mild spit of wind. It was starting to die down.

Sarrez smiled, visibly full of wine and cheer. Azetla nearly laughed to see him.

"Are you only just now back from the Colonel's?" he asked in surprise.

"Oh, Azetla, you've stirred them up like a poker in the fire. They were in awe of the exercise!"

Azetla's brow lowered. They weren't supposed to be in awe. The exercise was poorly executed to what it should have been. They were *supposed* to see how vulnerable Areo was. They were supposed to see the real dangers that their imaginary coup would provoke, and to see how desperately unprepared they were.

"Huh," he said under his breath.

Sarrez paid no mind, pulling something out of his satchel. "Take this. Joseph told me you wouldn't make it to mess." He handed Azetla a large, thin round of afi-bread filled with chuvia, garlic, onions, and roasted lamb, redolent of cloves, cumin, coriander, and cinnamon.

Azetla slowly took what was offered, always embarrassed in his gratitude toward Sarrez. "Thank you, Nimer."

Self-consciously, but dutifully, he washed his hands again. He said his prayer of thanks and for the day of rest—the longer version—then began to eat with relish.

Sarrez sat down with an ill-balanced slump of contentedness. He set one foot against the ground, one elbow upon his knee, and waved away Azetla's offer to share the meal. "Oh I had my fill. They eat like kings at the villa, let me tell you. And Rokh Imal brings all manner of honeyed delicacies each time he comes. If you really must send me there every so often, I will try my best to tolerate it."

Azetla laughed.

Sarrez had been frustrated, at first, with the certain role he had to play. He was the one with the highest blood, the most respectable background, the enviable lineage. So, whenever Azetla felt that his own voice or presence would be more of an obstruction, Sarrez's appeasing demeanor was offered instead. He thought of it as being a nursemaid of sorts, sent in to manage them, guide them, and tell them, "*no, don't touch that.*"

"Does Everson still tease you for a spy?" Azetla asked.

Sarrez shrugged and shook his head. "Not anymore. A useless one, I'd be. Everyone knows who I speak for and who I report to. They forgot a little at the beginning, *sooo* certain I shared all their feelings about...well, *you*. But they don't forget now. They don't tell me anything they don't want you to hear." Sarrez's smile receded slightly. "The Sahr devil is a better thing for spying, since no one has any idea who it speaks for, but when Imal and Rahummi are there, they have to use *it* to speak. But then, that's the whole problem, isn't it."

Azetla nodded silently. That was one small part of the problem.

"Well," he said, after swallowing another bite. "What *did* they say?"

"Oh, you know Colonel Everson. He just makes a thousand insincere remarks and mocks everything. But you could see that, under it all, he was thinking hard. Lord Verris asked a million questions. He obviously doesn't want to *believe* we'll ever have to come to blows, but he saw it, Azetla. He saw it. But no, listen to this!" Clearly Sarrez did not realize he was all but shouting in Azetla's ear. "What *they* said isn't even the thing! They had Captain Ishelor at the dinner, you see."

Sarrez looked at Azetla with almost mischievous joy. Azetla's eyes widened and he gestured fervently at Sarrez to continue.

"He said all the derisive things he usually says—you've heard them all a thousand times and half of them I used to say myself—but, at the end, he said 'I'll give the jackal this: he takes training seriously and he doesn't flinch this way or that.' *Ah-ha!*"

Sarrez slapped his hand on Azetla's shoulder, giddy with his news. Azetla could not refrain from smiling.

And it wasn't because of Captain Ishelor.

It was because of Sarrez.

Sarrez who really was quite drunk, actually.

Sarrez who had spent years hating Azetla. Who had almost driven a sword into his throat.

Sarrez the Makar, whose whole history and lineage taught him to hold Mashevis in utter contempt.

Nimer Sarrez whose friendship and loyalty Azetla now had, after all these long, awful years.

He needed both. He deserved neither. Guilt and fear blotted out the brief moment of joy.

3

Mali Colha took her new shawl, covered her hair in Trekoan fashion, and set out into the blazing sun. A sentry at the south residency gate gave her a slight bow as she departed. She still found it strange that they did that. Who did the soldiers think she was? Some high-blood set upon hard times? But living under the generosity of Colonel Everson, and being a northerner, she was treated differently than the local women. Differently than Khala too.

She tried not to trouble herself with it too much.

Mali crossed the south road, and skirted around the training field—she did not like going there—until she reached the Trekoan quarter of the outpost. She stood before a little brown hovel with small windows which were meant to keep the heat out. There were no adornments except for one crude carving in the lintel of the door, the meaning of which Mali never remembered to ask.

Stepping inside, Mali called out a greeting in Janbari Trekoan. She received a joyful response.

"Mali-le, Mali-le! How are you?"

The old midwife reached out to Mali and kissed her cheeks.

Mali answered in simple Trekoan—"I am very well"—and then, as usual, Sidara spoke on, and Mali comprehended little or none. She had lived in this hovel, with this old woman of the spry step and mirthful eyes, for the first three weeks of her life at Areo. She had loathed the smallness, the dark, the incessant dust, the farness from all she knew. The place Mali lived now was open, light, and beautiful. Full of Maurowan tapestries, Makarish elegance, and a Tusian-style balcony that overlooked one of the Colonel's desert gardens. Her duties were very few.

Nevertheless, in this cramped brown room, the midwife Sidara had comforted Mali when she cried and ached for home and feared for her father and for Anna. Sidara had wrapped her in her arms, sang her sweet Trekoan poems, and given her pleasant, distracting tasks. She made her fennel tea when her monthly aches came, putting in a costly share of honey which she ought not to have spared. She listened to Mali's complaints even though she understood no Maurowan.

So even after Azetla made good on his word and finagled a position for Mali's father as an under-steward, Mali visited Sidara. Each time, Mali expended her handful of Trekoan phrases right away, then set about to help Sidara with a few tasks that her late daughter used to do. Sidara would talk and sing. And it was comforting.

Sidara stepped out for a moment to check on a young woman in the early stage of labor saying—or at least Mali inferred—that she would be back soon. Mali decided to remain and finish hanging the herbs, boiling the washcloths, and mending the old woman's two spare articles of clothing. There was a different sort of peace here than fine food and copper vases could offer. Freedom from Anna's constant, wild pestering. Escape from her father's excruciating confusion. Everything about Areo worsened his memory, for he had none of the touchstones that made life real and certain to him.

The senior stewards were kind to him and gave him simple, regular tasks.

It cut Mali to the heart.

She drew in a deep breath as the scent of rosemary permeated the air.

Hearing a rustle outside, she turned. With a startling commotion, two soldiers stumbled through the low door.

"Hey-oh, Mali dear!" Joseph said. "Didn't expect to see you here. Where's the midwife lady?"

"Checking on a birth," Mali said, smiling to see a familiar face. "What's happened?"

The second man hung on Joseph's shoulder, bloody and bruised. He winced as Joseph helped him to the ground.

"Well, you see, it turns out Azetla and I have been doing our training *all wrong*. We had a mock assault exercise a month ago—hardly any injuries! Skirmishes last week—only a few bruises and scrapes! Today, hand-to-hand—all goes well! But Corporal Nuss here, he doesn't like that. High standards, this one. Thinks that nothing's earned if you don't break a bone or two. So he goes and starts a scuffle with some of the Juniper soldiers. Gets his nose broken, ribs gashed, and two fingers cracked."

"I think Sidara will be back any minute," Mali said. The Trekoan midwives were famous for their medical skill, and Sidara was the best of them, so this happened often.

"Good," Joseph said. "I'll leave him here and have someone to retrieve the idiot when she's done with him." He looked down at the young soldier. "And then you'll have to deal with Azetla."

Joseph left with scarcely a nod, as if he was in a hurry, and Mali was suddenly alone with the injured soldier. She felt a little strange. She continued with her work, but the silence was awkward and she could not bear it after a while.

"A bad fight was it?" she said uneasily as she woke the coals in the clay oven and set water to boil. She figured Sidara would need that, at least.

The young man smiled, then winced. "It happens sometimes."

"And what became of the other fellow?"

Years at the inn had taught her that men generally liked to be asked this question.

"The other *two* you mean? They fared better by their numbers." He winced again. "But they'll need more than a midwife if they chance at me again, by Serivash and Shouma and all the bloody Gods of Maurow."

Mali nodded sympathetically to his bravado, keeping her hands active to any random task she could invent. *This* was why she avoided the training fields, the mess tents, and even the war games that most everyone else on the outpost found exciting and loved to watch. She had no place. No purpose. At her father's inn, she rested in her work as clay in a mold. If she idled sometimes and chatted with the soldiers in a rather free way, it was only because of the freedom her position gave her. She belonged in a way. She had been something *to* them, so that she might be a part of them.

Here she was nothing to them. She had no community. No camaraderie. No work which could bring either about. She felt distanced even from those soldiers whom she might have called friends in the old life. Her new life was simple and dazedly calm, as a pool cut off from its tributary, shrinking every day from dryness.

As always, when such thoughts came to her, a steady stream of resentment flowed toward him who brought all this about, and she relished the tang of it. She resented Azetla for bringing her to live in Sidara's hovel, and she resented him almost as much for removing her from it, even though it was to have been a great effort from him and a great kindness from the Colonel. She was debris, carried along by Azetla's current.

Colonel Everson's current?

The Corra James' current.

Oh. It did not matter.

Here she was. And she must do *something*. Indeed, when Mali glanced back at Corporal Nuss, he was staring at her as though he expected her to do something right now. Mali glanced at the pot—the water began to simmer—then fiddled with the honey balm. After a moment of consideration, she pulled the stopper on the flask of arak. The sharp-sweet scent of anise drifted out, slapping her senses awake.

There was a little she could do before Sidara returned. Just commonsense things.

Mali pulled a few clean rags out of the corner basket, all of them stained a dull brown-red from the blood of many labors. All boiled a long hour to practically and ritually cleanse them. With the blade of her finger, she wiped the dusty top layer off the honey balm and set it beside Nuss. Next, a bowl of blistering hot water. Finally she doused a rag in the spicy-smelling alcohol.

Kneeling beside Nuss, she ignored his attentive and curious eyes, and focused on his wounds. He recoiled even before she touched him.

"Those rags have been covered in women's birth blood," he said in a mixture of embarrassment and disgust.

Mali almost laughed; her unease broke then as easily as the shell of an egg.

"Yes," she said. "As were *you*, once. Please be still. Sidara will be here soon and she'll right you."

The soldier still looked wary. Mali began to clean the gash in his side and—she was pleased—she did not flinch at his flinches.

"Blood is blood, anyhow," she added calmly. "What is your given name, Nuss? I don't think I've ever known it."

"Wydan."

"Ah. Please move your arm, Wydan. No...the other way."

She had nearly finished cleaning and balming the first wound—alcohol, water, alcohol, honey, just as she had seen Sidara do—when Wydan Nuss went rigid and a look of either terror or fury came over his face. Mali's heart raced. What had she done? Had she injured him somehow?

But his eyes were fixed on the entryway. Mali turned. A figure had slipped noiselessly through the door and when Mali saw who it was, her hands froze in their task.

The Sahr devil took a few languid steps until it reached them, then knelt and looked Mali in the eye. Mali would have dearly loved to look down, or away, or anywhere else. But she rather got the feeling that this was precisely what the Sahr wanted. Perhaps she did not meet the Sahr's gaze with strength, but she did meet it.

"Well," the Sahr said. "Go on."

Mali's fingers fumbled about for a moment but, through sheer force of will, she resumed her task. She soon found the initial terror dissipate, though the wariness remained, her shoulders taut to the point of discomfort. The Sahr slowly eased to a cross-legged sit, and watched Mali with lowered eyebrows. The scrutiny was almost more than Mali could stand. If only Sidara would return *now*.

Mali began to rinse the blood off of Nuss's nose and mouth. She tensed as the Sahr lifted its hands and pointed.

"Put it back," it said.

Mali glanced briefly at the Sahr.

"I—don't..."

"Put it back. Find the angle and shove it back right," it said.

The Sahr tapped its forefinger against its own nose, then pointed at Nuss once more. There was a cruel little smile on its face as it watched Mali come to comprehension. What a horrible notion. Jerk a man's nose about in hopes that it came right? The Sahr simply wanted to torture him. And her. Mali remained still, which was the closest to defiance she could manage.

"Watch," the Sahr said.

It knelt toward Nuss, whose whole face hardened with dread. Slowly—even gently—it began to feel the form of the bloody nose. The Sahr grabbed Mali's hand and pulled it until Mali was forced to run her fingers over the break. It showed her how to form her palms as an arrow's point over the nose and how she should pull it tightly down toward the jaw. Mali was too afraid to refuse, and Nuss didn't dare say a word. He blew out all the blood and mucous from his nose at the Sahr's instruction, his eyes watering from pain as he did so. Mali looked away.

"Stop that," the Sahr said coolly. "Now do it."

Mali tented her fingers firmly over the nose and tried to concentrate. For a moment she felt the Sahr's gaze as steel to her back, holding her against the fire, but then she shook her head and cleared her thoughts. She sucked her cheeks in and jerked downward.

Nuss let out a coughing shout and leaned his head back against the wall. *Oh Gods.* She had done it too hard, by blood. Or wrongly. She gritted her teeth.

"He'll feel dizzy for a moment," the Sahr said, after inspecting Nuss and raising its eyebrows in seeming satisfaction. "Wash it with cool water."

"What...what did I just do?" Mali said. The Sahr might be satisfied, but she was *not*.

The Sahr smiled.

"Depends. The West Hushai tribe has a ritual of breaking the nose of their new Shamans and then 'cracking it whole' as they call it—putting it back. If the nose heals straight, it is a good omen. They are accepted. If not, they must suffer other trials. A Hushai would read this boy's character in a few weeks by his nose. But as far as *I'm* concerned, you've mended a mild break, and the Gods are merely amused by the whole thing. They like to see us break our bodies to get a drop of favor from them."

Mali eased away from the Sahr like one might from a predatory animal and grabbed the bowl of fresh well water. As she soaked a clean rag, Sidara came in at last. She was covered in a more celebratory sort of blood, gladness pouring from her face. The birth must have come much faster than expected and ended well. Sidara had a smile for Mali, a curious glance for Nuss, and a spit of contempt for the Sahr.

Many of the Trekoans did that habitually when they passed the Sahr. It wasn't even real, they just made a spitting *sound*, and walked on with not the least break in step or attitude. Like the opposite of a customary sign of reverence and just as perfunctory. A superstitious warding off of evil.

After Sidara had warded the Sahr off, or whatever it was, she began to converse with the Sahr in rapid Janbari Trekoan as pleasantly and effusively as ever.

While they spoke, Azetla stepped into the room. Joseph followed him.

Mali loved and hated them in that moment, so relieved was she that they were there. Now they would extract the Sahr and leave everyone in peace. Surely.

But Azetla crossed his arms and waited for Sidara to finish speaking. Then he waited still more as the Sahr looked at Nuss and began to translate.

"Lean your head back," it said to him. "And unclench your fists. Now. Slowly, slowly, explain what happened."

"Two soldiers from Red Carth battalion were spinning their stupid tongues," he began in an odd and stuffy voice. "Going on about 'the bloody jackal' and 'the bloody Black Wren.' I spoke my piece against it, but tried to keep my hands to myself. But they just wouldn't shut up. So I...I barely punched him, Azetla. Not a tenth of what I wanted to do. They came back at me. They put me down, and ran a knife against my ribs, then bolted when the rest of their squad came out. That's when Lieutenant Drivas reported it to Lead Sergeant Radabe."

The Sahr translated this to Trekoan for Sidara, who worked far more nimbly and thoroughly over the wounds than Mali had. She tisked her tongue, nodding her head, and muttering in motherly sympathy.

Azetla, however, had no sympathy.

"This is exactly the sort of thing I've told you is unacceptable, Nuss," he said. His voice was calm and low, but it still fell harshly on the ears.

Nuss writhed a little under Azetla's gaze.

"I'm sorry," he said, barely audible. "But what was I supposed to do?"

"You're supposed to ignore them, Nuss," Azetla said. He let out a sigh of frustration and knelt down to the young Corporal's level. "I need you hale and whole. And I need you to show them by action how they should be, not by threat."

"But, Azetla...the things they *said* about you..."

"What, is that new?"

"No," Nuss said slowly. "But it wears one down after a while."

Azetla rolled his jaw as he stood back up. "Does it now?"

Nuss cast his eyes to the ground sheepishly. Then he winced as Sidara tested each of his injured fingers. She set one—Mali watched closely—and left the other alone. Nuss was sweating profusely from the pain.

Azetla leaned over to Joseph as Sidara inspected her work. "What did Lieutenant Drivas *do*?"

"He halved their rations for three days and put them to digging the new privy trenches," Joseph said in a low voice. "I didn't tell him to do it. He did it on his own before I even spoke to him."

Azetla rubbed the knuckle of his thumb against the cedar lion's head that hung from his neck. He gripped it briefly then released it. Mali remembered how, when she was much younger, she had thought the bit of wood was an amulet of jackal magic, and feared it. She had a vague notion, gleaned from who-knows-where, that jackals pretended piety but really lived by means of bloody and seditious enchantments. Azetla touched it often, like a totem. But Khala had laughed at Mali when she asked if it was magic.

"If only," Khala had said. "It is not, nor was it ever meant to be, magic. It's just one of many crude religious symbols—like the North Star for the Nagonans—and it's very dull and exceptionally *old-fashioned*. In the Mashevi quarter, only the elderly men still carry them about. Azetla is ridiculous that way."

Mali doubted at first, but she had come to believe Khala. If the trinket had any magic in it, it was only the magic of comfort. Azetla dropped his hand from the lion's head and folded his arms again.

"You know we have to give you the same punishment as Drivas gave his men, Nuss. And you know why."

Nuss stared at the ground. Joseph gave Azetla a sharp look.

"I know, Joseph. But that's how it has to be. All three broke the rules. We can't show partiality."

"Ah, Azetla…" Joseph stopped himself.

But they would not argue in front of Nuss, or Mali for that matter. They stepped beyond the doorway and spoke in low voices; Mali heard no more. The tension in the room had Mali fairly aching for a purpose, so she knelt beside Sidara and, by a touch of the hand, asked that she might help. Sidara, full of kindness, began to hand her things to put away, letting out a steady stream of Trekoan.

"She says the boy will be all right," the Sahr translated. "And that you did a good job caring for him."

Mali smiled at Sidara, and began carrying the dirty things to the basket that hung against the window. The Sahr's gaze followed Mali, eyes narrowed. It stood up as Azetla and Joseph returned.

The Sahr's voice was low, but Mali heard, and she supposed she was meant to hear.

"That girl needs to go under Sidara's hand. Then you could have something very like a real physician. You'll need more of those when the time comes."

Mali went rigid as the Sahr gestured at her.

"She is not mine to use or command," Azetla said coldly. "And it's not your place to suggest it."

"As you please." The Sahr shrugged. "But the Nagonan is right. The boy's punishment should be moderated, since he drew no weapon. Your fear of bias in favor of your own is in danger of reaching bias in the opposite direction. I hear the talk that goes round the corners and under the tables. In Maurowan and in Makarish."

And the Sahr left.

"*That's* what I was trying to tell you word for word," Joseph muttered. "I hate it when that bloody devil agrees with me."

"I know you do," Azetla said. Surprisingly, and ever-so-briefly, he smiled. Then he turned, grave as ever. "Mali, I apologize. You needn't worry about the Sahr. I won't allow it to—"

"I'll do it," Mali said. Her voice came out thin, so she cleared her throat. "I can do it. I will. If Sidara will have me, and if you will employ me."

Azetla was taken aback. He seemed poised to protest, and Mali dreaded it because she was not sure if she could withstand him, he was so like a wedge and steady hammer. But his look softened as if he saw, somehow, that it was simply his lot to be defeated in many small things today.

"Do you understand what that would be? Is that really what you want, Mali?"

Mali looked at her hands, lightly stained with blood. Then she lifted her eyes, warm resolution coursing through her veins.

"I took care of your men before, didn't I? I can take care of them again, in a new way."

Azetla looked at her, narrowed his eyes, and nodded.

"Very well. At your word."

A week later, Mali had returned herself and all her scant belongings to Sidara's hovel.

Two weeks later she attended her first Trekoan birth.

Three weeks, she lanced her first infection.

In the fourth week, the Sahr watched Mali treat a scorpion sting, and called her something for the first time. She had never used Mali's actual name. Not once. This time she called Mali, *Taya*. Mali asked widely, but never discovered the exact meaning of the word only that it was not Trekoan or Makarish. It was, she suspected, the Sahr's native tongue. But the Sahr used it like a title. A profession. A purpose.

Others began to call her Taya as well. "You think your arm is broken? Go get the Taya. Taya Mali."

And she felt joy and belonging in that vile Sahr devil's word. She would not relinquish it for her life.

4

*B*lood, salt, then blood again. That was his sister's way into life, the welcome that covered her skin. First the blood of life from Birai's womb. Then the coarse salt cleanse of the Trekoan midwife. Then the blood of death, from the midwife's own throat.

Around this last memory there was no haze or gap at all. It was etched as if on stone, limned as if by fire, stained into the depths of him. Each time he recalled it, he revived its strength. These days he brought the memory before his mind often, trying desperately to understand now what he could not have grasped then.

Aadin's father, Sa'ased, waited till the midwife had done all her care and curative work. Waited till Birai could stand on her feet. Then he did the slaughter. Quiet. In the dead of night. Cut the midwife's sing-song prayers off with a sharp knife by the glow of dim and dying fire.

Birai smeared the midwife's blood over the infant's body. A grotesque painting.

"Not for the Gods, this one. Not for anyone. Not for anything. Nothing. No one. Nowhere," Birai muttered in the cadence of a prayer, but by Aadin's heartbeat, it struck more like a shaman's chant for some terrible demon. It raised the hairs on his arm and made him want to *hide. Made him wish the light of day would cut through the night like a sword.*

"Do you really think you can hide her from the Gods? Even from Dimash?" Sa'ased whispered, his brow furrowed in worry.

"Just watch me," Birai said in a cold, harsh rasp. There was a look of predatory vengeance in her eye. "The old spirits of deception and illusion can hide from the Gods. So can she. She will. I don't even care what happens to her. Maybe she is cursed, maybe she is salvaged. But let her die some other way, some other day. I will not break my vow."

Quickly they gathered themselves, Birai heedless of her own blood, the wakeful infant firmly strapped, Sereya dragged by the hand, Aadin bid to keep pace. He thought nothing, at the time, of picking up the scarlet thread that had been cut from the baby's wrist; the strands were fine and bright and elegantly braided together. He slipped it into his pouch.

This, he regretted bitterly.

Why, why, why? Why had they done this? Why had his parents withheld that death-born girl from the fires of Dimash? Any true Shihrayan, native to the crags of the high desert, could see that she was a curse—a shikk. This happened all the time. Many children were born curses, either by omen, by flaw, by deformity, or by prophecy. They all went to the fires. Dimash was ever ravenous for the flesh of the weak, the broken, the tainted, the unwanted; his flames devoured all that could abate the strength of Shihra.

Yet Birai was as stubborn as stone. And Sa'ased stood with her.

They had given a child to Dimash before. Throat slit. Body cast into the blaze. Why not this time?

He did not know. At the time, he did not care. She was not much to him then. Another sound in the hut, another mouth to feed, another raid in the lowlands to survive, another cry at night.

By the black stones, how lightly we regard the steady trickle of water that cuts through our lives. Thus are great wadis made.

There were sinister rumors about the girl even then, but Sa'ased and Birai turned deaf ears to them. They stood their ground.

And at night, in a deep, scraped voice, Birai would sing the old Ghoshri lullaby.

"They'll have to slit my throat to get to you, they will, they will,
They'll have to slit my throat to get to you, they will, they will.
Though the knife draw deep, none will, none will.
Though the knife draw deep, none will, none will."

The girl was never taken to a shaman to be blessed and named. Never taken to the holy black stones to be dedicated. No drop of blood from her went into Dimash's hand. Not the least gashing of the palm. Birai gave them nothing to know, nothing to see, nothing to taste.

As the girl was kept from the fire, so she was kept from the Gods, a secret sin.

The girl herself grew and smiled and laughed and was stronger and wilder than she had any right to be.

From the first, she took all of it as a game. A challenge. She would clap her hands, cast stones at the sky, and get the Gods' attention. She would pry her name out from between their teeth one of these days, for why shouldn't they relent? She would argue them down. She would coax them.

Oh, she knew what she was, and she was not afraid; she was wayward and blasphemous long before she was old enough to understand why.

***

Azetla's voice was raw with shouting and his feet ached, but he kept moving.

"Full Column!" He shouted for the tenth time, moving quickly over the ground to parallel the soldiers as they pushed up the steep hill at a steady lope.

"Tri-Line!"

The eight hundred soldiers melted from a standard column, out into a frontal attack formation, staggered three forms deep. They were getting faster.

"Phalanx by fives!"

The lower officers echoed him, and their voices also cracked from effort and waterless throats.

"Dragon's Head!"

They rippled out into a wedge, shields at front. Azetla was breathing heavy as they breached the top of the rocky hill, returning to the main road that led back to Areo.

"Flank!"

"Full Column!"

He pulled the Juniper battalion Captain back out to the side and handed him the signal flag which Azetla had been snapping up and back at the rhythm of the morphing formations.

"Now just with the flags. No words. Keep the pace."

"Yes, Commander," Ishelor nodded.

This time, Azetla stood back and watched from the peak of the hill. He could see the battalion, the full stretch of the road, and the tall southern gates of Areo. The Juniper, the Red Carth, and the Sojj all moved smoothly through the various formations. The signaled pattern—Full Column, Tri-Line, Phalanx, Dragon's Head, Flank, all executed one immediately after the other—was a Maurowan parade display used mostly for show. But Azetla had never seen its like for hammering the essentials into the blood and muscles, for training the men's ears to voice and eyes to signal, and for holding form over coarse terrain.

And, by salt, it was working. He took a deep breath and walked, long-strided, down the road, watching the battalions unfold, ripple into pleats, harden into wide forms, and re-fold, all while moving forward at a taxing pace. Azetla perhaps should not have spent this long running flags for the drills—he had seven other battalions and a hundred other tasks—but sometimes he still wrestled against the difference between six hundred men and six thousand.

Five months at Areo. He should be used to it by now.

He had been merciless with them today and stretched himself thin as well. He doubted they sensed the urgency with which he worked, but they knew him to be dogged, and they certainly believed him to be untiring.

If only the latter were true. He had slept so little last night and his voice was nearly gone.

With a waved signal, he left Captain Ishelor to finish the drills. He did notice the still figure looking down from the rampart as he approached the north gate, so it did not surprise him that, shortly after returning, Verris' personal guards approached him.

"Lord Colonel Verris would speak with you now."

Azetla gave a faint nod and followed them. Verris never scheduled meetings. He demanded them at random and *at once*, and it often seemed like a purposeful imposition on Azetla's time and patience. He presumed it was Verris' way of exerting control where he could, given that he was in control of almost nothing else. To Verris' credit, he came to observe at the training fields nearly every day and he always asked questions; he did not shirk his duty in the least.

The guards directed Azetla to the observation pavilion at the west training field, and both departed at the flick of Lord Verris' hand.

"Yes, my lord?" Azetla said with a bow.

Verris—to Azetla's surprise—bid Azetla sit.

"I've been watching the skirmish training all week. I see the purpose—training them to protect the signalmen while still moving forward in the objective—but I wonder why you set them as like against like," Verris said.

"I'm not sure I understand," Azetla replied slowly. But he did understand. He just needed Verris to say the thing out loud. It would give Azetla the chance to take this man by the neck and make him see what he did not want to see.

"You set the two teams against each other, but both fight using Maurowan signals, tactics, training, and equipment. We are in the Trekoan desert. Shouldn't one be Maurowan and the other be Trekoan?"

"If Rokh Imal brings new tribal soldiers to Areo, we will train them in our signals and equipment, just as we have the Areo battalions. And we will integrate their methods into ours."

"That's not what I meant."

Azetla knew that well enough. He waited.

"If these soldiers are called upon for some reason, it won't be against Maurowans."

Azetla drew one slow breath and released it.

"Yes, it will be, my lord. Surely you know that."

Lord Verris flinched.

"If you intend to see your plans through to their end, you will have to face your own," Azetla added calmly.

Pressing his jaw tight, Verris watched the signalmen evade their "attackers."

"That is only the worst-case scenario. We didn't come here to start a *war*," Verris said in a cold voice. "But to gather ourselves, to keep safe, to be ready. To wait."

"Wait for what?"

"For the right opportunity."

Azetla let silence prevail for a few moments. He saw Lord Verris' fingers tense and fidget at his leg as he surely felt the true meaning of his own words break the illusion.

"My lord, you can huddle inside the walls of Areo, hoping for a chance to turn another moderately wealthy lord or savvy colonel to your favor, hoping that Riada doesn't sniff you out or your Corra doesn't give you up. Or...you can take ground."

Lord Verris breathed out hard through his nose. "That was never the plan, jackal."

Azetla signaled the drill leader, who reset the skirmish to a fresh attack pattern. "Your plan was never going to work, my lord."

Verris looked at Azetla, his eyes wide and burning. "You haven't the faintest idea—"

"Yes I do, my lord," Azetla interrupted, his voice calm. "Slowly, slowly, you would have touted James over the Emperor until you had enough support in the court and among the people. You would have spread rumors that Riada tended toward the old madness to which his father succumbed. Riada would weaken; James would seem the stronger. Then you would have used all this to pressure Riada into making concessions—one after the other—until he conceded himself into a corner he could not escape. Only then would the army stand and show itself, a symbol on the field of a victory already won in court."

Verris looked pale, his fingers curled to fists.

"But it's no good, my lord," Azetla said. "Emperor Riada is the one person in all the world upon whom that will never, ever work. You are trying to beat him at the games he plays best. Words. Stratagems. Court. Favor. Power. Persuasion. Better to take him to a field he has neglected."

For a moment, anger boiled in Verris' face, and he struggled to calm it. Azetla had been so careful all these months not to twist too hard against this joint, because the danger of it had been too great. He said "yes, my lord" and "of course, my lord" and bowed. But time was running out.

Verris pressed his lips together and began to speak, his voice betraying only the slightest tremor of emotion. "You think that the Emperor will be a fool on the battlefield simply because he is unassailable in the court?"

"Riada is not a fool of any kind, no matter what happens. But he walks on the victory of his great grandfathers. It has been a long time since Maurow has fought a real fight near its very front door. All it has had to do is flick off a few flies once in a while, and the strong become weak the moment they are convinced of their strength. Riada has never had any opportunity to question his martial power. Or to test it thus. If he has any blind spot—and I do say 'if'—*that* is where it would be, my lord."

Azetla lowered his voice and felt fire in his own chest as he spoke, for now he was trespassing beyond the words he needed Verris to hear and touching the edge of what he really wanted to say. "Please don't let this go to waste. Help me make this army into something more than mere fodder that Emperor Riada has to dig through to get to you when the time comes. Because that time *will* come. I swear it by salt."

Lord Verris was quiet a long time. His fingers tensed slowly, rhythmically, at his knees.

"I fear this reprieve has given you the wrong impression, jackal. You are still a common soldier of no rank whose life is in my hands. If I were in your position, I wouldn't dare speak so brazenly. You lay your neck at the knife," Verris said, each word slowly and carefully uttered.

"I know that, my lord. You remind me often. Nevertheless I *will* speak this way for my sake and for yours, because I think it's a miracle that your Corra is still alive—that all of us are still alive. And I don't think it will last."

Verris snapped his eyes closed as the sun cut through the corner of the pavilion's shade, his whole face wincing against the harsh light. The wind struck the cloth toying it in and out of place. The gap filled. The shade rested.

After a deep breath, Verris opened his eyes.

"You wish me to believe," he said, almost in a whisper. "That we are simply damned if we do and damned if we don't."

"Quite possibly," Azetla said. He breathed deep. "But we can make all of Trekoa a place Riada cannot go."

"What do you mean?"

"Slip it out from under him by Trekoan hands. You must leave no road, no city, no tribe, no outpost, and no well to him. The south—the *whole* of it—cannot be his. Some of this can be done now. Without his even knowing."

Verris stood up abruptly, full of nervous energy, needing to be above Azetla that he might look down.

"*I do not trust you, jackal.*"

Azetla leaned forward but did not stand, one elbow resting on the rail of the pavilion, the other on his knee.

"You don't need to trust me to know that I am telling the truth. I know what I am to you. A thorn. A worry. And a scapegoat." Verris blanched at that. "I work in the full light of that weakness. I can't easily hide it."

"No," Verris said with a rigid smile. "You practically flaunt it."

Azetla stepped past those words as being of no value to him.

"Did you ever consider that perhaps I need your success just as much as you do, if I am only an instrument that may be discarded or blamed at the least hint of failure? Or do you not realize that I have already given my blood on the field for Maurow, more than once? Blood for Maurow, which *hates* me."

Verris looked long at Azetla, then at the men on the training field, then into the distance. Azetla felt more words on his tongue, but judged that he had already used enough. He waited.

"*Merely knock the knife off the bedside table,*" Verris muttered.

"*So that when the hand reaches, it finds empty air,*" Azetla finished the quotation. How many times as a boy had he read the little book of battles and sayings from General Xichot of Tus? He read it even to his little sister, and she started using phrases from it to try and win arguments with him. Strange for that memory to come to him now.

"That is really what you think, Mashevi?"

"Yes, my lord. That is what I think. You must do as you see fit."

Azetla stood, gave a bow, and left without asking for dismissal.

For the first time, Lord Verris had acknowledged the state they were really in. Azetla should have been relieved, but a strange shadow crossed quickly over his thoughts.

The words in his mouth had tasted disconcertingly familiar: "*That is what I think. You must do as you see fit.*"

It was what Tzal usually said to him. When she needed him to think a certain thing and go a certain way, but wanted him to feel it was his own choice.

And he often did go that way. He did think that thing, in part. It did feel like his choice.

Well, she was better at this than him. He canvassed the notion, then laid it alongside so many other carefully gathered observations, that it might steep with them, gathering full strength. The men would ask for her blood again sooner or later, and he must have a better explanation than he had already given himself for his decision. He could not tell them what he himself did not know: what she truly was, what she truly wanted.

5

Orde Everson looked down from the balustrade. There was nothing much to look for, since the only guest today was Rahummi Bin-Deghan, Rokh Imal's nephew. He was an important young man, perhaps, but not an exotic offering—not likely to cause shocks or amusements of any kind.

And he did not like Orde very much.

After a casual glance, Orde noticed the Shihrayan. She leaned against the southeast column with a handful of dates and flashed a smile upward. Orde pursed his lips. She knew all his habits so damned well, he could never catch her unawares. He gave up on his perch.

"You're not really needed, you know," he called out as he rounded the column and walked down the steps. "Rahummi and I can usually make ourselves understood to one another without your help."

She took a date seed out of her mouth and put it in the pit bowl.

"Good morning to you too," she said. "As always, feel free to discard any of my words you don't need."

Orde rolled his eyes and put an olive in his mouth. No use pressing the point. Yes, he and Rahummi could navigate each other's gaps in language...but only as long as they kept to simple generalities.

The Shihrayan would enable a level of detail, clarity, and earnestness that Orde simply was not in the mood for.

He spat out the pit and resigned himself to a more tedious meal than he had expected. He could not even come up with one of his usual taunts for the Shihrayan. It took such a deft parry-and-jab to reach past armor and get to her skin—to make her flinch and strike back—and in all fairness, he had not yet had his morning's tea.

Looking at her sidelong, Orde realized for the first time how changed she was from that vicious little thing Rokh Imal had dragged in, purchased at such high cost from the south villages, indifferent to all Imal's attempts to cow her. But that was nine years ago now. She had barely been more than a child. Fifteen or sixteen years of age, he supposed.

In the desert, however, as in most places, as soon as a girl began to bleed she *was* no longer a child in the eyes of her people. And surely the Shihrayan had never really been one to begin with. Not in the usual way. The devilry must have been there from the beginning; she only refined it as time went on, offering various veneers for various situations, each more convincing than the last.

At first, Orde had teased Rokh Imal that he had been swindled. "*Look at this nothing-of-a-creature. Beat it all you like, I don't think it will do you any good.*" Had any so-called "salt-brick" ever turned out to be a *real* Sahr devil? He doubted it. It was a cheat.

But then she opened her mouth. Inhaled Orde's mannerisms, tone, turns-of-phrase. Took every word he said and gently laid it back before him that he might stumble over it. Drove him to thoughts he didn't mean to think. Snapped at his heels, cornered him, bricked him in. Smiled. Laughed. Enjoyed his surprise and confusion. She was *like* him. A dark mirror which he enjoyed peering into. A sly, amoral creature who always slipped out unscathed even if everyone around her fell.

He was riveted.

But familiarity bred folly first and then contempt. She would not play to his tune anymore. She would not amuse him if she could help it, and if she shouldered the conversation for everyone, then the conversation would taste only as she intended. She would withhold the flavors he wanted and give him the ones he did not. She liked to be the rock in the shoe. She liked to see him limp.

And he must suffer her today.

Rahummi arrived in formal war dress. That, Orde had expected. Rumors traveled fast.

What Orde did not anticipate was Rahummi's wife entering alongside him, visibly with child. Given that she was from the Hushai tribe, it was impossible to ignore her state; they did not conceal their condition as most other Trekoan women did, but adorned it with blue cloth, with beading and copper. She looked as though she might call for a midwife at any moment.

Rahummi had never brought his wife to Areo before. Orde's curiosity and worry were both piqued.

"Run off then, little devil," Everson said under his breath in Maurowan. "Looks like you won't be wanted after all."

Calmly and without concern, the Shihrayan addressed Rahummi's wife. "Do you want me to leave, Naima?"

Or at least that's what Orde thought she said, but the Hushai dialect was a difficult one for him to understand

Naima smiled slightly.

"No," she said in a soft voice, swaying back and forth as if standing still with her great burden was an uncomfortable task. "The desert God is great, and I have no fear."

Orde washed away his surprise as quickly as it fell upon him. He demanded that no one stand on ceremony. Let the young woman sit down and be given comforts immediately. He gave Rahummi his smiles and his greetings and all the meandering trivialities that one must give in Trekoa, but inside he found himself crackling with irritation.

Why on earth would Naima suffer the Shihrayan devil to stay, when she was in such a condition?

Trekoan women who were with child—and who knew what the Shihrayan was—considered her presence a very evil omen. They would not let her touch them, wash upstream from them, nor cross their path with the sun ahead, lest her shadow fall over the child, cursing it. It all sounded very sweet and pious that Naima should rely solely on her god for good fortune, but Orde preferred it when the Trekoans relied on their superstitions; then, at least, he knew what he was dealing with.

He doubted the Shihrayan cared one whit about Naima's comfort or safety. It always irritated him when she put on a gentle or deferential mask. He resented it, and he didn't believe it for a second. The character she played for Rahummi was dull to Orde: calm, warm, with only a few benign jokes at each other's expense. The two of them had the odd kinship of being brought under Rokh Imal's harsh rule at the same time, albeit in drastically different positions. She played older sister to him and played it well. As far as Orde could tell, Rahummi believed it without question, despite all she had done.

All sat. All ate. There was something like conversation. There had been raids and skirmishes, yes, and Rahummi believed that worse was coming. But do not trouble the morning yet. Instead, break bread first. Speak of everyday things. Yes, the child was due any day now, thank the God of the desert. The midwife Sidara of Areo was of such great renown, and Rahummi wished the most skilled hands for Naima, naturally.

Most of the time, the Shihrayan said nothing but what must pass through her mouth. Only when the subject of the Ghallaz came up—Naima's tribal home—did she and the Trekoans have a little chattering amongst themselves. The Shihrayan spoke in Hushai. Naima laughed; Rahummi shook his head with amusement. There was something about a skirmish four years back, and about Naima and Rahummi sending romantic messages to one another through the Shihrayan. But Orde did not understand more than that, because the little devil made sure to leave him outside of it.

After a while, Naima excused herself to rest, and no one could possibly object. Then Rahummi—with lengthy expressions of gratitude—left that he might see to her, without having said much more than Orde could have guessed on his own.

The Shihrayan came to her feet in an easy, languid motion and started eastward.

"I suppose the jackal ought to be informed that Rahummi has arrived," Orde said, walking alongside her.

"He already knows," she said.

Orde breathed a laugh.

"You do skitter back and forth like a rat, with little morsels in your mouth. Everyone jumps when you show up because you *might* tell them something that *seems* helpful," Orde said.

She only shrugged and kept her pace.

"Well you certainly have that jackal in hand."

"No, I don't," she said, scraping the leather band on her wrist, then twisting it around once. Twice.

Orde raised his eyebrows. "So it's the other way around?"

"There's no debt in either direction," she said in a flat voice.

She was getting irritated. He had the track.

"But you have nowhere else to go." He watched for a reaction. "So now it's just two pariahs trying to survive off one another's backs. No way that goes wrong."

She smiled slightly.

"You keep forgetting, Everson...*it doesn't actually matter*. In the end, none of this has anything to do with me."

"Nothing ever does," he said, enjoying himself much more now. "But here you are."

They had reached the wall marking off the south training field. The Shihrayan, reminding Orde of the old days when she was ever scrambling up things like a goat, pulled herself atop the wall and sat in a crouch. The hum of soldiers gathering could be heard beyond the stone.

"The Mashevi will listen to me or he won't. He'll do as he pleases. But this is the first time I am here under no ownership, and no obligation. Don't be so sure you know what that looks like." She brushed her thumb across the band on her neck. "I see your pavilion is ready for you. Shade, wine, and plenty of distance. There'll be sweat and mild hardships out there today, and I know you don't like to get too close to such things."

She walked away, atop the wall, toward the west gateway.

Orde did go to his pavilion where the overhang blocked the harshest sun and, by luck, the crosswind so happened to blow through. He was quite comfortable as he watched the soldiers fill the field's edges. A young lieutenant set the men in order to begin the matches. Azetla slipped onto the training field, ledgers ever in hand. The Shihrayan sat on the far wall just behind him.

Smiling to himself, Orde settled into his chair, unbothered. The Shihrayan's darts glanced off. He'd managed to raise *her* hackles: difficult to do, generally good sport, and always revealing. She liked to believe she kept herself such a great secret, the little devil.

<hr>

Azetla watched the first fight with real enjoyment; he did not write anything down, he didn't say a word. He allowed himself a quarter hour of no hurry and no calculation. Crowds of Trekoans and soldiers began to gather round, and some shouted or jeered, fanning the competitive flames. The sparring was fun to do, fun to watch, and the livening effect of it flowed across the field like a breeze.

After the third round of matches, and with some reluctance, Azetla brought the day's docket back to the front of his mind.

"Is Rahummi coming to the fields?" he asked, keeping his eyes on the nearest hand-to-hand match.

"Eventually," Tzal said. "He'll want to talk to you without Everson around at least once."

She stayed on the wall behind him. She tended to keep to the edges, as if she would rather people forget that she was there while her words were somehow everywhere.

"Rokh Imal's always come to Areo himself rather than send Rahummi alone. Does it signify a problem? Have I offended him?"

When she did not answer, Azetla turned back to look at her. It was a complicated matter. Under a veneer of mutual respect, and despite so many shared beliefs, Azetla and Rokh Imal did not always understand each other. Rokh Imal had a Mashevi ideal in mind, and it had become clear that Azetla did not conform to it. He was harsh and blunt and had lived long among Maurowans. As for Rokh Imal, his pride of place was so great that it nearly blinded him.

"Well?" he said.

"You may or may not have offended him—I don't know—but his sending Rahummi is *not* a slight."

She slipped down from the wall and came to where he stood. "Rahummi is Imal's favorite."

"Over his own son?"

"Well, no. He's the useful favorite who can be spared for dangerous things."

"Such as tribal unrest," Azetla said.

"That is what the northerners like to call it, yes. Qatlan and Saqiran shake spears, but hold off. It starts with the smaller tribes under their protection. Rahummi will tell you how it stands."

"Don't *you* already know?"

She always "already knew" whether she acted like it or not. Azetla never doubted that she had done violence on Rokh Imal's behalf when she was his; but far more than that, she had been eye, and ear, and tongue.

"I'll leave it to him," she said. "There's the matter of dignity."

Azetla could not remotely discern the presence or degree of sarcasm.

"You don't usually give Rokh Imal the same dignity."

She conceded that with a slight tilt of the head and no interest in explaining herself.

A soldier in the match nearest them executed a nimble evasion of a staff strike, and brought his opponent to the ground with a grip on the neck and a sharp outside trip of the foot.

"Oof, that was deft," Tzal muttered in Trekoan, apparently watching with the same simple satisfaction that anyone else would have in a good, clean sparring match. Maybe it was artifice, maybe it was genuine. He had chosen what track to take with her and part of that meant not letting himself belabor that particular question at every small juncture.

He cheered Corporal Nuss with a full-throated shout when he won his match with four strike points and not a single one scored against him.

Azetla had always enjoyed sparring, even—or especially—when he was a boy. It astonished his mother, who had liked to believe his nature too serious and calm, his bent too studious for such things. But all his cousins were louder and rougher than he, and they knocked each other about as often as they were let. It felt like kindness and generosity to wrestle with them for, otherwise, there was an unspoken distance separating him from them.

He lost most of the time. Was never very good at it. Life in the Black Wren had managed to push him toward the middle of the pack, though not much farther.

Even so, it had always been a fine and seemly thing to test skill against skill and shake hands afterward. There was a secret joy in it, a hint of some rugged paradise, with the hellish strains scrubbed out of it; all the strength, vitality, ferocity, and camaraderie of the fight, without the death, shriveling, collapse, and emptiness of war.

Azetla had seen enough of the latter throughout the years so as to leach away some of the joy. Those on the field who had not yet tasted that gall would know it soon. But for now, they cheerfully admired one another's nicks and bruises under the hot bright sun. They passed the water around, gave advice for the next fight, and brushed the salt dust off their faces before going at it again.

"I don't understand why your rules dictate a fresh start anytime someone hits the ground. You can kill someone from the ground," Tzal said.

"Dozens of feet and hooves, spread out? Maybe. Thousands of them, pressed shoulder to shoulder? Less likely." He watched as her eyes flitted from one fight to the next and then seemed to rest on nothing in particular. "What? Wondering how you'd do in a clean, fair fight like this?"

She raised her eyebrows. "I do my level best to never get in a fair fight."

He almost smiled. "You know what I meant."

"I have no earthly idea," she said. She gestured across the field toward Joseph, who signaled Azetla twice. The officers' matches would start soon. Azetla raised his arm in acknowledgment. He had debated the merits of participating, but calculated that he had accrued enough good will to lose a match without losing much else.

"After this, I'm free to speak with Rahummi whenever he wishes," he said.

Tzal gave a scant nod, determined—for some reason—to say as little as possible today. She still watched, twisting the leather slave band around her wrist.

He could have dogged her till he got something out of her. It worked occasionally, but he decided against it. Shaking his shoulders back a few times, he drew and released several long, slow breaths. It amused him that, even now, a formal sparring match could still make him a little nervous. Istamo, Ishelor, then Sarrez. Ironically, the only match that didn't concern him was the one he was certain he would lose.

Sarrez knew not to hold back.

55

6

*O*ther children came after that cursed one, their blood palmed on the stone, their names blessed and pronounced by a shaman, showing that the Gods saw them. There was a new wife brought in and mild war between the two sets of children. The shikk liked the fight of it until Dotiya was born, then she liked Dotiya, and made peace.

But Aadin was the oldest and a son; all of them had to follow him, skirt around him, accommodate him, and do exactly as he said. He had tremendous power in his very small sphere.

Yet his second sister tested his strength. That cheerful bad omen.

She hounded Aadin. Teased him. Pestered him. He would knock her down as hard as he could, and she would come right back. She laughed all the time, made the little ones laugh. Even made Aadin smile in spite of himself; he did not remember exactly how or why. She was like a strange shoot growing out from between the rocks. One wondered: where was her soil? Why did she thrive so? That she lived at all was an exception to rule, but why was she so raucous about it? Sometimes it seemed like she was about to burn up with aliveness, flames to the sky, heat to the wind.

Outside of their village of several dozen, she was deemed an errant word, a slip of the hand. Accidents do happen. But inside, she carried Dotiya on her back chanting loudly, and drew elaborate stories in the *dirt floor with Sereya, using sticks and stones and bits of cloth to make characters and terrain. Even in those stories, there had been a strength and vividness to her every word. One simply had to listen.*

So she was a creature of limbo, a thing that did as she pleased while everyone else held their breath, waiting to see what the answer to her would be. Was there some remaining contamination of foreign soil and foreign god? Was she damned or not? Was blood and deception enough to shield her from the Gods who ought to have consumed her?

It seemed so at first. The Gods turned a blind eye and a deaf ear to the shikk. Life was harsh, but it went on apace. One could almost forget the lowland tents and the dreadful omens.

That was their folly. His mother's. His father's. And, in the end, his very own. They had stowed a red coal in dry grass. The least bit of wind would bring it to flames. How could they be surprised when smoke began to fill the sky? Little by little, more and more, till it filled the lungs.

She was nine years old when Izkher was given his name at the black stones. She watched from afar, up the crag, for she was not allowed to go near such holy and god-ridden things. When there was blood on the black stones, the Gods were wide awake, the demons lurked, and the spirits waited like arrows resting anxiously in a drawn string.

After the ceremony, Aadin found a huddle of older, high-village Illari boys and reveled with them. They stole drink and temple girls; Aadin was dizzied and half sick from it all. Some of the things they did frightened him, young backwater that he was.

Unsteady on his feet, he stumbled over the shikk's pallet when he returned to camp.

It was empty. He instantly knew why.

Stupid girl. She was going to do something dangerous. He just knew it.

He lurched from camp up the trail to the holy stones.

She had climbed the holy rocks, up, up, up both the slick and the rough till she sat as high on the obsidian as she could reach. He could hear her voice, calm and conversational, drifting with the night breeze.

"Honestly, how much blood do you need?" she said. "When are you satisfied? What does it take to open your eyes and keep them open? I'm right here, looking at you. Your black teeth. Blood on both palms and all over your blank face. So what's my name?"

Her words zig-zagged from Shihrayan to the bits of Makarish and Trekoan she had learned in the outer villages, offering each language as a possible key to a lock. Which one would open the Gods' ears to her?

Aadin's blood still froze when he thought back on it. Her voice, lacking the full precision and richness it grew into later, nevertheless cut high and sharp into the night, like a shard to the throat.

"So go on, you cowards. Name me, or kill *me. Watch and see if I care which. And if you're too dull to do either, I'll go to that desert god who touched my wrist at first. That one you're all so afraid of? I'll catch him by the neck and I'll tell him the same thing I'm telling you. Then we'll know who is who. Are you alive? Then show me. WAKE UP!"*

Her words filled Aadin with a fear he could not grasp, it was so like a slithering creature winding about in his chest. Why hadn't the Gods struck her dead then and there? They should have. Aadin's stomach heaved. He went to hands and knees, and vomited.

She heard him. Started from her perch. Scrambled down.

The shikk crouched next to him as he looked up, sweaty and woozy.

"I told you that you shouldn't go off with those high-village boys," she said. Her palms were gashed. Blood dripped onto her knees. And she smiled wide in the moonlight. "What's my name, Aadin?"

Bloody shikk. She shouldn't be able to make him afraid like this.

"Zaraje," he spat. A disgusting word for a lowlander. Someone foreign-born.

She just laughed and said it again. "What's my name?"

"You won't just get yourself killed, you idiot," he slurred. His mouth tasted foul. The fear churned in his gut and he just wanted to forget

everything and go to sleep. "You'll get all of us killed. You can't touch the black stones! Climb on them!? It's desecration. How dare you? You can't make the Gods do what you want. You can't coerce them. You can't threaten them. You can't turn them one way or the other."

"Oh?" She jerked her chin, grinning. "Just watch me."

And that was the answer.

In time, Aadin would learn the truth of it more than anyone else. The omens had not lied. She was born to hot wind, choking dust, and dry lightning. She was a cursed Zaraje. Coated in deception. Thoughtlessly blasphemous. And unafraid.

Tzal made her way around the edge of the crowds until she reached the other end of the field. She intended to watch Azetla's matches more closely than she had the others. What it would tell her, she didn't know, but she knew she had missed something about this Mashevi and felt like she was walking around with the corner of her eye blind.

She usually understood people quickly, drew them as maps in her mind; everyone was navigable eventually. But she had handled Azetla more timidly than was her wont—it had seemed necessary at the time—and she was beginning to think this had been a mistake. She learned best when she could land a blow and provoke a reaction. But she'd been circling, taut, without striking much.

He beat Captain Istamo in hand-to-hand, and that chiefly by speed. Istamo was strong, but more than a decade older and simply could not keep the pace. Azetla brought him to the ground cleanly in the end. Almost politely. When the match was called, Azetla reached down and pulled Istamo back to his feet. They clapped each other on the shoulder, smiling, telling each other cheery kindnesses such as "that last strike was a near thing" and "no, it never had a chance!"

Her brother would sometimes reach down and pull her up like that after he'd knocked her down. But it was a toss of the coin as to whether he would smile that same warm way and share his water, or grab her jaw so hard that she felt like it was going to crack in his hand: "*do not let that happen again.*" She watched for every tic, every step, every narrowing of the eye that might tell her what sort of day it was going to be. Not that she could do anything about it, she just liked to be ready.

Now Azetla and Captain Ishelor fitted on the bits of leather armor and each took their staves. Staff-fighting was a northern art of which Tzal had seen very little, but she gleaned that the rule-sets were more strict for these matches, since a staff blow to the head was not a trifling matter. After rapping their staves together twice—an opening formality—Azetla immediately switched to his left-handed stance.

He attempted the first strike. Failed. Ishelor landed his, straight to the chest. And from there it went at breakneck speed. They did precious little "dancing" and the score counter was kept quite busy. Ishelor struck *hard*. As if he meant not merely to win, but to harm, and even rapped Azetla on the ear once so that blood trickled to his collar. Maybe an accident, maybe not. The counter prepared to flag it as a disqualifying blow, but then didn't for some reason.

The rules of these fights seemed like complete nonsense to her.

In any case, Azetla's pace and strength held. He was less fluid than Ishelor, but more consistent. Ishelor began to grow tired. Azetla did not.

It was a narrow win with a simple answer. Endurance over skill. Azetla pulled Ishelor back to his feet too, but neither smiled. Just a nod of acknowledgment.

Azetla lost to Sarrez, of course. But it was a dignified loss, not so quick as to be a complete embarrassment. Tzal made careful note that, should she ever have need to draw her knife on that Makar, she would never, ever face him square. Or in daylight. The two soldiers gripped each other at the back of the head afterward, touching brows briefly. The Black Wren men often did that with each other.

At that moment, she tasted a bit of contempt in her mouth. She swirled it around her tongue. It was of a certain vintage that—if you lingered over it—had an envious aftertaste. Azetla thought of himself as "outside," but he was surrounded by brothers. Brothers who walked past what he was rather than using it as a joint to twist, or a knife to drive you with. They had simply decided he was worth the cost.

Tzal lifted her shoulders and slipped back through the cheerful crowd of onlookers. Rahummi was nowhere to be seen, so she stepped outside the gate and walked in the shadow of the wall toward Azetla's headquarters. It was terribly dark in the tiny room, walking in from the midday sun as she had. She unhooked the inner canvas of the windows and, once her eyes adjusted, ran her hands along the coils of vellum and reed paper.

She found the maps she wanted right away. Azetla's meticulous system of organization ensured that her inability to read was no hindrance to her. East to west. Terrain maps first, political second, historical, narrative, then sketch.

Today, she wanted the maps of Masheva. There were certain places repeatedly mentioned in Azetla's holy writs—villages or mountains or shrines, she did not know—and she wanted to find out where or what they were. She didn't like when a word came to her ear with blank meaning, surrounded by no color or scent or sound. Not that she could have read the words even if she found them.

There were only two maps of the region: a large one of the whole tribal south, wherein Masheva was rendered with the least detail of all four provinces, and a historical map of Masheva as it was during the golden age of the Tusian Empire.

Neither offered anything in the way of terrain or tribes as far as she could tell. If she had a third map, perhaps she could begin to triangulate *something* but, try as she might, she could only go as far as the East Trekoan hill country in her mind's eye. She could smell the fragrant dry grasses that crackled under her feet, and she could see the faint circles around the hills rutted by grazing paths. Then, the picture faded to black.

She knelt next to the clay flat, fingers tracing edges, trying to see what would not be seen. She did not bother looking up when Azetla came in, but saw the light pour through and settle in the room as he tied the door open. He circled round, noted the object of her interest with nothing more than slightly raised eyebrows, then crouched over the basin of water to wash the crusted salt and dried blood off his face.

Tzal used her small finger to measure, trying to create a scale for herself based on known distances. But the proportions on both maps were too imprecise.

When Azetla sat down across from her at the north end of the table, she looked him over. His face was still bright with exertion, his demeanor that of someone wholly refreshed by a pleasant exhaustion.

"These aren't any use," she said brusquely.

"I know."

"Why don't you mark out the tribal areas, at least?"

"Those aren't worth correcting. Anyhow, all the ancestral claims were broken apart during the Tusian Empire. Corvee labor moved everyone around and these days the distinctions between tribes are...few."

She worked her way around his words until she found a place to grip.

"The Trekoans have a saying about that: 'all spices are made dust beneath the pestle, and you can never again extract the cumin from the clove.'"

"Well it wouldn't serve us to be in the same state as Trekoans, fractured along a dozen lines," he said.

"Of course not. But it makes sense now: why you are able to ingratiate yourself with northerners so well."

His expression changed abruptly, though his relaxed posture remained.

"What's that supposed to mean?"

"Those distinctions don't mean much to them either," she said softly. "You know, I always got the impression that the reason you hated that King of yours so dearly was because he was always currying favor with Maurowans. Trying to alleviate their contempt. Trying to prove himself to them. That sort of thing. And yet..." She fluttered her fingers over the symbol of Areo outpost.

Gods, that took him by the throat. His jaw drew tight, and the look in his eye was nothing less than horror. A breath from the nose like a bull, shoulders raised taut. All that rare joy and ease gone, as if the door had been shut and the windows battened down.

It was a little more than she had bargained for, actually. She sat back and waited, somewhat uneasily. When Azetla spoke again, his words were slow and deliberate.

"If you're taking soundings—if there is something you're trying to find out by goading—why not just *ask*?"

"As if a curated answer would mean anything."

"Really?" he said. "Every last word out of your mouth is cut to exact size, and every tilt of your head. You dole out and withhold information to pull and push. First you give generously because you think it will save you, and now you hold back because don't want to lose your place here—"

The sound of footsteps and the distinct clink-and-rustle of Trekoan war dress drew their eyes toward the door. Tzal stood up.

"I can't lose what I don't have."

She said it quietly, and in Mashevi. She was fairly certain she said it right.

Whatever expression passed over Azetla's face was gone as soon as it came; she knew nothing by it. He stood also. Rahummi entered, full of warmth and greetings and—after a moment—numerous words that Tzal must render for him.

"Let's take a walk, my-brother," Rahummi said.

So he and Azetla walked, with Tzal immediately behind them, settling into her usual place of comfort: being the means of conversation but not a participant in it. It was customary that the translator be treated as mere furnishing, and Tzal never minded it. She could see and think and be, while very little attention was paid her.

To her absolute fascination, people usually seemed to forget that she was there; she held all their words in her hands till she was as strong and invisible as the wind.

Azetla was still not accustomed to this way of doing things. Every now and then he looked back to see her expression as she spoke, to gauge her tone against her posture. It was poor etiquette, but Rahummi did not begrudge him his inexperience; he used to do the same with her when they were young, and each time Rokh Imal would flick him in the middle of his forehead to stop him till he learned not to look back at her.

"There *was* a skirmish between Janbaris and Numayris last week. Four killed. They always attack Janbar first, to antagonize us. They want to see if Saqiran will fulfill our duty to Janbar, which," Rahummi gave Azetla a fierce look, "of course, we *will*."

Ah Rahummi, no need to sound so defensive. The Mashevi doesn't know.

"But that is a separate matter from what I have really come to tell you. Rokh Imal wishes to give you more men. That you will train them as you train these Maurowans."

Azetla gave a slow nod.

"He had mentioned that some time ago. I am willing to do it, but Colonel Everson..."

"My uncle has decided he would rather ask forgiveness than permission. He has known the Colonel many years and he believes he'll not have the will to say no once three thousand Saqirani and Janbari fighters arrive at the gates."

Azetla's brow furrowed. He looked back at Tzal.

"Three thousand? Are you sure he said three thousand?"

"Of course I'm sure," she said.

Rahummi smiled at Azetla.

"My-brother, you must understand. Maurow thinks of us in dozens. But you must not let their thinking confuse you. We can be thousands. Under the right circumstances, we might be tens of thousands. Over the last several years we have broken off the yoke of Qatlan," now Rahummi did glance at Tzal with a soft smile, "and contempt for the greater yoke has grown with that small taste of freedom."

Azetla looked at Rahummi, then to the road. He was quiet for half the length of the south training field.

"Three thousand men will put Areo at its fullest capacity," he said at last. "There's the matter of supplies."

"Bir Herash and Oyesh-Dir-Min-Yazha will assist in all necessary provisions. Now come, there is one more thing I must show you."

Rahummi veered toward the south stables. Tzal grew curious. He had already said all she knew to expect, albeit with a number she had not anticipated, and he also made those omissions she knew he would make. What was left?

The three of them entered the south stables. They were finer than the north ones, built wide and airy for the privileged North Trekoan breeds, which the Maurowans coveted for being taller than most desert horses, yet hardy like them.

Rahummi walked past his horses and past Tzal's own Nashuv. He made a gesture at the chief stableman who opened the stall and, by a slim sheep's skin bridle, presented a seal bay warhorse. Tzal let out a coarse laugh.

"What the hell are you doing, Rahummi?" she breathed in Hushai dialect.

He glanced at her, did not answer, then spoke to Azetla.

"This is a gift from Rokh Imal, my-brother. Named Barra, and sired by Qowah of Sanchi," Rahummi said, his voice suddenly full of pomp and circumstance.

"He doesn't know what that means," Tzal muttered after translating.

Rahummi looked at her once again, this time with strange frustration. Almost a pleading. He replied directly to her in Hushai dialect.

"I am doing what was put into my hands to do, and saying what was put in my mouth to say."

She stood back, chastened. Those were *her* words—old ones—shot back at her. Well-aimed too. So Tzal translated. Habit made her take on Rahummi's inflection, though Azetla had easily read the tension. He looked faintly wary of it all, questions flitting across his face.

Questions she did not have to answer.

Rahummi gave a speech regarding the extravagant gift. And perhaps the speech was not so aggravating as it seemed—*perhaps*—but every word bore the stamp of Rokh Imal, not Rahummi himself. She could practically hear his voice and see his expression: a pride that had fear at the back of it and a piety that washed only the part of the hand that others saw. If a bit of her own derision infiltrated her voice, she didn't think it noticeable.

"And with this gift, may you always remember your God, and never forget your people," Rahummi concluded.

This was a common ceremonial phrase among the Trekoans who served the Mashevi God, but Azetla tensed as though it was a reprimand.

"Thank you," he said stiffly. "I'm honored."

Rahummi relaxed, his duty done, and smiled. "Would you like to try his paces with me?"

Tzal translated and reached to take Nashuv from his stall.

"No." Rahummi held his hand up to her. "No, Shihrayan, I don't need you anymore. You can leave."

"But he won't—"

"Leave me to it. My Maurowan is a little better these days. Let me stumble around a little if needs be. I'll manage."

She dropped her hand from the stall latch.

"If you say so."

Azetla watched her leave with slight confusion. She heard their disjointed attempts at conversation as she stepped back into the sunlight. She went straight through the south gate to the Oraq plateau. She had climbed it so many times, she probably could have done it in pitch black if she had to.

None of this should surprise her.

She had been gone two years; Rahummi must have worked very hard to extricate his reputation from hers, for they had always been at each other's side in her days under Rokh Imal. But that was then. He'd bleached the cloth clean and must be careful not to dirty it again.

She brushed away the sting of it. Rahummi used to be the first to ask for her help, and without begrudging that she could give it. And when he was with Rokha Ayla, he had sometimes called her Tzal. He never did that now.

She climbed as fast as she could. When she sat at the top, berated by the wind, she had silence in her head for a while, and streaks of dried salt on her arms and around her mouth. When the thoughts roused again, numerous and aggravating as flies on the skin, she went back, taking the harder way down.

7

Azetla had instructed the watch to rouse him a little earlier than usual and was briefly disoriented by the grip on his shoulder. His eyes resisted opening as if the lids were stuck together. He pushed himself upward slowly, sore and lightly bruised from yesterday's sparring. When he managed to pry open his eyes, he saw moonlight brightly framing the window-cloth, and felt how still the air was.

He dressed, prayed, and put on his sagam. He left his Maurowan sword beside his bed; the official day did not start for an hour. He felt around in the basket which contained his few personal possessions and—after a moment of hesitation—grabbed the coil of parchment.

The watch greeted him and gave him a cup of coffee, as they always did, and Tzal was already there when he reached the watchfire pit, as she almost always was these days. There was much she did that was unpredictable. She would come, she would leave, she would help him, or she would stand back a while to watch him stumble in the dark. But Azetla took careful note of those habits she fell to most often, and under what circumstances she did so.

During the day, if she was absent, it was best to look up. The ramparts. The south balcony of Everson's residence. The plateaus outside the gates. He knew that most people took to the high places to beseech their gods, but since Tzal held hers in contempt, he doubted that was the reason.

Also, she always woke early and scrounged through Everson's kitchen for better fare than could be got by the men in the barracks. And then, God alone knew what she used to do half the time, but for the last month, she always came and sat by the watchfire.

The two of them hardly talked in the traditional sense. She would teach him how to say something in Trekoan, he would muddle it, she would correct him, and he would muddle a little less. Eventually he would relinquish the same phrase in Mashevi. She did not need much correction. He supposed he could have resented this disparity but it was strangely soothing to have all words returned to him strong, clear, and intact, as if they had been born there.

He handed her the coffee. She tasted it slowly, shook her head, then gave it back.

"They need to ask the Trekoans how to do it," she said.

"They work with what they have," he said dryly. "Listen, you know exactly why you can't have any official place in—"

"Oh for blood's sake that was just a statement of fact," she said with tired irritation. "A comment, not a complaint."

Azetla rolled his jaw and sat down.

"The point is, I've taken care not to ask too often for your help and certainly never to demand it. I don't have a right to and, practically speaking, I can't afford to make my survival here dependent on you."

She stared at the fire, saying nothing.

"But now I need you to tell me what Rahummi would not," he said.

"And what *did* Rahummi tell you?" she asked. She reached over for the coffee, giving it a second chance.

"Nothing more about the skirmishes." *A little bit about you, though, when pressed.* He wasn't going to mention that. "A great deal about the horse."

Tzal gave a sigh. "Yes, yes. The horse."

"It's the extravagance of it that concerns me..." Azetla said.

Tzal nodded. "It should. Trekoans don't often *gift* such a thing unless it comes with a tether. It's a great honor, but one you might have done better not to accept."

"It creates a debt."

"Yes. You don't owe him anything now because you don't *have* anything. Should a day come when you do, you will. He'll do even more than that, just like he would for a horse he thinks will win a race...or a war," Tzal continued. Her voice was low and soft as she turned the leather band on her wrist round and round. "He expects training and battle and the taking of ground. He expects a subordinate, not a superior, and for you to be his ally first, before Maurow or anyone else. He'll never exactly demand something a person can't give...but with Barra, he makes a strong wager on you. And no one likes to lose a wager."

Azetla rested his elbows on his knees and lowered his head. So often he had been forced to simplify his aims: *can I come out of this alive?* But now, more than ever, the quieter and more driving question was allowed to crawl to the surface: *can I come out of this with any shred of honor?* He was already playing both sides against the middle. He was already steeped beyond recovery in lies of omission.

The Mashevi sages had the right of it; rarely was it a sudden plunge to deceit and hypocrisy. One simply acclimated to the gentle slope downward, each step carefully justified, and you learned not to look up to see how far down you had come. You liked to imagine that, whatever the loss, it would be easy to recover. As soon as you got the chance.

Tzal may not have understood fully, but her instincts had told her the truth; there was no crueler barb she could have offered than to compare him to *that man*; Keved Aver, King of Masheva. He was everything Azetla hated, and everything he feared he would become. A coward. A liar. An apostate. A man who would sacrifice anyone and anything to *keep his place*.

"That's not all Rahummi didn't tell you." Tzal's voice came strangely soft, dispersing his thoughts.

Azetla turned with weary apprehension.

"In his defense, he'll never tell you something that might put his uncle to shame." She gave a half-hearted smile. "He lets me do that for him."

"Well?"

"There are three tribes south of Areo whose loyalty Rokh Imal might lose. Soon. Ishaan, Sirawal, and Ukhaf. They're weak and very small, so when larger tribes had need, his obligations to the little ones fell by the wayside. This happened more than once, and they've grown bitter and desperate. There are rumors they've allowed Qatlan to pass through their land and use their wells. Rokh Imal claims that they will hold to him because 'right is on his side' but the truth is, he doesn't see much value in them."

"You think I have to restore his reputation with them?" Azetla said slowly, chewing on the information.

Tzal waved her hand as if he was missing the point.

"If it makes you feel better to be appealed to on the basis of honor, then broken vows *are* at stake. Imal has failed them. But there is a practical matter of no interest to him; you have to go through their land to get to Cozona outpost."

He tensed slightly, and tried to mask it with a sip of coffee. But there was really no point. She would see and go on seeing with the eye of one who has learned to hunt for survival in a barren place. When he looked at his maps, she followed the trail his eyes made across the parchment.

"Look, it's no difference to me—" she began.

He gave her a wry look.

"But for once I'd say Rokh Imal has the right of it. Ask for forgiveness, not permission."

"I would've liked to have more information by now."

"What? Qatlan's numbers, encampments, that sort of thing?" she said. She grabbed the coil of parchment from his side and began, carefully, to slip off the binding braids.

"Yes," he answered slowly. "And I don't know what Qatlan *knows*."

Tzal pulled the parchment open across her knees and, after a moment of confusion, raised her eyebrows. It was Masheva she held, not Trekoa. Azetla rested his mouth against his fist and watched. She drank a long, fine draught of the map before she spoke.

"The scale and key are different. I don't understand them."

"Well it's not Maurowan made. I can explain them to you."

"It's well-crafted."

"Like I said. It's not Maurowan made."

She gave half a smile as she ran her palm just above the illustrated border.

Azetla waited to hear her criticize it. The rich detail, elegant drawings, and unnecessary anecdotes all showed that the map had not been made by a strategist, but by a cartographer a little too deeply enamored of his subject in the abstract. A faded splash of indigo gave color to the Goshesh Sea. The capital, Rinayim, out of great affection and honor, had been drawn well out of scale, with the likeness of the temple ruin at its center.

He saw her note each of these things, and trace the distance between the borderlands she knew, and the coast that she did not. Azetla took a sharp pleasure, quiet and thief-like, in seeing someone relish the thing he relished.

"It's not a military map," he said. "But the important parts—the roads, towns, terrain, and regions—they're accurate."

She nodded, eyes still fixed, but straining a little by firelight. "If only all Everson's maps were like this."

"I'd have brought it out yesterday but you were more interested in antagonizing me, so I didn't have the chance," Azetla said.

She breathed a laugh and Azetla supposed it was because she didn't believe him. After a few moments, she rolled the map again with slow precision and handed it back to him. Without a word, she left the firepit, swallowed by the dark outside of it.

She would raid Everson's kitchens, and come back at her leisure, as usual.

Except she did not come back. Not that morning. Not that afternoon. Not by nightfall.

Nashuv was gone from the stables, and the Shihrayan was gone from Areo.

"He killed it."

"No, he didn't. He would've told us."

"I don't think he even *wants* to kill it."

"He doesn't. It's too useful."

"That's the problem."

"Look, the Commander knows what he's doing, even if—"

"—well, one way or the other, it's gone, isn't it?"

Sergeant Burre Lachlan stood outside the light of the watchfire for a few moments, listening to the young men have their argument. They were an interesting mix. Nuss, Isilia, and Vrai from the Black Wren, ready to defend their jackal against all charges—even against all reason. Mavoz and Lukios from Juniper, lukewarm on the subject. Idhan from Sojj Pine, a Makar, still trying desperately to hold the jackal in as much contempt as he felt necessary.

But the jackal wasn't the true subject of the night.

"Well, good riddance, I guess. But I honestly don't believe it really is a devil," Idhan said.

"How can you say that?" Nuss exclaimed. "I was there! I was in Sahr territory. I saw it with my own eyes. Running down the rocks like an ibex!" Nuss was passionate, but he was not angry. That was the interesting thing to Sergeant Lachlan. None of them were angry.

The boys no longer sounded like wary enemies. The clannishness of the battalions was chiefly on the surface, all in good fun. They had the antagonism, the ease, the warmth, the raw annoyance of brothers. Sergeant Lachlan, with his long years and his gray head, rather liked the sound of it.

The damn jackal was sewing them together, one stitch at a time, with a deft hand. And that devil, whatever would become of it, had sharpened the needle and handed him the thread. Lachlan was amazed by this, in spite of himself.

"You're an idiot, Idhan. Everyone and their grandmother knows it's a devil. That isn't the question. What *happened* to it? That's what I want to know."

Sergeant Lachlan thought it best to step in now.

"The Commander didn't kill the devil," he said. The young ones looked up from the fire. "And he didn't send it away. It was no longer bound, that's all."

"He should have killed it, Sergeant," Vrai muttered.

"Maybe. Maybe not." Nuss shook his head thoughtfully. "The Trekoans say it can't die."

Lachlan did not know about that. To his eyes, the Sahr looked like a thing that could die.

To his eyes it looked like a thing that had every intention of dying. Only it had very high standards, Colonel Everson once told Lachlan. "Oh, she wants the Gods to be the ones to do it, you know."

8

Tzal shifted her weight and slowed Nashuv, pulling him up. He breathed hard and there were flecks of foam at the edge of his mouth. She waited until she was sure the Janbari men had spotted her, then slipped down and led Nashuv by the reins with a loose grip. The sleeve of the outer robe she wore hung down to her knuckles so that the Makarish tattoo on her hand was mostly concealed. The head covering was the same as that which a West Trekoan woman of low status would wear. Her appearance ought to have been utterly nondescript.

But there was no question that the Janbari men who met her at the crest of Yavash hill had marked her as a concern. Their swords were already drawn.

"This is your fault," she whispered to Nashuv.

A Sanchi lineage horse was hard to miss. But the truth was, she could never maneuver through Trekoa as freely as she had those first years under Rokh Imal. Back then, no one knew who or what she was and, if they heard a rumor, they did not believe it. If they saw her, she was of no interest until all the damage she intended to do—and all the knowledge she intended to extract—was accomplished.

When anonymity was gone she was forced to use notoriety and that was much harder. Anonymity made no claims. Notoriety had to prove itself. There was every possibility she could not live up to her own reputation. Honestly, she was a little out of practice. There was a steady turning in her stomach, like some pestle swiveling round and round and round in the mortar. She opened her mouth and ran her tongue across the edges of her teeth where she felt the residual pressure of clenching. She rapped her fingers rhythmically against her thigh and turned the slave band on her wrist.

When she had been younger, in Shihra, there was only raw terror in every violent encounter, collapsing exhaustion after. But in Trekoa she had learned to make the flutter of nerves before danger work in her favor. She took her own tension and drew it like an arrow and bowstring, supple and well-aimed.

"God's holy blessing to all his children," the first Janbari man said, his tone ice-cold. "Who are you and what business do you have in Yavash?"

"I've come to speak to your seer."

"Are you here as the hand of Saqiran?" the older Janbari man said.

She did not know this man's name, but she recognized him. And it was clear now that he recognized her too.

"No."

"The hand of Areo?"

She took a deep breath, feigning a thoughtful pause.

"No."

"He'll know if you're lying."

She smiled. "Good. Then we have nothing to worry about."

The five of them encircled her, driving her forward with their swords low and ready. Now there was nothing feigned at all in her breathing or her posture, both gone taut. She snaked her hand up, slowly, slowly, toward Nashuv's mane, then down to the canvas flap of his saddle.

"Calm, calm, Nashuv." She tisked as the tips of her fingers felt the metal handle of her old Trekoan knife. Nashuv trod on, pulling his head up only once or twice. Tzal ran her thumb back and forth over the scored knob of metal under the canvas. She breathed in and out with the motion and kept her eyes moving from one man to the next.

The one to the left and slightly behind her was young. And nervous.

Tzal reached up to remove her head covering. The man stiffened, eyes skittish. But when the head covering fell, and nothing happened, he settled back into his stride. She continued to do a dozen small, meaningless movements—wipe her forehead, adjust her shift, stroke Nashuv, change grips on the reins—until their instinct to worry and react dulled. She walked with a lazy posture and a weary gaze. "*Calm, calm,*" she silently told them, as with a soft stroke. "*I'm truly nothing to worry about. Nothing at all.*"

If she wound up with five dead Janbaris on the slope of Yavash and no seer to speak to she would have failed before she even started.

She felt a slight revulsion upon seeing the Seer's black-red tent. She had come here a handful of times, when Rokh Imal was desperate enough to hand her a little gold, honey, or spices, and tell her to "find out one way or another and don't tell me." He liked being able to deny that he had consulted a demon-haunted seer.

The heat bore down on her as she waited outside the tent. When she was let in—pushed in—the cloth fell dark behind her and the air turned thick with the heavy sweetness of incense. Tzal coughed and felt a dizziness which took tremendous focus to fight off.

The Seer sat just outside the light of the dim lamp and the dark red glow of incense, in the safety of shadow. Even so, she could see the streak of blood from his own palm, smeared across his blind eyes, just as the seers in South Makaria and even in outer Shihra did. She could hear the tick of long fingernails against the copper divining bowl. The same sound from the Shaman of Dimash before an execution or an exile, the same rhythm she herself tapped when trying to stir up someone else's nerves.

She hated everything about this man. He used all her own tricks and it turned her stomach.

"Speak your name and village," he said in a calm voice. It always started out that way—soothing and pleasant—but his tenor would gradually change and start to feel like a needle in the ear, a cold scraping down the spine.

"None," she said.

He smiled, and out came a laugh, thick as a bog. "Is that who I think it is?" He tapped the woven mat in front of him twice then gestured upward. "Then you will certainly not have come empty-handed."

From her satchel she drew two quarter-bricks of salt, and a pound of whole spices. As the Janbari man next to her described the payment to him, she laid the offering on the mat, expecting the Seer to scoff at how little she brought.

What she did not expect was for his hand to dart out, snatch her wrist, and pull her down toward him. She caught herself with her knee, her left hand slipping to hilt. But she did not draw. She pulled back, but was met with a startling amount of strength, and fingernails burrowing into skin.

Still, she did not draw.

"If it's not enough, just send me on my way."

Again the thick, syrupy laugh. "Oh it's not nearly enough, but I have no intention of sending you on your way. I know you could kill me right now if you wanted, but that is exactly why I'm not afraid of you, devil. Why so cautious? You *need* something from me, so I'm going to get what I want from *you*."

His forefinger plucked at the Saqirani slave band on her wrist. "First, I would very much like to know who owns you right now."

With visceral disgust, she twisted her hand till his wrist bent and he could not hold on any longer. She sat back against her heels and said nothing. Information was one of his favorite currencies and she had to find some way to inflate the value of the little she meant to part with. She was, as the saying went, trying to buy a Sanchi horse with a lame donkey.

"Everyone said Rokh Imal renounced you...but it seems you didn't renounce him?" He massaged his wrist. "You poor, stupid creature. You think his half-hearted piety casts some light over you, but you're no better than me, Shihrayan. You were stitched into darkness from birth. You'll never get out."

Tzal's head ached from the incense. His tone of voice was already taking its turn, as if from clear air to dust storm.

"Do you want to know what I came to ask?" she said.

"I want to know what is going on at Areo."

"What does Qatlan *think* is going on?"

The Seer was very quiet after that. He was Janbari-born. He ought to have some loyalty to Saqiran and Janbar, if only for the sake of his own safety. But a seer was like a depression in the ground, to which people found themselves slipping from all directions, and to which information would inevitably drain to form a sinking pool of mud for everyone to claw through.

He could not admit out loud that he ever dealt with Qatlan. He could not be known for it.

But she knew.

She knew a great deal about him that she held behind her back. That he was a shepherd in Ma'at-jouf until an infection took his sight. That his family's poverty drove him from a pious youth toward the Makarish spirits and gods. That much of his "divining" was like her own "devilry": he was deft with words and manner and manipulation.

Yet she did not think him a fraud. She knew that if you told the demons you would like to hear their voices...they would let you. And then they would not stop letting you.

"I have nothing for you," he said in a flat voice. "But give me what I ask, and allow me a few weeks."

She reached over and began to wrap up the bricks of salt and the spices.

"I'm not going to wait around for your informants or your spirits. I came for what's in stock."

"In a hurry, I see." The Seer smiled.

He flicked his hand at the Janbari soldier. The man glanced hesitantly at Tzal, then departed. The Seer began to scrape his fingernail round and round in the divining bowl, and the texture of the copper gave a rhythm to the sound—*skkkil-tic-tic, skkkil-tic-tic*—and it made her nauseous. She knew there were real, foul spirits. She had felt them before, like hands clawing over the mouth, a whirlpool pulling you down, or even a foul metal taste in her mouth when she spoke and knew for a fact that no one could help but listen and succumb. It didn't happen often, but it did happen.

Her hands turned to fists where they rested on her thighs and the thick, oppressive sweetness of the air dragged dark sounds and sights through her mind; agarwood and camphor, screams and burning flesh, blood running down the stones of Dimash, a broken body on the lintel of a door. All this haze surrounded by the clear knowledge that she herself was the cause of it all.

She braced against the oppressive atmosphere and felt a rush of relief when the copper-scraping sound stopped abruptly.

The Seer laughed at her.

"I have barely even begun to knock on the door of the dark, Sahr devil, and you're already flinching. Why are you so afraid of your own nature?"

He reached out and took the salt and spices.

"I will tell you what I already know, because it is small enough to meet you at your price. Qatlan sends a runner to Pardish market every few days. A Numayri fellow. He sits and listens to the Saqirani gossip, never opens his mouth, sells a few trinkets, then goes home. He takes the Mahwar trail, I'm told. Perhaps today, perhaps tomorrow. Get ahold of him, and you may find out what Qatlan knows."

She rapped her hand on the low table in acknowledgment.

"That's all I need."

She turned to leave.

"*Wait*," he growled. "Pay the rest. Is it really a Mashevi, an actual easterner, commanding the soldiers at Areo?"

"Yes."

"And for his sake you came here today."

She chewed longer on that one.

"Yes."

"Then I wish you well, Sahr."

She let out a sharp breath through her nose.

"No really, I do." He laughed. "Go. I hope you find all the throats you wish to slit. Soak yourself in blood till you drown in it. And enjoy it while you can. Because on this road, all that fire you're trying to scrape back to life will be snuffed out, and everything you cherish now will turn to ash for you. Even the words in your mouth."

Tzal walked out of the tent without reply or the least scrap of cold farewell. She sucked in the clear air outside.

His voice had changed at the last. The needle stabbing into the ear. The words clung to her as she left, cobwebs on the skin. Hours later it was impossible to be certain she had brushed them all off.

9

*I*t was easy to disown the shikk. This, the family and village did publicly. It was harder to want to do it. And hardest of all to force her to disown them. She was of the clan of Haddar. Of the tribe of Illari. She refused to relinquish these truths, no matter that she was thrust out from under the shelter they were meant to provide.

She was sap to the skin, not so easily washed off.

She was ten when Sa'ased was obliged to turn her out and send her to the leper village, Kivaj, on the edge of Shihra. This was the place for problems and refuse, and she was hardly the first to be sent there. Yet over and over again she made the rough two-hour climb back to Yaqil. Aadin woke to her lying next to Dotiya, Dotiya's fingers gripping the shikk's ragged tunic like a blanket, shoulder nestling into her ribs. And when Dotiya cried in the night, as she sometimes did, the shikk would sing the same song Birai had sung over her.

No beating or threat deterred her. She took every strike like granite. A true Shihrayan, he must admit. When she looked too lean and ragged, Aadin discovered how weak he was; he would fill her arms with what little they had before he cuffed her hard and sent her back.

But it could not possibly have gone on like that, this half-hearted turning of the back.

When the summer burned to its height, and the water shrank into mud, she was attacked in the outer lowlands. By a fellow Illari. For her food or for being a curse, Aadin never knew. It was a miracle she lived. She dragged herself home, all bruises and blood. It was a few days before she was on her feet again.

Aadin did not know if the anger he felt was more toward her or toward the Illari who ambushed her; they seemed about the same. Either way, it was not going to happen again.

That day, he took charge. Let Birai and Sa'ased be innocent of her. She would belong to him. As a soldier to his captain, a slave to his master, a dog to the hunter, she would be his creature.

He would drag her across every rock of Shihra and the low desert. Whatever harm came to her would be by his own hand, not anyone else's. If she would not let them let her go, then Aadin would take her and put her to his own use. She would learn to raid and thieve and barter and swindle in the lowlands, as all outer village Shihrayans must do in desperate times. This would be her purpose and her place.

With her tongue and tenacity, she was well-suited to it.

"This, Zaraje, is how you shall be one of us while not one of us. You can only belong by the skin of your teeth, from afar, as long as you make yourself valuable. And, by blood, you will learn to watch your own back."

She had made him afraid; she would fear him too. Aadin would be to her like a virulent infection, nearly killing her so that no one else would ever *be able to do it.*

Her eyelids pulled down to close and her head lolled. She flicked herself hard against the cheekbones and across the forehead, circling her eyes with firm pressure. Forced her posture straight again.

It became easier when the sun rose, then harder again when the mid-morning heat set in.

Her vision blurred, and the whole desert turned into a tawny haze, but a flicker of movement caused her to blink hard and try to focus.

A pack donkey. A boy. Headed west on the Mahwar trail.

That woke her up like water dashed over the head.

It had taken her six hours to get to Mahwar, and nearly an hour to climb her old lookout, limbs sore and aching afterward. Every inch of her was stiff from her perch, but she scuttled down the northeast face of the butte. She circled partway round and jumped at last onto the Mahwar, not half a mile behind him.

She closed the distance slowly. She was almost breathing down his neck before he seemed to sense that he was not alone. The boy glanced back, his wavy black hair falling across his forehead, nearly to his eyes. Couldn't possibly be more than seventeen years old, she thought, and a wiry, underfed seventeen at that.

He stopped and stared.

In this part of the desert, a woman who traveled alone was either a fool, a whore, or a jinn. The confused look in the boy's wide eyes told her that he had not yet decided which.

"Gods greet you stranger, will you share a meal with me? Some water?" she called in a plain, neutral voice. Not too clever, lest she suggest jinn. Not too drawing, lest she suggest a woman of the roadside.

The boy remained wary. His shoulders were raised high, his mouth drawn. He looked ahead to the path—a rugged one—and she saw the shimmer of flight in his eye. Yet he did not run. He made his donkey a wall between them, and talked over the animal's shoulder.

"I...I don't have much," he said.

"Neither do I. But I'll share it if you'll break bread with me. Please."

That time her voice was strained, plaintive. She spoke with the gentle lilt and the omitted consonants of the Barad tribe which ought to make him feel, if only unconsciously, a little safer. It was the closest dialect to the Numayri one, which was her secret favorite.

She marked her route around the donkey's hind legs. She was ready to chase. But the boy stayed.

She was relieved. And a little sad.

What followed was one those strange things that she had experienced many times, but which she could not explain to anyone, not even herself.

She lied and lied, but it all tasted true. She played a role, but it felt as solid as her own back teeth—which had been gritted with uncertainty only a moment ago—and as real and intrinsic as her own blood, flowing in her body. She was a young Baradi woman, shamed by her family for reasons she dare not explain, seeking a new life in Maurow. She was sad and lonely and halfway innocent.

It was easy to fall from one voice to the next, from one sympathy to another, and there was nothing to stop her from the shift and the plunge, because it seemed there was no bedrock in her. Or if she had it, she had yet to meet it.

The boy laid out a scant bit of dried goat meat, a small barley cake, and a share of his water. She laid plump dates, several rounds of fried, spiced chuvia, and her share of water. It truly was all she had left. The boy prayed a little prayer to the desert God—this surprised her since most Numayris followed the Gods of West Makar—then he ate ravenously. Without his noticing, she let him have the greater portion. She refilled his cup each time he drained it till hers was nearly empty.

"It is strange, you being out here alone," he said through a bite. He looked askance at her, still uncomfortable for all their shared and meager hospitality. "Where are you going?"

"I don't know yet."

The boy knit his brow and finally managed to look her in the eye with a childlike shyness.

"You ought to go to the main road and meet with a caravan. These trails are contested territory."

"It is good advice," she said, her voice even softer than before.

He finished eating. There was no reason to delay any longer. She felt the dread and distaste so strongly for a moment, but when the Numayri boy reached forward for the mealcloth, she grasped his wrist. He did not even try to pull back. He froze in fear.

"Listen very carefully and answer every question exactly. How many times have you carried market gossip to Qatlan?"

He tried to jump to his feet. She jerked him down and he tripped against the rocky ground. She pulled him beneath her, her knee in his spine, his arm pinned behind him, ready to be wrenched like a lever till it broke.

"I'm sorry, little one. Under other circumstances I might have brought it out of you gently, and you could have gone on your way none the wiser. But I'm in a hurry. What have you told Qatlan about the outpost?"

His voice came thick, jaw pressed to the ground, dust coating his mouth.

"I told them everything I heard. I don't know what mattered and what didn't. They sent me because I...I can remember word-for-word."

"What made them ask for *more*?"

"They wanted to know about the jackal. They asked about him over and over. I told them he was a Maurowan soldier. That he answered to the Colonels. But they also answer to him. And I told them that he was alone."

"What do you mean 'alone'?"

"He has no band of jackals with him, no kin, no one of his own kind. He is alone."

The boy made a sudden writhing movement, but she was ready for it, bracing with her foot against the ground and bearing her weight down on him till he gave up. It was strange; he did not seem to realize that a more sustained effort really might shake her off. He didn't understand how badly he needed to do it. *I wish you would fight harder. It makes it so much easier.*

"What else did they want?"

"They wanted to know why the Colonel at Areo had changed so many things in the last months."

"And did you find an answer for them?"

Silence. She heard his breaths rasp and chop; he was trying not to cry. He really was barely more than a child.

"Not before now."

"What do you have for them *today*?"

"The men at the market all say...they say that Areo—that the jackal—will overturn Qatlan. Any day now, the war will start. Where Qatlan has been the right hand of Maurow, Saqiran will take its place. Qatlan will be destroyed, and perhaps we Numayris with them. It is a coup."

She moved her hand slowly back along the ground toward her belt. The rumors were somehow both true and false at the same bloody time.

"I won't tell them," he whispered. "Please. *Please.* I'm Numayri, not Qatlani. Please. My family follows the desert God. The Mashevi God. I won't tell them. I won't say anything!"

"I know you won't."

She drew the knife. Took him by the chin. Pulled the blade hard across the throat, leaving no need for a second attempt.

He really tried to fight at the last, but it was too late. She felt the life go out beneath her, like a sinking, sinking, sinking to the ground until, so suddenly and strangely, the body was just a thing, lying there, ready for the vultures and dust and time to take it away.

She raided the donkey's satchels. She raided the body. No reason not to.

"Listen, little one: if your God is what the Mashevi says he is, all is rest and light from here," she whispered in Shihrayan to the corpse.

She found the little knife looped on his belt. "And I won't mangle you. I don't need to."

"By blood, why did you tie these so tight?" she said, working over the knots in the cord of his belt. She inadvertently glanced at the boy's face. It had no life or expression or character remaining and yet, even in its blankness, it reminded her of something. She turned away quickly before she could think what it was.

The halo of blood sat around the boy's head on the slab of rock, unabsorbed. A bit ran down and wetted the knee of her trousers and the hem of her shift.

"I know how your people fear being unburied. A curse, right? Animals tarnishing the body, making it unholy. But I'll tell you the truth." Against all need or reason, she lowered her voice to a whisper. "If the Gods really do adhere to curses marked on the body, then it will be far worse for me than for anyone I ever marred. Have that as your vengeance, little one."

She finally got the knot loose, and slipped the knife off. After a brief inspection, she pocketed it. It was a little small for his hand, or hers. He must have had it since he was young. She looked at the boy's face one last time, and then departed her native tongue for his.

"That's it. Your God is with you, maybe. Now let's go."

It took nearly an hour to get the body up so that she could drop it into the crevice. The vultures might give it away, eventually, but whoever wanted that body would have to hunt hard for it.

She wanted to collapse when she got back to the trail, but she knew that if she sat down it would be impossible to get back up. She reached the village of Gori at sunset, and paid the young woman for the care of her horse, Nashuv, and retrieved him. She paid with the clay and copper beads she had taken out of the boy's satchel.

Her empty stomach nagged at her as she rode all night under the three-quarters moon. She had the truthful excuse that time was of the essence. But she would have done it either way. There were many fierce thoughts driving at her back and, if she dared slow down, they would catch and swallow her whole.

Every village south of Areo bore traces of Qatlani incursion. Bead-work on girls' wrists with Qatlani-style etching. Anise and cam-phor incense. The villagers' ambiguous responses when asked about the ruling tribe. A reluctance to send their goats—and their young herders—too far from sight. An uneasy, fearful atmosphere.

They were bracing for whatever was coming, uncertain what that might be, or who to trust. But they did not expect to be helped or protected. They did not expect to matter to anyone but themselves.

Nearing the largest village, Sijaya, Tzal kept to the outskirts, settling herself by a small cut of rock. From there she could see the road, the village, and the hazy line of Wadi Obin to the south. She sat with the last of her water.

This time, her efforts were useless. Sleep struck her hard and put her down.

She awoke disoriented, not quite remembering where she was. Nashuv snuffling warning. Voices closing in on her quickly. The sudden pressure of a knee against her ribs. She went still as the dead.

"There's blood on the body, but it's warm," one whispered.

Qatlani dialect.

"It's a *Sanchi* horse, and if this—"

No. That was already more than they needed to know.

Tzal turned to her hip, clutched the leg, and buried her knife deep in the Qatlani's thigh. His sword hilt cracked against her shoulder as she ran him down, driving him with the handle of her knife. When he hit the ground, she held coiled to him, rolling his body directly on top of hers.

His spine took the sword blow meant for her.

The other Qatlani shouted and lunged just as Tzal twisted herself out from under the body; she barely caught the next strike with her short-sword. The hilt jarred her palm and the next blow nearly made her arm go numb.

She kicked and scrambled again, trying to get to her feet. Trying to run, run, *run*. She managed to get to a knee when the third swing came. She felt the hilt casing loosen around the blade, biting into her hand. She dropped it and bolted.

Bloody, stupid, shoddy weapon.

There was no way to know how close a thing it was. All she knew was that she felt the heaving sensation of an almost-fall at a cliff's edge, and she heard the metal cutting through the air at her back. She ran with all she had, zig-zagging up the rise. Across rock, soft dust, then rock again. She heard him lose his footing. Once. A second time. He fell further and further behind.

Night was an easy, nimble thing for Tzal because it was so often forced on her. Once she had her hand at the saddle, she could have pulled herself atop Nashuv and ridden blindfolded.

The sword was gone, though.

Her knees bit into Nashuv's flanks and he flew, circling back after she pulled her bow.

It took several attempts, but at last she saw the shadow of the man collapse in the dark. He staggered up. Tried again. She sent another arrow. He did not rise that time. She jumped down and slit the throat for certainty.

It seemed to take a very long time to get back to her feet. To shake the sudden watery limpness out of her arms. But she couldn't leave the bodies here.

Get up.

Get up.

It was four or five miles to the entrance of Wadi Busla.

She moved quickly, even though it felt like she was walking against a headwind. She could thank her brother for that. Aadin hated to be slowed down. She used to feel a visceral panic if she found herself falling behind for fear of what he would do.

As dawn broke, she dumped the bodies where the flow of the river was lively, if shallow.

She might reach Areo before dusk.

Weary thoughts began to worm into her mind as Nashuv's rhythm lulled her. She had achieved what she set out to accomplish. Some by work and some by luck, but she got what she wanted. She usually did.

It troubled her sometimes.

The mind and muscles atrophy when they meet no resistance and, besides, who is to say that the Gods don't let you have your own way just to see you snared by it.

Azetla did not realize how the light had gone till he finished writing the message. It always took him so long to choose each exact word and even the spacing of the words. His eyes ached. He slid the bit of reed paper into a deep mortar crack behind his pallet, then lit the lamps that hung over the headquarters table. He sat against the edge, going over the message in his head, making sure—absolutely sure—that each letter, each diacritical mark served its purpose.

Joseph came in with evening rations and a fiery scowl.

"You've heard," he said, his tone almost accusatory.

Azetla nodded.

"I've spent the last three days saying 'glad and good riddance.' The others too." Joseph slid the Trekoan map aside and set the bowl of food down. "But you never said anything at all."

No, he had not. And he wasn't going to say anything now.

Azetla rinsed his hands and whispered his prayers before dipping the bread into the chuvia. He had, at first, no idea whether or not Tzal would come back, and the question of *what* she was doing was even more fraught. Azetla steeled himself for some consequence and walked through the last three days with a quiet drum of anxiety below the surface of his skin.

But for all that, he didn't say "good riddance." He never even thought it.

Joseph dipped his bread into the bowl, trying to discover the gristly, crusted bits of meat mixed somewhere in there. "It's bad enough you're overplaying your hand—"

"Joseph, I'm not—"

"I wasn't done," Joseph said. "Every day you're bolder with the colonels, pushing them, provoking them, telling *them* what to do. All these Areo men are starting to believe they're actually ready for a war they could never, ever win. You've got the Trekoans bringing out their war dress—"

"You don't even know what—"

"And you've tolerated that Sahr jinn far too long. You should have killed it in the first place, but each time you listen to it, use it, let it help you, you make it more and more necessary. You *acclimate* to it and force us all to do the same."

Azetla took his time finishing the bite in his mouth, holding the anger at bay.

"I've heard those words before," he said, making his voice as pointedly calm as Joseph's had been angry. "But usually it was 'jackal' instead of 'jinn.'"

Joseph's eyes widened.

"*That's* how you want to classify yourself, Azetla? Really? Well the one who chose to ignore that warning is dead now, so who knows what he would say?"

The words went straight to the chest, knocking the wind out of Azetla's lungs. Joseph winced and looked at the ground.

"I didn't mean—"

The cloth door rustled and Tzal stepped in. Probably she had been waiting outside listening, though she offered no particular expression. She crossed the room wordlessly, took a handful of troop markers from the bowl on the desk, and began to place them—black for ten, yellow for a hundred—at various locations on the map of south Trekoa which was spread on the clay flat.

She looked awful. All her clothes were filthy, there was dried blood in her nailbeds and on her neck, even though it was clear by her damp hair and sleeves that she had tried to wash it off. The circles under her eyes were dark as fresh bruises and her scabbard was slung, but empty.

"There," she said, looking up. "These ones I know for certain—and these over here are conjecture."

She stood, meeting Joseph's unwavering glare, though she spoke to Azetla. "And if you don't want to lose the Ishaani villages—and their sister tribes—you need to meet with their Rokh right *now*."

Azetla scanned the Qatlani clusters on the map.

"Why didn't you *tell* me what you were doing?" he said.

If you had explained your actions, then I would have been able to explain mine.

Tzal rested her hands on the low table, leaning heavily, then stood straight again.

"I don't have to tell you anything. I'm not one of your soldiers. Besides, there was every chance I'd come back with nothing worth knowing. As it is." She gestured at the map. "Take it or leave it. If the latter, you will be handing thousands of dunams of land over to Qatlan. Within the week."

She walked toward the door.

"Tzal..."

She shook her head and waved his words away. "Just send word once you make up your mind."

There was a tight, miserable silence in the wake of her departure. Joseph crouched down and looked at the Qatlani troops concentrated just south of Areo.

"So that's why you pulled the Juniper officers into the last meeting."

Azetla nodded.

"And that's what you and Rahummi Bin-Deghan have been talking about."

Another nod.

"You knew the Sahr was doing this."

"No. I hoped she was."

Joseph let out a deep sigh. He was no fool. He understood nearly all that Azetla did not say.

"When do we leave?"

"Tomorrow."

10

The day Emperor Riada Sivolne was informed of the Sahr jinn's escape from the inn he knew—quietly and without pointless agonizing—that he would eventually have to kill his brother James.

Of course, it had always been a complicated question of "if." Now it was made simple, a mere question of "when."

Nothing was known. Nothing was proved. And James continued to *seem* his aimless, imbecilic self, doing exactly as he was told and showing little interest in the high court. But chieftains and kings and Emperors dying at the hands of their own kin was so common a tale as to be told in coffee houses as both a truism and a jest.

It wasn't as though the two of them had ever been anything like friends. But for the last few months, Riada kept him close and handled him gently. He hadn't gained much by it. Now he needed a different tactic.

"Tell my brother he may enter," Riada said, gesturing at his scribe. "Then leave us."

"Yes, Your Highness."

James stepped in with a deep bow, dressed and groomed with no particular care, and wearing a look of faint confusion.

"Honor to you and the Gods who uphold you, Your Highness," James rattled off in a stiff, formal tone. However, as soon as Riada indicated that he may, James relaxed into one of the cushioned chairs. Riada remained standing.

"What is it you wish of me?" James said.

"Only a quick word. Do you intend to come to tonight's gathering?"

"I hadn't really thought about it. I'll go if you like," he said in a resigned tone.

"You don't want to?" Riada said, his amazement absolutely genuine.

He simply could not comprehend this man. Sharp as Riada's mind was, wide as his intellect could roam, it could not reach as far as James. James, who would rather play Arratul with his nursemaid than attend either councils *or* festivals. James who was passive and plain and had described his lone act of valor, venturing to the devil's lands, as "well, very exhausting."

"No, not particularly," James replied. "Everyone will want me to tell stories about the jinn and it is so arduous to avoid the discussion. The only thing they want from me, I cannot give."

Riada spoke as gently as he was able, "This time, I will tell you what to say. And I will have you come."

"Oh," James said, disappointed. "But why?"

Riada smiled. "I like to keep my eye on you, for one." It always disarmed people to tell them what they assumed he must wish to hide. "And, besides, it's good for you. If you use the words I give you, you'll save some face."

Narrowing his eyes, James gave a dull nod.

"The jackals will be there, you know."

James sat straight now, his curiosity piqued. "King Aver?"

"He *and* his wife, in fact. And a handful of backwater Mashevi nobles."

"I thought they hated coming here."

"Oh, Gods, James. They do. With every fiber of their being," Riada said with satisfaction.

"Then why are they here for some lesser holiday that has nothing to do with them?"

"Because King Keved Aver always comes when he is called," Riada said softly.

He watched James shift and squirm in his chair as he realized that he too must come when called.

"Why...why do you want him here?"

"I have several concerns to discuss regarding that Mashevi coastline of mine," Riada said. "Concerns for which couriers are insufficient. It has been a long time since they have come to Piarago and, every now and then, I prefer to observe them with my own eyes. To make my own assessments. I know no better way to be certain of actions and intentions than to look a man in the eye and talk plainly to him."

James nodded unevenly, shoulders hunched, looking like a child waiting for the part where he would be boxed on the ears and told off.

"But still," James said, tilting his head. "Why must they come to the formal gatherings? No one wants them."

Riada smiled, for the strength of his own thoughts and plans was a heady thing.

"That's half the purpose, James. There's nothing so gratifying in all the world as watching Keved Aver twist under the light of his irrelevance."

"If he is so irrelevant why must he be reminded of it?" James muttered. "He probably knows it well enough. Seems almost petty, really."

Riada gave a cool laugh at what almost sounded like boldness, however accidental. "Be that as it may...even I like to indulge myself in a delicious taste once in a while. It's not only because he's Mashevi, though that would be enough. He's spineless. An infinite coward."

He could taste the hatred on his tongue, sharp and full of brine.

"But he sits on your coastline," James said.

"Yes. Yes, he does."

"And if he were any less of a coward, that would be a problem."

Riada raised his eyebrows.

Now, James, who put those words in your mouth? They're certainly not yours.

"True. But a weak spine bends both ways. That sort of person can be cowed, but can't be trusted. Lady Beranadon, for instance…she's very difficult to deal with, but she and her family can be relied upon to have firm beliefs, and to live up to them. I always prefer an unwieldy person who actually means what they say rather than a pliable one who never means anything at all."

James contemplated these words with a dazed look—he seemed to draw words in at the pace of molasses. Riada's mind was a torrent, and it was always with great difficulty that he had to wait for others to climb to the conclusions he had long since reached.

"I suppose." James sighed thoughtfully and sagged his shoulders. Riada's irritation flared. James was as guileless, uninterested, and uninteresting as he had ever been, and yet somehow he still managed to give Riada nothing into which he could sink his teeth. Nothing which he did not already know.

The Beranadon family had always made James nervous.

He always hated formal gatherings.

He always bemoaned his ineptitude.

Six months Riada had been trying to draw his brother, turn the man inside out, sift him through, and put meat onto all the bones of suspicion Riada held in his hands. And here James slopped around like weak soup with no shape and no strong taste for the tongue. One could gag on the insipidity of him.

"What is it you would like me to say about the Sahr, Your Highness?" James said.

"The truth, for the most part. You caught a Sahr jinn. Dragged the near-corpse of it to Piarago. It attempted escape. It killed several guards and inn-people. Then it *died*."

"What? You...I..."

James floundered in such a stupid, exasperating way.

"The Black Wren burned it to ash on their way to Areo."

"But..."

"Does this contradict anything you have already said in the months since you returned?"

"Riada, you know I haven't said *anything* to *anyone* about *any* of it."

"Good."

"But certainly there are rumors that—"

"Do you honestly think I've allowed the rumors to run amok all this time? Such things must always be shepherded. And as you swore silence before, now you will swear by this. You'll be quite popular tonight, I daresay."

The dread on James' face was not quite as entertaining as it ought to have been, but it would have to sate.

"You may go," Riada said.

James departed in that distracted, slovenly way of his. When he was gone, Riada pressed his teeth together in frustration. What had he expected to get from James this time? Whatever it was, he had not got it.

An hour later, the disappointment still left a slight aftertaste. With purposeful care, Riada shaved his chin—he always did that task himself—and dabbed it with oil. His mind circled the problem, prodded at it, and proceeded to other problems while his servants dressed, perfumed, and decoratively armed him.

He wore his favorite knife. The only one that had seen blood. It was simpler than the rest of his accessories, a commonplace Laritoni battle knife. He'd won it playing Sinja-Arratul, the Bigharan version of the game, when he was ten years old. The important feature of the knife was who he'd won it *from*.

Most of the other children wagered necklaces, sashes, bracelets. And, since Riada almost always won, he courteously returned these items lest he beggar all the youths of the court. But when Keved Aver's son, Samuel, stepped up and wagered his plain carrying knife, Riada kept the prize and all its attendant satisfaction.

It did not take the jackal boy long, however, to come back and try again next time he was in Piarago. He wanted the knife back and he would have got it too, if Riada had ever been willing to set it back down in wager, because Aver won often as not. Riada quickly learned that when playing games of strategy against Samuel Aver, he must never put down something he could not afford to lose.

Riada brushed his fingers over the reminder of his first victory and stood ready. A little too early. He must, of course, arrive last of all.

The room would fill slowly. The Mashevis would arrive among the first so that their cold reception might be from as small a crowd as possible. Lady Beranadon would arrive late for the opposite reason. Then James, and their sister's family. The tables would be full of food, the air full of music, and the crowd full of Riada's aides, who collected conversation and would bring the choicest bits to Riada's ears later on.

His servant told him, at last, that it was time.

The music broke off just before he stepped into the grand pavilion. The silence had savor and strength to it. A crier made the announcement.

"Lord of the Ten Lands, Sovereign of the Maurowan Empire, Ruler of the Gods' City, Piarago: Emperor Riada Edward Daris Sivolne. *Give honor!*"

The crowd sank in hundreds of deep bows. Riada walked across the mosaic entrance without looking aside to the right or to the left.

He walked up the stone steps of the Imperial dais and a breeze ran across him as he turned to face his subjects.

He took his seat. Raised his right hand. The sea of people began to ripple and flow once again. Drums returned. Then northern flute and southern oud. When the tension of his own presence had ebbed sufficiently, and he had drunk in all that his savvy aides had to report, he took to the crowds himself. A warm greeting here, a kindness there, he doled himself out in respectable portions to the appropriate audiences. He did not linger with the Beranadon family for long, not because they were unimportant but because they were rather too important. They must be acknowledged, but had enough potent brightness of their own. He would not lend them his.

Their wealth and clout was nearly a straitjacket to him. His father had failed to dilute their influence, and Riada was left to both control and conciliate them. An arduous task. The easy answer was for him to marry Lady Kathryn, but there was a grave danger in putting someone so strong and ambitious directly against his skin. The Lady would rule all that she touched, which was why Riada had never let her come too close.

In any case, she was not what interested him right now.

What he really wanted, and with a great hunger, was the jackals. Riada derived a sharp pleasure from watching how Keved Aver tried to ingratiate himself, and then how subtly yet surely he was rejected by nearly everyone. Riada needed to see this happen before his eyes, because King Aver always looked stronger and wiser and better at first glance than he was in truth. His back was straight, his frame was strong. His beard was graying, but the hair on his head was still chiefly black, as when he was young. He always became a coward when pressed, but he managed to project a dignified manner so long as nothing was at stake.

He had not lowered his eyes. His tone had not yet turned beggarly and cloying. Riada wondered if Keved seemed so well tonight because the presence of his wife shamed him into holding his head high. Riada remembered little of Eliana Aver from his boyhood, and she had not been to Piarago in over a decade. Her hatred of his people and his city was well known.

She was, Riada decided, a perfect opportunity.

"Noben," Riada gestured to his chief advisor.

"Yes, Your Highness?"

"I need you to take King Aver to one of the adjacent rooms and have a talk with him."

Noben was bewildered. "Regarding what, Your Highness?"

"Oh I don't give a damn. Just keep him occupied. Tell my sister to have his wife sent to me. I'll be in Serivash's shrine."

"But—"

Riada gave a sharp glance, and Noben held his tongue.

"Of course, Your Highness."

There were a number of shrines and alcoves through the north and west ends of the pavilion which were used for liaisons of all lurid kinds during such a festival. Riada lounged on the couch beside a vivid fresco of the old Maurowan pantheon. He liked to have the Gods at his back when faced with those that hated them.

Eliana Aver arrived with a calm, unreadable expression, two Mashevi women trailing her.

"I wish to speak to you alone," Riada said coolly.

The attending women stiffened and gave each other nervous glances; southerners were so easily scandalized.

"I have no choice but to honor your request, though it is a dishonorable one," the jackal queen said.

Exquisite.

She was the opposite of Keved. She was *exactly* what he wanted. Riada kept himself from smiling as the ladies left. Eliana stood tall and stately, her gray-streaked hair braided, the beauty and dignity of her age flawlessly worn. Embroidered purple cloth was woven throughout the braid, calling to mind the traditional head covering without truly being one. Everyone knew that she had been dragged to Keved's throne from that lank desert gully called the Limila River, barely old enough to bleed. The fact that she had such good bearing was a lovely surprise.

"Have you enjoyed the feast?" Riada said.

Eliana Aver pursed her lips.

"Well, of course not," Riada said in mock sympathy. "Not with food you refuse to touch, and company which refuses to touch you."

"What do you want of me, Your Highness?" Her accent was soft and her Maurowan words crystal clear. This impressed Riada because Keved's accent was mercilessly thick, and all his children were like him, speaking Maurowan as if it hurt their teeth.

"I want to know about these rabble-rousers in Masheva," he said.

"The fishermen? Or the Nairim?"

"They use the name 'goatherd' these days."

She frowned and her voice came out flat and cold. "Popular with the scholars, religious masters, and on the coast. Loosely organized, I think, and no marked threat to our city or our stability," she said. "That is all I know, Your Highness. May I go now?"

Ah, this was exhilarating. She hated him so much, it crackled off her like fire. Why was she not afraid? She really, really should be.

"No. Please sit. Even if you are not in the high assembly, surely you hear the same rumors that I do. It causes worry. I may have to send aid."

"You mean soldiers," she said.

"If you cannot keep your people in check, someone has to do it. The ports are admirably run, but your city...is rather too close to my ports and too bestirred for my taste."

"That has nothing to do with the Nairim or the 'goatherd,' whoever that may be, Your Highness. It has to do with the corvee labor. You draft fathers from their homes to build your roads and arenas and aqueducts."

"There is a draft in every province, but only yours complains so loudly of it."

"Forgive us for not living up to our reputation of being a people easily cowed," Eliana said.

She glanced down at the ground for a brief moment, as if suddenly remembering that her bold words might have deadly consequences. Not for herself, perhaps, but for others.

"I mean to say that the draft of indentured labor seems to have fallen upon us in something of a disproportion," she said, more gently this time.

Riada folded his hands. "I see why Keved found that strange, new interpretation of law and restricted you from the high assembly,"

"Indeed? I thought that was your doing."

"Perhaps it should have been. The truth is your name was never worth mentioning in my father's eyes, but I am willing to acknowledge that he may have had blind spots." Riada carefully pieced his thoughts together. "I did always wonder why Samuel was so *utterly* unlike his father in every way that mattered. I was a fool not to have considered the real source of his arrogance. He took that ragged desert pride of yours and returned it tenfold."

He caught the flash of anger in her eyes and the slow way she rolled her jaw. Samuel Aver used to do that too.

"If pride is all I taught him, then I failed. Not that it made any difference in the end."

Riada feigned bewilderment. "My dear lady, whatever can you mean? I'm told the man is a great scholar of Okiziu and has all the opportunity in the world to become a good and righteous king."

"Stop it," she whispered.

"But he really should come to court if he is to prepare for his role..."

"Why are you doing this?"

"Because I think it might be time to retire the façade."

"By all means, Your Highness, with my most ardent support," she said in a low, harsh voice. "It is *you* and your father before you who have long pretended that my son is still alive. Why were you so afraid to be known for your handiwork? Why shouldn't everyone know that you would execute a boy for all the imaginary crimes he has yet to commit?"

"*I had nothing to do with it*," Riada said sharply, then policed his manner. "My father's determination and your husband's acquiescence was more than enough to seal his fate directly over my head. I was only a boy myself."

A strange look flashed across her face, and her posture nearly faltered. But she righted herself quickly.

"You've had nine years as Emperor to undo the lie."

"And you've had even longer," he said with a rigid smile.

Her brazenness no longer amused. Rarely did anyone ever speak thus to him, like a mother admonishing a child. What had begun as savory was turning bitter in a hurry. He had meddled with something he had not fully understood. That was his mistake. This woman cared for nothing but that Riada should taste her contempt.

Did she not realize that was precisely what sealed her son's fate?

"For all your self-righteousness, you have played the same game," Riada continued, taking a sip of wine and deciding to give the conversation its final heading. "My father allowed your people to believe that Samuel Aver still lives because Keved begged him to. He claimed that he could not possibly manage without being able to wield the power of that ancient and beloved name. But he has not wielded it. He can barely get his hands around it."

"In fact, I believe others have begun to realize that the name is valuable without the actual man inside it." Riada stood, walked across, and leaned down over her. She was forced to look up, and she could not shrink back. There was nowhere but the wall. He liked the fear in her eyes. He had never been able to get it from her son. "They are using that name to send your people into precisely the treacherous frenzies Keved claimed he would stop. Your people are brandishing that name and dying by it. If anyone—goatherd, fisherman, or scholar—begins to use it even a little more effectively, then many more will die. Surely you do not want that?"

Eliana Aver looked at him with quiet ferocity but did not speak.

"Tell Keved that he has until your spring festival to find out what story he will tell—a sunken Okiziu ship, perhaps? It will have a lovely, symbolic quality. Your people discard all their leaven, and you get to discard this lie, and give Samuel the dignity of his passing."

She let a livid breath out through her nose. "Don't speak his name as though you didn't hate him and celebrate his death."

"I will speak however I choose. Especially if you fail to speak as *I* command."

Slowly she stood. She gave the necessary bow. She met his eyes with iron.

"Understood. Now, may I go, Your Highness?"

Riada hesitated. He had said that which he had set out to say; why did he feel bereft? He had sent his daggers, and they seemed to hit their mark, but he had no satisfaction. *Again.*

"You may go."

She lifted her head and turned.

"I didn't hate him," Riada said quietly once her back was to him. "Not so entirely. I thought him a worthy challenge. But he *did* hate me. And he hated Keved even more. Your husband may be a coward, but he is not stupid. He saw what was coming."

She stiffened. But she did not look back.

Riada sat down, alone in the lamplit room, the statue of Serivash at his side, her eyes looking down on him with all their violence and desire.

It had not been his decision, this whole affair. He had been left to guess what really happened until more than a year after Keved's son had been executed. That was when the old Emperor's madness led him to speak of matters he might rather have kept secret.

But still, it was probably for the best. Things would have been much, much worse if Samuel Aver was still alive—for Riada, certainly. And for his jackals too.

Queen Eliana may have had fire on her tongue tonight, but Riada had them all by the throat. And he would never, ever let them feel relief. The moment he did, they would bite deep, and flood Maurow with poison.

<hr>

James had no choice but to smile and greet. He had to say the things Riada told him to say, and doing so made him vastly more interesting to others than he would have preferred. But as soon as he could, he slumped on an unoccupied couch, like an old drunk. In fact, he was stone-cold sober. He pretended at the wine, swirling it, touching it to his lips, but he was afraid that even the least impairment would lead him to make some mistake or other.

He watched the Beranadons and his other court allies, but dare not speak to any of them except with slight and formal words. He watched Riada's "spies" wander around, collecting conversation. He watched the lamplight flicker warmly. Once, for a moment, the terror in his chest ebbed, his mind retreated to blankness, his ears simply took in the low, sweet strings and high, tender flutes.

But then he saw Riada order the Mashevi Queen to a side chamber—*what the devils does he want with her?*—and the hot streak of fear shot back, quickening the blood in his veins. He remembered the jackal soldier of the Black Wren with the same gasping dread that one remembers a candle mindlessly left too near the bedclothes.

Thank the Gods Verris had forced him to snuff *that* fire out. Who knew what might have happened if James had kept the jackal Commander? The man would right now be doing who knows what, provoking who knows who, inciting worry and rumors and cutting everything off at the knees. Oh Gods. Verris had the right of it.

Where there were jackals, Riada's attention became heightened. Obsessive. Relentless. He had been that way since they were boys, always antagonizing and being antagonized by Keved's eldest son, as if he thought to prove himself by it. As if...well, as if he was afraid, actually.

He made people stand close to him when he was afraid of them.

And he had been making James stand very close of late.

When Riada finally came out of the alcove—long after the Mashevi Queen departed—he looked pale. He mingled and smiled and spoke and laughed. But the trouble sat right there, in and around his eyes, flashing bright with each occasional glance toward the jackals. And, once only, he shot a glance toward James.

It was rare that James *knew* a thing. He was told things. Assented to them. Allowed himself to be faintly convinced. Wondered. Made guesses. Felt a fool. Made new guesses. Only acted on something if someone made him do it by flattering him or trapping him.

But tonight he knew one thing with a dull, lead-like certainty. He knew that Riada was on the hunt, quickening his pace, craving a victim.

And the moment he closed in on his prey there would be no warning.

James must leave Piarago *now*.

11

Khala stepped out of the tent on the fourth and final morning of the journey. She pulled the Trekoan shawl tightly about her shoulders and thought little of her uncovered head since most of the soldiers were still asleep. She had never been very particular about that sort of thing anyway, to Azetla's mild dismay. But he was long past the point of saying anything about it.

The air bit her cheeks with nighttime cool, the breeze brushed a sharp herby scent across her nose, and if Khala strained her eyes and imagination she felt she could see the very first hint of dawn to the east.

"Good morning, my-sister. Are you ready for your grand task?"

Khala gave a half-hearted laugh as she turned toward the voice of Lieutenant Sarrez. Azetla had assigned him to keep care and watch over her during the journey southward since she was the only woman in the company; after the second day he had taken to calling her "my-sister" in Mashevi style. Khala would rather he used her given name as Joseph did, but he seemed to think that would be too familiar.

Her eyes adjusted and she began to see the shadows of his face, smiling, offering assurance. Khala drew her hand through her hair and down her shoulder, as if to set it right.

"It would be a shame if I weren't ready, my lord, since I believe my duty is to do *nothing* with all my might. The bloody Sahr devil made that quite clear. I'm to be a doll on display, mouth painted shut."

Lord Sarrez scoffed.

"Not at all. A totem, rather. A very good luck charm."

"Well I suppose when your commander is a jackal with no rank and your guide is a devil with no scruples, you need all the luck you can get."

She could feel rather than see his uncomfortable surprise. He faltered at a response; the man had expected honey but found vinegar instead. Khala spoke quickly to sand down the rough edge she had cut.

"Thank you, though. For your kindness, Lord Sarrez." She smiled. The light became a surer thing, and she knew he could see her. "Not that you had any choice in the matter."

"I realize that my kindness has not always been a guarantee," he said softly.

Khala rushed to fill the uneasy silence that rested on the end of his words.

"He never complained about you. Not to me."

"I'm sure he didn't. But you must have known how it was."

Khala looked at the man who had been Azetla's cruelest enemy and tormentor, and she could scarcely believe that this face—too easy on the eyes for anyone's good—belonged to *that* Makarish bastard from all those years ago. She remembered overhearing Azetla one time, with a shaking in his voice: "He'll kill me if he gets the chance, Joseph. I know he will." And Joseph gave no word of comfort, because none was possible.

And now Azetla trusted Lord Nimer Sarrez—a Makar—with his life. And with Khala's.

"Whenever you find him, my lord, will you tell him I need to speak with him?" she said.

"Of course." He smiled again and departed with a slight bow of his head, as if she really was the great lady she must pretend to be today.

The light grew. The wind cut through her clothes, carrying the voices of waking soldiers into her ears. Khala covered her hair and watched the day's rocky trail come into clearer and clearer view. She waited.

Azetla came at last, looking tired and distracted.

"Thankful you could finally grace me with your presence, *Commander*," she said.

He raised an eyebrow at her tone, but said nothing. He led her toward the headquarters tent, the only one tall enough to stand in. She stepped through and saw how barren the space was. Azetla's thin pallet lay in the corner with a pack, a writing box, a scabbard, and nothing more. She saw the impressions where others had slept, but their pallets were already packed.

"Well, you asked for me," Azetla said.

"I know that devil is going to come in here and show me what I must do. But I won't be left alone for it to slither around me, mock me, and threaten me."

A fierceness came to Azetla's eyes, sudden as lightning.

"Did she threaten you? What did she say?"

In truth, the Sahr scarcely ever said a single word to Khala, good or bad.

"I'm supposed to assume it won't threaten me simply because it hasn't done so yet?"

The flash faded. Quietly, Azetla stooped and began to roll his pallet. He did not speak again until he had tightened the strap.

"Khala, you know I wouldn't tolerate her to threaten you even once, near or far."

"I also know that you've barely spoken a word to me since we came to Areo. I've no doubt you'll do your duty by me, but a duty is all I am to you."

His shoulders fell wearily, exhaustion pouring down his posture. "That is not true."

She wanted tell him all the reasons she knew it *was* true, and drive each one into him like a nail. Her mother had been a woman of the night, and Khala had been raised without prayers and rituals. She was not pious, nor would she pretend to be. She knew only the broadest customs of her people, and felt no compelling need to set herself apart with them. She was worldly. She knew more of men than he cared to contemplate. She did not speak Mashevi very well.

She was not like his real sisters.

Yes, she remembered that one time he had a little more wine than the scant sips he was accustomed to. And he knew she remembered. He almost never spoke of his life before Piarago, though any fool could guess that he had come from privilege.

But just that one time he had looked at Khala sadly and told her that she "made him think of his sisters."

She'd asked him, "How so?"

He floundered. Muttered. Scrambled to cover for the mistake of mentioning that which he was so careful not to mention.

Even so, Khala understood what he tried not to say. She made him think of his sisters in contrast. She, the half pagan, raised in hardship, of little knowledge and little propriety, against his sisters: the pious, wise, elegant, and educated women Khala presumed them to be. She was a stand-in for something he had lost, and what a disappointment she turned out to be.

Of course he never actually said any of this. But Khala felt it from him. She watched as he strapped on his Maurowan sword and the little Trekoan knife.

"I'm sorry, Khala," he said, his voice rough from the cold, dry air. "You're here because of me. I'll own that. And I've had very little time to spare for you or others. But you're not a child, and it's not like you ever listen to a word I say anyway so if—"

The tent flaps slid apart and the Sahr stepped in. A large embroidered satchel was slung over its left shoulder. Its right hand carried Azetla's sagam, loosely gripped by the sheath. It gave Khala a brief glance then, handing the sagam to Azetla, spoke in swift, quiet Trekoan.

That voice was so cool and pleasant if you didn't know who owned it.

Contempt slowly filled Khala's chest as she listened, uncomprehending, till it spilled into every part of her body like liquid fire. Throughout the journey, when the Sahr and Azetla spoke, it was in Trekoan. Or Mashevi. In Maurowan only when they reached an impasse. Khala longed for Azetla to struggle over the words that he might fall to ones that Khala knew, but the Sahr was ruthless even in that small way; it did not often let him escape to the familiar. For its own part, it clambered up the Mashevi language as a ladder with missing rungs, or a wall with crumbling rock. However, Azetla admitted to Khala, it rarely slipped.

So Khala had ridden beside them, nervous at being atop a horse for the first time in her life, cut off from half of their conversations, appalled at Azetla's relaxed, easy manner with this jinn devil. He was not buckled and braced and armored the way he usually was.

It worried her. Everyone else handled the Sahr as with tongs and hooks, happy to let Azetla be the chief snake charmer. He seemed so skillful in the task, the others hardly seemed to worry about being bitten anymore. But didn't he realize it could still bite *him*?

"No. There was no report about it," Azetla whispered to the Sahr, taking his sagam slowly in hand. "And we will speak in Maurowan for the time being."

He gave Khala a nod of apology.

"If you like," the Sahr said.

It opened the satchel and began to hand Khala all the articles of clothing she was to wear: an embroidered underdress, and a crimson-dyed outer shift, an intricately woven shawl, a waist sash with purple thread for tassels at the bottom, and copper bangles with jasper and carnelian inlay. The headcloth was deepest blue, stitched and adorned so delicately that even Khala would have struggled to match its quality, and she was skilled at her craft. Khala ran her fingers over the silky threads while the Sahr laid out the bangles in the precise order that they ought to be worn on the wrist and ankles.

Khala had never touched so much wealth in all her life, let alone worn it against her skin.

Azetla stepped out for only the brief moments required for her to change the underdress, but returned immediately at her request, and remained. He could be relied on to keep his word, if not to keep cheerful company. The best he could offer her was an occasional stiff glance of assurance. In fairness to him, he had never been skilled at giving comfort or gladness.

The Sahr gave Khala specific directions; the Ishaani people were apparently notorious for their fastidiousness regarding dress. One end of the sash must reach the ankle, the other must be in line with the knee. Carnelian closest to the heart, Jasper only on the right hand.

The Sahr also began to ready itself, but in a very different way. It changed its outer dress so that it looked less like a Trekoan rider and more like a common villager. It pulled the knot of its hair down and began to braid it like the Trekoan house slaves who scrubbed the marble at Areo outpost.

Thus Khala dressed upward to look like the sister of a powerful army commander, someone both valuable and vulnerable enough to signify good will and peaceful intent. But she must neither do nor say anything.

And the Sahr dressed downward, to look like something worth neither care nor notice, even though its tongue would guide the whole day like a rudder on a ship.

"There's blood at your collar," Azetla said under his breath. He was staring fixedly at the rhythmic movement of the Sahr's hands as it wove its hair, left-over-right, right-over-left. Only now did Khala also notice the almost invisible dried stain at the Sahr's collarbone.

The Sahr glanced and shrugged dismissively. "The coat will cover it."

"What did you do?"

"Nothing. It's from before."

"*Nothing*?"

Khala fixed the clasps of copper on her wrists slowly, her eyes dropping to the ground. She pulled the bangles up and down with nervous fingers. Azetla rarely raised his voice when he was angry. He merely turned the whole bloody room to ice.

The Sahr finished the braid in a smooth, unhurried way. "Nothing."

It stood up and brushed itself off, turning toward Khala. "Stop fiddling with that copper. Ishaanis wear a great deal of jewelry, but there are rules; don't compliment them on theirs, and don't draw attention to yours."

The Sahr adjusted the blooded seam at its collarbone once, then slipped out. Azetla stared off into nowhere for a moment, his arms folded, the icy air still hanging about him. But soon he looked up, and gave Khala that faint and rare smile of his. A small gift, but she would take it.

"I'm sorry I've put you in this position." He reached out to her hand so that she might step carefully. The finery belonged to Rahummi Bin-Deghan's wife, not to Khala, and it must be returned as it was given. "You look like the women of Aram-Tal. Fine and elegant. Not that it helps."

Khala smiled back. "Oh, it helps."

It was truer than she meant. Many eyes were on her as she walked carefully through the camp. Lieutenant Sarrez helped her onto the horse and she had the rather delicious experience of watching a man realize he had been staring just a moment too long.

From the moment they entered the Ishaani village of Sijaya, Khala knew that something was happening that she could not hope to understand. The words that were spoken had some meaning beyond what reached her ears. Even the Maurowan banners and the tassels that hung from the poles seemed to signify more or other than what they claimed.

The Rokh of the village received them coldly. Yes, he invited Azetla to the meeting tent. Yes, he laid a generous table before them. And, yes, Trekoan pleasantries were exchanged ad nauseum.

But contempt curled softly around Rokh Idayir's every word. Khala could hear it even before translation, but the Sahr brought to bear all that was cold and dry and bitter with perfect clarity.

Khala flinched when Azetla abruptly deviated from the meandering Trekoan path.

"Rokh Idayir, you have asked me about my journey, you have confessed shame for your exceptional hospitality, while I have said it is an honor. You have signaled welcome; I have spoken gratitude. But hear me: my words are in earnest. Are yours?"

Rokh Idayir's small, wiry frame rose, filled with sudden strength. Azetla had sheared the lock from the door, and all that was within broke loose.

"Who are you to request my inmost thoughts? Why do I owe you anything beyond remarks about the weather and the road? Explain it! Explain this to me!" The Rokh hit the table with the palm of his hand. "They say you are a Mashevi. *They say*. But you are dressed like a Maurowan. You descend upon us like them, with barely a message of warning. You will have demands, no doubt. You will want what we cannot give. You will cause provocation and leave us to fend for ourselves. And you will try to claim that Saqiran is righteous and faithful when we know they will abandon us rather than spare even one drop of their own blood on our behalf."

The Sahr took on Rokh Idayir's ferocious tone to perfection. But Khala heard grief and terror too, trickling across and through and underneath every phrase. Was it the Rokh's voice that told her that? Or was it the Sahr's? Khala never looked at its face, so she hardly knew.

But from the force of it, she felt certain of one thing. Azetla would fail here.

It seemed he knew it too, for he did not answer right away. The silence simmered and crackled. Khala began to wish that the Ishaanis followed Saqirani custom and kept the women on the screened side of the meeting tent. Then she should not have to worry about what her face and hands and breaths might say.

"Forgive me, my-Rokh," Azetla said, tilting his head in something like a bow. A soft and humble voice took his words and gave them to the Rokh. "It seems that indeed I have come a little like a Maurowan. They have owned me for nearly half my life. I am not easily rid of their ways."

Those words pricked Khala's ears. He had never described himself thus before. *Owned.*

They pricked the Rokh's ears as well.

"You are a debt conscript."

"Yes, my-Rokh. Beholden to Maurow." His voice hardened a little. "But I am *not* Maurowan. And not Saqirani, for that matter."

"Yet you have the war embroidery of Saqiran tied below your banners."

Azetla's eyes flicked almost imperceptibly downward, scarcely a blink. Others might not notice, but Khala did. His posture and expression remained perfectly calm.

"Rokh Imal Bin-Zari is my ally, but I am not here to plead his case."

Rokh Idayir scoffed audibly. "No?"

"I'm here to plead my own."

"Well then you have wasted your time, easterner, because I need not entangle myself with you on top of everything. Maurow stands over and above us, flicking us off like flies if we brush too close. Qatlan harasses and robs us. Saqiran neglects us. But you, Mashevi? You are neither good nor bad to me that I should even have to decide about you. If you are not here to threaten as Maurow or entreat as Saqiran, then leave our village in peace. And knowing what happens when that salt-brick is around—" he shot a hateful eye at the Sahr "—peace will soon be very hard to come by."

There was not the least hitch or change in the Sahr's voice at these last words. Yet Khala could not help but glance its way. It sat to Azetla's right, but back a pace from the meeting table, as if to signify that it was present but not a part. It looked unusually taut—as if it was about to spring to its feet, though it sat perfectly still.

"You need not blame those who surround me, nor those who came before me, for what has not yet happened," Azetla said. "But you are wise to smell the smoke before the fire."

The Rokh paused at that but Khala barely glanced at him. Her eyes flitted from Azetla to the Sahr. Azetla was taut now too. Khala's skin began to tingle. What was happening here?

Azetla continued.

"My-Rokh I have come to ask that—"

"*No*, easterner. No. I cannot. You ancestors brought your God and his stories to us. We thank you. But there is nothing else we want from you. And if you've come to say 'woe to you if you don't do as I ask, for Qatlan will come down upon you,' it is without meaning. Qatlan will do as they please never mind you. Perhaps it is them you should entreat, since they are the ones who claim to do Maurow's bidding."

It was going so wrong. Khala wanted to shut her eyes, but she could not pull her gaze from the Sahr. No longer was it so perfectly still. Its thumb quietly pushed the leather slave band round and round on its wrists. Its eyes cut toward the opening of the tent. Its fingers slipped down to its bow and began tapping. Curling. Gripping.

A heartbeat before the shouts of alarm rang out, the Sahr was halfway to its feet.

12

All Azetla's thoughts clattered to the ground, swept off a table that must instantly be put to another use. The cry of warning quickly gave way to a ram's horn, blasting from the south end of the village.

Azetla knew what this was. One glance at Tzal's ready posture confirmed it. There was not the least mote of apology in her eyes when he shoved his sagam into her hand as hard as he could. Anger boiled through him in that moment, but that too must be swept from the table.

Tzal slung her bow and walked out of the tent. Piercing light and chaotic sound broke through. Trekoan horses barreled past, goats scattering and bleating. The villagers rushed toward the meeting tent for safety, making a thick, muddy river of fear through which Azetla had to wade.

"The runner's out?" Azetla said as he finally reached the reins of his horse.

Tzal nodded, her eyes scanning from the date grove to the road.

"Good. They can't have seen Sarrez's detachment."

"They wouldn't attack if they had." Tzal was atop Nashuv in one fluid motion.

"Unless there are more than you thought."

She brought Nashuv in the opposite direction, brushing past Barra's withers. "Don't leave any alive if you can help it. It'll do the trick."

He made no attempt to respond. Any more words for her were a waste of his time and breath and reason. His men were his chief concern now.

The old hands—they would be able to anticipate his orders. But the newer soldiers and Saqiranis? *God forgive me.* He urged Barra southwest toward the sound of the warning call, and the tangled rush of horses.

He called an arrow's head formation. As the riders and foot soldiers coalesced into clear lines, Azetla's heartbeat jolted.

The Qatlani soldiers were already roaring across the gully, and it was giving them no trouble, so shallow was the water just now. More than a hundred riders.

He had no idea how they got so close in such flat terrain without being noticed, but he did remember all that Tzal told him about Qatlan. The first wave was usually the smallest, and they always came like a pincer: there would be more coming soon, clamping down from another direction.

There was no time for him to do anything about it, except draw his sword and give the one shout of command. The grit of the sound was still in his throat as the ugly clash engulfed him, brown water lashing up his legs and into his eyes. His men broke against the Qatlanis in a shamble of flesh and metal and horse and churned mud. If a man could think of it in that instant, he would say it sounded like death in the ears. But he usually could not.

Blood rushed through the body in that strange fervid way, seizing it and hurling it into task. The hands adopted procedures, following their lessons-made-instinct, while the mind clicked with unnatural speed from assessment to action. The heart seemed to be beating in all parts, in all limbs, in all organs.

But without objective, all that brief strength and surreal clarity was worthless. Azetla cut down into a Qatlani rider then he drew Barra backward. By every stroke and false retreat, Azetla pressed, then pulled, the enemy, funneling the Qatlanis into the paths between the date palms. Narrow corridors. Away from the center of the Ishaani village.

With a jerky motion, almost losing his balance, Azetla sliced across the spine of a rider, driven against him by another writhing horse. Barra, with his great size, trampled those who fell into the rutted rows. The Qatlanis tried to scatter the battlefield, but Azetla's men forced it to remain concentrated. Bodies cluttered the grove paths. Every time the Qatlanis tried to slither out of Azetla's noose, his men tightened it. He shouted commands, and the lieutenants echoed them.

How many men he was losing, he did not yet want to know. How many villagers would be taken was impossible to guess. But it was certain as stone that the Qatlanis had expected nothing like the resistance they'd been given. Some of them were already trying to edge back toward the river.

Azetla cast his left hand up, the sword halting a blow from the Qatlani's smaller blade. He hurled the man back and gutted him.

As best he could tell, the second wave still had not arrived.

Two unhorsed Qatlanis rushed toward Azetla, going for Barra's throat. Azetla swung his arm down, leaving the first man's neck riven and bloody. The man fell after a stumbling attempt to lift his arm again, then writhed on the ground under Barra's feet. Azetla brought the edge of his blade directly onto the second man's skull. That one dropped cold and did not move at all, like a marionette whose strings had been cut all at once.

Azetla braced, but no fresh blow came. He found that he was counting the men around him and was late to discern the meaning of his instincts. He never counted unless it was all but over. Every soldier around him was one of his own.

He called out to Rahummi, and to his three lieutenants. After several echoes from the grove to the tributary, all answered.

Soon he realized what had really happened. The daterows had obstructed his vision at the last, and he had not seen Sarrez's companies fly in. *They* shattered the Qatlani reinforcements to a man. *They* had initiated the alarm. He could not have known it, but the battle was half won before he ever drew his sword.

The moment Sarrez had reached the village, he'd made a decisive end of it.

A few Qatlani stragglers did flee to the river, but they did not escape. They met a Mashevi sagam in a Shihrayan hand. Tzal kept along the west riverbank, circling out and around to the south bend, further and further till she could not be seen.

She had said to leave none alive. She meant it.

Azetla would have to deal with her later.

He slid down from Barra and picked his way back toward the village to find Sarrez. Along the way, he set each tribal leader and each lieutenant to the task of accounting for their men. There would be a faint, scraping itch through all his thoughts until he knew how many he had lost.

"I have all thirty of my riders, though five are wounded," Rahummi reported when Azetla reached the meeting tent.

Azetla did not yet allow himself to feel relieved. He had forced his men to favor the Trekoans as one favors a hurt leg. Protected until they could be proven. He pulled out his ledger and made a mark.

"Good. Have you seen Sarrez?"

"No, I haven't."

Two of Captain Ishelor's men were killed. Six wounded. That was out of his sixty. Ishelor's eyes dropped briefly to the ground as he said the names of his dead. His tone was strained. It was possible he had never lost men before.

"Have you given your report to Sarrez?" Azetla said quietly as he marked the numbers and names. He had no notion of how to comfort the man. Precious little good it would do to tell Ishelor how well he had done today. It was hard to hear "good job" when you had the dead freshly at your feet. Accolades would have to wait.

"Well...no. Because he's in the tent with the other wounded."

Azetla looked up from his ledger.

"What?"

"He's wounded, Commander. That's all I was told."

"Take me to him."

Ishelor led him through the crowds of villagers, whose current of movement was confused and inexplicable in the wake of danger. Azetla stepped into a large tent toward the edge of the village, which was usually the gathering place for the women.

Some three dozen men covered the ground. Most sat upright with nothing more than a scrape. A few would die within the hour.

Sarrez was one of the upright. Azetla's hand relaxed on the wooden corner of his ledger. He sat next to Sarrez with no regard for the Ishaani women who tried to shoo him out.

"By salt, Sarrez, how bad is it?"

"Not bad at all." Sarrez pointed to the wrapping on his leg. "A gash. A stupid mistake on my part. Avoidable. And the women here have been giving me far more fuss than the wound warrants, I tell you. But your sister was made to come in here and help, and she's kept an eye on me. I'm well enough."

The relief Azetla felt was so complete, he could have leaned back against the tent post, closed his eyes, and slept within it. If he were let. Which he would not be.

Joseph brought in the next account. While Azetla annotated his ledger, Khala came by with fresh-drawn water for Sarrez, who thanked her warmly. She offered some to Joseph as well.

"You're all right?" Azetla asked. He heard how curt his voice sounded, but he could not amend it.

"Yes." Khala glanced at Azetla, the smile falling from her face. "I was terrified when it was all happening, hiding in the tent. But it only lasted a few minutes. These Ishaani women, though! They've not given me a minute's rest since. They berated me for removing the outer garments and rolling up the sleeves in front of the men, but I'm trying not to ruin Naima's finery with blood."

Soon after, Lieutenant Carihua brought the final report.

Out of four hundred men, Azetla had lost eighteen. As of now. Forty-some were wounded.

But Azetla's men had killed no less than a hundred and thirty Qatlanis. In fact, that was a conservative estimate.

Under any other circumstances, it would be an astonishing triumph, worth jars upon jars of wine. A tale to tell for years and years to come. It had been a slaughter of the enemy. Everyone had done *beautifully*. They had proved their skill and Azetla's handiwork.

Tzal alone had taken more men from him in the Shihrayan crags than he had lost today.

And Tzal was the reason he could taste no hint of victory.

Few as they were—and thank God—he had spent lives he ought not to have spent today, as a con-man bargains with money he does not yet have in his pocket.

⁂

Khala did not think on the why of it at first, but she was relieved when Azetla finally left the recovery tent. He had kept Joseph and Sarrez completely occupied, leaving her no excuse to linger. The Ishaani midwives took firm charge of her for the remainder of the afternoon and, as far as Khala could tell, they relished it. They regarded her as a high-born woman being forced to muss her dainty hands. She was between anger and amusement at the absurdity of it, but she played her part.

There was a brief period where they admired her for not being too delicate for ugly tasks and shocking sights. But among the older women, it quickly turned into a question of what must be wrong with her that she had no delicacy at *all*? Was she not ashamed to see the men laid utterly bare with their wounds? Why did she not flinch, gasp, show tears in her eyes that the women could then laugh together about the weakness of the well-born?

She would not be able to make them content, nor would she try. They were nothing to her anyway. She did her tasks at such a pace as pleased herself and avoided having to clean filth and vomit by being extremely aware of such situations, and making sure she was suddenly too busy to attend to them.

When Azetla had been gone for some time, she took her meal by way of serving some of the wounded men, then slipping off with a portion for herself. And one for Lord Sarrez. He had been moved to a partitioned area of the tent as soon as they recognized his name: the Zawish tribe was the most powerful in Makaria, and the Sarrez clan one of the wealthiest and most famous therein. To these villagers, he may as well be a king. They certainly treated him like one, even though he was a Makar.

That made it all the more strange how kindly he received her when she slipped through the linen. She was Mashevi, which ought to have been offense enough. And she was of no birth. Worse than that, actually. She did not even know her father's name, only that he was the sort of man that saw a sin in lying with a pagan woman, but somehow no sin in taking a prostitute of his own kind. He had paid extra coin to be sure of the goods.

Azetla had been so profoundly offended when Khala told him all of this that Khala nearly laughed, for it was simply a joke to her now, if a coarse and bitter one.

She was reasonably confident that Lord Sarrez knew none of this and was thankful for it.

"They gave you a reprieve at last?" Lord Sarrez said, taking the food she brought with a gracious nod.

"Not exactly, my lord. I took one without asking. I hope you won't think less of me."

He smiled faintly, some thought flitting behind his eyes. "No, of course not. I think if you hide here and eat, you won't be troubled for at least a few minutes."

That was precisely what she had hoped he would say. Tucking Naima's elegant garments beneath the midwife's apron, and stretching out her arm, Khala began to eat the simple meal. She tried not to show how ravenous she actually was.

"You don't observe the rituals?" Lord Sarrez said.

Khala lifted her eyes from the olives and chuvia; the dipped bread was just shy of her lips. The garlicky smell rose into her nostrils. She found herself staring at the Makar with a flush of embarrassment she had not felt in a long time, and it made her hesitate.

"Azetla cleans his hands at meals then has these little—I don't know—prayers or something. In Mashevi. I mean, he's not always able to do them, but—"

"I only do them when Azetla is present, my lord," she admitted demurely. "But I would rather you didn't tell him that."

Lord Sarrez seemed genuinely surprised. The memory flashed through her mind's eye: Azetla as a lean and taciturn teenaged boy, desperately trying to teach her the prayers and prophets and sacraments and holy days. And she, a begrudging student who had survived in Maurow by being like, and did not wish to be made unalike.

"Azetla is very pious and very particular and I...I simply cannot keep up with him, my lord. I have stopped trying. Surely you have heard him complain of me being half a pagan or some such."

"He has never said a single unkind word about you, rest assured."

"Well, he is a man of great restraint, my lord."

She said it a little too sharply, perhaps.

But Lord Sarrez only smiled. "In the Black Wren, we are loose with the formalities. You don't have to say 'my lord' with every single phrase."

"I wouldn't know what else to say, my lord."

"My given name is Nimer."

Khala's cheeks burned with far keener embarrassment than before. "I can't call you that."

"Well I won't force you," he said warmly. "But you may if you can manage it. You might recall that Azetla is my commander right now, not my subordinate."

Khala managed to raise her eyes again and look at him. "Until we fled Piarago, I didn't know what he was. I didn't understand his position."

"Well," Lord Sarrez sighed. "He didn't exactly have one. And it was never easy to understand. He sets himself apart. Often to his detriment. Once in a while, to his benefit."

Sarrez watched her as she ate both lamb and crumbled cheese with her bread all at once. Another thing she did that Azetla would not do. Her upbringing had not lent itself to such stringent measures as keeping certain types of food separated. Naturally she could not tolerate the thought of swine, and hated seeing their butchered carcasses in North City, but almost all southerners avoided *that*, Mashevi, Makar, or Trekoan.

"I do not mean to cast Azetla into a bad light," she said. "He did not fail me. Not in care or instruction. I just..."

Nimer smiled again, warmly. "I am not Mashevi, Khala. You think I am staring at you because you are skirting rules which I only half understand to begin with. No. All I am thinking is this: Azetla has always been the sole source of my idea of all Mashevis. And now...he is not. You do not malign him, you simply bring nuance."

When Khala rose to leave, she was keenly conscious of every movement of her fingers as she took the bowls away, of the way the copper fell down her arm, of the bits of hair that came out from her head covering and stuck to the side of her face. She was conscious of it all. And, she felt certain, so was Nimer Sarrez.

13

*A*adin *remembered the beginning of the end clearly. It was painted with strokes of meticulous color and detail in his mind. Strangely, it was the good years that were indistinct; a haze of light and warmth and freedom, interspersed with those fragments of affection that Shihrayans but rarely permit themselves.*

The shikk was at Aadin's heel always. In Trekoa, in Makaria, in trades and thefts and simple ambushes. She made the tasks easy, the way she drank in lowland languages and poured them back out, believable in every word and expression. It dazed him a little to watch her do it.

For the most part, Aadin dealt ruthlessly with her. Just as he should. She was not allowed to make mistakes. If his anger rose, if she provoked him as she loved to do, he did not hold back. He scarcely knew how, and what good would it have done her? Only now did he realize that even at his most brutal, it would never have been enough. He could never be as cruel to her as Shihra would be. Shame on him. But he had been so young; some weakness might be allowed for.

On the good days, where there was cheer, the two of them raced and fought and provoked and attacked one another. The one form of play that a Shihrayan child could always find. She never won, of course. Tried till she was black and blue, though. Then went on blaspheming through bloody lips, and scrambling away from his grasp with a limp, and a dogged laugh.

Eventually she was not quite so small, and Aadin had to actually try a little. The crooked fourth finger on his left hand and the scar on his right calf served as a reminder that she would use his own tricks against him if he gave her even the slightest chance. He had to keep his wits about him, for she was deceptive, brutal, and difficult to corner.

To his credit. That was his whole intent.

When they were in the lowlands, she sometimes alarmed him as her tongue and manner turned to a given task. He began to think she wasn't merely hidden by the spirit of deception, but was slick with it. Made of it. Breathed it. It flowed through her blood, whether she knew it or not—whether she wanted it to or not.

By then, all of outer Shihra knew that she was some sort of curse, bound to break out sooner or later. But no one touched her. Not when the seasons flowed by without calamity, rains came on time, and live-stock gave good birth and good milk. Why risk it? Shihrayans tended to live like prey even when all was well, every step calculated, shoulders braced, always certain that one false movement would bring the Gods' claws and teeth to bear.

He remembered it was still dark when he woke her that morning. She had snuck into Yaqil again, and Dotiya had crawled over to her, listened to her stories, then fallen back asleep.

Aadin knelt hard against her ribcage.

"Wake up, Zaraje."

When he called her Zaraje it was to tell her that he was in a cold, hard mood; she was quick to her feet. The light grew over them as they descended from Shihra in silence. He saw the woven grass bracelet on her wrist, which Dotiya had painstakingly crafted for her. He saw the yellow and red yarn braided throughout her hair. The dots of henna on the side of her nose and the lobe of her ear, where piercings ought to be. Scrounged attempts at a grown woman's proper trappings.

He said nothing about any of it; she seemed disappointed at his indifference. She did not know that Birai and Sereya had already told him. She bled now. She could not feign to be a child anymore. Perhaps, they advised, Aadin should now disentangle his name from her as the rest of them had so carefully done. Wash his hands of her at last. Leave her to her fate.

Soon. Soon, *he always told himself.* Fool.

Two days they traveled thus, and the air was turning cold, threatening winter rains.

"There." Aadin pointed to the flock of goats on the hills below, watched over by a young boy.

The shikk nodded. "I'll get the goats and meet you back at the wadi entrance."

"No, Zaraje. Not this time."

He remembered taking a deep, resolved breath. He could almost feel the tightness in his chest, even now, so many years later. Why? It should have been such a small matter.

"I'll get the herd. You deal with the herder. Good, cold mercy, understand?"

He could still see the look of shock on her face—and her hurried attempt to conceal it from him—because he had never made her do this before. In all fairness, he had never quite done it himself.

She challenged him, tried to convince him that she could find a way around it, but Aadin stood firm.

She did manage to catch the boy by surprise. He saw her instincts take over once he hit the ground, for she had learned how to use her whole body first like a hammer to strike and then like a snake to grip. Her hands shook when she pulled the knife across his neck and she had to do it three times before it truly did the trick. She sat next to the body for a long time, and Aadin noticed that the boy was no bigger than she was—rail-thin, ill-used, a slave.

She said nothing to him for the rest of the day. So be it. A Shihrayan ought to be able to kill a foreigner in cold blood and she of all people must be willing.

The journey back up into Shihra was very slow, for the goats were unwieldy.

"You still have blood on your neck and hands. We'll wash and rest at Batina spring. Good, Zare?"

It was his attempt at a peace offering. Shortening the word Zaraje until it meant nothing but sounded softer, kinder. She always liked it when he did that, because he said it like a real name.

"Why should I wash it off?" She gave him a strange, vicious smile. "Shouldn't I be proud that I could kill a starving little Zaraje while he sat on a rock? Aren't you proud that you can knock me down when you outweigh me by two carons of oil? We Shihrayans are so brave. So strong. So fearless. Good thing we're not weaklings like those—"

Aadin struck her so hard she stumbled backward. He caught her by the arm, pinned it behind her, and drew his knife. His sister went still as the dead.

"Easy for you to call Shihra a place of cowards when I'm the one who's been shielding you from her. You have always lived outside even when you were among us. You will never understand, Zare."

He slipped the knife under the delicate green and reddish-brown weave of grass on her wrist and cut it off, nicking her at the wrist-bone. She barely flinched. He cut the braided yarn from her hair, and several strands came along with it. She tried to get away from him, but he held her firm.

"So stop acting like you can change this. Stop playing at being someone who—" He bit his words, his own anger clogging his throat.

"No, Aadin, that's it. You had it plainly. Stop playing at being someone."

He let her go with a shove. Neither spoke after that. They reached the outer edge of the leper camp at dusk. That was where they first heard the rumor. An illness was spreading through the western villages of Shihra. They were burning bodies, both the living and the dead, a bloodthirsty frenzy building up on the horizon.

And the rains so fervently promised by the skies never did come.

It was nearly dusk when Tzal returned to Sijaya, quietly slipping about as if she could be of no interest to anyone for any reason. She was a mere villager, weary from the day. Nothing she did was of consequence.

What struck Azetla was how effective it was. His own soldiers knew what she was, yet they scarcely seemed to mark her. She walked in a more shambling way than she usually did with an inattentive expression. In this manner she received a pour of water and a portion of food in the village center. She sat in an empty corner and ate. The light began to fall, the village fires began to rise, and Azetla waited.

When Tzal rose and walked through the date grove to the braided stream of the Limila, Azetla stood and followed.

She moved north along the bank till she came to the place where the village women did their washing. Abandoned now, but for a few forgotten scraps of cloth hanging from a line of rope, and the water was very low.

Instead of dipping her hands and face in the water, she stood ankle-deep, water leeching up the hem of her loose trousers. She set her hands against her hips, stared at the flat, dark western bank, and let out a long breath.

"What?" she said.

"You know what."

He stepped out of the grove, and over a dark patch on the ground which was probably blood. The fading light made it difficult to be sure.

Tzal crouched down and began to wash her face and arms. Her left shoulder sagged lower than the right, stiffening her movements.

"So we're going to pretend you didn't know what would happen?" she said coolly. "Because you prepared for it perfectly."

"I would have done that either way," Azetla said. "That's my chief duty."

"And having prepared for it, how many did you think you would lose if the worst happened?"

"I don't kn—"

"No, you had a number in your head. That's your duty as well. How many?"

"Sixty. Seventy. Based on what you told me."

"And how many did you lose?"

"As of a half hour ago, twenty."

A self-satisfied smile stirred across her face as she began to scour the blood and dust from her neck, then from her hair.

"Don't you dare treat those dead men like coins won in a bet."

"Azetla, it's not—"

"You took them from me, you bloody Sahr devil. And you had no right to do it."

Tzal's hands stilled, her hair and sleeves dripping. "No, I *gave* you Rokh Idayir."

"I was given no chance to win his confidence in the first place!"

She stood up and faced him, acting as though she was thoughtfully scrutinizing him though he never really believed that anymore. Every word she said always rested in her mouth, waiting, long before he finished speaking.

"Ah, Azetla." She shook her head faintly. "You think a little too highly of yourself. I don't care how grave and sincere your manner, I don't care how eloquent your speeches, earnest your attempts, or compelling your convictions...you *never* could have done it."

"*You can't know that.*"

"Yes, I can."

"I've gained unlikelier confidences than this, all without putting hand to hilt."

"Azetla, that man has been betrayed and abandoned so many times, since before either of us was born, up to this very day. He had absolutely no reason to trust you. You had nothing to offer him but a promise which his whole experience tells him he *cannot* believe. Not unless he wants to see sons slaughtered, daughters abused, and tents burned. There was only ever one way this was going to work, and that was to put blood on the ground for him."

Azetla grabbed Tzal's sagging shoulder and jerked it toward him. "It was never your call to make."

She winced, but made no effort to step back or pry his hand off. She just stared at him, tired, stubborn, and cruelly indifferent to how much each body in the ground weighed on him. These very first ones, most of all. The anger simmered, simmered, and slowly seeped out all over him. He almost savored it, as a strong drink burning down the throat. He so rarely let himself linger over it.

"You took my men's lives out of my hands and you didn't say a word."

"I didn't think I needed to. I thought you understood. You couldn't be seen to intentionally risk your men—and their trust—over something seemingly so small. So I did it for you and you get to keep your pious hands clean. That's how it *works*. Now let go."

Her voice was calm and unconcerned, which galled him all the more. He did not let go.

With a breath of laughter, her right hand reached out and grabbed the cord to his lion's head. She pulled till the precious bit of cedar was clenched in her fist and the cord bit into his neck. Instinctively he dropped his grip and pried the lion's head out of her hand. Pressed it back to his chest. Wound his fingers tight over the shape of the face. He felt his unsteadiness keenly.

No doubt Tzal saw it too. She had a good eye for moments of weakness, failure, and confusion. She didn't always use them right away. She pocketed them. And since she seemed to learn more by what he tried to hide than what he meant to show, he didn't try to brick himself up to make any front.

She slumped a little after he let her go, kneading her shoulder.

"Is that from today?" he said coldly. "Or from the last time you disappeared without saying anything?"

"Well, today didn't *help*, that's for certain."

"You never told me where you went. What you did."

Tzal stretched her arm around, fiddling with her range of motion, digging around the shoulder blade with her opposite hand. Then, with gritted teeth and a slow exhale, she sat down against one of the date palms. "I didn't think it mattered as long as you got what you needed. Like I said, this is how it works."

"How *what* works?"

She did not answer right away. She adjusted her shoulder, winced, and adjusted it again.

"I guess I figured Rahummi already told you all this. Rokh Imal found himself in a lot of bad corners during the worst years. I got him out of a few of them. Whatever...un-pious things I had to do, he pretended not to know about it. Imal is still deemed a virtuous and honorable man—to most—but if all my actions were accorded to him, he wouldn't be. That's the silent bargain we had. And he would have gotten rid of me long before he did if I hadn't done exactly what he needed me to do without saying a word."

"I don't care how Rokh Imal dealt with you, or how much guilt he was willing to eat to get what he wanted. I have to account for you. And I have to account for *them*. Whether you realize it or not, it all goes on my head—"

"No, you—"

"If I understand right, it 'worked that way' until it didn't, and I'm not dropping down a cliff with an unknown length of rope."

Tzal gave a lopsided shrug. "All you have to do is tell me to leave. And I will."

"It's not as though anyone asked you to stay in the first place."

She laughed a little.

"True. But no one forced me out and that's as close to an invitation as I get."

Azetla shook his head, and looked southward through the short, stocky grove of date palms. He could hear music and merriment of the village of Sijaya, and he could see the flicker of many fires. Celebratory fires. Azetla lost few. Ishaan lost none.

He looked back.

"Well then," he said in a calm voice. "Do you *want* to stay?"

She scoffed. "What I want isn't relevant."

Azetla stepped closer and looked down.

"Answer the question."

He could have drawn a knife on her and she wouldn't have blinked an eye. But this made her balk. For the first time that he could remember she did not like to meet—or defeat—his gaze. She cut her eyes downward. Clenched her jaw. Practically squirmed.

When she finally spoke, the words were only just audible, tacked with resentment.

"Obviously I want to stay."

"*Obviously* nothing. You play like you know exactly what's going on in my head—and maybe you do—but I haven't the faintest idea what's going on in yours."

He folded his arms.

"Anyway. That's beside the point. If you want to stay, you have to abide by my rules. You already know what's next. We start the task of driving Qatlan out of the whole region, except this time you're not going to float in and out like a vapor, doing whatever seems best to you. You're going to do what *I* tell you. No more. No less."

She was still looking at the ground, slow to let her words fall from her mouth. "I'm usually most effective when left to my own devices."

"I don't doubt that. But I'm willing to suffer some inefficiencies," he said. "You like to play at being this and being that? Well you can play at being a soldier for a little while. Do you understand?"

The silence was even longer this time. He had expected her to bristle under these words. She would look for a way to win, to gain the upper hand, to guilt, or confuse, or unbalance him. But he was set like flint now and he had his objective.

"You are always telling me 'do as you please, makes no difference to me,'" he said. Begrudgingly she tilted her head up to look at him. "So now I'll say it to you. It's your choice. Do as you please. But I will not say it makes no difference, because I know what you're capable of and I know what I'd be losing."

He crouched down so that she would be sure to see him by what little light was left. So that she would know he meant every word, as if by salt.

"Either way, what happened today will not happen again. I would rather put a thousand men at risk, than have little handfuls of them sacrificed behind my back."

She loosed her jaw, and bent her mouth into a faint smile. "Behind your back? You're sticking to that?"

He ignored those words as best he could, and waited.

"All right," she said. "The left hand will know what the right is doing, I promise."

"Good." He stood up again and held out his hand. "My sagam."

"I have to disarm also?" she said dryly as she dragged herself to a stand.

"After today there's more than enough enemy swords to scrounge from. Find whatever suits you. And anyway, I've already sent for three hundred more men from Areo. They'll come with supplies."

With visible reluctance, Tzal began to undo the buckle and loose the sagam.

"And what about the other message you sent off?" she said quietly. "Eastward, I think."

Inwardly, a heavy stone dropped in his stomach, and his heart raced. Outwardly he moved not a hair, leaving his hand outstretched for the sagam. He said nothing.

"It's the second time you've done that," she said.

It was the fourth. He felt a dim pride that she'd missed any.

He flicked his fingers again. "The sagam."

The sheath hung in her hand. Her fingertip ran across the stitching. With a sharp sigh, she laid it in his palm.

"So, if a 'soldier,' what are my orders?"

"The local envoys of Sirawal, Ukhaf, and Fajeen are coming to Sijaya tomorrow. I'll need you for that."

She gave half a nod and stood quiet. Her frame was still a little uneven. She leaned eastward as if she was going to leave, then paused.

"I really did think you knew what was supposed to happen today."

He said nothing. Stood still until she disappeared through the grove and for several minutes beyond. The light was truly gone now. He turned the sagam over in his hand.

He didn't *know*. But he was letting himself off on a technicality. He had willfully not known. And that was not like him. All of her advice—which he followed—implied that this meeting could provoke an attack. So had every last detail of his preparation.

He had seen it all in the periphery of his vision, but simply refused to turn his head. Because he had needed this success so desperately, yet had dreaded putting these men to battle with the word of his own mouth. Not the word of Captain Hodge, or Colonel Everson, or Lord Verris. His own.

What a coward.

His whole life had been pressed in relentless resistance against that word. *Coward.* And there was the foul imprint of it on his very skin. God have mercy. *Well, sling it over your shoulder and walk,* he told himself; *the thing is done now.* He'd started it. *Allowed her to start it.*

But he would not shirk again, by salt.

That still left the problem of Tzal. A problem that grew strange new layers with each passing day. He supposed he already knew the solution. But that too had been resting in his periphery, uneasy on the eye, unsettling to the mind.

Azetla walked south along the braided stream till the din of the village grew faint. He made himself look everything—all the worst of it—in the eye. Especially the parts that made him wince with shame or try to skirt his own thoughts. He knelt at the edge of the water. Listened to the soft sound of it. Wrung his thoughts out and left them to dry. With a somewhat reluctant tongue, he prayed the favorite song of the Tusian exiles; a praise of God, a plea for wisdom, and the traditional reading to initiate the high holiday and its requisite fast.

Only one day of fasting, but it posed problems. How to hold an entire day of negotiations when the chief form of hospitality was conducted through food? He would be seen as cold and heartless for refusing to partake.

He'd had reasons—even lawful ones—to violate this particular fast throughout the last many years. But he'd never done it. Even during long, forced marches, no bite had touched his tongue from dusk to dusk. He had some foolish, futile pride in this accomplishment. However, he had often violated the high holy day and the day of rest with work. The sages permitted this, for he had been as a captive in a foreign land.

But was that still entirely true? He had no man of the law, no teacher to give him a hard, firm answer, a clear instruction, a reprieve from responsibility for the state of his soul before God. He had only the confusing push and pull of what was needed, what he thought was right, and what he could get away with. He hated it.

Well, either way, he would not break the fast.

He prayed the old song again, slowly this time, muttering his own feeble prayer after. Then, he was quiet. In the stillness, silt settled, waters grew clear. The weight and precision of unclouded sight pressed—gently, firmly—down upon him.

When he rose, his knees protested. His back hurt, and there was a deep bruise in his ribs acquired—somehow—during the skirmish. He walked slowly back to the fires of Sijaya, mouthing the last verse of the song over and over. It was the rail by which he steadied himself as he went on.

Azetla sometimes doubted whether the God of Masheva ever spoke straight into the soul of someone fallen so far from home and holiness as he. Usually silence and ambiguity engulfed his prayers.

Tonight he was reminded that it was sometimes easier to endure the silence than it was to have it broken. For then, something might be told to you—or asked of you—and it would show all the more how much of a coward and a hypocrite you really are.

14

Joseph Radabe watched the Gora road. He attempted to count the Qatlani riders as they passed, distant little specks building into a swarm. There was no indication that they marked Joseph and his riders, but he doubted it would do them much good if they had. The Sahr had scouted yesterday. Expect about two hundred, it said.

Seemed accurate. Again.

They all needed the Sahr to be right. Everyone was already in position. But, against his own good sense, Joseph almost craved the day that it proved lethally wrong; he had all the words saved up. He could imagine, and almost taste, the miserable satisfaction he would feel.

How else could the Sahr be pried out of Azetla's hands and put to dust?

Joseph glanced southward toward the solitary peak of the otherwise long, low rock formation. It provided his men a little cover. Very little. The Qatlanis would travel within the shadow of that jagged peak in a few minutes. The Sahr devil was perched somewhere up there with a bow and a bundle of shafts. Azetla always made sure to give it discrete tasks, so that no one officer was ever forced to be in charge of it, and he was careful never to make it the crux of any battle plan.

Joseph was glad of that at least. He needn't have anything to do with it.

The swarm moved swiftly. The Qatlanis began to disappear around the southern knuckle of the rock formation.

Any moment now.

Joseph took a sip of water from his water-skin and swirled it slowly before swallowing. He did this three times exactly, as he always did before a battle. He tied his Darubhet—a little red symbol of Serivash—onto his pauldron, and kissed it. Then he raised his right hand and held it there, waiting. He curled his fingers nervously against his palm. Took deep breaths. Four seconds to inhale, five to exhale.

Come on. Come on.

Waiting for the dangerous thing was worse than simply doing it.

His arm flew down the moment he heard the first spit of the ram's horn.

Joseph's riders tore eastward from behind their scant concealment and spread out like a flock of rooks, wheeling in unison, drawing space in and out among each other without ever losing their collective form.

They careened not toward the enemy, but toward the enemy's retreat.

Joseph could not see it, nor could he think on it for more than a moment, but just beyond the low cut of rock, Azetla had ambushed the Qatlani riders. Azetla's job was to take the wind out of them, and send them running straight to Joseph.

He had to reach their avenue of escape before they did, though they knew this desert far better than he. They were better riders, too. Joseph galloped across the rugged plain and he felt the tension in his knees, holding to the horse, and in his fingers, clenching the reins a little harder than he ought. He had trained on horseback, some. But only in the last few weeks had he fought that way.

Joseph shouted to his signalman—"veer southward, fan out"—and caught the enemy flutter in the corner of his eye. He had hoped Azetla would hold them down a little longer than that. But the Qatlanis were proving more skittish and disorganized than Joseph expected. They didn't have the mettle for a long fight. But they were terrifying as long as they lasted.

Here they bloody come.

They claimed to have the blood of horse-gods in their veins. The Sahr—itself uncanny on horseback—spoke over and again of their unmatchable skill. Through the dust and wind that tore at his eyes, Joseph could see it. The Qatlanis did not ride over the ragged desert; they slipped over it like silk against skin, as though the rocks, gulches, and cuts that littered the open land simply melted before them.

Half the Qatlanis veered off toward the gulch, the other half shot into Joseph's men.

Briefly, the net held. In a flash, he saw dozens of those great, famous horsemen fall. Sacks of meal, slumping, collapsing, hitting the dust, ground under a mill of hooves.

Joseph raised his hand to his signalman. The signal flags swirled throughout the ranks. Holes appeared in the net, as they were meant to. Joseph retreated with his men and called a new formation. Brody's signal flared, then Ishelor's. A freshly woven net.

This one did not hold at all. The Qatlanis were frantic and ferocious. They pushed through the formation before Joseph could call the order, and a small swarm of them reached all the way to his command point. He jigged his horse back and forth to keep from being pummeled by other horses and leaned hard in the saddle. For one horrible instant he was certain he would lose his seat.

He clung. He righted himself. Flung his sword arm across a man with terrible force, but little precision. It bit into the man's arms and gashed his ribcage. The Qatlani wheeled to flee, only to meet another blow from Lieutenant Carihua; the enemy dropped.

The Qatlanis were scattering and fleeing in a dozen directions. They wanted *out*.

Joseph shouted to the signalman. Shouted again. A third time. The flags whirled. And Joseph's men gave chase.

Now Joseph felt strong in his seat, and sure with his hand. He and Carihua ran one down. Then another, working in tandem. Carihua sliced at a man's back, Joseph cut off the man's breath. He was famous for his brutal blows, tearing open necks and cracking bones. This, he knew how to do.

As they neared the gulch, Joseph pulled up his horse.

The signalman's flag was sweeping the sky even before Joseph's voice hit the air. The rest of the Qatlanis fled. No breath of fight left in them. Joseph called formation. Called a count. Gathered the wounded, of which there were few.

Carihua pulled up next to him, gesturing to Ishelor across the way.

"That good enough?"

Joseph nodded. "Better be. We got more of them than I'd hoped—demons on horseback these bloody tribesmen."

Carihua grunted agreement.

As they rode back to the Ishaani village of Sijaya, Joseph saw the Sahr devil slip down from its perch, pull onto its horse, and head for the gulch.

Azetla always told it to hunt down the enemy stragglers after the battle was over to siphon things out of them; even vultures and devils must be sated, perhaps. The Sahr always came back with plenty of blood on its sleeves and plenty of words in its mouth. Maybe it told Azetla how many it killed, but Joseph never asked. He was determined not to count it among the number of his men, nor to mark any of its victories as his.

Tzal returned to Sijaya before dusk, headachy, irritated, her left shoulder on fire from holding the bow at odd angles. It was still healing from a few weeks ago. She took Nashuv to the stream, its waters low and brown with winter rains still a month or more coming.

Tzal rolled her sleeves up to the elbow and rubbed the horse down. Slow, methodical motion. No need to think or talk. Just breathe and brush and click her tongue softly at Nashuv to soothe him. She looked at the blood on her wrist, forearm. Palms and nailbeds. Then she folded her arms and waited for Nashuv to settle and shake out. He scorned the mud also, determined to wait for well water in a trough.

Five assaults in six days. A swath of success about forty miles wide, cutting over halfway toward the Maurowan outpost of Cozona. Give it another week and Qatlan would be as scarce in south Trekoa as a brick of ice.

Azetla did not waste time. And Tzal liked to see herself proved right, even if she couldn't quite see how he was going to pull it off. He shared and planned and spoke clearly with his senior men. Almost, almost everything. The blank spots on the canvas were few, but that made them all the brighter and more fascinating to her. What was he holding back?

Regardless, she played along. Eventually he would cool off and let her do as she pleased. Everyone always did, because practicality won out over principle. It was not to her liking to be assigned specific tasks in specific places, to go there and no further, to give a full account of herself. She liked to roam to and fro, looking for little chances, bits to gather, victories to scavenge. She preferred considerable room for interpretation in everything. The fewer delineations, the better.

Azetla liked every meaning of every word to be clear. He liked to know everything in firm black strokes on parchment, at sharp right angles, and in columns. With annotations. Residue of ink ever on his left hand, like a scribe's.

Also, he liked to stand quiet and still. Blank-faced. Bow and nod. Then go for the throat.

She did like that, actually.

Tzal watered Nashuv and took him to the matting of dry reeds and redgrass alongside the other Sanchi horses. She scrubbed herself over the village wash-troughs. Took food from the soldiers' mess. Sat in the outskirts, listening to the goats and distant music, eyes half closed against spits of wind and a burnished bronze sunset.

A shadow crossed in front of her. Then stilled.

"I caught three," she said. Took a bite and a sip of water. Squinted up at Azetla. "They said the same things as the others. I let one go with my words in his mouth. That more or less what you wanted?"

"Meeting at the south command tent," he said.

"When?"

"Right now."

She stopped eating. "Did something change?"

He gave a faint nod and turned, expecting her to jump and follow.

By the time she arrived in the tent, the bronze sky was turning to char and smoke, thin clouds blanketing the last light. She had finished eating at what she liked to think was a pace of perfect medium. Neither pointedly slow nor fast. She had walked at that same pace. It even took a bit of concentration, to be honest; just long enough to stir up a faint irritation in the tent's air.

Joseph Radabe. Nimer Sarrez. Azetla.

And no one else. Not even Rahummi. No one for whom she must translate; no reason for her presence.

"You shouldn't have waited on my account," she said, looking from face to face.

"I didn't really have a choice," Azetla said. The others looked at him with as much surprise as she felt. He sat. The others did the same. Tzal remained standing, arms folded.

"We've received a courier from Areo," Azetla began. "The Corra James feared for his life and has fled Piarago. He is well on his way to the outpost, and he will be accompanied by many of his supporters."

Joseph lowered his head to his hands. "Oh Gods."

Sarrez blinked as if the lamp had dimmed and he could not quite see. "Then...then we are unmasked."

"So it would seem."

There was a death-like silence. Tzal could almost taste their dread on her own tongue.

"So...must we return to Areo immediately?" Sarrez said, trying to shake the daze off himself.

"That's the opposite of what we're going to do," Azetla said firmly. "We're going to walk straight down the path we just cleared for ourselves."

Joseph's head was still buried in his hands, though his fingers tensed against his scalp.

"It's too soon, Azetla." His voice rose up, faintly muffled but undeniably livid. "We go to Cozona outpost, we're no longer attacking the Emperor's proxies. We're attacking the Emperor himself! We can't do it. It's too dangerous and too soon..."

"Either we do it when it seems too soon for them, or when it's *undoubtedly* too late for us. There is no sliver of an instant more perfect than this very minute. We have days, at best, to work before the other outposts know the truth. Hiding behind the walls of Areo won't do us any good in the long run. Might as well be fish in a net, waiting for the cinch and pull."

"You brought us into this," Joseph muttered under his breath.

Azetla rolled his jaw slightly, but his voice came as clear and calm as before. "They would have made our battalion their creature with or without me. You *know* that. Be as angry as you like, Joseph, but don't pretend you can't see what we must do."

Sarrez was staring at the oil lamp in the center of the room, brow heavily furrowed. "Did the courier say anything else?"

"The Corra managed to send messages to his supporters throughout Makaria and West Maurow. There will be more soldiers arriving on his heels; it's unclear how many. Maybe as few as five thousand. Perhaps as many as twenty thousand. I won't rely on the numbers till I see them set foot in front of me."

"So. Cozona," Sarrez said, looking from the lamp to Azetla.

Azetla waited.

Slowly Joseph lifted his head, offering a flint-hard eye to Azetla. "Cozona."

"We have two thousand more men from Areo already on their way. In two days we'll join them at Jashna and move out from there…"

Joseph lifted his fingers and flicked them in the air. Azetla went silent, and tilted his head, waiting for Joseph to speak.

"First explain to me: why *does* that devil have to be in here for this?"

Azetla rested his left palm on his knee and looked Tzal in the eye.

"She's going to let us in the gate."

Astonishment flared through her, and she rushed to snuff out the effects. Slowly she unfolded her arms and set them akimbo. Let them believe she knew what the hell he was talking about. She did not.

"*Azetla,*" Joseph said through his teeth.

With a sigh Azetla set down the ledger he had been holding. He nodded at Joseph in a conciliatory way.

"Tzal, how many times have you been to Cozona?"

Everyone's eyes cut to her.

"A handful," she answered.

"And you stayed there days, weeks, even months at a time alongside Colonel Everson, did you not?"

"Yes."

"Then you know it well."

She pursed her lips. "Reasonably well."

"And the local population. The tribes that work on the outpost and live in its outskirts."

They had talked about all of this over the last month. Mere scraps and dustings of conversation. Azetla was making much more of it than he should. But he must have talked to Everson. And Rahummi. From the beginning he'd been bleeding them for information about her.

"Janbar, West Shayal, a few clans of Lir Ruhhal. But there are many Qatlanis also. And they're given the most important positions."

"But the others will ally with us."

Tzal almost laughed. "That's a gamble."

"Not really. I'm sending you ahead of us. Prepare the ground. Prepare our allies. Empty outpost towers as we arrive. Shatter the axles and hamstring the horses, so to speak. Give the signal for us and make sure the gates stay open. Do anything and everything you can without raising the alarm. I mean to take Cozona quickly and quietly."

For once, Tzal struggled to summon words to her mouth. It was all she could do to keep a neutral expression.

"I am leaving you to your own devices, you see. So I expect you will be effective," Azetla said. He was perfectly calm in voice and expression, but it was all on the surface. She could feel bright anger coming off him, as off fresh-fired metal, distorting the air with quiet heat. "Can you do this? All of it?"

She looked awry of his face. Ran her tongue along her teeth to keep from clenching them, but she got her words out this time. "How many days do I have?"

"Six, from tomorrow morning. You'll have to move quickly to get there in time."

Tzal lifted her eyes, fashioned a smile, and slacked her posture to one of comfortable certainty.

"All right, easterner. You'll have it. All of it. Down to the word."

He did not respond at first. She searched him to find any hint of hesitation, any tic in the eyes to show that he had actually expected her to balk, to hedge, to negotiate him down toward reason. Toward reality.

Maybe there was something. Maybe not. But it didn't matter.

If he wasn't bluffing, then neither was she.

"Well then," he said after a time. "Let's get to work."

Azetla had thought it all through, Joseph couldn't deny that. He always had an eye for this sort of thing, and was quick to move in on a target once he selected it.

The Sahr slipped out as soon as the meeting was over. Sarrez also.

Azetla turned to Joseph once they were alone and gestured wearily at him. "Go on. Out with it."

"Oh, there's a thousand things I didn't say, most of them because I already know your answers. It's one of the most obnoxious things about it: ready answers for every objection, as if you'd studied our words before we spoke them."

Joseph felt the bitterness on his tongue and let it fall out freely as a confession. Azetla listened with a sad, infuriating patience.

"I never wanted this, Azetla. I know many of the men did, but it was supposed to simmer, never boil. We don't get to come back from this. And you? You least of all. Your people? Don't you know they'll eat every consequence?"

His eyes flashed at that. Of course he knew. Still, he was quiet.

"I hate all of this, but at least...at least I know why. I understand the corner we're in. I can see all that. But that *blasted* Sahr devil. Why would you trust—"

"I never said I trusted her."

"This whole plan rests on that Sahr-jinn doing—"

"No, it doesn't," Azetla said sharply. "There are two methods in place. One if she succeeds, one if she fails."

"But what if it does neither. What if the Sahr simply betrays you?"

Azetla spoke quiet and firm as he began sliding his ledgers into his satchel. "That's the one thing I'm certain she won't do."

"You've no right to be certain about that. You act like you understand that jinn-creature, like you know what it really is."

"No, I don't. But I do know what she wants, and this is how she gets it."

"Gets *what*? That devil is going to die if it actually does everything you've asked and—"

"Then what's it to you? We'll still take Cozona—though admittedly at far greater cost—and everyone will be satisfied that it's over the Shihrayan's dead body. Won't you be glad?"

Joseph muttered his exasperation.

"I know what you think you're doing, Azetla..."

"Then you know what I need from you."

"You need something I'm not sure I can give."

Azetla nodded gently and gave a look of such absolute understanding that Joseph's frustration ebbed.

"Just remember how it was, and what it took," Azetla said. "That's all I ask."

"As long as you remember what that devil took from *us*."

Azetla's hard gaze faltered to the ground.

"I will remember that till the day I die."

15

The rains were long in coming, and meager when they arrived. The illness spread through Shihra. Many little ones went into the fires of Dimash, though the great God was not sated; the curse did not lift. And why not? The shamans bled and tranced and divined.

Because the curse lives among us, they said. We must root it out.

The fever glanced off his sister, as most things seemed to. She was on her feet sooner than the others. Izkher died. Dotiya nearly died as well, and she never quite recovered her strength afterward.

This time, when Zare climbed from the leper camp up to Yaqil, Aadin showed no mercy. He found her, singing in a whisper, running cool water over Dotiya's head. Sereya kept her back turned, awake but saying nothing; would never let Zare touch her, but she always quieted to hear her voice. Motti sang along with the shikk without understanding what he sang. Some Trekoan ditty.

The others slept in the dark, unknowing or pretending not to know.

Aadin grabbed her by the shoulder. Dragged her out. Struck her in the face each time she tried to open her mouth.

"They will kill us all if they know you are here. You want Dotiya to live? Don't come back."

"But, Aadin." Her voice came out cracked and dry. "They won't let me stay outside Kivaj anymore."

So even the lepers would not have her now. The fact brought no pity to him, only more anger. Indeed, he learned that day that he was never so angry at her—never so glad to see her stumble—as when he feared for her. Not for the first time, he wondered if he would be the one to kill her in the end.

Again and again he'd thought this. Again and again, he did not do it.

"Go down to the lowlands." He stepped toward her. She flinched back. That's how he knew he'd already won. "Go to the foreigners, Zaraje. You were born to them. You know how to sound like them. You know how to get what you need from them."

"But if she—"

"Leave Dotiya to me. For now, the only good you can do us is to have nothing to do with us. For all we know you really are the cause of all this. Go beg to that desert god and see if he will take you. We cannot."

He often saw in his mind's eye the stubborn, defiant look on her face. The beginning of a thought that Aadin would one day see come to grievous fruition.

But she went.

Over the next five months, the fever flared bright through Shihra, then dwindled to a smolder. The drought persisted. In the wake of such a winter, raids and feuds and violence broke out between the tribes of Shihra. The tribe of Kopka—always the most powerful—sought to survive off the back of the other tribes, especially the Illari tribesman who traversed the lowlands in desperate times and were tainted thereby.

Aadin hunted the other tribes. He slit throats. He protected his village. He took what could be taken. He proved the Illari reputation of fierce cunning and bloodthirst. Made a name for himself, young as he was. Aadin, son of Sa'ased, brother to a curse, was not to be trifled with.

He was not surprised when she came back in spring. Drawn, as it were, by the sounds of danger.

This time, Aadin did not lash out or drive her away. He had a plan. He put a sword in her hand and set her on the hunt, to vengeance and stealth and theft. For the rest of the feud she was not "shikk" or "zaraje" to their village. She was the swift and quiet shadow who watched over them. She was Zare. She was his sister. She was Illari. She was—very nearly—one of them.

He supposed it made sense now, all these years later, as he tried to remember everything through the haze of heavy drink on a dark, cold night like this. During the feud, the more brutal she was the more her own people tolerated her. She burned bright with the satisfaction of it. All too bright. Like something frenzied that cannot possibly last.

She no longer balked when told to slit an unsuspecting throat in cold blood. It was an opportunity to prove herself. When the Illaris dove into the lowlands to raid for food, she used her tongue on their behalf, then the rest of them drew swords and left the whole village with not a breath in it.

The feud ended strangely. Not as in the old times. The new Usarin gathered all the tribes together as few before him had ever been able to do. Aadin was given a Kopka woman for a wife. Nitzma. Sereya was given to a man of Serde. Through many such marriages, and more sacrifices, a semblance of peace was cobbled together.

There was a small chance Zare might also have made peace. But she was still herself; she could not leave the Gods alone.

It was still dark when Azetla stood, bowing his head several times at a gentle rhythm, and said his prayers quietly over a tent full of sleepers. He reached for his sagam and the little scroll of holy songs. Paused to hear the peaceful rustle about him. Made his way carefully through the pallets and came out into the cool, clear night. He recognized the horse, Nashuv, as he passed through the stabling.

She had not left yet.

Sijaya had no marked heights, so he had some trouble finding her at first. But, if not heights, then fires. And he found her at the south watchfire. She sat too close, as though she could not get warm, two mismatched swords at her feet. One was from the Maurowan armory, the other scavenged from a Qatlani rider. She had gone back and forth between them all week long, satisfied with neither.

As usual, she took no notice of his arrival.

Azetla sat down and began to read from the little scroll, as if it were any bit of early morning, before any kind of day. Tzal didn't translate. She didn't have to anymore. Rokh Imal had only the three small scrolls—twenty of the songs, one minor prophet, and a short reading of court law. Azetla had read them again and again, till he knew the Trekoan words well, and could have recited the original Mashevi almost from memory.

By now, Tzal could probably do the same. She had translated them for him so many times. But he did not read now to hear. He read to be heard, in a low, plain voice. A short lament, praises spoken from dust and ashes.

Grief and anger were the commonest things in holy writ, he found.

Tzal made no acknowledgment of him or his words. She did not even correct his pronunciation. She carried on, mending the seam in her outer garment. The one she wore when she meant to be perceived as a common Trekoan slave woman.

He finished the passage.

She bit the thread and packed the needle away.

With an irritable motion, she pulled through her hair. Swift hands wove the strands into a plain braid.

"The watch should have extra rations—" Azetla began.

For the first time since he came into the light of the fire, she looked at him, and did so with utter contempt. "I've got everything I need."

No doubt. She never asked for anything she could quietly take, and never took less than what she wanted. She stood and pulled on the threadbare outer garment. Then she tied the pale blue sash, shoulder to hip, and about the waist.

"Do you have a ritual?" Azetla closed the scroll gently.

"What do you mean?"

"Every man I know has at least one, before a battle. Joseph kisses his darubhet. I have a certain prayer I like to say. But I've never seen you do any particular thing."

"I make a point not to. No amusing little dances for the Gods. If I catch myself forming a habit, I break it."

"And that isn't terrifying?"

Her hands stilled as they reached for her belt.

"Of course it's terrifying," she said in a low voice.

"Then never doing the same thing twice *is* your ritual." Azetla stood and crossed the few steps between them. "Denying one thing out of spite usually just means succumbing to its opposite. It must be exhausting to always twist against everything, no matter the direction it sends you."

Derision filled her countenance as from a well, sourced deep. She picked up the Maurowan and Qatlani swords, eyeing both with discontent.

"What's your point, Mashevi?" Her voice was cold and pelting, like winter rain.

There really wasn't much use in coming at her sideways.

"Do you actually *want* to die? Because you could have just said 'no' and walked away."

"You knew full well I wouldn't do that," she said. "Besides, I like to give the Gods chances to do something, good or bad. Mine like to turn their backs and shield their eyes. And your God..."

She smiled a little.

"Maybe your God is not so skittish? Your poems like to say he's unchanging. So by what wiles or rites can I expect to influence him?

He does as he wills and I'll do what I said. And should his will be against me?" She shrugged. "Then if he is what you claim him to be, I die by the hand of a god worth fighting. I lose. Losing is an answer. There are worse things that can happen."

Azetla let out a faint sigh of exasperation. He could never tell if she meant what she said, or just spoke this way out of habit. Like picking at a scab. Chewing on fingernails. A dog that bites at every hand, whether it means to feed or beat.

"What's worse than God's wrath aimed at you?" he said.

"Indifference, Azetla," she said, as if speaking to an idiot. "If your God said he would neither love you nor hate you, but would simply walk past you as though you were not there, you would be content?"

Azetla closed his mouth.

"The Gods of my people won't even touch me, whether I honor them or insult them. Your God made sure of that."

"Careful when you speak of the God of Masheva," Azetla said. "He is far too holy."

"For me," Tzal spat.

"For anyone."

"Then what use is he to you?" she said coolly.

At any other time, that would have riled him to offense, just as it was intended to. But he had a purpose here and it steadied him. Also, she said those words in Mashevi. In the high poetic form with a native-sounding Rinayimi lilt. Because that was all she knew. He had strong and deeply mixed feelings whenever she did that.

"Tzal, you're asking what use is the sun when you can't look right at it."

She stared at him for a moment, then shook her head, determined to make as little as possible of what he said. She put on her belt without attaching either sheath. Slinging both the Maurowan and the Qatlani swords by the straps, she turned in the direction of the stabling. It was an hour till daylight, but Tzal preferred to set out in the dark.

"Tzal."

She did not break stride. "What?"

"You'll take this."

She glanced at the sagam in his left hand and scoffed. "What in all the desert do you mean by that?"

With an impatience borne chiefly of exhaustion, he grasped her arm and shoved the sagam into her palm.

"I mean exactly what I say."

She stood still. Wrapped her fingers around the upper band of the sagam sheath. Her eyes narrowed. Slowly and without a word, she donned it, leaving the others behind. Not a mote of gladness or gratitude in her face, however. Just the same steady contempt.

"Rather undermines your purpose to lend me this, doesn't it?" she said.

"Think of it however you will. Just make good."

She raised her eyebrows slightly, quickened her pace, and broke off in her own direction. Azetla turned back to his. He was grateful he had far too much work to do. There was no time at all to let his mind wander or worry or doubt.

<hr>

If she was willing to ride a few hours in the dark each night, and hold a stubborn pace, she could have reached Cozona in just under three days. But on the first day, she spotted the Qatlani scout; he ought not make it home with word of any kind. That cost her the better part of a morning.

Then, on the second day, she woke and felt the air whip about her. The dust at her feet rose in a pinkish-yellow haze. It would be a red day. She hurried to cover what ground she could. By late afternoon she had to give up and shelter in the tattered traveler's tents outside a small village. The canvas did little to shield her from the dust.

As the sun sank, the day grew deep, deep red, like the fiery inside of a hearth oven. The cloth over Tzal's face felt useless. She could taste the dust on her tongue, feel the grit in her teeth, and hear the rasp in her throat. She could barely open her eyes.

She had a poor kind of sleep. The dust began to calm during the second watch of the night. She departed somewhere around the third watch, coated in pale desert powder. The sky turned murky, and a scant rain proceeded. Just enough to make mud out of everything, including Tzal and Nashuv.

Daylight broke on the fourth day over a small Shayali village. Tzal waited until the women had drawn their morning water, then she approached and drew. Washed herself, her clothes, and Nashuv, each as thoroughly as she could. Hid the sagam within the saddlebags. Tucked a knife within her long outer tunic. She wrapped her hands with cloth to conceal the Makarish tattoos on her thumb and wrist.

When she reached the narrow market gate of Cozona, she led Nashuv in by the bridle.

With the same precise care that one might pull on a damask garment, gently thread the leather string through each aperture, and smooth the cloth down, Tzal dressed herself with all the mannerisms of a respectable, business-minded Trekoan slave, come to the famous Cozona market with a Sanchi horse and heavy saddlebags of small goods.

She glanced over at the main gate as she made her way with the mid-morning crowds. It was wide enough for ten or twelve men to enter on horseback at once, but it was only opened for ceremonial purposes. It would be the least easily solved of all her problems.

"List of goods," a Maurowan officer said wearily, looking not at Tzal, but over the top of her head.

"Embroidered sashes, salt, dates," Tzal answered. Everything she could beg, borrow, or steal—mostly steal—in the wee hours of the morning before leaving Sijaya.

"Is the horse going to market?"

"No, sir. He is a gift."

"For?"

"Rokh Youra of Shayal."

The soldier took a pair of shears from his satchel.

"Make him mind."

Tzal soothed Nashuv with a stroke on the neck and soft clicks of her tongue. The soldier cut a jagged section of Nashuv's mane. Tzal winced, though she'd known it was coming. Now Nashuv could not appear in market, for no tax had been paid on him. The smaller goods were allowed to pass uninspected. One way or the other, she would not have to worry about the departure tax.

Nashuv tossed his head at her and snorted as the soldier waved them through.

"A blow to your pride, ah?" she whispered to her horse in Shihrayan. "You'll get used to it. It's never our job to look fine, you know."

She had thought to cover her hair with the blue sash, but then she would seem too high ranked a slave to be clad as poorly as she was and it would make confusion. Best to keep her hair uncovered and her sleeves tacked up to the elbow. Nashuv already made her more ostentatious than she liked to be. She sat just outside the market circle, so that she could take in its sights and aromas, but not be accused of trying to sell an untaxed Sanchi gelding. She listened like one basking in the sun, calm and still. She whispered Shayali Trekoan dialect, warming her tongue to it.

The scent of cardamom and clove and honeyed ginger touched her nostrils as she counted the watchtowers on the walls, piercing through the all-pervasive atmosphere of livestock and sweat-stiff cloth. She watched the changing of the guard at the nearest post, marking their numbers and procedures. Cozona was larger than Areo. More a city than an outpost. A city of soldiers. A dozen tribes were represented at market, but two rivals were most prominent. Shayal and Qatlan.

She lowered her head into her hands, letting each anxious thought out in a long, long breath. Just for a moment. Then she righted herself.

Why am I doing this?

You want to see what will happen. For spite. To make them keep you a little longer.

No chance it works. More likely I get my throat slit.

You say that all the time.

And yet...

And yet letting her live was the one thing the Gods did with stunning consistency, no matter how she spit upon them or plied them or bled for them or blasphemed against them. She just ran on, headlong, waiting to hit whatever stone would eventually crack her open and lay her out. None yet had. And she was fairly certain she couldn't stop herself of her own accord. She would sometimes imagine herself acting differently—craft the words, envision the voice, sense the strength of decision—but when the moment came, the deep-rutted habits always won out. On she went.

She was utterly beholden to herself. And she was getting out of hand.

More than that, she was weary of herself. Sick to the back teeth. Even of all the things she called her strengths. No, *especially* those. All her vigor applied in any and every direction, only to meet so little resistance. It made her reel. Someday she would lose track of what she was or was supposed to be at any given moment. She would go on slipping from one voice to another, one manner to the next, with all the stomach-turning speed of falling down and down. She was pretty sure if she set to scraping it all off, she'd have scraped herself into nothing. No last debris of truth to salvage out of all the things she actually wasn't.

Discovering this old thread of thought wrapping ever more tightly around her mind, she cut it off as with a knife, and let it all fall to the ground. It would grow back later, whenever she was too still and too quiet.

She chewed dates and spit their seeds to give her hands and mouth something to do. Her eyelids were heavy, and her muscles sore, so she had to work hard to take the sights in and translate them into something meaningful, something she could use.

At last, she saw a man of seventy or so come to the cheap corner of the market. He moved like one blind, or near to it, and laid a mat for his wares. By his dress, he was South Shayali of the Tal region. He had a soft, intermittent smile aimed in no particular direction, as if his own thoughts simply pleased him. His neighboring sellers shared their hot cardamom tea with him, and a few laughs.

Now here was a good place to start.

"Good morning, grandfather!" she said as she approached his mat. "I have not seen patterns like this in a long time."

He felt about and held up one of the traditional bracelets of tightly woven thread, dotted with beads.

"You are from Ibrem-tal?" the man said in happy surprise.

"I was born very near there. In Qeim-tal."

She suspected that would be the last fully true thing she would say for the rest of the day. The old man exclaimed. How good it was to hear the lilt and words of home! He welcomed her warmly. They shared their meals. Especially at the beginning, Tzal scarcely needed to ask a question. He spoke to her as though she was a relative, and could be refused no good thing whatsoever, especially not the rich gossip of Cozona, the squabbles among the tribes, which Maurowan soldiers were helpful, and which ones were best avoided.

In a warm, fatherly way and on a dozen matters both desperately important and deliciously irrelevant, he spoke and spoke and spoke. With the contentment of a no-one girl from a nothing place, she drank and drank and drank it in. Every last word.

16

Of all the many small tasks and preparations Tzal accomplished that day, it amused her that the easiest one of all was gaining entry to the military stabling. A proud and stubborn slave of any Trekoan Rokh would not allow a Sanchi horse to be stabled with mules and donkeys and the like. It was offensive and ridiculous.

Maurowans tended to agree.

She need only pay the cost and present the little clay marker they gave her and the stabling—which was at the back side of the cavalry barracks—was hers. She examined every corner thoroughly, retreating to Nashuv's row any time some soldier glanced at her with either curiosity or suspicion.

Most of the floor was planked wood, laid over a pit, to act as a natural drain. Some of the dividers were wood, some stone. Some roofing was thatch, some clay and tile. All of Cozona had this patch-work quality and, some years ago, Tzal discovered the story of it. When Cozona was commissioned, a Cullitonian was assigned as chief builder. In his land, great places are made of logs and beams. He quickly ran out of funds, and also discovered that cold-weather wood does not wear well in the desert. The gaps were filled with stone, brick, and clay. So Cozona stood, a strange, proud place as mixed in its very walls as it was in its people.

Tzal counted the horses. She hid a few items and made small marks on four wood posts. Then she took her clay marker and stepped out into the last of dusk. Every scrap of roof cost coin, and the narrow stone alleys in the Trekoan sector were patrolled for troublemakers and "debris." It took her a long time to find a place to sit down. A little shadowy corner that the patrols seemed to skirt.

She leaned her head back against the clay bricks. She pulled her cloak over her shoulders, and used the length of it to wedge against the wall, making a soft place for her jaw to tilt. Her eyes could scarcely be kept open. Her ears heard, but her mind made less and less meaning out of the sounds as it slouched toward sleep. Music, laughter, sandal scuffles, and voices demanding this or that; it all crackled about her like a soft, warm fire, neither thought about nor tended to.

"*Now*! Get up and come with me."

The words came to her as if they had drifted. She realized that they had been repeated two or three times.

She pried her eyes open and looked at the shape which hovered over her. She could discern nothing of the face, dark as it was, but the dialect and clothing were Shayali without a doubt. Her shoulders sank slightly against the bricks; someone had recognized her. No good would come of that.

"You'll have to give me a reason," she said, closing her eyes and affecting a daze of exhaustion that was not far from reality.

"Rokh Youra of Nahro sent me to retrieve you." The man hiked his shoulders in a readying way; his hand rested on his belt-knife.

Now she really did open her eyes and sit up just a little.

"Retrieve me why?" she said.

"For...for the sake of the peace of Cozona."

"That's all Youra told you? And retrieve me *how*, exactly?"

"By any means necessary."

"Ah. So not a friendly invitation, I take it?"

He did not answer. He seemed a little uncertain about himself.

"You don't know who I am, do you?"

A pause. Shifting feet. "You have to come with me."

"Well." She shook her head and lifted her hands. "Do your best."

He hesitated. But only for a moment.

She always felt Aadin's voice in her head when this happened; his words had spanned minutes or an hour, days or years, but the action they induced lasted only seconds.

If some clumsy idiot comes at you...

The Shayali was not clumsy, but he was uneasy.

He tries to grab your wrist to keep you from striking or reaching a weapon...

Regular as the sunrise.

Snatch the arm and yank it—no, no, no, do it much harder than that, Zare—take him where he was already going. He will feel like to fall.

The knife nicked her shoulder when she dragged his arm across her chest.

And kick the leg out from under him. Gods, ram it! Into the bone, Zare.

The Shayali gave a bark of pain and lost his balance.

He'll practically fall into your lap, his neck yours for the taking. But you better be quick and decisive about it. If he is strong, you won't get another chance.

That was the problem with all Aadin's methods. They required one, and only one, conclusion. And Tzal needed something else tonight.

She cracked the back of the Shayali's hand against the gravelly walkway. Two, three times, till she got the knife out. But by that time she'd lost most of the little control she had over the man, her left arm looped about his neck, her right hand pulling the knife toward his ribs.

"I'm not going to kill you," she growled in his ear. "But be still, by blood."

She almost held her breath. He was not a small man, he was much stronger than her, and she needed him to heed her threat before she lost all ability to threaten.

He stilled abruptly, less mindful of the knife than of how his neck was clamped in the crook of her arm. She heard a raspy, gurgling sound; instantly she released him and scrambled to an arm's distance. She kept his knife, though.

He stumbled to his feet.

"What bad water has been drawn up that Youra would treat an envoy of Rokh Imal's like a criminal?"

She had mixed up the North and South Shayali idioms. That irritated her.

"That is a question for my Rokh." The man cradled his sore wrist, but stood firm. "If I do not return with you, he will send another."

Tzal smiled a little. The man had not been wise enough to reason with her *before* he tried to force her, but he was no coward. She had not met many Shayalis that were.

"He told you nothing at all of *why*?" she said.

"He said that you might argue. But you would come."

Tzal laughed, and it was half genuine. The Shayali man tensed as she turned to gather her things.

"I don't think you happen to be in Youra's good graces right now. You've had a bad trick played on you," she said. "Go on. Lead me to him."

The man's shoulders fell slightly and Tzal knew by the way he moved his head that he was struck with shame. But, Shayalis bore embarrassment with the same poise as they bore fear. He made a faint gesture, cast a wary look, then walked northward. Not, as Tzal would have guessed, further into the Trekoan sector, but out toward the northern villas of the dignitaries.

The room she entered was, but for its occupants, a place of decidedly Maurowan style. She took care not to show her surprise, but she did look the room over, piece by piece, and took her time, so that the Shayalis would notice her noticing and be curious about her curious glances.

Rokh Youra had always been a troublemaker and a tricky one. Friendly with Maurowans, curious of their way of life. A fierce fighter, a tepid ally to Rokh Imal, with two firm hatreds of which Tzal knew. He hated the tribe of Qatlan from his inmost being, and all the more for having to live peacefully beside them in Cozona.

And he hated Tzal. Rokh Imal's use of a Shihrayan—real or suspected—nearly broke Shayal from the fighting coalition four years back. It was a desperate problem for her just now; he was the only person in Cozona who could have been any real use to her.

She gave no gesture of respect, no semblance of greeting. Instead she cast down the Shayali's knife with a jerk of her hand. It thunked dully on the dirt floor.

"A bit cruel sending someone after me without telling him who or why."

"It need not have been cruel, unless you chose to render it so, devil," Rokh Youra said.

He did not stand from his lush seat on the ground, but sat tall and active, like a man who could—and indeed might at any moment—leap to his feet. There was hardly any gray in his beard; Youra was young for a Rokh. He looked from her wrist to her neck, narrowing his eyes.

Tzal kept her hands at her side so that her fingers did not drift toward the slave bands; they tended to itch under scrutiny. In the past, the signs of ownership had been such an advantage. Even now they served her, opening tents and convincing many to tolerate her who otherwise would not. But the lie they told wasn't necessarily the one she wanted to tell right now.

She didn't even know what would work on Youra: lie or truth. It felt like blindness, not knowing what he needed to hear. She could not run across, climb through, divert, or capture his intentions; she would have to step slowly with dragging feet, feeling about with fingertips. There was a slight ache in her jaw. Teeth grinding. She loosed them. Pried her body out of tension and into a careless posture.

"Why are you here, salt-brick?" Youra said.

Tzal's eyes took another long, slow tour of the room before she answered. "It's nothing to do with you."

"Yet you threw my name out of your mouth the moment you walked through the gates."

She smiled faintly. "It was just the first one that came to mind."

"I can have you put out of Cozona this very minute, and I do not care how many men it takes to do it. So answer me, devil, and do not play about: are you here on behalf of Rokh Imal, or on behalf of Colonel Everson?"

The strange fervor in his voice gave her something. A faint texture beneath the palm as she felt along. She dropped to the floor and sat, cross-legged.

"Neither."

Confusion passed through his eyes only briefly and then his posture was more alive than ever.

"There really is a jackal, then."

Tzal raised her eyebrows. "A *jackal*? You've a very northern lilt these days, Youra."

"You can't beat me with that stick anymore, devil. I have too many people under my care, and if I don't keep myself in the Maurowan ear, Qatlan has it all to themselves. I won't be ashamed of vying for my own."

Peering at Youra's face, combing through his gestures, Tzal wondered if Youra and Azetla would not easily tolerate one another. They were too alike. Azetla was calmer waters, perhaps, but both teemed with inexorable certainty. It resided in the very frame of their bones, holding them upright. Let it be righteousness or merely self-righteousness; Tzal did not like to differentiate. In any case, two of a trade rarely agree.

Suddenly, Rokh Youra made a gesture and gave one of his compatriots a purposeful look. Most of the Trekoans left the room. Those that remained, stood at the door, as if to bar it. The lay of the land came clearer to her now, all scarps and loose gravel. There would be no recovery from a misstep; even retreat did not seem safe.

"Every time you turn up, I wish to rid Trekoa of you forever. Yet always you come bearing someone else's name and strike it up as a shield," Youra said, leaning forward. "But I do not know this Mashevi. And I am not convinced that his name—whatever that may be—ought to hold me back."

Tzal looked at her hands, resting lightly in her lap. Lightly only by severe effort. She ran her thumb against the callouses of her palm and smiled a little.

"You must do what you think is right," she said, turning her eyes up at him, scrupulously placid. "And it might not do you any harm. The Mashevi was practically forced to take me in hand—he did not much like it. There's every chance it would be a relief to his conscience if I came here, failed, and got my throat slit."

She had no idea if that was true. But it very well could be.

"In any case," she continued. "He will accomplish what he set out to do. With or without me."

That was probably true too, but she laced her voice with the bite of absolute certainty; the effect was instantaneous. Rokh Youra looked at her with a bitter hatred. The first sign of his defeat. He stood up and paced toward her, away, and back to her again.

"Now, of course, you want me to ask what he plans to do."

Tzal shrugged and stood to face him. "Perhaps it will be easier for you if you don't ask. Just hide here and nose about for whatever scraps the northerners brush from Qatlan's table."

He slapped her with all his strength.

Through the hot sting on her jaw and the salt taste of blood in her mouth, she knew she'd won.

There was a strangeness to it; this was the closest Rokh Youra had ever come to treating her as an equal, or even human—as someone who deserved reprimand because there was a real possibility of shame and repentance. It was that, more than any flash of pain, which held her silent for several seconds longer than she intended.

"Well?" he said, almost desperately.

"He will cut Qatlan out of Maurow's right hand once and for all. And even *that* hand will not come out unscathed."

Youra's eyes widened.

"Get out of here!" he barked.

She nodded in compliance. The men parted from the door reluctantly.

"I have one last question for you, Youra."

"I said *get out*."

"Do they open the gates for Trekoan ceremonies like they used to? Funerals and weddings and the like?"

He gritted his teeth, kept his silence, and would have had her taken bodily out of the room. But she smiled at the answer he gave without giving, and slipped out into the dark courtyard. The men outside watched her with curiosity as she left.

When alone, she laughed; forced and shaky at first, then half manic. Once in a while she felt a harsh tang in her mouth as she spoke; it tasted as though her words were drugged, leaving the hearer no choice but to imbibe and succumb. In those moments—she tried not to think about them too much—she felt like exactly what they believed her to be. A real devil, fire-full and damned.

She reveled in it. Was queasy from it. And then, she went hollow.

Tzal took a long draught of water to satisfy her dust-dry mouth and slept like the dead.

17

The timing of it all was the hardest part. She could only guess. But she did not second-guess. What good would *that* do?

She put the torch to the stables during the third watch of the second night. In seven prepared places so that the fire would spread rapidly; she had to move fast to get herself and Nashuv out. The heat was already billowing out as from a high summer sun when she threw down the gate latches. Some horses would get out. Some would not. If the fire took the way she intended, many soldiers and many hours would be needed to douse it.

At the very least, she should have excellent disarray for a while. The four bodies she left in there—one stableboy and three cavalrymen—would not be found soon, and when they were, the fire would be blamed for their corpses. As for the fire itself? Few would question it. It was a miracle the place had not burned down long since.

Tzal set Nashuv to run with a whistle and a low tisk. He knew how to take care of himself, and he must be nowhere near her from here on out. She watched him leap away from the surging heat and turn toward the Trekoan quarter. She could barely stand to remain where she was, for her face felt like coals were pressed against it. Still, she looked back.

The fire took. Better even than she had hoped.

She moved quickly and carefully along the common ways until she came to the tower entry she had selected the day before. It was manned no more or less than any other entry, but it fulfilled the crucial requirements. It was isolated. On the north wall, near the eastern corner. And, thirty meters west, was an alcove full of supplies—arrows, signal torches, axes, and spears. At least, that was how they were stocked as of three years ago.

Lastly, there was a good place nearby to wait without much chance of being noticed, just behind the well-house. She slumped down to a sit. Instantly she felt the weight and weariness seize her limbs, like a trap sprung. Even the muscles of her face did not seem to have the strength for expression, for she had been this sort of person and that, leaning from one dialect to another all day and night. Never mind that she could count on one hand the hours of sleep she had had since arriving,

It was still dark. She was now far away from the desperate rush and noise she had brought about. She had to scrape her short, torn fingernails into her palms and pour her precious store of water down the back of her neck to keep her eyes open. She counted. She tried to translate her thoughts to Mashevi, and heard Azetla's calm, corrective voice each time she was uncertain of word or structure. Always in a reading cadence; always the harsh, ponderous syllables, which he savored.

The hour was interminable and halfway through it, she had to stand. All her body felt like lead. She suspected she slept a few seconds here and there, because she found herself beginning to sway. She felt, rather than saw, the first hint of dawn; there was always a rush of cooler air leading the first rays of the sun.

Out of her slim hip bag she drew three leaves—two mint, one chobi—jammed them to her back teeth and bit down. It wasn't enough to have much of an effect. Probably less than coffee or ghasnin tea. But the smell and taste of the two together pulled up memories of long, dangerous waitings in the Shihrayan lowlands. It put her mind in the path of action.

It was, she thought grudgingly, a little like a ritual. One kept for only the most uncertain tasks done in a bruised and weary state.

She clung to the shadow of the well-house, taut now. She did not have to wait long. Two morning guards slogged toward their post, one of them still fiddling with his buckle. Up the dark narrow stair, they went to their stretch of catwalk between two wall-towers. Three men came down, chatting as they trotted off the steps. The first two left, and the third lingered, rapping his tired heels against the wall and glancing about for his replacement who had been dead now for two hours. The man's eyes began to glaze, so ready for drinks and wife and sleep and whatever other comforts he had in life.

Instead he got his head cracked against the stone. A Mashevi sagam through the gut and a Trekoan knife across the throat. He didn't have a chance to make much noise. The dark was still strong enough that she had been able to move in until almost the very last second.

She did not wait to see if he'd been heard. She lugged the body up to the first landing and left it there. No one would see it until the head watchman came through. By then—one way or the other—it wouldn't matter.

She paused on the landing, just to get her breaths under control. To listen.

Nothing.

Nothing.

A faint, casual scuff of a boot some distance above her.

And then nothing again.

One silent step at a time—careful, careful—up the dark, low-roofed stairwell. She could see now; the faintest dawn-light was falling down from the lip of the stair. Her heart kept trying to go too fast, and all she could do to abate it was to press out long, slow breaths and adjust her hilt-grips. *Firm and supple, not a death grip, Zare.*

When she came out into the open, she saw the shape of one soldier cast against the dark blue of morning. He leaned into the wall, looking out over the desert as if drawn by the beauty of it.

Hand over mouth. Jerk back. Throat slit.

She caught him as he dropped and draped him down the top steps. No shapes or shadows yet, to either left or right.

Tzal shook her hand out where his teeth had practically bit into her middle finger. It seemed a very long time that she crouched behind the supply alcove waiting for the last of the three, but it was probably a mere minute. Time slowed horribly, then sped up, as if it had lost control of itself.

The third soldier almost got off a real shout before being silenced. Tzal flinched, bracing for the sound of alarm.

But none came.

Sagam in one hand, knife in the other, she trod the catwalk to the next tower as if she were the soldier assigned to it.

Three bodies later, she was rapidly losing the last of the dark. She had to move so gradually, to wait so carefully, to halt and hide and dispense of all fluidity and momentum with each kill. One at a time. *Zare, you're strong enough for what you are, but don't be so stupid. Almost anyone carrying a sword will beat you in size or strength. Never go for an enemy head-on, and always disperse them first, so you can deal with them one at a time. Like we did at Ozib. You have to stop* doing *this. I don't know why you think you can just go however you like and still come out alive.*

Two towers cleared. Waiting in the alcoves was the worst part. She would feel the sticking dust-dryness in her mouth, the slackness pulling on her limbs the way it always did when a struggle was finished. Then she steeled herself to hear the distant voices. They came—calm, cheerful, irritable, or indifferent, but not afraid—and she knew that she could proceed.

She held back for the right moment, guessing, guessing, then slipped out. Each quiet death gave her a split second of relief. But then she had to start all over and do it again. And again. Until it couldn't be done anymore. Until she failed and was known. And then what? She would be caught in the narrow trap which was now quietly feeding victims to her one by unsuspecting one.

The problems started after she passed the third tower. She had to start leaving the bodies where they lay, rather than pulling them into the stairwells, and all the while light was spreading invasively into her night, taking away her ability to hide and stalk. Her only advantage.

She thought she had timed this one so perfectly. A large soldier walked with what she thought was a distracted air. She darted out of the stairwell.

In an instant, he turned on her. His hands leapt at her throat as she drove her sagam into his belly. A shout broke from his mouth, piercing through the cold air, as he stumbled into her. The whole of his weight and all the strength in his arms put her to the ground. She let go of the sagam, hooked her fingers into his lower jaw, and jerked. He cried out again, but kept his grip on her throat. He tried to crack her head back against the ground and almost succeeded.

She dug her Trekoan knife into his side with muted strength. Again and again and again.

Gray clouded in at the edges of her sight from the relentless pressure on her throat. Her fingers were going numb from his teeth. Something was wrong with her arm. Only by virtue of being smaller than him was she able to twist her legs underneath, pull them up, and kick into his wound with all she had left. His head flared up, his fingers relented, and she flung the knife across the throat. Twice. Three times. Till all the life left him for good.

She pushed and shimmied herself out from under nearly two hundred pounds of corpse and stumbled to her feet. Recovered the sagam. Looked both long, deadly directions down the catwalk, unsure of which would prove worse. She hadn't gotten anywhere near as far as she needed to, and the light had overtaken her at last.

She still needed to cast the signal: twenty feet of scarlet cloth which she wore crossed over her shoulders and bound about her waist.

From the west, Tzal could see a cluster of soldiers far away down the catwalk.

Suddenly the sound of alarm broke out: the bell and the trumpet passing down their word of warning from west to east.

From west to east. It took her a moment to know the meaning. She was not the cause of the alarm.

Azetla was.

Firm, supple grip. She stepped over the corpse and counted the soldiers in view, channeled almost into single file as they were. Now they saw something amiss. Now they hurried. She did not know if Youra had accomplished what he said he would do. She did not know how far her fire spread. She did not know how she would get out of the towers.

But the signal *would* be cast.

Azetla had never felt so bewildered before in a battle that he had yet to fight. He felt as if he was being carried, over water, at a speed so sudden and swift and perfect he wondered what must go wrong, and when.

First, under the dark of night and by the graces of the nearby tribes, Azetla had been able to move four thousand men almost to the very gates of Cozona. Scouts from the previous day told him that Cozona *seemed* to remain in a state of peaceful ignorance; it was possible they did not yet know that the Corra James had fled Piarago, or that war was breathing quietly, patiently on their doorstep. Indeed, the siege ladders were already hidden at the ancient altar of

Amaqesh, just beyond the periphery of what a tower guard could see.

Dawn grew near and Azetla began to advance in the faint light, knowing that at any moment the guards on Cozona's walls must see them and know what had come. Suddenly, one of his scouts galloped back to him, voice almost giddily desperate.

"The gate is open!" the scout said, sounding incredulous even at his own words.

"No, it's not," Joseph barked, shaking his head forcefully.

"A small procession of Shayalis came through, as on a funeral day. It *is* open. *Just now.*"

The words hit like a wild sea wind, driving hard at Azetla's back.

He did not waste a breath. He filled the night air with his call. The thunder of hoof and foot broke out as Azetla's army spilled toward the outpost. The sun breached the horizon and cast its light over all his men as they met the wall, the whole body of them moving just as it should. He saw the great gate, now embattled, three-quarters open. He saw the market entrance, instantly overrun by his own. Then, as he drove the rear company toward the walls, he caught the flare of that scarlet strip, hanging down the wall. Fourth tower from the east.

That far, she had made it.

That far was cleared.

His men would start there.

Only minutes later, through a thin sputter of arrows, Azetla himself reached the gate with the final column. They entered bedlam. Hundreds of Trekoans dispersed from the square as if they had been in celebration or protest, and their very presence muddled the movements of Cozona's soldiers.

Azetla's men engulfed the frenzied infantrymen. The cavalrymen were strangely few, which made it all the easier. Azetla's calls to his signal-bearer were carried, with beautiful swiftness, all around the square and through the main thoroughfares. Juniper battalion flooded the walls and its towers where they had been cleared. The Black Wren advanced toward the General's villa.

Azetla and his column spread through the thick belly of Cozona where troops had attempted to form for defense. After fighting to the main storehouse, Azetla leapt from Barra. Climbed to the roof. From the height, he flung his voice and his signals. He could see everything. The fitted stones of Maurow were sloshed with red. His men were strong and sure. The walls were almost his.

The enemy collapsed. Men were fighting with no coherent purpose or form, fleeing with nowhere to go, surrendering without having received any orders to do so. Cozona felt smaller and smaller as the dead filled the open space, and there was a strong, acrid smell of smoke hanging thick throughout the air. Numerous soldiers tried to hide in the Trekoan sector—the only place to be passed over by the assault. They were hunted down, one by one.

Azetla saw it in the end. As swift as the surrender was, it would have been even more so had the men of Cozona been more organized. They scarcely knew how to go about it. Azetla did not stop to marvel at the furious victory—the kind that a man might imagine but has no right to expect. Not till after.

After he had commissioned men to pursue and destroy any messenger.

After he hurriedly put pen to reed paper and sent two separate couriers.

After he had spoken to the Rokhs of Shayal, Janbar, and Lir Ruhhal, each of whom advised him as to who among the surrendered officers might be made allies and could thus be spared.

After he had counted his dead—one hundred and eighty-nine—and his wounded.

After he knew how many he had killed: nearly a thousand.

After he had executed Riada's loyal General. The resident Colonel he questioned and, by his own discernment, spared. For now.

After his men had eaten and been given instructions for the morrow.

Then and only then did he pick the whole course of the day up from the ground and study it warily, working hard to step around his own astonishment and see things clearly. He listened to the surrendered soldiers make their confession: it was as if they had been handed over to this mismatched army by an invisible hand, they said. Fire broke out. Horses trapped in the flames. Everyone distracted. Watchmen missing. The Shayalis betraying them so abruptly and so utterly. All at once. It was like a curse. From devils or demons, who knew?

Azetla knew. Not a true demon, by his reckoning. But awfully close.

There had been no promise of her success. Not from his God, and certainly not by reason or circumstance. But he had known with quiet conviction that he must put her to the task and read the answer for himself. Was the risk of her one worth taking to the full?

He had not expected the answer to be so absolute.

Azetla sat down at the work table of General Monteche. The thought fluttered briefly through his mind; last night the man had put his desk and accoutrements in order, his cup set at the edge with the smell of arvine tea still resting in it. And he'd gone to bed. An hour ago Azetla had him executed. There was no regret in this, only a terrible gravity. The thought passed on. The gravity remained.

Slowly, with somewhat mired focus, Azetla began to examine Monteche's scrolls and tablets. Tax and trade. Rosters and livestock. Stores and finances. Correspondence. And a bit of what appeared to be personal poetry. More than once Azetla found himself staring just awry of the words he read, as if lost in thought. But there was no thought he was aware of. Just a faint, distracted unease.

The lamp was guttering and his hands rubbing against strained eyes when she came at long last.

She was worse for wear, though she moved steadily enough. A swift glance from head to foot showed no sign of serious injury, though who could be sure. A bruise and slight swelling on the jaw. Bits of dried blood on the hands. The same shoulder that had sagged in Ishaan sagged once again.

Tzal looked at him as if she was sighting along the arrow of a drawn bow.

"Do you need a physician?" he asked.

"No. Is there anything else *you* need?"

Before he could give an answer—and it wasn't as though she really wanted one—she loosed the sagam from her belt and cast it on the table with a clatter.

"You're not even willing to kill me yourself, so what on earth makes you think you can do it by proxy?"

Azetla sighed and gently pulled the scroll he'd been reading out from under the sagam sheath.

"Many of my men would have been very glad to see you fail against a sharp edge here," he said quietly. "But they saw something else today. And it's enough."

For a moment her words, already high upon the tongue, seemed to falter. She narrowed her eyes.

"I doubt it."

"Look, Tzal, I don't need them to like you. I don't even exactly need them to trust you. I just need them to let me trust you. I won't be badgered at every turn."

He glanced at his sagam, resting in front him, then back at Tzal.

"For now, that will have to suffice."

18

His servant, Adi, woke him while it was still dark. James was used to it now. Dutifully he dressed. Dutifully he ate and drank while they readied his horse, rolled his pallet, and filled his water skins. His servants, his guards, and his exorbitantly expensive Trekoan guide all executed their tasks with a clean, quiet swiftness that James rather admired. Not for the first time in his life, he imagined how fine it would be to have a strong skill in one or two things—be they ever so simple—and tend only to that.

In a matter of minutes, the camp was swept from the ground, as if it never was. Then it fell behind them. James savored the short minutes between departure and sunrise; being in the dark made him feel invisible and alone. No one was looking at him or to him. And the less light, the less thought, he supposed.

But this was the last morning. A heavy fact. As wearying as the hurried journey through Trekoa had been on his body, it had been such a reprieve to his mind. Nine days he prepared for his flight, barely sleeping for fear that Riada would be ready to move before James was. Now the dread action had been taken. The consequences were out of his control. Until he got to Areo, he could do absolutely nothing but blindly follow the Trekoan guide, and do what his guards and servants told him.

He still could not believe he had made it out of the city. He was almost bewildered that he was alive at all, leaving aside the fact that he had stolen two entire brigades from Riada's western coast. Well. Wesley Verris had stolen them. The work of that had been done months ago, and James scarcely knew how much was loyalty and how much was bribery. All James had to do was say "now is the time" and "there is the place."

It had been nearly impossible to warn his remaining allies in the city. James knew how closely he was being watched and, if nothing else, he had learned not to trust any servant or slave whose placement had not been overseen by Lord Verris.

Subtlety was not his strength. But he tried. He really did try.

The night he left, he thought he would vomit from terror. So many of the little details which Wesley would have handled were left to James alone. *He* had to choose who to trust. *He* had to decide upon the hour. *He* had to put money into a palm to be put into another palm. *He* had to walk out of that door of his own volition.

He had to rely on the work of his own hands.

James had thought he would recoil and slump when he saw the walls of Areo outpost, as from the jaws of a beast intent on snatching him up. But that was not what happened. Under a dull gray sky that never released a single drop of rain, he saw the outpost as a speck in the distance, slowly growing into great sand-colored ramparts. He heaved a deep sigh and simply accepted that he was here. Much would be demanded of him. Many voices would crowd into his head. But he had made it this far.

And if all hell was to break loose, he probably had some hours before it did so. There was every chance he'd have time to bathe in hot water, eat hot food, drink wine, and sleep deep in a soft bed. The anxious drumbeat in his stomach would come back, no doubt, but he need not seek it out.

He had to wait a brief while at the foot of Areo's walls, as the guard sought to verify that, indeed, the Corra of all Maurow might really be here at the least of all Trekoan outposts. From the seat on his mare, James craned his neck and stared up to the top of the ramparts. He rather liked the smallness they imposed on him. Their sturdiness. The way they cut against the sky.

Then he passed through them. Without word and without ceremony, he was suddenly in command of all he saw. Whether he wanted to be or not.

It couldn't have been more than an hour after his arrival that the summons came. James had washed the dust from his face. He had tea brought and clean clothes laid out. He was sitting in a cushioned chair, eyes a bit heavy, thinking that when the Trekoan servant returned, he would order a bath to be drawn.

But it was a Laritoni officer who arrived instead. With deep bows and many respects, he asked that His Highness the Corra come dine with the Colonel of the outpost.

It occurred to James that he could wave his hand and say that he would do nothing of the sort. He was tired. The Colonel could come to him. All this could be handled tomorrow, anyway. *And send for Lord Verris, while you're at it, Captain. He ought to be here.*

James certainly had the right.

But he did not do it. He rose and told the Laritoni Captain to "lead the way."

Maybe it was simply because he was very good at coming when called. Or because he was faintly curious, remembering almost nothing of Orde Everson from when he was at court. But there was a chance it was something else. For the last several months he had had to face Riada again and again and again, all while brimful of terror and secrets. He taught himself not to avoid Riada, not to prolong things, not to escape, because he feared this would arouse suspicion.

Some old reluctance in him broke. He was no longer so afraid to face a man who was cleverer and more knowledgeable than he was, while tired and uncertain himself. He had done it so many times. How much easier to do it with a man who was supposed to be his actual ally. He could drink wine without feigning sips. He was allowed to have errant words and ask stupid questions.

Colonel Everson stood and bowed deeply when James entered the airy portico. James couldn't have said that he actually recognized the man, so little had they known each other amid the sea of high-born people in Piarago. He was several years older than James and had been in the tribal south a long time. James thought he almost had a bit of their look to him. His manners, however, were all high court. Aloof, confident, deft with his words, and sharp with the eyes.

"It is a great honor to have you here, my Corra," Everson said, gesturing to a chair.

James took the proffered seat without hesitation.

"I think it is also a great peril to have me here. But I am glad to have arrived safely," James said.

"Peril, yes." Colonel Everson smiled. "But expected and prepared for, Your Highness."

The Colonel was a sensible man. He gave light talk as James ate his food, and James enjoyed the way his appetite gave even the most unfamiliar dishes wonderful savor. It was only as James began to lean back and settle to his wine that he noticed something amiss.

"Where is Lord Verris? Has he not been told of my arrival?"

"Of course he has been told, Your Highness. I believe he will be here very soon indeed. Since the two brigades arrived ahead of you, we have had some…logistical challenges. Such things have kept him very busy."

James nodded in acceptance and took another sip of wine.

Colonel Everson made a gesture to one of his servants.

"And do you have any questions for me, Your Highness?" the Colonel asked gently.

Oh.

James was supposed to be asking questions. Getting reports. Making assessments. Issuing commands. He felt his shoulders and neck tighten immediately. He knew next to nothing about the goings-on of the last several months. It had not been safe to send or receive messages.

"I'm sure I should have a thousand, but I cannot think where to start," he said.

"I understand. And, of course, Lord Verris will have his reports and they will be quite thorough. I *can* tell you, at the very least, that we have had wonderful success thanks to your decision."

James nodded thoughtlessly, but then blinked.

"What decision?"

And what "success?"

"Letting that Mashevi take command. A shocking thing to do, but it turned out to be a master stroke."

James set down his cup of wine. His eyes and mind both strained as they focused on Colonel Everson. He must have misunderstood.

"What?"

"Lord Verris told me that he didn't want the Mashevi in command of the Black Wren, but that you argued for allowing it. Did you not?"

"I...I did. But he's dead. He's supposed to be dead. I wrote it."

Almost against his will, but for the Gods' sake he wrote it!

"Yes, Your Highness. I received the execution order, but you worded in a way that left some small room for my discretion. 'Howsoever you choose,' you said. I wanted to honor both the order and its intent," Everson took a sip of wine and a thoughtful bite of lamb. "We've held it lightly over his head, with beautiful results. Do you want to keep it or rescind it?"

How calm. How casual. How carefully crafted.

James rummaged wildly through his mind looking for the memory of the execution order. He had not remembered leaving it so ambiguous.

"And the truth is," Everson went on. "I liked your plan better than Verris'. I don't say this to disparage him. Naturally he sees the value in the Mashevi now more than ever. But it turned out you had the right idea in the first place."

James held up his hand shaking his head.

"Wait, stop, *stop*. You are trying to tell me what my own thoughts were. It is not your place to do that. I signed an order with my own hand. You didn't follow it?"

"Your Highness, I understood that—"

"You let him live."

Until now Colonel Everson had seemed all smiles and warmth and lightness. Some faint sobriety shadowed his face now. He was slower to answer.

"Yes, Your Highness. I did. And I do not regret it."

James scarcely understood the horror he felt. Was it because his order was cast aside, even though he had never wanted to give it? Or was it because the Mashevi, that untapped danger, had been long buried in his mind, and was now restored to life.

"And you left him in command of the Black Wren," James said, almost in despair.

"He's in command of a great deal more than that, Your Highness."

Now James began to understand. Everson's laid-out bits of flattery to soften the blow. James put his hand to his forehead and felt his teeth clench hard enough to ache.

"How did he engineer *that*?"

Colonel Everson hesitated briefly.

"I chose to spare him and use him in the way I thought would best serve you, Your Highness. In your execution order—"

"I know what I wrote, Everson. Regardless of any hesitation I may have so foolishly expressed, I am fairly certain I did not say 'feel free to put everything I've risked my life for into the hands of *that jackal*.'"

There was the faintest flinch in Everson's calm demeanor, but it resolved with a somewhat condescending and reassuring smile.

"That *jackal*? Forgive me, Your Highness, you are not afraid of him, are you?"

"Yes! I am. And you're not?"

"I don't entirely subscribe to the Emperor's view of Mashevis. But I do find his blind contempt for them incredibly useful. When trouble comes, they are all he sees, if you under—"

"I understand your meaning," James said sharply. "And don't bother implying things. Just state them. I'm much too tired for all that. The simple fact is you disobeyed my order."

The silence that ensued was an uncomfortable one. While Everson's posture remained relaxed, there was lively calculation in his eyes. It occurred to James that Colonel Everson had expected a more flaccid response. Seven months ago, he might have received one. But James had spent all this long while teaching himself to be glad of the execution order, to feel justified in it, detailing its necessity with the ritual regularity of prayer.

Now all that was being ripped from him. *Again.*

It was infuriating. By the time James finally caught the stroke, he found everyone else had pushed into a different current.

"Yes, Your Highness, and forgive me," Colonel Everson stated at last, in a cool, soothing voice. "I stayed the execution and gave my account to Lord Verris. I made what I consider to be a battlefield decision."

James scoffed.

"I had thousands of new men to command, tens of thousands of Trekoans to placate, and the Shihrayan made it clear that—"

Everson broke off and turned as Wesley Verris burst into the room. Wesley rushed over to James, knelt clean to the ground, and looked up at him with what James wanted to believe was earnest gladness. He was not quite sure anymore.

"Thank the Gods you have arrived safely, Your Highness. I came as soon as I knew."

James rested a hand on his shoulder and urged him to rise and take his seat. On the long journey James had pictured how relieved he would be to finally have Wesley back at his elbow, telling him what was happening and what he must do. Kind and grateful words he had in store, but they died quickly on his tongue.

"Wesley, is what the Colonel told me about that Mashevi true?"

Wesley nodded severely. There was a brief glance exchanged between the two Colonels, actual and honorary, and James began to think that Verris' delay might have been contrived on purpose.

"And you approve?"

Wesley pressed his lips together, and did not quite shake his head.

"*Wesley.*"

"Approve? How could I say it, Your Highness? Yet I see no way around it. And I cannot dispute the results."

Here he glanced at Colonel Everson once more, eyes wide.

"A courier arrived moments ago. Azetla has taken Cozona."

James looked at Wesley. He reeled as when too many cupfuls of wine hit the head at once; the whole world tilts and spins, the mind is dizzy and detached, and the stomach threatens revolt.

"Taken?" He managed to utter the word in a child's plaintive voice.

"By force, Your Highness, and with small loss of life. Hidud outpost will be next. I think Azetla will—"

James stood abruptly. Wesley closed his mouth, and Colonel Everson stilled.

"I arrived here grave and somber, thinking that I brought such terrible danger down to your door," James said slowly, staring at his hands which braced against the table. Fine-grained olive wood, polished to a shine. "But it turns out that all this while you were dragging the danger purposefully in my direction and without my knowledge. You've started a war!"

Oh Gods.

"Your Highness—" Verris began with a deep bow.

James put his hand up. "When will the jackal return to Areo?"

"In a few days, Your Highness."

"The moment he sets foot in the gate, bring him to me."

"Your Highness, what are you going to—"

"I will do as I see fit. Just as you two have apparently done." He shook back his shoulders. "Straight to me. Understand?"

They both bowed and acknowledged, but James' back was already to them. He was half sick with worry and fury when he reached his apartments—maybe there really had been too much wine—and he scarcely knew himself.

Why was he stricken so? He had always been so glad to let others make the decisions for him. He couldn't have expected them to be idle all these long months. But that they should yank him one way—"*the jackal must be killed and you must sit peacefully in Piarago*"—then yank him another—"*the jackal is our commander and we have lit the fires of war*"—how dare they? *How dare they?* They cared only that he complied, not that he thought, or understood, or gave his honest, calculated consent.

He could have struck something or someone. But it was not in his nature to bruise his knuckles against the wall, so he sat in quiet fury on his bed. Sat until the fury flickered down into weary confusion.

By blood—and he had not even *wanted* to kill the Mashevi in the first place!

Now the Mashevi was his General. All James possessed, that jackal wielded.

Why is Riada always right?

He sank into his bed, certain now that the wine had done much of tonight's work, both boldness and folly.

I am at war with my brother.

Then his wine-thick thoughts admitted—at long last—something he always managed to hide from himself.

And I can't possibly win.

19

Aadin was not there when it happened, and he always wondered if his sister had told the whole, true story. Her stubbornness often came alive in the most irrational ways; her pride took a strange, useless cant. She would as soon lie against herself as tell some truth with the least hint of pleading. Or perhaps it was that she omitted all exonerating facts because she wanted to see if anyone else would be willing to offer them.

He simply did not want to believe it was so entirely her own fault. Yet it was.

All his efforts thrown off the cliff, because Zare was a stupid child who would burn a shrine down just to prove she could. Could her anger at the Gods really have been so deep and so cold?

On this dark night, waiting for the sound of drops—the first of the rains should have come by now—Aadin began to realize that he never understood her as well as he thought. No matter how he pushed and pulled, she was not his creature, not the work of his hands. She was something else altogether.

The Usarin had been forcing peace throughout Shihra by the twisting of so many joints. Most villages had succumbed. Aadin's village of Yaqil found less and less use for the shikk. They wondered how it was they had ever had any need for a fifteen-year-old girl whom the Gods rejected. She had been good only for quiet, calculated tasks on which they dare not waste their fighting men, and who would have mourned her?

First, one of their cousins accused her of bringing leprosy from Kivaj.

She was stripped and thoroughly examined, proving her skin clean and brown from head to toe. Aadin had the good sense to stand by and let matters fall as they would, but the hatred he felt for that cousin abided to this very day.

The next incident made things far worse. Dotiya came back from the spring-well, tearful, with a red mark on her cheek. She had been harassed on Zare's behalf; they threatened far worse than they did. Aadin had to act quickly; he took hold of his shikk sister—she fought desperately hard—brought her to collapse with his arm around her throat, and tied her down so tight it left bruises. Whether she killed or was killed, it would have been the end.

He told Dotiya to hold her damned mouth shut, for she was always talking about Zare. About how her beloved Zare did not fear the Gods because she was born outside their hands. Stupid girl. He dealt with Dotiya, then he dealt with Dotiya's tormentors. Only then did he let Zare go. He thought he had done right. She seemed to see sense. Seemed. She said she was going back to Kivaj. Said.

After that day, all he knew for certain was that she had gone up to the holy stones at Deshe in broad daylight. Palmed the stone with blood. Climbed atop it just as she had once done. And waited. Waited for someone—anyone—on whom she might take vengeance.

The bulk of the matter he still did not really know.

The end of it was that a shaman, his temple girl, and his young apprentice were all killed. And the eldest son of the great Usarin was left limping, his face scarred for life.

All this was told to him. The Usarin and his people came to the village of Yaqil to find her. Never had the Usarin come so near the lowlands. Never had Yaqil been of any import. Little Zare, once a merely local curse, had finally drawn the fierce, retaliatory attention she so longed for, from the very heart of Shihra.

Aadin did not have to hand her over. She did it herself, quite freely.

She went to her knees, though there was not a drop of humility or concession in her face.

"Everything you wish to accuse me of, holy Usarin, I have surely done," she said. "And I would do it again."

Aadin knew it would be just and right to wash the black stones with every last drop of her blood. So he put his shaking hands behind his back. And his sister put her forehead to the ground.

But the Usarin grabbed her by the hair and jerked her head back, till her eyes bored into his.

"You thought you could get such cheap mercy, shikk?" The Usarin's voice was as cold and jagged as the black stone itself. "Only the weak and the small get that. And only those we choose to call our own."

Azetla worked beyond the hours of daylight, straining over lamps till Joseph urged him to rest. When the words ran together in his ears or blurred before his eyes, he conceded. All of it had to be done, and quickly. In some small sense, the endless, pelting, driving tasks were a form of relief.

It used to be that he had good governance over his thoughts and there was no reason why, when presented with a bit of silence or rest, his mind should not also keep quiet. It used to do so easily enough. But for the past week or so there were wild and wayward thoughts of all kinds, snaking through and darting about in so many exasperating directions. Toward things infinitely beyond his control. Toward things done that could not be undone. Toward troubles he was willfully bringing on himself, and troubles he did not yet understand. Toward distraction and folly and longing and all that which could turn sight murky-gray. It was a strange and ever-changing barrage.

Perhaps the exhaustion was as much problem as it was solution. Yet it was good to fall asleep at night with the belated evening prayer tumbling quietly from his tongue. He was never certain he finished it, few as the words were.

The most difficult and tedious work had been creating a command structure for Cozona out of the remnants of its former occupants, the most capable of his own men, and the chief Rokhs of the region. He had to fashion something that would not collapse the moment he left and which would do for him what it had failed to do for Riada.

Rahummi executed his role flawlessly, treating with all the nearby tribes so that Azetla's army grew by far more than it had lost. Before each tent meeting, Rahummi sat with Tzal to plan his words and tactics; she struck him with all the arguments she thought he would face, and shaped for him the coercions she thought he might need to employ. It became clear to Azetla that this was a pattern the two of them had formed long ago, and fell to naturally. Azetla saw no reason to interfere; it was utterly effective.

Finally, the third day after the battle, a quarter of Azetla's southern army was nearly ready to march. Through Sijaya to retrieve Khala and bow to Rokh Idayir. Then on to Areo to swell their ranks with fresh troops and replenish supplies. Then swiftly to the next outpost which, if Tzal and the Shayali riders had done their jobs, would have nothing but rumors to nourish and prepare them. The rest of the army would meet them along the way.

At dawn, Azetla held his last meeting with those of his officers and allies who must hold and wield Cozona for him. The moment of relinquishment was always a hard one; his love for precision and control made it so. It was one of the dangers of his temperament and he knew that. But now it was done. He stepped out of the guardhouse, took his meal from the common pots, and seated himself where he could be easily seen, should anyone need him, but set apart from the roil of men and market and preparation.

He ate his food with what felt like leisure. Fifteen entire minutes, it must have been. He watched the Trekoans lay out their wares for the day. It intrigued him that the people of Shayal and Janbar and Lir Ruhhal behaved as if no more than a light rain had washed over them, when in fact the entire outpost had changed hands and there was still blood on the edge of the stones. If anything, they were especially industrious today, for it was the last chance to sell to such a sizable and diverse crowd.

The market gate opened. The scouts and outer watch returned from the night's work.

Azetla paused at his meal and watched them, one by one.

Tzal was nearly the last to come in. On foot, not horseback, which meant she had taken the ravine again. There was some pagan superstition associated with Doshas ravine and the local tribes did not like going there at daytime, let alone at night. "*Let the Sahr devil do it*," Rokh Youra had said. "*An ibex with no scruples and no soul*," he called her. "*What else is she good for?*"

Azetla watched as she crossed the dusty market yard, accepting a portion from the common pots and then—to his surprise—she turned to the cheap corner of the market, a stone's throw away. Without invitation, she sat down next to an old, blind man who sold trinkets. Bracelets, earrings, hair dressings, all made of common materials for women of common means. Tzal spoke to him, though Azetla could not make out any of what she said through the muck of market noise.

He only saw that the Shayali man brightened at the sound of her voice. They shared their meals and cups. She admired and praised his wares. Both used many similar gestures to punctuate their conversation, hold a comfortable silence, then resume talking. It mesmerized Azetla. It was like nothing so much as an uncle, or even a father, taking joy in his daughter. The old man was so *glad* of her. He made wry faces, and seemed to tell jokes.

Once he made a gesture, feigning to convey a secret. She bit the inside of her cheek, straining to hold back a smile. But it broke out, full and bright and just shy of laughter. No shadow of the gallows or of contempt was found there.

What was the point of this performance? The old, blind man couldn't see her face, or notice how completely she incorporated his every mannerism. Her voice alone could convince someone of nearly anything. He had no doubt that the man heard *home* when she spoke to him. The sense of it was so strong when she spoke Mashevi to Azetla that it was almost unbearable. She took whatever words she was given, massaged them like some bit of cold clay until it took a warm shape. And when the words came back they did not sound rote or parroted. They sounded like they were really hers, native-grown on the tongue, known from childhood.

The old Shayali man tried to give her a little bracelet with wooden beads as she stood to depart. She pretended to accept, but slipped it back among his wares a moment later. Then, she knelt and touched her forehead to his palm—a uniquely south Shayali gesture—and turned toward the stables. Who knew what imaginary person she had been to the old man?

What dazed Azetla was that he would have believed it too. Every word out of her mouth. He would have acted just the same as the old man, duped by a warmth and sincerity that seemed so plain and hearth-steady.

The deceit was at work on him even now, and he didn't know from which angle he ought to fight it. It seemed to him that the person she played to the old man was the one she most liked being. Maybe even one she really wished she was.

He shouldn't believe that. That was telling himself what he wanted to hear.

Azetla took time he did not quite have to bid respectful goodbyes to all the Trekoan Rokhs, Shaykhs, and officials. Respectful, but brisk, with most delicacies stripped from his words. From here on out he must speak as a commander and a Mashevi; he had acclimated to them, now they must acclimate to him.

Because he was not like Tzal. To speak precisely in the local tenor—to elaborate and lilt and flourish and make every minute adjustment of manner—wore him to the bone. He did it when he knew he should, to the best of his meager ability. But now he must be free to work with all his faculties. They must let him be blunt and quick and pragmatic.

His army marched out at mid-morning, under a graying sky. A second contingent, led by Rahummi Bin-Deghan, would follow in two or three days. His duty was to make sure all the administrative mortar Azetla had so quickly laid down would cure properly. And also to be elaborate and slow-paced where Azetla could not afford to be.

They marched to the far edge of dusk, camping outside the town of Kol-adar. Azetla received the reports at a trickle from the advance scouts. As usual, Tzal was the last to return. Azetla was unrolling his pallet against the edge of an old well-wall when he heard her voice come up behind him.

"I saw no Qatlanis on my route," she said. "But at the wells, women were talking about Cozona. They don't know the whole of what happened yet."

Azetla stood and turned to her.

"I offered a watered-down story for them to tell, which they seemed to take," she added. "But don't expect it to last."

He gave a tired nod.

"And what were you to them that they believed you so readily?" he said.

"The first time, a Janbari woman, returning from Cozona market. Then a Saqirani slave, ironically enough."

She rested a shoulder against the well-wall, lopsided, rubbing her palm over her eyes then turning her slave band round on her wrist.

"And what about the Shayali man from this morning," Azetla said coldly. "What were you to him?"

"A girl born in south Shayal who left home because of 'the Sahr devils.'"

It was the strange little laugh she gave which set him off like kindling. He planted his hand against the wall next to her.

"You'd already emptied him like a jar, got all you could from him. What was the point of it? To mock him? To amuse yourself that he could not know with whom he was breaking bread?"

She raised her eyebrows faintly at the vehemence in his voice, and the way he stepped in to corner her.

"Don't worry. I'm sure someone's told him his error by now," she said.

Her calloused tone of voice abraded against what little, exhausted good sense he had left.

"Oh for God's sake Tzal, can you say even one plain, true thing?"

"Azetla...almost everything I've ever said to you has been true."

He breathed out sharply through his nose.

"On a technicality, maybe."

"What? That's not good enough? What else is it that I owe you?"

Azetla rolled his jaw and lifted his hands, conceding. "Absolutely nothing."

He pushed away from the wall. Knelt to his pallet, smoothed it, and set about preparing for sleep with barely a fragment of control over himself. And all she did was look down and watch him as though he'd lost his mind.

"What are you waiting for?" he said, feverishly ready to set his head down and set his mind right. "It's not as though you need to be dismissed."

"I really was born in south Shayal," she said. "A village called Qeim-tal."

"Tzal, it doesn't matter, just—"

"It does matter. It wasn't supposed to happen. It almost cost me my life and it did cost someone else theirs. But I *was* born in Qeim-tal. Later, theirs was the first dialect of Trekoan I ever learned. I know Tal."

"But you are not Shayali." Azetla said it with neither accusation nor disappointment.

Tzal shook her head. "The point is I had some truth for thread, even if the rest was made out of whole cloth."

"You understand why it galls, don't you? To watch you turn in and out of shape like clay on a wheel? To Everson, you are flippant and mocking; to Rokh Imal, a heartless devil; and to Rahummi..." He waved the last of these away for not quite matching the tone of his accusation. "Everyone thinks you're what they need you to be."

Tzal smiled faintly, sitting down against the wall.

"You say that as though that isn't what everyone does to everyone," she said.

"No one thinks I'm what they want me to be, Tzal. I can't pretend with your finesse." He paused, straightening himself. "I just want to know which costume you don for me."

"Azetla..." But she shook her head and closed her mouth again.

"Exactly," he said. His throat was dry, his voice weary. "See, in my arrogance, I think *I'm* the one who sees you right. But that's what everyone thinks. So which illusion are you casting? I realize it won't help me know what you are, but at least I'll know what you think *I* am."

Tzal was quiet a long time. Her arm rested heavily on a raised knee and she looked off to the side as if she was really thinking of how to answer Azetla. But he questioned everything, his perception most of all. She looked tired too. Or she was simply mirroring his state? He saw her do that all the time. The small fire crackled low and he almost lost sight of his question by the time she spoke.

"I was the pariah for you. No difficulty in that and no lie either, but I threw myself into it and drove it at you pretty hard. I had to. You were the only opportunity I could see."

She looked at him sidelong. "But I'm not doing that now."

"I know," he said, keeping his voice low and quiet. "You always drop a gambit when it's used up."

"Look, it's not always on purpose Azetla. My tongue just drifts to whatever tone or dialect—whatever cut or angle—will do the trick. Sometimes before I've even thought about it. It's not that I don't realize, it's just...look, I don't know. But I'm alive because of it."

He didn't doubt that for one moment.

"I've been honest with you, Azetla. And if that honesty was being used as a lever to pry from you what I wanted, so what then? It's certainly not the worst one can get from me."

She came to a kneel; a sharp, cold smile cut across her face.

"Besides," she slipped into Mashevi, her voice low and all too near, "something tells me that this demand for pure, unvarnished truth does not work both ways."

She waved her finger softly between them. No chance, looking him dead in the eyes as she did, that any flicker of shame or fear escaped her notice. For once in his life, holding his gaze steady was not an easy thing. Holding his tongue, he could hardly help.

"That's what I thought," she said with a gentle tisk.

She stood, drew a deep breath, and looked up.

"We'll get a rain tonight. First real one."

And she was gone.

He fell asleep in the midst of his prayers again, with the word "hypocrite" hiding under every mouthed syllable, making the rhythm sluggish.

Drops of rain woke him sometime during third watch. He pulled his goatskin roll over his head only to wake what seemed like a heartbeat later, surrounded by biting air and mud as thick as clay.

20

—◦—

Lady Kathryn Beranadon and all her accompaniment reached Areo two days after His Highness the Corra. She despised the place. Not for what it was—she could scarcely take that into account—but for what it was not. It was not Piarago. It was not the center of the world. It was not her home. Her high birth and delicate work in the court slipped like dust through her fingers. They meant nothing here.

She had seen the danger. She had understood James' inept attempts at warning. It had been at her own fierce urging that her father finally agreed to collect a small coterie and flee. She did this. She chose it. It was, for now, the way things must be. But it was a bitter herb set between her teeth.

Each evening she took her meal with Lord Colonel Everson, Lord Verris, and the Corra James. Sometimes another officer or two would attend. Once, a local woman dined with them. Kathryn could not remember her name, only that she had a brand-new infant strapped to her chest. She wore bright colors with garish jewelry, and spoke not a word of Maurowan. Those evenings were especially tedious because Colonel Everson kept cutting either from Maurowan to give brief summaries to the local, or from Trekoan to give brief summaries to Kathryn.

Yet even when her father and his men retired early to bed, and all that remained were Kathryn, James, and the Colonels, it was clear to Kathryn that all the real meat and salt of the conversation was being reserved for her departure. Colonel Everson was witty and swift of tongue, happy to talk court and politics with humorous warmth. It sated her to a point, and that point was the moment she arrived in her room and realized that they had soaked heavily in matters that were of high price in Piarago, but that she knew little to nothing about what was going on right here in this rough, wind-bedraggled place.

She rose on the fifth morning with grim determination. She performed her usual daily routine, socializing with all the high-blood women of Areo, and dining with the Corra. But as the afternoon waned, she called for an armed escort; she would know her surroundings. In Piarago she could order a sedan with the snap of her fingers, but here she must be content to go about on foot like some mountain shepherdess.

When the escort arrived with a knock at her door, it was not the smart, young pair of lieutenants she had been expecting, but Colonel Orde Everson.

"Your girl said you wanted to look about the place. I thought you could join me on my afternoon rounds, my lady. Kill two birds with one stone," he said cheerfully.

Kathryn accepted his offer with manufactured warmth. She had wanted to gather her own impressions before having everything carefully curated for her. She did not wish to have her curiosity satisfied too quickly and too easily. This Everson liked to do that; he was always heading her questions off at the pass.

Why? she wondered. She was no less a part of this than he.

Kathryn followed him past the villa stables and out the gate. The stones of the road and all the edges of the buildings were mucky from the night's rain, little though there had been. The wind carried some of the worst smells from the barracks and privies until Kathryn reached for her lavender-soaked cloth. She waved it under her nose.

Colonel Everson noticed this, smiled mildly, but made no comment.

Always amused. Always cool and casual. Always a ready smile, this one. Kathryn did not like it. He had a trickster's look to him, but there was a precision to his lightheartedness that hinted she ought to take him seriously. He was something she did not quite recognize, which was a problem for her; Kathryn could usually classify a species of man on sight.

He took her to the Trekoan sector first, right to the little village market. The smell of spices, coffee, breads, incense, and smoked choba overtook the other rotten odors. The launderers walked by with piled baskets of lye-scrubbed cloth, and old men with gnarled hands sold fine clay wares. Still, to her eyes, it was a dirty, disordered place.

The women on their woven mats eyed her with none of the awe or fascination she was accustomed to. They gave but one or two faintly curious glances, and then went back to their business. She would have supposed herself a more exotic offering than *that*. But no. This was an outpost. Many northerners had come and gone; she was faceless to them.

The women chattered and laughed and sang in their incomprehensible language. She disliked their manner immensely, though she could not have said why. Some of the older men *did* stare, but not in a way that Kathryn preferred. The brown, bare-footed children played games and dashed around, heedless of her.

Suddenly she felt tired, a prickly feeling in her eyes. She hated it all. Everything was doubly foreign to her; common and southern, and she knew nothing of either. Colonel Everson took no notice. He spoke casually to the locals as he walked through, giving intermittent asides to her. Coppers tossed in pity, it felt like.

Kathryn gave a start and pulled away when a boy of twelve or so came alongside her suddenly. He was dirty-ish, had smells about him that Kathryn did not recognize, and he babbled aggressively to her.

"He wants your earring," Colonel Everson said, looking rather amused.

"My earrings? I—"

"He just wants one of them. He says he would give it back before you leave."

"Why on earth?" she said, putting her hand to her ear.

"It's related to a local custom. They—how do I explain it—it's like putting up for security, or proving honor or showing good will. But I think this boy is just trying to put one over on you."

"How do I tell him 'no' and 'please leave'?" Kathryn said calmly.

Everson grinned and said a few words to the boy who strolled away unhurriedly, not much chastised.

"Not to worry," Everson said pleasantly. "The boy can't possibly know that your earrings are worth more than all he owns or ever will own."

Kathryn opted to neither rise nor balk at the gentle provocation in his tone. She simply ignored it, fixing her eyes on the boy who still lingered nearby. He promptly struck up an argument with a girl who, upon closer inspection, was no native of Areo market. She was a sunburned, freckle-faced northern girl who yelled back at the boy in an atrocious mixture of Maurowan and whatever local tongue. The boy made a face in response and then bolted away.

The northern girl gave Kathryn a fleeting glance of curiosity, but upon seeing the Colonel, she ran right up to him, bold as a bull. She plunged into a deep bow and, with a lively face, she said, "My lord, I haven't done anything wrong."

"Really?" Everson said, a smile twitching at the corner of his mouth. "Little one, I haven't the faintest notion what you should or should not be doing...or of where you should and should not be. Confess your innocence to someone else."

"It's just that I didn't tell anyone I was coming to market, my lord. And I was meant to be in the kitchens."

"Ah. I see," Everson said.

The girl looked up at the Colonel hoping for pardon, but she received none.

"Carry on, Anna. Just know that the longer you stay away, the stricter Niri will be with you."

"Aye, my lord," the little girl replied, glancing uncertainly at Kathryn once more. "My lord?"

Kathryn was somewhat surprised to see how patiently Colonel Everson engaged with the dirty, brash, common girl. Why he gave her his attention at all was beyond Kathryn but, for the moment, it intrigued rather than offended her.

"Yes, little one?"

"I only came to market to find out when the others are coming home and *Salil*," the girl pointed furiously in the former direction of the earring-begging boy, "...doesn't believe that I got my knife from the Sahr, though I swore to him by blood and by salt."

Everson laughed.

"By blood *and* by salt! Dear Gods. Let me see the knife." The girl handed it to him. A little of the mirth receded from his face. "She gave this to you?"

The girl nodded with her whole being.

"When?"

"The day before they left, my lord. I was a little afraid, but when I tried to tell Azetla, he was busy and all the soldiers—"

Everson cut in sharply, as if he had quite suddenly run out of patience for all this. "Don't go troubling soldiers and whoever else about trifles. Back to Niri."

The girl bowed and obeyed very quickly, for he had used a lordly tone that time and at some point in her life she had learned to heed *that*.

"You encourage this sort of informality?" Kathryn said, watching the girl's bare heels kick up behind her as she ran off.

Everson shrugged.

"It depends, my lady. With that one? Yes. She is the daughter of one of my stewards, always underfoot, and known by everyone from highest to lowest. A smart thing, full of fascinating jibber-jabber. I hardly mind her, and often she tells me things that surprise me."

"She said *Sahr*."

Everson gestured at the path for Kathryn to follow. "That she did."

Kathryn's chest tightened. "So does that mean—"

"A subject for another time, my lady."

She did not like that answer. Through the market, past the barracks, and to the observing pavilion at the training field, Everson remained perfectly warm and evasive. She waited until he sat in the tented shade—sipping tea and finessing olive pits out of his mouth—to shed her placid manner.

"What is the purpose of your managing me with gloved hands?"

"My lady?"

"You think I cannot stomach to hear the grisly details of that into which I have willingly entered? Do you think I am here for amusements? You won't tell me anything about this commander of yours. You demur at the mention of a Sahr devil as if you fear I'll faint. Is my reputation in the court so weak?"

Everson took a pit from between his teeth, and smiled like the trickster she first took him for.

"Your reputation is iron shrouded in silk, my lady, do not worry. They say even the Emperor knows to be cautious around you."

She held her head erect; he spoke the truth, but it felt like mockery coming from him. Everson looked at her a long while, in a calculating sort of way. Like Riada used to do. This, at last, she liked. "But we are in the realm of ends justifying means, and there are things that even you might want to brace for."

And then he was no longer looking at her but past her with an opaque expression.

Kathryn turned and saw the Laritoni Captain—Istamo, she thought it was—walking into the wind at a hurried pace.

"They're here. Nearly at the gates."

The Colonel's eyes flashed with excitement. He gave a sharp nod.

"Have Brighton deal with placing everyone—hardly an inch left to set a bedroll anymore." Istamo nodded. "And you bring the Commander straightaway."

Istamo and Everson exchanged the briefest of looks. Kathryn knew little by it, except that now important matters were laid fresh on the table, and she must find out how in the world to procure an invitation.

✦

Azetla's headquarters room had almost twice as many people in it as it was ever meant to fit. Everyone was exhausted, and there was a dull roar of chatter, weary laughter, and pressing matters. Tzal slid down the wall, sitting quiet and cross-legged. Her ankles were kicked two or three times on accident. She found the chaos rather pleasant seeing as nothing that went on pertained to her, and nothing was required of her at that precise moment. It was the first such instance in weeks.

Logistics were life and death, Azetla liked to say. Tzal was happy to leave him to it.

She leaned her head back and rested her eyes, listening to Azetla answer so many rapid-fire questions, and delegate so many unexpected tasks. He lobbed orders like little toq-balls and—to their credit—the officers caught them all neatly until it was just Joseph, Sarrez, Ishelor, and herself remaining.

"Let's do this quickly," Azetla said, spreading out the largest Trekoan map on the stone. "Then it will be ready as soon as they ask for it, and we can all get a little rest."

Tzal pulled herself to a stand and leaned over the map. It was one Azetla had commissioned several weeks ago, and it was beautiful. Her own descriptions were inked there, with precision and elegance. Everything was to scale. She wanted desperately to trace her hands across every known and familiar thing, but she folded her arms tightly and inhaled it with her eyes.

Azetla began placing cubes and stones, with Joseph and Sarrez questioning and advising alterations.

They did not get very far before the door-cloth parted.

"His Highness the Corra bids you come." Captain Istamo entered, speaking and standing in an unusually stiff manner.

Azetla looked up from the map. He let out a sigh. Nodded.

"Do I have time to make myself presentable?"

"You are to come immediately."

Azetla threw Istamo a questioning look; Istamo shook his head.

"I don't know, Azetla. I simply don't know. Neither does the Colonel. But you best be quick."

He gave a field salute and left. Tzal couldn't remember if he'd ever given Azetla any such gesture. By the look on Azetla's face, she thought not.

Azetla washed his face and hands. Righted his baldric. Rolled the map and took it in hand.

"We'll go back through it first thing tomorrow." And he hurried out into the dusky light.

Tzal set her arms akimbo. Looked at the doorway. Grabbed a marker stone and turned it round in her fingers. Suddenly, and with great irritation, Joseph scooped all the discarded marker stones into his hand.

"Well *go*," he said, tilting his head toward the cloth door. "You can get away with things we can't."

Sarrez gave a faint nod of agreement. "Just in case."

Tzal dropped the stone on the table and strode out the door. It's not like she needed their sanction. She'd have done it anyway, and they knew that.

She caught up to Azetla just before he reached the villa gate. She crooked her finger at him to follow her the long way round. Without a word they made their way past the south garden and through the kitchens. Azetla had walked to half-certain death here once, and he did it headlong. Maybe he fancied some "virtue" in it, some idiotic proof that he put his faith in his God, not in his circumstances. But Tzal believed in coming from the periphery, on your own terms, and without warning. Also, if possible, best to have someone waiting in the wings, hand on hilt.

She moved swiftly through the dark, narrow servant's passageway. Azetla stumbled slowly behind her. Then she waited for him. She had slipped up and down these passageways hundreds of times, eyes closed, ears open. She hadn't thought about the uneven bits of stone, or the turnings for a long time.

When he reached her, she stopped him silently, lifting her hand against his shoulder. She fixed her eyes on the heavy cloth door, her ears to the sound emanating from beyond it. There was one bare slit of light coming through and, against it, Tzal pressed her fingers together in a Mashevi gesture she had often seen Azetla use. *Wait and be quiet.*

Everson, Verris, and their Corra were in the peristyle. All talking about Azetla. Everson, flippantly. Verris, begrudgingly. The Corra...she was not sure. Nothing shocking was said. Little that could be pocketed for later use, and they seemed to be at the end of their conversation rather than the beginning. The simple whiff of it all was that Everson was trying to convince the Corra that one could indeed play with fire without being burned, given deft hands, and the Corra was not convinced any hands present were deft enough for the task.

What Azetla thought of it all, Tzal couldn't guess. He was look-ing at her the whole time, as if she must understand more by their words than he could. Doubtful, though she tried. Once she was convinced that there was nothing worthwhile to be had, she lowered her hand and turned aside. Azetla slid past her and flicked open the door.

21

J ames had time enough to steel himself. Time enough to think through what sort of man he was to be to the Mashevi when he came. Not cold with quiet threats, like Riada. Nor taut with anger and defensiveness like Verris. Nor sly and casual like Everson. No. None of these.

He had survived Riada chiefly by wearing his own face. He could survive this bloody jackal too. James had learned how to be afraid of someone and still speak what thoughts of his were allowed, and hold back the simmering things that were not. And he was the one in authority here.

Remember that. No matter what that jackal says, you remember it.

By this token, James felt like he was the only one who wasn't flustered by the jackal when he stepped quietly through the slave's entrance, unannounced, unescorted, seemingly unimportant. For Everson and Verris this clearly created a crack in the atmosphere of the room which required patching up. They wanted to justify or explain or amend his way of coming.

James did not care in the slightest.

Let the man come loud or quiet, from east or west, dressed like a general or dressed like a tackman. It changed nothing. He was a red coal in the dry grass and they all knew it, even the jackal himself.

Azetla bowed. Proper and deep. Raised his head and looked James in the eye.

"Your Highness."

James had ordered this man's execution. And the man knew it. James' heart hurried a little at the implications of this—his first hurdle to jump. There should be no hemming and hawing on the subject. No apologies. No caveats. He doubted the jackal even wanted them. James might not grasp all, but he thought he grasped something of Azetla's nature. The man would have things plain and simple, if possible.

Well, so would James.

"You two can leave." He waved his hand at his colonels.

They were startled. Wesley in his demonstrative manner. Orde in his subtler way, pausing coolly with his cup of wine partway to his lips, eyebrows softly raised.

"Having had my life in your hands for these last months, you two have played a bit carelessly with it to my reckoning. You've already said all you had to say. You told me what you think and why you acted as you did. So leave your words here to do their work. I want to speak to the Mashevi alone."

Many months it had been since either of these men had been around someone who could give them an order, and it was clear that neither of them had expected James to do anything of the sort. They stood. Glanced at their unfinished meals, and moved in a slow-ish way toward the outer columns.

"Keep to the courtyard," James said, working a decisiveness into his voice that was not natural to his tongue. It rustled and wavered just slightly. "I'll call you in when I need you again."

James kept his eyes on the jackal the whole time, until the last echoing footstep drifted out of the peristyle.

The jackal had sense enough to wait in silence. James was long in breaking it, not because he wished to draw it out, but because he was still not sure what he wanted to say. He had practiced many sharp and strong words—so they'd seemed to his own ear in his own chambers—but they didn't feel quite right now that he was faced with a real person. He didn't want to make a long speech. He wanted to have a conversation.

"So, jackal, I let you convince me to allow you your place. Then I let Lord Verris convince me to take your life. Now I'm supposed to let Lord Everson convince me you should hold all our lives in your hands."

"I think he also means to convince you that I make a very good scapegoat in case of failure, though I don't think it will work as cleanly as that."

Never one to shy from the raw side of the bargain, this jackal. James felt himself tense, but he breathed it down.

"No, I don't think so either. In any case I don't think I'm in the mood to be convinced of anything right now. Not of you. Not of your actions. All I know for certain is that you've done things that can't be undone. You've sent a signal to the sky declaring us traitors for all the world to see."

"Your Highness, you did that when you fled Piarago."

The words blocked James like a stone. That—that was true. He could not go around it.

"I won't say I didn't act on my own, Your Highness. I certainly did. Indeed, I doubt you would have approved had you been here; we had to be swift and aggressive and everything shy of reckless to take advantage of that narrow window before, as you put it, the whole world could see."

The jackal wasn't saying anything James didn't know, in some sense. Yet he spoke in a way that seemed to burn off the mist and show things in their natural shape, undistorted by shadow and haze. Ah, but this was what James feared. Being so easily swayed.

He shook his head and sighed. "The lords have cut their angle. But I want to hear it from you. Tell me what you've done. What you mean to do. And what it will take. No cant. No flattery. No sly omissions."

Azetla gave a soldier's brisk nod. "Help me clear this—scoot those down."

Surprised, but having no interest in taking offense, James shoved the cups and the platter to the far edge of the table. Azetla moved the wineskins and the heavy pot. Then he unrolled the large Trekoan map. A fine thing it was, with wells and tribal markings, wadi trailheads, and even very small villages. James had never seen one quite like it.

"This is Everson's?"

"No. I had it made in Juniper battalion…" The jackal paused oddly, almost in hesitation. "Most of this information came from the Shihrayan. The Sahr, that is."

James' heart gave a slight jump. Yet another thing he had allowed himself not to think about too much, rearing its viper head.

"It's still here? Still alive?"

"Yes. And useful. Though probably not in the ways Riada anticipated."

Gods. What does that even mean? The jackal did not explain. He simply smoothed the land of Trekoa out before James and began to tell the story of their battles. Those accomplished. And those yet to accomplish. All with terrible swiftness, Azetla said. Not a moment to lose.

"It's like the date-seed game children play. When the count runs down, you have what you have; you can gather no more. The one with too few in his hands when the betting comes is out of the game. Areo by itself would be an easy target for Riada. The whole of Trekoa and South Makaria—that will require everything Riada has. Every dunam of ground we take increases the cost for him, slows him down, forces him to take precautions, to wait for more troops.

And we inhale his own army as we go, keeping what can be kept, and discarding what can't be."

James listened intently to the jackal's rough, easterly voice, and watched his hands travel knowingly across the map. It all made sense. He could see it plainly. Azetla had that skill. He knew how to put the scattered mosaic together till the image came bright and clear. He spoke to James as if he were one of his officers, and they were laying out a battle plan in which James would be expected to participate. And take charge.

Like a blow to the head, James realized that was *exactly* what was happening.

For the space of ten panicky breaths, James was terrified and his ears stopped taking in the jackal's words. All the clarity he'd had mere seconds ago blurred, as did the lines on the map. In that moment it all became far too real. And, by blood, it was too much. The scope was too great. It was more than a man could take in. Too many ifs, too many this's, too many thats, and a jackal, and a devil, and *oh Gods...*

But James caught himself in the tumbling of mind and forcibly held it off.

So too did Azetla, in his way. Gruffly, he shouldered James out of the limp.

"Your Highness, I need you to tell me about the senior officers in Hidud and Golmouth."

James took a very long, deep breath. Looked from the map to Azetla's face.

"Names?" James breathed.

"At Hidud we have General Avinroe and Colonels Diebha and Walenti. Golmouth is Colonel Pachten and Senior Captain Tol."

James took his time in answering. "I don't know much about Walenti or Pachten except that they have land recently granted on the North Makarish coast. Could make them beholden to Riada, though they are of lower blood and outer circles."

Azetla began making notes on his ledger.

Marks of fate, James realized. Annotations toward life or death.

"Diebha is Nagonan. He used to be a lieutenant in an old battalion until it was decommissioned. He was very bitter about it. He might be worth courting."

A curt nod. A swift mark. Azetla gestured for James to continue.

"Tol, I cannot tell you. I never met the man." James paused, fully aware that the word of his mouth bore reprieves and executions for men he barely knew. Azetla took it all plainly and sincerely. "Avinroe is high-blood. *Old* blood. Of ancient Tus. He would never ally with us in a thousand years."

Always clawing for the highest seat of favor, Avinroe. Swift to abandon a friend or step on him for a stool, as he had done to James. Tamhet Avinroe was not a man James wanted as ally. Azetla glanced up from his ledger at the unavoidable trace of vehemence in James' voice.

"Are you sure, Your Highness?"

"More sure of that than I am of anything else," James said sharply.

"Good."

"Do you—do you put them to the sword right away?"

Azetla nodded. He was so calm and practical. It made James uneasy.

"It's a cold-blooded necessity and a foul burden. But I'm asking you these questions so as to lighten that burden however I can. Don't want to kill a man if I don't have to."

For once James heard exactly what wasn't spoken. And he answered in kind.

"But sometimes it is necessary. Just as you said."

"Well, what are you going to do then?" The Mashevi pulled a folded document from his satchel and handed it to James.

With no pleasure, James read the words of his own hand. A bit long for an execution order. There was tepidness and hesitation in the phrasing, but the death sentence was there in simple black ink and lightly angled letters.

"A pointless question. I've been cornered, haven't I?"

"Not a particularly enjoyable position to be in, I'll admit," Azetla said. Cool as autumn, pointed as a needle. "Are you going to keep that pinned over my head just for show? Or do you really want to see it done?"

James felt leaden all over, so that all his movements were very deliberate. So too, his thoughts. Slow, heavy, but set in a clear direction. He put the execution order to the soft flame of the lamp. Waited till it charred halfway up. Then set it in a bowl with traces of spiced oil to finish its quiet journey to ashes.

"This is not a healthy alliance for either of us, I don't think," James said softly.

Azetla did not answer. For he certainly knew it to be true. He was only the enemy of his enemy. A strong current in the desired direction. For now.

"Well. Call them back in, Mashevi. If I'm to be swayed, let it be in three directions at once so I can triangulate and find the center."

Azetla gave a faint but seemingly genuine smile at those words, bowed, and walked toward the courtyard to retrieve the colonels.

James liked and did not like that the jackal should smile. He liked and did not like that they should seem—*seem!*—to have all this simplicity, plainness, and soldierly honesty laid on the table. It was a soothing, warm draught laced with terrible danger and complication. It was confusion. Old frustration and uncertainty, which usually led to apathy. He just couldn't afford that this time.

The execution order smoldered, but did not quite burn.

Perhaps James would still have to do that which he thought he'd already done. All the justifications he had so carefully taught himself, all the sense he had worked so hard to find in that senseless order, all the peace of mind he accrued in believing that the jackal was removed from the board—these things he must keep, tucked away, until they might be needed again.

Don't forget. Don't let yourself forget. If you need an anchor, let this be it. He's only the enemy of your enemy. This is no friend.

Nearly two hours Tzal stood in that dark corridor. If she sat down too long, sleep would threaten her. If she moved too much, she would have been heard. Her muscles were tight from strained still-ness. Perhaps she could have left sooner, but she needed to be sure. As soon as Everson and Verris were brought back in, they kept mucking it up. They wanted so badly to cover Azetla in some impos-sibly bright sheen, to save their own skins and justify their choices. But each time, Azetla deliberately rubbed off the glamour, saying simply, "this also is what I have done, this is how I have done it, this is what I am going to do next...and these are the likeliest points of failure. And *this* is what will be required of you when the time comes."

He made no promises or sweeping statements and he never de-fended himself.

No surprise there. But it was satisfying to her ear, just as it is satisfying to the eye to watch a skilled trailman walk any which way, not because the trail was hard, but because the feet were sure.

At one point, Azetla explained how he expected Riada to think, what he believed Riada would do next. This affected the Corra's voice and tone in a strange way. It pricked Tzal's ears. For most of the night the Corra's voice was weariness spiked with hostility. Deter-mination weighed down by uncertainty. Such a strange, wandering mixture. Did he not know how naked the timbre of his voice was? She could hear every doubt, every longing, every fear, plain as day. But when Azetla began to describe Riada—assess him, *speak* for him—all the meandering threads of the Corra's tone snapped into one graspable rope. Thoughtful, earnest, engaged.

Azetla's words rang true to him. This, he understood. Here was terrain the Corra recognized. Here was an enemy he had actually faced and survived.

Tzal wasn't sure what to conclude from this, so she set it to the back of her mind to simmer for the time being.

Eventually the Corra declared it was time to retire. He was, he said, "satisfied."

Tzal, on the other hand, was not.

As soon as Azetla was dismissed—Captain Istamo left with him as a courtesy, so Azetla was not alone—Tzal jogged up through the passageway. She crossed the upper balcony, went back down past the baths, then through the north peristyle. Rarely did she have cause to come all the way through to these residential wings, reserved for guests and coteries of the highest officers. Istamo's family lived among these rooms. So now did the Corra.

She watched from across the peristyle. The Corra returned with a personal guard and two servants. No frenzy of soldiers. No atmosphere of paranoia. He called for no one and sent no one out. Tzal listened from the edge of the open-air corridor, hearing little to nothing. She combed back over the evening's conversations. She hardly knew what she was looking for, except certainty perhaps. That impossible thing.

Tzal saw the figure approach out of the corner of her eye.

"Would you come to my mistress?"

A Trekoan slave girl stood three columns away from Tzal. She was a young thing, the top of her head would barely hit Tzal's shoulder if she came up next to her, which the girl resolutely would not do.

"What?" Tzal said.

"She's asked for you." The girl was whisper-shouting and looking at Tzal with absolute terror.

"Who's asked for me?"

"Naima, daughter of Ghassanin...that woman from the Ghal-laz."

Rahummi's wife. Tzal relaxed her shoulders with a sigh.

"Show me to her."

The girl skittered ahead, careful to keep a firm distance, while Tzal followed.

The northern Corra himself could not have had finer apartments than Naima had. Mosaic floors; elegantly embroidered partitions; high, flower-shaped windows with heavy battening hatches for dust storms. There was a hearth fire, and three lamps lit. A grand, cushioned chair, draped with woven blankets, and a bed large enough for a whole family.

Naima sat on the floor, disheveled. There was a baby's cry. The slave girl promptly left.

22

Naima knew herself to be beyond dignity; she made no attempt to conceal her desperation.

"Where is Rahummi?"

Her little one gave another stirring cry and Naima began to loosen the wrap and draw the child out.

"He is well, Naima. No one told you? Just a few days behind us."

Naima shook her head, jaw clenched. She knew that someone would have been obliged to come to her with ill news. Her fear had been rushing and intense, but shallow. The relief did not taste as sweet or touch as deeply as she had hoped. All the things this fear had distracted her from were instantly there to greet her.

"*Why?*" she barked, looking at the Shihrayan with all the fury she dare not spend on anyone else.

"There were things he could do that Azetla could not."

"Why couldn't *you* have done it?"

She offset the sharpness of her voice with especially gentle hands as she painstakingly put her daughter to her breast and stroked her cheek. The babe latched and suckled easily this time, which was a blessed relief. Almost instantly, pain came to her belly, so like the pain of labor, and she tensed from head to toe to bear it till it passed.

"*Well?*" she said raspily.

"Naima, no one listens to me unless I am speaking as someone else or for someone else. The Shayalis least of all. Only Rahummi could have done it and done it *properly* because he was speaking for himself and for his people. You know how skilled he is in those situations."

"That's supposed to comfort me?"

The Shihrayan narrowed her eyes at Naima's vehemence. She looked at her in that terrible, scrutinous way which saw everything. *Everything*. The ugly sleepless shadows under Naima's eyes, the tell-tale redness of weeping, as if Naima were the first new mother to ever have to worry about a man at war, even though no harm had come to him. As if she were not living in luxury unimaginable to most of her people. As if her daughter was dead instead of living, nursing vigorously, precious and soft as silk.

Naima looked at the ground. So she had some shame left. Enough to fill the room, reach out beyond it, and bring a Shihrayan devil in that she might be a witness to it.

"Naima, where are your women?" the Shihrayan said at last.

The tears broke free, silent and profuse. She tried not to let her throat seize or her body shake, lest her baby break the latch and oh, then, *then*, the arduous effort of righting her and the bitter frustration when she failed. Then the creeping fear that something was wrong. Then the longing for her mother and sisters, for her home in the Ghallaz, for her people, the Hushai, and their ways which she knew and understood, and which were ruthlessly mocked by Saqirani slave girls and Janbari laundresses when they thought she could not hear.

The Shihrayan sat down on the floor, near to Naima, which was what she desperately wanted her to do.

"Rokha Ayla was supposed to come with Rokh Imal yesterday, but he said she took ill. I almost wonder if she simply didn't want—"

"If she was able to come, she would have," the Shihrayan said firmly.

Naima did not argue, but she was not so sure. The Shihrayan was not there when Rahummi brought Naima at last to Bir Herash. Rokha Ayla had been so cold at first, even though she assented to the marriage. That her nephew should marry a Hushai woman was a mild scandal. Everyone knew it, and Naima felt it.

"My own mother would crawl here on her knees if she knew," Naima said, stroking her daughter's wisps of black hair. "But the Colonel allows no couriers of any kind to be sent that way right now. It's too dangerous, he says."

"He is right."

"The midwife was kind, and also that northern woman you call Taya. They were as God's hands to me, but as soon as they saw all was well, they were gone. And these Saqirani women..." Naima felt a boiling in her chest just to mention them. "Why do they despise me so? My people are immodest, are they? Our women are whores? My prayers are wrong, somehow? *I* am a savage? *They* kiss Maurowan statues, then look at me as if I were little better than an animal. They know nothing about the Ghallaz, yet they hate me."

"Then let them hate you. But still let them give you what you need." The Shihrayan paused with faint hesitation. "That's what I do."

Naima looked up sharply, horrified. The Shihrayan smiled.

"Don't worry. You're not fallen so far as this. They hate you because you actually represent them to the high-bloods and all the important people here...and they fear you represent them wrongly. If you were not part of them, they would not care what you did or how you dressed."

The child was asleep. After a while, Naima gently broke the latch and rested that perfect head on her shoulder. She smelled impossibly sweet, and Naima could not help but press her cheek against the child's warm skin and feel her small breath.

"No one here knows Hushai customs."

Except you, Shihrayan. Oh please say something familiar. Please pretend. You're so good at it. Let me imagine that I am not alone. She had pride enough not to say these words, but if her eyes begged it, let God decide.

"And these women pretend not to understand Hushai dialect," she added, shaking her head.

"Oh Naima, they *don't* understand it. At all."

The Shihrayan had been slowly drifting from whatever dialect she had been using toward Hushai, but now she used it firmly and purposefully.

"It was one of the hardest I ever had to learn," the Shihrayan said. "But worth it for the fire-songs alone. How does it go? The one for a birth?"

"Which one? There are dozens."

"The one that says, 'does the gully flood, does it wash away our paths, we don't know till morning, something-something...'?"

There. The Shihrayan heard Naima's plea. She pretended for her. She sidled into the sound and the words and the manner, playing along. Knowing this, Naima drank it in, parched woman that she was.

"With only one voice, no drum, and no gudar it will sound strange, but I do love that one."

Warmth trickled through Naima's throat as she sang the ghen-wa—the little fire-song. The tears came again, but of a sweeter kind. The Shihrayan listened, calm and intent. The song was meant to pierce and the Shihrayan indeed looked struck. She was very good at that. For the first time, Naima noticed that the shadows under the Shihrayan's eyes were as dark as Naima's own, the weariness in her posture drawing her limbs and eyelids down every so often.

But Naima was so glad to have sung and to have been heard by someone who knew the song that such things were easy to dismiss.

Afterward, the Shihrayan asked the little questions that someone ought to ask, offered the little admirations one ought to offer, mentioned what other Hushai rituals she knew in leading ways so that Naima might fill in all that the Shihrayan did not know to say. The whole thing was a deft, soothing falsehood. Thin, but truly warm.

"Rahummi will want to name her right away." Naima sighed.

"If it was a boy, on the eighth day, yes. He's even more serious about those things than Rokh Imal, especially since Azetla came. For a girl you *might* convince him to wait. A month is not such bad luck, is it?"

Naima sucked in through her teeth.

"We like to wait a year for best luck."

"So do we." The Shihrayan pursed her lips and looked down. She had broken the illusion.

Years ago the Shihrayan told Naima that the rocky, narrow places of the Ghallaz reminded her of Shihra. Many things among the Hushai did, in fact. Naima remembered it clear as daylight, because it was—until now—the only time she had ever spoken of her home or people in Naima's presence. Naima had taken severe offense at her home being compared to the devil's lands, and the Shihrayan never said another word about it.

She looked long at the Shihrayan, who had been turning the slave band on her wrist round and round with mindless fingers. But then the Shihrayan stopped and pressed her hands to the floor ready to rise and depart.

"What is it he calls you?" Naima said.

The Shihrayan adjusted her sash as she stood, the short-sword resting against her leg.

"Rahummi? He doesn't call me anything in particular these days."

"I meant the Mashevi."

It amused her to see the flicker of surprise on the Shihrayan's face. "Tzal."

Naima nodded. "I've heard it from Rokha Ayla before. Rahummi used to call you that too."

"Yes. He did. Every now and then."

"I don't dislike it."

"Neither do I." She smiled a little then glanced behind her. "Will that girl come back when I leave?"

"Yes. With fresh wrappings. The blood just comes and comes."

"It will slow."

Naima nodded again, this time to show that she knew the conversation was ending and the Shihrayan—Tzal—must go.

"Will Rahummi be disappointed?" she called out as Tzal hit the shadow of the doorway. For Saqiran was the same as Hushai in this. Everyone always prayed for a son.

"No. He'll be infatuated, and I'll never hear the end of it."

Naima smiled and she knew it was true. She forgot to say, "keep watch over him." But then, there was no need. Tzal had always done so.

"What a terrifying older sister to have," Naima once teased Rahummi.

"Yes," he'd answered, holding Naima close and tracing his fingers along her shoulder. "But so long as she's dangerous, little else is."

⁂

Junior Colonel Joar Peterson had to bow his head slightly to enter the room; southerners seemed short to him, and they certainly kept their doors that way. He was early on purpose and found himself alone in the room. There was little by way of furnishings, just a shelf of scrolls, and a stone flat on which lay a very beautiful map of Trekoa. He admired it.

It was difficult to wait, so tense was he with curiosity. He had arrived at Areo so recently, and all was still fresh and new to him and his men.

Colonel Everson had told him very little about the southern commander. The name was one he'd never heard of and could not recall now. But he had united dozens of Trekoan tribes to an unprecedented degree. He caught a Sahr devil, so they said. And he'd taken Cozona outpost paying only a pittance of blood for it.

Only at the end did Everson tell them—warn them?—that the man was a jackal.

He did not wish them to be blindsided.

Colonel Truillon expressed his disgust passionately. But Joar held his tongue.

He wanted to look the man in the eye once before the proceedings. He would make his own judgments. There were not many jackals in his homeland, beside the icy sea cliffs of Berdan. He had been told of their craftiness, their wiles, their nameless God, and their bizarre rites. But for his own part, he could not easily tell one southerner from another, and he had become more suspicious than ever of all the things Maurowans claimed and believed.

He had been in awe of Maurow when he left his cliff-side clan to fill their provincial quota. Twenty-five years later, as a colonel who could never be a general because he had only paid for his citizenship rather than been born to it, he wondered if he had signed onto a leaking vessel. He wished to repair rather than abandon ship, but how much cargo would have to be jettisoned to achieve it? Were the tools and materials available sturdy to the task?

And who was the real Captain of the ship?

As he traced his eyes across the southern and eastern borders of Trekoa, a cheerful clatter entered the room. Several southerners and two Nagonans walked through, bowls of burghul and dried fish in their hands. One greeted him. Another asked his name. They offered him the only thing in the room which approximated a chair; they all sat comfortably on the floor. Even the austere, elderly one with the woven band about his head—to whom Joar felt the need to offer special deference—tucked his robes and sat upon the woven mat.

Immediately between them, the southerners procured a small vessel and began scraping portions of their food into it. They offered it to him, and the cups from their hands full of a dark drink which all the southerners loved but which he could not stand.

He coolly declined. One of them—a soldier of no rank, and not much more than thirty years—urged him again, saying they would all be honored to share the meal. Joar refused more firmly. The soldier with no rank conceded with a bow and flicked a little gesture to discourage the others from pressing the matter further.

That was such a difficulty about southerners. Hospitality, they called it, but Joar felt it as an insult and a coercion. As if he needed their scraps. As if he would stand to be in someone's debt. To offer your cup to someone was to imply they had none of their own. How could they not see that? He was no subject for their ridiculous, ritual shows of charity.

Once again, the soldier with no rank spoke out and asked Joar questions. About his experience. The state of his men's readiness for war. What he knew of the southern desert. The soldier asked these questions calmly and soberly. There was no disrespect in his manner. But Joar wondered at the impertinence of his doing so when his betters surrounded him and said nothing.

He did not immediately understand—so trained were his eyes to rank—but he should have. Who could blame him for not knowing? He was accustomed to dealing with men who looked over the tops of other men's heads and paid to have their rank panels embroidered in gold so that they could not possibly be ignored. Not a youngish southerner, commonly dressed, with a manner that reminded him more of a well-trained steward than a general—the sort who quietly shouldered his way through problems and was calmly readying to bring you that one needful thing you had not yet thought to ask for.

He began to understand when the woman came in. He recognized her immediately. Tattoos on her hand, slave bands on her wrist, ankle, and neck. She had been in the halls and among the servants in the early morning. But she had been wearing a woman's shift then, not a rider's. And she had not been armed.

Her appearance at that time, and the free way she moved about and spoke to everyone struck him. He had called in one of his own slave girls and asked whose she was.

"I have no idea, my lord," Egri said. "But she was very helpful. Told us who to talk to and how to get things. Some Trekoan phrases to get us by."

"Did she ply you with questions?"

"A few. She'd never seen Berdan people before, my lord. She was intrigued."

"What was her name?"

"I..." Egri faltered. "Forgive me, my lord. She did not say."

He coolly advised his people to keep themselves to themselves. Nobles liked to pry by means of their slaves, and they should be mindful. Joar had nothing he needed to hide, but nothing he wished to share. It was quite that simple. Of course he collected all the bits of gossip his own people had gathered and tried to piece them together.

So to see that same woman now, her brown cheek crusted in salt-dust from dried sweat, mud crawling up her hem, sword hanging lightly at her hip—he guessed what she was. All his slaves had heard that the Sahr devil took the form of a woman. They heard it could make you do whatever it said but was itself beholden to no one.

Except maybe—*maybe*—the southern commander. Some thought that. No one was sure.

Joar's spine tingled.

The Sahr spoke to the young soldier with no rank in a language Joar did not know. The soldier nodded. Asked a question. She shrugged in answer, adjusting one of the stone markers on the map. The soldier handed her the bowl of burghul and fish which Joar had refused. He shared his cup with her, just as all the others did with each other.

If there was a slave here and a master, Joar could not see it. The Sahr devil—if she was that—smiled easily. The jackal—if he was that—did not. Neither were awed when the Corra entered the room, with all the highest officers following him. The Sahr devil simply began speaking translations into the ear of the old chieftain as the young soldier stood up, stepped forward, and made himself known with a firm bow.

And there it was, so simply. Azetla, he called himself. A jackal soldier with no rank, several years Joar's junior, was the commander of the armies at Areo. And Cozona.

Hidud was next, he said. It would be the most difficult and he demonstrated why. But from Hidud, Akva-nish, and Ustiral would be laid open to them. If Tus and Nurica could be convinced to declare neutrality, Riada would be hamstrung from nearly every direction.

Most questions, Azetla answered directly. On a few, he deferred. A matter to be discussed another time. Joar looked to the Corra James to insist, but he did not.

"Colonels Peterson and Truillon. Do you understand your role, and are you prepared for it?"

Colonel Truillon nodded, but he looked displeased. Joar knew why. He tapped the charcoal sketch of the Commander's battle plan.

"The role you've assigned us in this assault is insultingly trivial. As if you did not trust us to do what we have all our lives been doing."

"I have no doubt as to the abilities of you and your men, Colonel Peterson. I suspect that you, however, have many doubts about me. His Highness the Corra can command you to follow my orders, but he cannot force trust. If it were me, I would want to see the Commander proved before I put my men fully into his care."

The quiet voice of the Sahr devil echoed in another language, but somehow with the exact same tenor. Calm, grave, sincere. And irrefutable. A voice that did not need approval or admiration, for it was used to doing without.

Almost against his will, Joar Peterson was pleased. He looked Azetla in the eye.

"My men and I are ready."

23

Azetla remembered, so many years ago, asking Captain Hodge why he had no wish to be a colonel or, someday, a general. He could easily afford the costs, and he had many connections who would vouch for him.

"The higher your rank, my boy, the further you have to stand back from your men. I don't think my eyes are good enough for all that. Besides, the generals I know spend most of the days at tables and at their papers. It's not a life for me."

Azetla had not really believed him. There were stories of great Mashevi generals—in the days when Masheva had such things—and they rode out and fought among their men and wiped the blood from their swords. The annals of the old Kings and their warriors gave very little indication of idleness.

"They leave the boring parts out, my boy," Hodge had said with a grin on his face.

"It is holy writ, sir. God does not lie," Azetla had said, so quick to misunderstand in those days.

He had been deeply angered when Hodge laughed at him. "Well I would guess then, that your god has a sense of story, which is to his credit." And he laughed again.

The memory embarrassed and saddened Azetla.

Of course it *was* holy writ. And God does *not* lie. But boys with barely a scratch of hair on their faces don't understand much, especially not the boy who is convinced he understands everything.

Azetla was experiencing it now. At tables and papers. From dawn to dusk. Every tedious bit of it was of dire importance. Supplying enough food for all these men was becoming a near impossibility. The routes were rough with winter mud. The Beranadon coffers were deep, but not endless. Joseph brought reports on the new Colonels—Peterson and Truillon—and on the state of their men: well-trained, but little tried. Rahummi hadn't returned from Co-zona, so Qadi would stand in his place over the Trekoan riders until Rahummi came, and there were squabbles boiling up between the tribes about position. Qadi didn't have Rahummi's finesse. They were to leave for Hidud in two days, the barest minimum that Azetla needed. He could afford to wait no longer. Rahummi would have to catch up.

Then at the end of the day, around dusk, Tzal would come. Like a thief turning out pockets, she handed him all her careful gleanings. She told him what she thought all these fragments of information meant. How she managed to gather all she did baffled him: by now even the newer arrivals knew who and what she was. There was no one left to deceive. Yet all manner of people spoke to her. And listened to her. She always managed to pry them open.

She did the same to Azetla, he was well aware.

Over the last weeks of battle and travel this meeting, of sorts, had become a commonplace thing. She did not always have something to tell, yet she still came to say so. If there was any bit of food or drink to be scrounged, they had it. She always spoke in Mashevi as much as she possibly could and he always corrected her words and handed her new ones. She gave her counsel on certain matters. Occasionally she would advise something he rejected out of hand—like bringing Mali Colha along as a battlefield physician—but much of it was worth chewing on.

Azetla looked up at the cloth door. It was well past dark now. He was tired and wasting oil to keep a lamp lit. Tzal would leave first thing in the morning, two days ahead of the rest, so if she didn't come now, he would not see her until he had taken Hidud. Or failed to take it.

Well. There was nothing for it. He unwrapped the dozen dry oatcakes. Little oil they had, and no honey, but nothing should go to waste. Rations were poor and would continue to be so until the next caravan arrived from Tus. He had eaten two of them by the time she pushed through the door.

"If you'd have waited, I have salt and dates," she said.

"How on earth?"

"Everson has his private stores."

No surprise there. Everson was a man who did not like to be even slightly deprived of his comforts, and planned meticulously around them. Why he let Tzal pilfer, Azetla never fully understood, since there was nothing but smiling contempt between those two.

Tzal sat and ate with unabashed hunger. Azetla lingered a good long while over the pit of a date until she slowed down, pressing a finger of salt to her teeth, and savoring it.

"You haven't gone to see Naima yet," she said abruptly.

"I haven't had the least chance, Tzal, and you know it."

"You need to. Before you leave."

"I thought you said that to go without a birth gift would be an insult. We have nothing to give."

She reached over and pressed something into his hand. It was a simple woven tassel with a few cheap clay beads. It was a little like the ones that hung from Naima's shawls, though quite inferior.

"How—"

"I didn't steal it," she said sharply. "And it isn't worth anything. But it's a Hushai tradition to fringe the girl's first shawl, and you acknowledging that tradition will be the most important part. You keep telling me how invaluable Rahummi has been, and how much more difficult Qadi is to deal with. Show Naima that you mean it."

Azetla raised an eyebrow at the chastisement in her voice; it did not bother him.

"First thing in the morning."

Tzal picked up the last date and held it toward Azetla. He waved it away.

"If the goods from Tus don't come soon, even Everson is going to have to thin out his table," Tzal said. "He gave another banquet for the high-bloods tonight, but there can't be many more like it."

"Is that why you took so long?"

"Not exactly. Everson was in a certain mood. Poking and prodding at me. Trying to get who knows what sort of reaction. Asking questions he's already asked you, to weigh our answers against each other. When he gets nervous he likes to antagonize."

"I've noticed," Azetla said. He put the barest bit of salt to his teeth also and handed the palm-bowl back to Tzal. "Well, if there's anything else, say it now and say it quick, because it's late."

Tzal swallowed her water and nodded.

"I think Lachlan and Ishelor did a good job with their end, showing how things really look under your methods. Looks like Peterson will be the easiest for you to work with. Truillon will need more time. The real problem is the one called 'Lady Kathryn.' She's angling at the Corra's elbow all the time, and Verris' too. She *despises* you. Not too subtle about it either. Also I think it's fairly clear that it's she, not her father, who takes the lead."

Azetla nodded. This, he knew already. Tzal spoke mostly in Mashevi, and made only a few mistakes. He added the corrections directly on top of her words, because that was how she liked it to be done.

"I wouldn't waste too much of your effort on Lady Kathryn. She's not going to change her mind," he said.

"So she doesn't matter?"

"No, she matters a great deal. There's just nothing we can do about it. We have to hope that James and the Colonels leverage their weight against her, and do so wisely."

"I think that *is* the problem. She feels like they're not giving her an equal hand in an affair that she's financing. The more they resist her opinions, the more demeaned she feels, the more uneasy. Maybe she'll question the whole thing."

"Who's telling you this? Everson?"

Tzal snorted. "No. He's too busy trying to work his wiles and wits on her. She's a hard nut for him to crack."

"Then who is this coming from?"

Abruptly, Tzal traded Mashevi for Maurowan.

"I spoke to the Lady's servant girl. She told me all this."

"And she knew who she was talking to."

"More or less," Tzal said.

He could tell that if he asked the next question, he was going to get an answer he didn't like. Consciously or not, she was using her broadest, most neutral Maurowan accent and pushing the slave band at her wrist up and down in a scraping motion. Every time she did that, he wanted to yank her wrist and cut the damned thing off. The bands irritated him immensely, those stupid bits of half-truth she wore "just in case."

"Tzal, *why* would she tell you all this?"

"She has a high opinion of the Black Wren, and especially of you. There was a boy that she was fond of…"

Azetla closed his eyes and let his head rest back against the wall. Dersha. The name came into his mind like a jab. Cheerful, bright little Dersha. He had loved a girl named Timaa. A servant of Lady Beranadon.

Azetla thought about his Captain all the time. About his life. His wounds. His death. Always conscious of the hands that did it, for they were ever near him.

About Dersha, he had thought very little. A few sad and fleeting thoughts.

"How long before you realized that you killed the boy she was talking about?" Azetla muttered.

"About halfway through. She didn't know how he died, and I didn't tell her. I'm sure someone else will."

Tzal stood up and folded her arms.

"I told her you set aside some of his things."

He didn't ask how she knew that. He remembered. She had been tied up like a dead thing, eyes glazed, when Azetla carried Dersha's body, laid it down, and whispered over him the prayer of mourning. With miserable numbness, he had collected the knife, the little copper charms which used to offend him so, and the woven sash Dersha's mother had made. He had thought, at the time, to give them to his family. He had them still. They were worth some small coin—far more than anything Azetla himself owned—but nothing in all the world could have induced him to sell those trinkets.

Tzal adjusted one of the stones on the map by an inch as she did any time a stone shifted too close to Shihra.

"I still think you should bring the Taya to Hidud," she said.

"Absolutely not."

She gave a half shrug and ducked out the door. What else was there to say? She had driven a cold knife through the air. There was no reviving it.

With heavy shoulders, Azetla stood up to put out the lamp. Before he doused it, he glanced at the barren spot on the map which was Shihra. He pressed the tips of his fingers to that dark place where Dersha was killed and Tzal taken, then beyond it to where no terrain features were marked because none had been known and Tzal would give none.

He probably could have fallen asleep the instant he lay down. But he forced himself to trace both the blessing and the mourning prayers with his mouth, for Dersha. He did not flatter himself that he did this merely out of the depth of his grief, good will, and fond memory. It was chiefly guilt. The kind that would have made it difficult to look Dersha's family—or that girl—in the eye. But not the kind that could induce him to act differently.

He was going to keep using Tzal at every single turn. He was going to keep expecting her to come at the end of the day to tell him something or nothing. He was going to keep listening to her, in Maurowan or Trekoan or Mashevi, and turn all her words over in his hands till he knew the full strength and shape of them.

That he knew decisively. He wasn't even ashamed of it.

But he was ashamed of how cool he had sometimes been toward Dersha, who loved Azetla and longed for his approval. How stiff and irritable he had been the first few times Dersha joined him in his prayers, fingering those pagan charms, but praying to "the God of the desert and of all" with ferocious sincerity. The boy was kind sometimes to the point of cloying, but earnest. So innocent and earnest. Azetla wished he'd been more patient with him, and sooner. He wished he'd taken his devotion for the God of Masheva more seriously, rather than judging him ignorant, illiterate, and child-like.

And he wished he'd protected Dersha from that half-dead devil who herded them out of Shihra in what he now knew to have been a purposeful and violent surrender. He had been careless. He had not understood at all.

After he spoke to Naima, he would give that servant girl Dersha's things. Take his portion of the blame from her. Then leave the judgment of it to God.

24

*A*adin had never witnessed a Kakht ceremony. It was rarely performed and nearly always done to powerful seers or shamans, not to nameless girls of poor families from the edge of Shihra. His mother told him about a long-long-ago feud in which Kakht was used as a weapon between the tribes, until so many shamans were cut off from their people that almost none were left. Then came drought and famine and terrible winds that drove people into the clefts of the rocks for hours, even days at a time. After that, Kakht was deemed a foolish thing to throw about over small disputes. Shihra could not be left so defenseless before the Gods and spirits.

So the shamans made their usual sacrifices. Blood trickled down the black stones. The unwanted went into the fire. The lowlanders stayed out. The rains came. Choba and fadi root grew. Raids were successful. The spirits were appeased. The Gods passed Shihra over. Let there be no missing stones in the wall lest the whole thing crumble.

But Aadin's sister always shouldered her way past such rules.

They took her up to the Usarin's village, where the air was thinner, colder, and dry as death. They did not tie her, for she went willingly, and they did not strike her except when she spoke; then they did it so quickly and brutally that she went to the ground and did not readily rise. She spoke twice. She might have done it a third time but, marching *behind with all the family, Aadin pled with his eyes that she stop provoking them.*

They heated the iron rods in a forge the likes of which Aadin had never seen. Shihra had very little art of metal; swords were rarely made, but stolen from the lowlands, then handed down many generations.

For once in her life, she did not fight or evade.

She went gingerly to her knees without a word.

She did not move a muscle when they tore her shift to expose her back.

What did she think was going to happen? That the Gods would crack the sky open for her again?

No. She had gambled all and was ready to lose all.

The look on her face was one Aadin could see in his mind's eye even to this very day, though he could not understand it or even describe it. Was it anger or relief? Despair or longing? Resignation or defiance? All of these things or none of them, perhaps; her look was like a tongue of flame to the eye, steady in its heat, but ever moving. That was how he attempted to explain it to his wife, Nitzma, when he was drunk enough to talk of things he vowed to forget.

She fixed her eyes ahead. Jaw clenched. She braced for the pain.

When the tip of the red-hot iron touched her shoulder, she convulsed. Her head dropped to the ground and, since her arms were being held, she could not catch herself. Face against the rocky dust she opened her mouth in a scream, only no sound came out. The iron burned across her shoulders and down along the spine; the dust smeared in her sweat and coated her gaping mouth as it pressed against the ground.

Why did she writhe and cry out silently like that? It was not like her. A sudden dread of the numinous kind blanketed Aadin, like a great dust storm. Surely it was not just the searing of the skin, but the wholeness of the agony; body, soul, and spirit, cut off once and forever from all the Gods and all her people and all her heritage, without any hope of return.

What was it like to have your soul seared and severed? He did not want to know.

She fell unconscious after. They left her to lay in the dirt while they arranged for the rest of the rite to be completed. A trading family from the village of Solkadh was elected by lots to take her to wherever their trades guided them—Makaria or Trekoa—and sell her, provided she lived that long.

With that, his sister was gone. Gone as if she had been erased from the earth. No one needed to be counseled not to speak her name; she had none. No one needed to be warned not to look for her; she would be sold to someone who would take her far beyond where any Shihrayan ever traveled. No one needed to be told not to display mourning; she had been separated from family and village long ago.

Dotiya was the only one little and foolish enough to gash her arms. She grew quiet. Thoughtful. Unwieldy. And she kept the whittled smokethorn doll the shikk had made long after she was too old for such things.

Some years later, Aadin's wife told him a rumor she heard about the shikk. The shamans had been reluctant to do the rite of Kakht as the Usarin's maimed son requested. So they left it to the Gods, by lots. Should they put her over the black stone, a slow sacrifice? Should they set the fierce men of the village on her to do as they liked until she died of their whims and wants? Or let it be Kakht?

They drew lots and the answer was Kakht. They drew again. Kakht. They called on another God. And another. Kakht.

Seven times they drew. Maybe ten. That night, two of them had dreams.

She heard it made them tremble with dread so that they feared her even as they obliterated her. It was almost as if the Gods had not discarded her in all their strength and power, nor even in their indifference, but had desperately scraped her off as something they simply could not bear to touch, could not bear to hear, could not bear to know.

General Tamhet Avinroe stood at the highest point of Hidud's walls, an odd turret on the east side. It had once been a ritual place in the golden age of the Tusian Empire, so legend had it. Then the Tusians built a military fortress around it just before the age of their last Emperor. The ruin of it was rebuilt by the Maurowans not long ago, and the view from the ancient turret made Tamhet wonder how Gods so capricious, so sly, and so wanton could have cobbled together amongst any of them a view so elegant, so precise, separated perfectly into lights and shadows, rises and falls, the innumerable shades of red and brown to his north, and the hint of that greener land of Tus at the furthest edge of his vision to the southeast.

Usually when he came up here it was to feel awe and peace.

Today it was to feel power and resolve.

It was not working like he'd hoped. The beauty would not enter into him today, would not be his servant. It was beholden to someone or something else. If it spoke any word to him at all, it was the eerie truth that he stood now where once a Tusian general stood—perhaps even General Xichot himself who wrote all the great works of strategy—thinking he was great and should never fall.

The fortress of Hidud had never been taken. But it had never really been attempted. It was only ever gently handed down from one great power to the next when the receding power saw no choice in the matter.

Tus was a shell of its ancient glory, able to keep its nominal independence only by a pact that held its army—if it could be called such—below a certain threshold. Every Imperial visit to Tus was also an Imperial inspection. No, the eagle wings of Old Tus were carefully clipped. She could not fly far and, besides, Maurow was her river of gold and she would not have that river dammed from her.

The Trekoans were more violent and unruly than the Tusians, but they could never gather themselves together to accomplish anything. When Tamhet was given Hidud outpost, the old retiring General told him, "*if ten tribes were brought together to place one rock on top of another rock, both rocks would be unmoved, but both painted blood-red.*" The last fifteen years had put no lie to that.

But the past fifteen days had. Rumors were flying around like locusts, stripping peace and sense from everyone, leaving them in turmoil.

Tamhet, however, kept his head. Some few years ago there had been a similar ruckus about a central tribe—Saqiran—making new alliances and pushing enemies out of their way. There were mutterings then too. The outposts implemented stricter protocol. Generals sent to Piarago to request more men. Riada demurred, saying to wait. Let them have their fight among themselves, but harshly punish any least violation of Maurowan law or obstruction to Maurowan commerce.

Uneasily they waited, pacing and planning. But, after a time, the tribal consolidation slowed. Came to a stop. The war between Saqiran and Qatlan ebbed to a squabble. The balance of Trekoan power had certainly shifted in the thrash, but it was once again at rest. The dark cloud had passed.

Tamhet convinced himself at first that this one would too. These rebel tribes and their dirt-poor, jackal-borrowed desert god could never quite scrape themselves together, could they? Look how hard they tried, though. Tamhet and his wife had a great deal of amusement over the matter.

But yesterday, the worst rumor was confirmed, and laughter ceased. Cozona had been taken. Not merely attacked, but swallowed whole. The myriad reports about Qatlan being driven out of all their lands hardened into unassailable fact.

Tamhet faced the matter with practicality. He could have commanded Qatlanis to fight for him, but they had all streamed out of his hand like water; he hadn't even understood it till now. Tus could provide no men because they were permitted no men so near the border. And the next nearest outpost of any size was Areo, over a week's hard ride away. The rumors of Areo had been difficult to prove, but it seemed wisest now to assume the most shocking of them was true; Areo would be of no help for Areo was the adder's nest itself.

How this had come to be, was a mystery. Had the Trekoans done it themselves? Or were they Maurowan rebels? Was Colonel Everson dead or had he become a part of it? Did they really think Maurow would not lift its dragon head and burn them all to ash?

Yet a beast of great size was slow to turn and meanwhile Tamhet was on his own.

Tamhet thought on the thin thread of his Tusian lineage. A thing to be both proud and ashamed of at once. General Xichot was Tusian; there was pride. Tus had fallen swiftly and almost at its own hand; there was shame. And fear. Tamhet believed he had faced all his trials well thus far; small skirmishes, marches, displays of power as a sharp reminder to those around him. This was a thicker task, but he had walls and his own Maurowan soldiers. When the rebels came they would be scraped off like fleas, and burned, the disease of them eradicated.

He would call upon the spirits of his great Tusian ancestors; he would call upon the Gods of Maurow.

With a lifted head and a confident stride, Tamhet went to the house shrine of the great warriors of Tus and of his name-God, Shouma, to burn incense and pray for victory should these rebels come. Dissatisfaction stirred in him still. So he went to his wife's shrine of Serivash, asking for her to spill the blood of the enemy, for that was what she most loved to do.

Then he fell to one of his hidden habits of late.

Without formalities or sacrifices or incense or any sign of respect, he spoke scornfully out over the balcony into the blackening night.

"There, you 'god of the desert,' I have made myself ready. You surely do like to toy with your followers...tease them with hopes, then shatter them. You gave those jackals their land for one blink of an eye, then sent half of them into exile for decades and centuries. What gain are you to them? A dry well, it seems."

He spoke as to a man who stood near him, and he let his words hit the air with all the curiosity and contempt he always felt when he did this. The Janbari Rokhs he dealt with spoke often of this desert god, ever threatening people with his holy wrath, ever deferring to the strange practices and demands that they inherited from the jackals and distorted in ways of their choosing. The so-called God of Masheva. Formless—or of many forms?—and with a name that could not be spoken. Tamhet had heard so many of their prayers and songs. They needled at him. Jibberish, really.

Having to wrestle so tirelessly with these tribes made him feel that he was actually in a match of wits with their god, to see who would win. And when Tamhet stood at the pinnacle of Hidud, he knew that he would be the victor. He felt all of Maurow and all of Tus—the seen and the unseen of each—standing at his back and running in his blood with vicious strength.

So sometimes he spoke to this god in this strange way, casting his line out into unknown waters, testing to see if this divinity had any life in him, any power, any truth. And every now and then, with a sharp tug of elation and terror, Tamhet did feel that he had been heard and would be given an answer. An answer he might not want and could not control. At such times, he assured himself, *no, it was your imagination; you will make your own answer. You will.*

A shout below interrupted his words. His heart hurried, just a little. His shoulders tensed. He told himself to hold his head high and be sure of his place.

"What is it?" Tamhet asked as the soldier jogged up the steps to meet him.

"We've received a courier, Lord General Avinroe. A Trekoan. We are having trouble understanding his dialect, but he brought this."

Lieutenant Goudin handed Tamhet a coil of parchment. Gold-edged, scarlet thread twisted about it, something terribly like the Sivolne seal rolled twice on the exterior.

"He came all the way from Piarago?"

"So he claimed, my lord. But that was all we could understand from him."

Tamhet wanted to tear at the message, but he slowed himself, hoping to show that he cared little about these petty rumors. He went at a languid pace to take a look at this courier.

The middle-aged Trekoan was being held, not inhospitably, in a small cell-room. After a wearisome back-and-forth, Tamhet gathered that the man was from the Ghallaz region, near Wadi Kilsayn. A Hushai. Tamhet knew a smattering of Hushai phrases from the three years he spent as a captain at Darton. But not enough to make a proper interrogation. Several times the man said "honor to the Emperor" in awkward phonetic Maurowan, eager to prove his allegiance.

Tamhet ordered that the Hushai man be housed, well-fed, and *very* well-guarded, just in case. Then, in private, by lamplight, he eyed the sealed coil. He opened it like a man who expected to hear the fate of a faraway loved one—dead or alive. Only let the answer be clear. Let it be as hard and unmoving as stone.

And so it was.

Brutal clarity, without escape. And if it was from the Emperor, as it seemed it must be, then all doubts, and all hopes, and all snide prayers to desert gods must be laid aside.

"...And so I command you General Avinroe, to be ready. Whether this rumored rabble comes first to you or first to Cozona cannot be known, but I do not allow that they should take one mote more of my southern ground. If they come to you, you will not hesitate. Use all you have to its fullest strength. It is my holy will and the will of the

Gods of all Maurow and of Carth. Show them our might. I want them slaughtered down to a man."

Nimer Sarrez looked up. Last night the sky had been clear and vivid with stars. He had imagined riding to the wall of Hidud in that still bright darkness and felt something a little like terror and a lot like awe come over him. It reminded him of taking a high commanding view at the edge of a cliff; standing on and being a part of grandeur, but small in the face of it and subject to its winds and ways.

But tonight the sky was black as pitch and felt low atop Nimer's head. The terror remained, but was weakened, blanched of any awe. A cold drizzle fell on his face, lasting just long enough to chill him and make his clothes chafe under the leather armor. He adjusted the wool neckcloth Khala had stitched for him so that it wouldn't catch on the gouged brass loop. He stroked the embroidered pattern with the edge of his finger. The wind picked up and he licked his chapped lips.

He ought to know by now that real things are always more, less, or other than you thought. It is rare for a man to partake in something great and *know* that he does it at the same time. Captain Hodge told him that once, in that gentle-rough voice of his which Nimer sorely missed.

Nimer looked back where the men clanked and breathed and stomped, covering the land like locusts. Planning to consume everything in their path. Leave the enemy nothing to live by. The dread jumped sudden and swift through his blood, but he caught it with deep breaths, tamed it with rhythmic prayers to Yaar and Shouma, and changed its name to anticipation.

Azetla rode next to Nimer, a steady, quiet shape in the dark. They did not have to be able to see each other's faces; knowing the other was there sufficed. They were close enough to pass words, but chose not to do so just now.

Nimer had chosen this. He would choose it yet. But he had not known or understood in the least when he chose, and he never could have guessed that the elusive "something" he had sought as a youth would look like this. If it had been told him, he would have scoffed and likely spat in contempt. *Set a coup against the Emperor? Ally with Trekoans? Follow a jackal?*

Nimer Sarrez had not been born to tribal life. His family was Makarish of blood, but chiefly Maurowan in custom and culture. Oh, they told all the old stories, and there were a few remnant traditions hinting at a time when the North Makarish had lived like their southern brethren, in villages or tents, enduring the hard life the hard land offered them. But it was all so far removed from Nimer and the Sarrez villa outside Piarago. It was not a real thing to him, nor the people real people. It was vapor.

But as he grew nearer to manhood, the life that he did not live but that might have been his only a few generations ago, took on the sharp, intoxicating flavor of a legend.

He yearned for it. Ached for it. He became certain that the past of his people must have had more truth to it, more richness, more strength. Briefly, as a youth, he floundered with drunkenness and women and troublemaking alongside many of his peers. But he wished to prove himself a true Makar—whatever that meant—and show that his family line was more than just a gold bangle on Maurow's long arm.

In the Black Wren, he had expected a pompous, self-important Maurowan captain. He was given a warm, hard, humble man.

He had expected rivals. He found brothers.

He had nearly murdered Azetla. Now he was purposefully following him into fire. Nimer was fairly certain that Azetla was the only person he knew who both could and would take this role. Gentle and kind, he sometimes seemed, on the surface. Perhaps gentle and kind most of the way through. But like a vein of gold cutting through the rock, he had a ruthless streak, bright and unmixed when you touched it.

Captain Hodge had that too. Maybe Azetla learned it from him.

He was good at keeping that calm veneer too, although Nimer knew that he experienced the same symptoms before a battle as everyone else, and the same sufferings after. Azetla told him as much. He did all the same things too; the breaths, the prayers, taking his thoughts by the shoulders and making them go where he wanted them to go. He said that when he was very new, Joseph used to bully and bark at him, making him do endless stupid little tasks or answer endless stupid little questions. He hated it, but it helped.

A torch struck a signal in Nimer's periphery. Azetla's voice followed it.

"Joseph!"

A slight rustle and shuffle of men and horse. Joseph and Azetla rode up next to the signal-bearer.

"This is where you break off," Azetla said. "I'll send a runner the moment we reach for our hilts."

Joseph nodded sharply. If Nimer had not known better, he would have thought Joseph was angry. But that was the face he wore when he turned to a fight. His eyes were furious with focus and his voice would hit like a hammer. It was a terror for new young soldiers who were accustomed only to his joking and laughter.

There was a sudden burst of torch signals, like fireflies from the north, flashing here and there down the east flank of the army.

"Does it look like what it's supposed to look like, Joseph?" Azetla asked.

Joseph wheeled around and looked out over the great breathing shadow that cloaked the land. He was a long time in answering.

"Yes. I'd believe it. As long as we really do put our shoulder to the stone."

Azetla nodded very slowly. "And we will."

That was as close as Azetla got, once the course was set, to asking for assurance. For it was his duty to give assurance to everyone else.

Joseph's contingent sheared away. The main army quickened pace. It was not long before the watchfires on the ramparts rose on the horizon like dull stars. Nimer listened for sounds of war and warning, but he could only hear all their own noise. What had been a gentle and vast rustling suddenly rumbled into his bones like thunder.

Nimer looked to Azetla as the signal torch dipped beside him. Azetla mouthed his usual prayer. Twice. Then Nimer saw the thumb of Azetla's left hand tap the lion's head, *tic-tic-tic*. Seven times. Nimer tensed, his body recognizing the meaning of it ahead of his mind. Even knowing what was coming, his heart leapt when Azetla's shout cut through the air.

The orders flashed fast and bright then.

"*Shields up.*"

The front line formed a wall, but the pace did not slack.

"*Runners out.*"

Six Trekoan horsemen burst off the formation: three toward Joseph, and three toward the Khafri village where the Sahr waited, long since ready.

"*Archers forward.*"

They strung their bows and formed their line behind the shield wall.

"*Double-pace.*"

Iron-tipped rain began to fall on them as they broke into a run. Hidud was not Cozona. Hidud was ready. Hidud had been waiting with bated breath.

25

Azetla's army surged forward, siege ladders and shields rushing along like rafts atop a river of men. He saw arrows from Hidud strike. He saw men fall to the ground. He saw it all, and yet it did not reach but the surface of his eye. A ruthless sieve in his mind strained out what it did not need. And what he needed right now was for ladders to raise, and men to reach the top.

He had to hold himself back with the cavalry, fully out of range; it was what he had dreaded most. What if, so removed, he misread the battle? What if the cold distance cost him more than he could afford? What if it made of him a coward? He had never done this before—commanded so many men that he must step so far back to see them all.

But the moment the battle started, all those questions dropped like stones, never to be picked up again. Azetla's thoughts and emotions stilled so as to take steady aim.

He saw so clearly.

He saw the unbelievable strength and ferocity of his own men as they rushed the walls.

And he saw that their task was, in every sense of the word, impossible.

But he already knew that.

They clambered up so fast, though, and fought so well, it seemed to alarm the enemy soldiers on the walls. His men stabbed the wrists of anyone trying to fell the ladders. They threw the hooks with vigor. No one balked. Swordsmen began to replace archers on the walls of Hidud. At this, Azetla's men moved still faster.

The quieted part of him might have bloomed with pride at them.

But as he was, he had no time for that, and little interest in it. He was riveted on the crucial marks, like a gambler watching the pieces turned over, calculating when the one he had bet on would show up—and how much it would cost him by the time it did.

He searched for weakness and slowness in Hidud's response. There was none. They hurled their strength back without hesitation. His soldiers had just begun, but already Azetla could see it was taking too long. He saw a smattering of his men reach the top of the wall and, ever so briefly, wreak havoc on the defenders there. But those few were swarmed and slaughtered.

His eyes could not linger on that. They must see the whole. *The whole.*

Azetla called for the three volleys of fire-arrows. He did not expect much damage from them, but that was not the point. They were to harass. To give his men slim moments to do their work. To make the enemy flinch, if only for a second.

With an echoing crack, two of the ladders were felled. Several men slammed down into to the rocky dust.

Azetla rolled the order around in his mouth like a pit, ready to spit it out.

Not yet. Not yet. You can't bluff without showing you can tell the truth first.

He held himself back as with a tight fist wrapped about the reins. Maybe, after all, his sieve was not as fine as he thought. Though his eyes were on the whole he managed to see individual deaths as dark flashes, over and over again. But then he let the images fall, and the whole come clear again.

A third ladder was thrown from the wall. It fractured on the stones beneath it, catching one of his Areo soldiers on a jagged piece of rock. Someone pulled the soldier out and back behind the firing line. It was a miracle neither took an arrow. Plenty of others did.

The Black Wren soldiers at the wall were being viciously pushed down. Slain. Thrown. All the vigor and all the training in the world could not erase the reality of coming from below, of struggling to place foot and hand, of meeting a stream of soldiers who seemed endless and endlessly fresh.

A Saqirani soldier fell straight from the top of the ramparts. Another was cut through the jaw by a broadsword, collapsing on the rungs, clogging up the ascent.

Even from the distance, Azetla could feel the fear building in his ranks. Like hair raised on the arms, or the smell of a storm on the wind. There was no denying it.

It was time.

He bit down hard; this was all about to get much, much worse.

Azetla snapped his hand at his signal-bearer and barked a mere word. This time the flag remained perfectly still. As it should. Azetla set Barra into a run, galloping from one end of the rear guard to the next, then back again, shouting like a man desperate to rally a flagging force.

Peterson cried out first. Azetla almost thought he did it too quickly, but the response of his men was slow, so it had the desired effect. By the time Azetla returned to the mark, Peterson's Bluerock men had abandoned their ladders. Shields dropped and dust kicked up as they fled the walls of Hidud. After a few hectic moments, Truillon and his Red Hawk men followed. For the half moment Azetla took it in, their retreat looked jagged, desperate, and disoriented.

They fled like bleeding that would not stop.

They fled like hirelings and treasure-seekers. Those who had no cause.

The Black Wren, the Red Carth, and riders of Saqiran remained. Fifteen hundred men together, when they'd started. Less than that by now.

The Black Wren heaved the ladders back to the stone. With shouts. With swagger. Yet with sudden and purposeful slowness. No one traversed now where an arrow could reach them. The no-man's land between stone's edge and firing range was abandoned.

Sarrez rode from his watch-point on the eastern flank.

"It has to be enough, Azetla. It's taking too long. Too many—"

"They have to believe it Sarrez," Azetla said briskly. *They have to believe it.* "And they won't believe it if it doesn't cost us."

Worry riddled Sarrez's posture. His lips pressed tight and his eyes skittered wildly over the battlefield.

"Keep steady, Sarrez. We're almost there."

One more minute. One more sacrifice. Cold, clear, and distant, Azetla knew exactly what the enemy on the ramparts needed to see. He held his men out with brutal focus. He could not take in Sarrez's grief or fear. He could not afford to.

It was true that there was something looming far, far in the back of his mind, from the other side of his soul. Present, but untouched, like shadow and shimmer darting through one's vision foretelling a cracking headache. It could be ignored for now.

But it would come for him later and it very well might lay him out if he wasn't careful.

His men were out of arrows now.

Another ladder fell. Three of the men who had been on it rose to their feet. The others did not.

Enough. It had to be enough. In that moment, the lie Azetla needed the General of Hidud to believe was sliding closer to the truth. He could not lose any more men.

"*Retreat!*"

The word echoed down the line in time with the ram's horn and signal flags to meet the ears and eyes of rapt lower commanders.

At last they could pull their men off of this death wall. At last they could abandon this hopeless assault. Men scattered from the wooden ladders and stone ramparts, roughshod but blisteringly fast. The ladders were abandoned, as were all the ropes and siegeworks.

The signals flared out again and the ram's horn pierced Azetla's ears, so near it was. The flags waved direction—*northeast*—and the horn told them what form to take. Wild and disordered the retreat seemed. But only at the outset. After the initial clamor, each man found his place, and not one abandoned his weapon or his footing.

A minute passed of strong and steady retreat.

Five minutes. Ten? Time lied profusely on the battlefield. One could never know how it was passing.

God of Masheva, it all rests on this. He had sent Tzal to the Khafri village to sway them, utilize them, and prepare for the last. He had sent the Hushai rider. He had thrown his men at a wall he knew he had no chance of taking and watched them bleed and die for it. What more could he have done?

The sun was just breaching the horizon, striking at their eyes. It had taken so long for so little time to pass.

He looked back again, his heart beating, his teeth grinding.

The distant gate began to shudder. Finally, it opened wide to spill its contents. A thousand. Then another thousand. On and on. Infantry and cavalry, the leaders of them bright with armor, and the rear guard impossible to see for the army of Hidud seemed to be infinite.

A trained, determined, overwhelming force flooded toward Azetla as if from a burst dam.

Azetla smiled wide.

He tapped his lion's head seven times. Full of satisfaction and vigor, he looked at Sarrez.

But Sarrez's face was drained of life. He kept glancing back, despairing of seeing the end of Hidud's soldiers. Azetla knew what he wanted to say. "*We can't, Azetla. It's too many.*" Sarrez almost opened his mouth, the muscles in his jaw working with dread and frustration.

Sarrez had always been like this. The best swordsman Azetla had ever met in his life, a ferocious fighter in the true moment of need, but always in danger of the moments in between. Given that bit of breath, he fell to the edge of uncertainty, fearing that what had to be done could not be done.

"Sarrez, *look at me*!" Azetla spoke loud and harsh, shifting his weight on Barra so that the horse closed in on Sarrez.

His gaze jerked back toward Azetla, and he reined his horse to parallel.

"The more that come here, the less there are there," Azetla said. "This is *exactly* what we want."

"I know," Sarrez replied in a pale voice.

"Then put your hand on your hilt, Lord Sarrez, and don't look back again until I tell you."

Azetla reached out his arm with a snap and a shout.

The signal flag flew out and over, out and over, out and over. The pace doubled. Azetla cut away from Sarrez and galloped Barra all the way around the western flank to the front of the retreat, catching the eye of his lieutenants, warning them of what was next by the work of his own arm; the signal flags must hide for a while. Once he had circled them like a hawk, he fell back to the rear guard.

The pace quickened in jerks and starts, the form of the men working over the terrain. Finally his officers had seen the bat-tle-mark; they bolted for it. Azetla pressed in the back, forcing all gaps to close as they ran. Keep tight. And hurry. *Hurry.*

They *had* to get to the gully before the Hidud cavalrymen reached their backs.

A thousand horses. *By salt.* Azetla had never dreamed Hidud had so many. Sarrez was not wrong to shudder at the sight. The thunder and dust-cloud of them could be felt in the bones and tasted on the tongue as they galloped at full war-tilt.

That was not something that fell through the sieve.

That could ruin everything.

Even without their cavalry, and even if Azetla made no single mistake, this next part would be a desperately narrow thing. He'd known that from the beginning. No step or signal could go to waste. Nothing missed. Even now, in his periphery, he could see the Hidud horsemen fanning out to engulf them. Beyond that, their infantry was the abyss into which Azetla's army was meant to fall.

His soldiers were sprinting now; he could see the mark with his own eyes. The terrain grew more treacherous, hiding and revealing itself, and even Azetla was surprised to find the gully suddenly cutting down underneath him.

When Barra had climbed up the north side of the dry riverbed, Azetla pulled to a dead stop and turned.

"Archers!"

His signal echoed in voices and flags, rippling out behind him.

Quivers replenished from the supplies hidden in the riverbed, the archers rushed through to the edge of the gully, taking position on the highest lip of that low ground. They barely had time to form the line before the Hidud cavalry came in range.

His archers executed the relay with precision. They fired one volley, fled a ten second sprint while the enemy slowed on the rocks and dips. Fired two more volleys. Then they dispersed in every direction, like thieves in the night, as the horses of Hidud crashed into Azetla's men.

There was barely a moment for his mind to perceive it, but it was worse than he expected. So much worse. His aiming mind briefly wavered. Sarrez was right. It was too many. Too many to control, to pull this way or that.

God of Masheva, make him swift, swifter than he's ever been before.

Barely did he allow his mind that thought, that prayer, before he took himself by the shoulders and made himself look squarely on the task. Only on that.

The Hidud riders took no interest in the foot soldiers, whether they crushed them or not. They went straight for the mounted commanders; Azetla was swarmed twice, by those trying to protect him and those trying to kill him. His signal-bearer speared the flag and drew his sword, and Azetla's right arm braced with the buckler. Rarely in his life had he fought shield-laden.

The first blow hit him like a hammer, jarring him all the way to his bones, then sliding off his pauldrons. But his body understood before his mind did; he swung his left hand back with clean force. Barra burst forward at Azetla's allowance, ramming into the dun before him as Azetla cut into the pit of the rider's raised arm. The sword dropped. Azetla struck his sword across the man's face, but didn't wait to see him fall.

Another square blow to the buckler, a last-second shift of the shoulder probably saving his life. Azetla leaned in the saddle and struck an unaimed blow with nothing but a hope of unbalancing one or the other of the two riders coming at him.

The first rider reeled and paused as if suddenly woozy. Azetla did not ponder why; he ran his sword past the man's teeth and into his skull. He nearly yanked him off the horse just to get the blade back.

There was only one moment where he wished he had his sagam in the bucklered hand, rather than a Trekoan long-knife. Its certain weight. Its perfect edge. But he knew where the sagam was, what task it would be set to, and he was satisfied. The Trekoan weapon was flightier in his palm, but it drew the blood he wanted. It did the task.

Out of the corner of his eye Azetla saw that the infantry of Hidud was catching up to its cavalry. They were more and more and more, far beyond any number Azetla could have accounted for. He tried, with every slash and strike, to extract himself to the edge of the fray so he could *see* the things he had to see. Were the Hidud cavalry floundering in the mud of Azetla's foot soldiers? How many officers were down? How many signal flags remained?

Each blow he blocked with that buckler rattled him till his whole arm throbbed with a bruise deep, deep in the muscle. For a terrible streak, each and every strike he made with his sword felt like grace and luck and desperation, never like skill.

But sometimes the body really was just that inch ahead of the mind.

He'll come any moment. Had to. Had to. It was time.

Now, he thought, as if the thought had the power of a ram's horn. Nothing but God himself is as sure and timely as Joseph Radabe. Azetla told this to himself. And he believed it.

He still could not extract himself, no matter how hard he tried. The terrain grew ever more uneven with bodies and bits of Maurowan armor. He saw, at an accidental glance, the face of a Juniper Sergeant, staring up from the ground. Eyes open, unalive, hand still curled about his hilt.

He cut two more Hidud soldiers down, but the last one was a near thing. Barra was limping now.

There was a sound like distant rain. He could not think about it.

It became a roar, and surrounded him. As soon as he understood the meaning of it, he saw his avenue through the deadly muck. He fought his way out and out and out until at last he could stand clear and see with his eyes what he heard with his ears.

There they were, wonderful and dreadful in the rising light. Joseph Radabe and Lieutenant Ishelor, each leading a tributary of nearly two thousand men. Joseph dove in to reinforce Azetla from the north, Ishelor lapped up the infantry from the south, blocking them off from their own gates.

Peterson and Truillon would not be far behind.

Then real rain began to fall, gently at first. Within moments the ground was sticky, churned mud. Everyone on both sides struggled for footing.

Azetla had lost his signal-bearer. His eyes hunted desperately until he found a flag, stuck in the ground as a pike. He took it up and held it level, waiting. He scanned the battlefield from the rise of rock to which he'd retreated, trying to read every paragraph, making sure he missed no crucial word, before he raised the flag and wrote the command against the gray sky.

His men had already dug a deep hole in the Hidud cavalry. A sound blow at the right point from Joseph's cavalry would collapse them into nothing.

Drive them into the gully! He flung the signal again and again.

A run of water was already snaking down the dry rocks.

The rain grew stronger and steadier, a true winter rain. The gully, an easy drunk, began to swell.

Azetla flung the signal flag again, forcing poor Barra to canter back and forth. He shouted himself hoarse. Only a few flags were left to respond from his own contingent.

But Joseph's signalmen were sharp and ready.

Ishelor's too. They saw. They took up the signal and spread it through the men as they drove the Hidud infantry down on the jagged riverbed. These men had the wild energy of those who had listened to the battle from afar, fresh-bodied and straining at the bit. Azetla caught Sarrez and, together, they pressed back from the north while Joseph and his men clawed in at the east, brutalizing the enemy command line. Truillon and Peterson rounded out the south.

There was no chance for the enemy to retreat, and the battle was too swift then for surrender. Azetla would have brooked none had it been offered.

The Maurowans of Hidud were slaughtered to a man.

26

Tzal sat on the stone roof of a village house in Khafri-Mai. Still, silent, and concentrated.

She listened in the dark as the threads of fire and shouts of war crashed against Hidud's ramparts. Then she watched as night receded at the edges—and Azetla's army receded from the walls. Out, out, out to the gully. A carefully staggered retreat. A set trap. And a very costly lure.

She traced every stage of the battle with the tip of her finger, following the pathway as it had been mapped for her beforehand, lining up each marker as it came. But one part depended on Hidud alone. Neither she nor Azetla nor anyone else could take another step until they made their choice.

For some minutes Tzal simply closed her eyes, felt the cool wind that foretold rain run across her skin. Made herself breathe long and deep. Over and over. Loosed the shoulders from their aching tension. Over and over.

The deep sound reached her ears from afar and her eyes snapped open.

She felt such a brutal satisfaction as she watched the gates of Hidud crack open and pour out its men to the last drop. She smiled—precisely as she did when people fell to her words against all their reason—and dropped from the low roof.

She'd doubted Azetla on this score. But he was right in the end. *Now let's see how many times you can go on being right. It can't last forever, I don't think.*

But he could just as soon say the same thing to her.

Rain began to hit her face at a spit as the light grew to fullness. The distance and gentle cuts of land marred her sight of the gully. She knew what was supposed to be happening right now, but her eyes could not prove it to her; she had traced her finger straight off the map.

Well. She could not know what she could not know. What mattered was that the Trekoan soldiers in this village were ready when the moment came and that the villagers themselves had been kept quiet until this moment. Hidud did not know that there was a tiny poniard already pointed at its ribs, ready to jab at the least touch. That there were lightweight siege ladders and ropes hidden in the guest tents. That the fighting men of Khafri, few though they were, would not come to Hidud's aid.

For two days she held the whole village in her palm while it kept trying to crawl out of her grip. She was not allowed to close her fist and crush them; she could barely afford to threaten them. They were no natural allies of Saqiran, their hatred of Maurow was less piquant than she would have liked—that would have been a fine sharp tool to pry with—and they did not easily trust her. To them, she was an anomaly at best, a demon at worst.

She was known.

More and more, this was a problem. Less and less could lilt and wit overcome it.

Rahummi might have had better luck, she thought, if only he had arrived sooner.

"Wake up. Let's go." Tzal gave Rahummi a good hard shove.

He nodded three or four times as if convincing himself that he was indeed awake. Then he dragged himself up.

"I'll get everybody in place—"

"Everyone is in place. It's all ready. I let you sleep a bit longer."

His brow furrowed as he dressed himself hurriedly and looked about.

"You shouldn't have done that."

Well, you shouldn't have ridden almost three days straight without sleep. Little good it did either of us. I corralled the whole village by the skin of my teeth and with no help from you.

"Just go speak to the village leader. Fill in the gaps. Soothe him and what-not so that we don't have to watch our backs while we run into arrows."

Rahummi tied his sash with a hard jerk of his hand and a sharp look toward her. But then he nodded and did as she said.

They both knew he could do a good job of it because he had spent seven years learning at her hand. He probably did not realize how much he had gleaned from her. At first, she had not even realized she was teaching. But she had been. Use this idiom with them, not that one. *Leave a little room for interpretation, Rahummi.* Change posture. Tilt words without breaking them, circle round here and cut straight there. Make someone beholden to you with little more than strong and carefully placed phrases. Only a hint of a threat, if needed.

But unlike Tzal, Rahummi had the name, position, and power to see his word through. What Tzal said was rarely meant to endure past the needs of the moment; as soon as she removed her hands, it all collapsed.

So let Rahummi supply the mortar and make it hold. She kicked the dust of that task off her feet, glad to be rid of it. She felt no need to tell Rahummi about the two villagers she caught trying to run out and warn Hidud last night. Tzal dealt with them quietly and carefully. No one heard. Those bodies would not be found till after today's question was answered. By then it wouldn't matter anyway.

A young man. And a woman some twenty years older than Tzal. They did it because they were afraid. They believed Maurow would prevail and the village would suffer blame. A perfectly reasonable assumption. But it rankled Tzal that she hadn't been convincing enough to keep them from running into her knife.

What good was she if her tongue failed? Who would suffer her if her words fell limp, or if she ran out of things to know that no one else knew?

No one.

Then what?

"By blood, he's swallowed them whole!"

Tzal ran over to where Rahummi stood at the edge of the village. The local Rokh stood beside him and saw. The Saqirani soldiers saw. The Janbari soldiers saw. An ignorant child could have seen it.

Yes. Azetla had swallowed them whole. It happened so fast! The army of Hidud was beaten into the mud and it would not rise.

The rain was coming stronger now and a shiver coursed through Tzal's body as the drops ran down her neck.

"Wait for the rider's signal!" Rahummi shouted to his soldiers, for they were all nearly jumping out of their skins, anxious to join in the battle that had been rumbling in their ears since before the sun began to rise.

Then he looked at Tzal. "Are you staying in the village?"

She shook her head. "I'm going over."

"That's what he told you to do?"

Tzal gave a look that sufficed for a nod. It was at least well within the bounds of what Azetla told her to do.

Rahummi glanced worriedly from her to the horizon, working his jaw. She knew what he was thinking. He was afraid she would make the same mistake as last time, making a sacrifice that was not hers to make, for the sake of a victory that was not hers to keep. But she did not want to hear it. She did not need the distraction.

"You saw Naima?" she said quickly before he could get a word out.

"Yes. And I held my daughter. For all of three minutes before I had to leave again."

"She looked strong."

Rahummi could not stop his smile. "That she did. I already know what her name should be, but Naima didn't want me to speak it to anyone yet."

"It's very bad luck."

Rahummi laughed. "Nonsense. You people who live in crags are very superstitious."

"We've got good reason. The Gods in the crags are tricky. Can't turn your back for even a second. Can't lose your footing."

"I don't think that—"

They both stood taut. A single rider broke off from the army as it rumbled back to the walls of Hidud. The rider angled toward Khafri-Mai and cut the signal clear as day.

"Finally," Tzal breathed in Shihrayan.

Rahummi barked the ready order; Trekoan in tongue, Maurowan in style and method. He had learned from Azetla, who had learned from the Empire, and they were going to take that learning and run it through Maurow's ribs.

Now everyone was exactly in place. There was that moment of creaking and shifting and firming of grips. Straining to begin.

Tzal stood just behind the ladders, set to follow them straight to the wall. She needed to get in quick, for her quarry would be the swiftest to flee and hide, the likeliest to cause long trouble, the worst lingering wound even in the midst of victory.

Her nails dug into her palm.

Her heart raced as it always did in the moment just before.

A final shout rose from Rahummi's throat. The ladders were shouldered and set swift sail for the ramparts.

Tzal ran behind, eyeing the top of the wall, fixed on it, pulling herself toward it.

Halfway to the wall. Still out of range of arrows.

A Saqirani stumbled badly all of a sudden and limped. The ladder lagged as the others tried to compensate for him. Tzal shouldered him out and took his place, the weight coming on her like a stone, slowing her. Just under ten minutes at a hard run from the village to the wall—she'd tested it—and the Hidud archers would have to make a choice between the trickle of ants running up their side, or the swarm that was even now pounding at their door.

The sound of an arrow biting into the ground not far to her left told her that at least someone thought the ants worth squashing.

Two men fell from underneath their ladders, struck by iron tips, and they were left where they fell. The wood bit hard into Tzal's neck and shoulder. Her legs burned to keep the pace, but they were nearly there. The sound of the wood thunking against the top of the stone, echoing all the way down the eastern wall, was a relief to body and mind.

The Janbaris leaped upon the ladders. Tzal stood back—for three breaths, then four—watching the furious upward rush, gauging how bad the fighting at the top would be. Then she joined the stream. She clambered up, feet half-steady on the rungs, grips half-shot from blood-rush.

She had never done anything like this before. Never climbed a wall to an enemy that was facing her, ready. As she neared the top, there was a clog of men and she had to cling there, nearly twenty feet in the air, with nowhere to advance, nowhere to retreat, and nothing into which she could dig her knife. The ladder groaned against the stone and shuddered; someone just above Tzal's head was fighting for control.

Being trapped put the hammer into her pulse. She had to press the stiffness out of her grip, crack through the catches in her joints. At last a foot moved. A scuffle cleared. Two rungs up, Tzal dug into the arm which tried to push her off, pulling herself over the stone lip and drawing the sagam.

With a clumsy swipe, she took what life was left of the enemy in front of her.

By nature, she wanted to slide through the deafening chaos without being a part of it. *Keep to the edges. Keep to the hazy edges.* She had always to find her own way and go about her own task. But the only way through was to fight within the rush of Azetla's army, growing ever thicker and ever faster even as she stood in its midst. She had to set her strokes with the current.

It was unnatural for her.

For those short minutes, atop the ramparts and on to the stairwells, she acted like a soldier: plain in purpose, concerned only with the Janbaris and Saqiranis who surrounded her, and the Maurowans and Qatlanis who tried desperately to beat them back up the cramped stairwell. She had to cut down in short, shallow motions so as not to harm or impede her own. To protect rather than advance. To clear the path rather than clamber through it, because otherwise no path could be sustained. It was hard to finish anything, or even start it. It was like having a hand tied or a foot weighted. Like having a bit in the mouth.

Bodies collected underfoot. You could not help but brace your heel against a dead man's jaw. Shouldering and cutting through, Tzal lurched ever closer to the front of the striking line, ever closer to the bottom of the stairwell. Sudden as a shutter snapping back, there was bright, cool air and level ground. She broke free of the clot of soldiers. There was still a gauntlet before her, but enough room now for her to move *her* way. To do as she pleased. She could slip through the cracks like smoke, cut down only that which slowed her, and leave the rest to those who listened to their commanders, watched their flags, and dangled dreams of home and glory and purpose in front of their eyes.

Soon she had clawed herself out of the belly of the tumult. She edged her way to the Qatlani quarter; the battle and din fell behind her. Once truly inside the quarter, it was uncannily quiet. How many were hiding? How many fought? How many fled? She could not begin to guess. The narrow walkways between the mud-and-brick might be more dangerous than even the ramparts by now.

She had a stroke of luck at first. She found two Qatlani shamans in a dark temple room. Three birds, dead on the floor, necks broken. Blood at the foot of some fierce statue. The shamans were old and easy to overpower. Today their god drank stronger blood than usual.

I guess I'm the answer your gods decided to give. But she recoiled at her own thought. She didn't like the idea that she was but a puppet for some Makarish god as cruel or crueler than her own. She made her eyes focus and her mind go silent.

Another hour of careful, painfully slow movement from one dark room to the next yielded another shaman, and four men who she recognized as informants and watchers. No one needed them about.

But she could not find the Rokhs.

She needed their throats especially. Rokh Calav. Rokh Mudha. And, most of all, Rokh Zaqahi. These were the names that plagued Rokh Imal all the years Tzal belonged to him. The last and best strength of Qatlan.

Further and further southward she went. Corner by corner, house by house, room by room. She killed any men she found who could not—or would not—answer her questions. They were caught off guard, hiding as they were, and only a few caused her real trouble. These were not the ones who knew how to fight. For the most part, she left the women and children alone. Let Azetla decide about them when the time came. He had strong beliefs about such things.

Her frustration grew the longer her quarry evaded her. Her ribs started to ache till it hurt to draw too deep a breath. She'd taken the butt of a spear on the wall, she remembered, but the pain of it was only now beginning to wake up and seep through. Her ankle was swollen and the sole of her foot strangely tender. She had no idea why. Her thirst became a distraction.

All this and she had gained so little. She did manage to scavenge a slight, sturdy bow, slung from one of her kills. Only three arrows to it, though. Not likely to be of much use.

After leaning and listening at a threshold in a decrepit corner, Tzal pushed her way through the cloth door into a small, dusty home. A Qatlani woman and several children sat on the floor. They stiffened when she entered, but most dropped their gazes and hunched their shoulders immediately after. They thought all this would pass over them like the dust of a red day.

"Are there any men cowering here?" she asked. Her tongue rolled to the sharp-sweet accent of south Qatlan, but her throat was dry, giving each word a rasp.

The woman shook her head wildly. Tzal looked in every corner to confirm it. Then she sat on the ground, sagam across her knees, eyes on the door.

"I need water."

The mother made a motion with her eyes and the eldest girl darted to the jar in the corner of the room and drew a cupful. Tzal risked a mild courtesy and took it with her right hand, removing it for those few seconds from the hilt. The young woman stared at the Makarish pattern on Tzal's hand as she did so. Tzal did not care. She had no intention of trying to convince these people she was any particular thing.

Tzal drank the water in a few swallows. She rested her palm on the sagam's hilt.

"Where are your Rokhs?" Tzal demanded.

Silence. But she had expected that.

"They were nowhere to be found on the battlefield. They are not fighting for you. They have left you to the likes of me."

She leaned her head back against the wall and closed her eyes. Only for a moment. Two moments. Waiting to see if one of them would feel a streak of bravery and try something. She wished they would. It might take the bad taste of what she was about to do out of her mouth. Eyes still closed, she gave a deep and earnest sigh.

"You're not going to tell me where they are."

She was saying it to herself, really.

"It's such a waste," she breathed in her native tongue.

No point in waiting any longer. She came to her feet. The mother instinctively coiled around the infant in her arms. But Tzal grabbed one of the other girls by the wrist, gripping hard enough to bruise deep. She was no more than eight years old, probably. The choice was arbitrary.

Well, that's not really true.

"I will give each and every one of them to whatever god it is you serve, until you tell me where those cowards are. If they hide like children, the children will be taken in their stead."

The little girl didn't scream. She cried so, so quietly.

It's Dotiya. She reminds you of Dotiya and you know it.

The mother would not look at Tzal. She stared wide-eyed at the ground and all she said was, "No. No. No."

She said it over and over again till Tzal wondered if she was becoming manic and, therefore, useless.

Tzal sheathed the sagam. Drew her knife. Then twisted the little girl's arm until she gave a sharp cry. For half a moment, the girl writhed and yanked and pulled with spirit. But then she gave up.

You should have done better than that, little one. I'm not bluffing this time.

Pushing the girl to the ground, pressing her elbow into the back of the child's neck, Tzal forced herself into the mother's line of sight.

"Give me something. Anything. And I will mark that door. This house will be left alone in peace."

Tzal began counting to thirty in her head. Longer than that and she would have to steel herself to the task all over again. *Ten. Eleven.* Her grip pulsed on the knife. *Seventeen. Eighteen.* She would have to make sure Azetla never found out about this.

But his God would still know.

Twenty-three. Twenty-four.

"I don't know! Gods, I don't know! But...if, maybe, at the aqueduct...if, it might...I don't know. *I don't know.* I've heard of escaped prisoners hiding in the aqueduct before, but I don't know if that's true. Maybe there is a way out through the waterway, I don't know. I don't think it can be true. I don't know. *Please.* I don't know." The woman's eye closed tight with tears and she rocked back and forth, clutching the infant till she might have smothered him.

Tzal all but collapsed with relief. As if she were the one who had been spared. She put the knife away immediately and pulled the girl up from the ground. The real terror and real hatred in the child's face were a wash of comfort over Tzal, for they were lively expressions. Tzal's arm felt limp and weak as she withdrew it; she'd had such a tight, miserable death grip on that child.

As she slipped out, Tzal hung a knotted strip of red cloth on the edge of the door. She had not lied about that. When Azetla's men came through, they would pass that door over. Rahummi and Qadi and the others had the same bits of cloth with them to be used at their discretion. But this was the only one Tzal had offered, and the only one she intended to give.

She ran south along the eastern wall till she came near the place she only vaguely remembered. Peering around a corner, she saw that it was guarded. There was a crafted lip of stone and several steps leading down to a pool of water. Beyond that a dark, narrow tunnel which drew from a spring half a mile beyond the walls of the fortress. Tzal had never been in that tunnel and, as far as she knew, it was made only for water to traverse, not for anything that breathes or wishes to live. Never before had she heard of it as a place of hiding, let alone of escape. She was frustrated with herself for taking so long; if the Rokhs of Qatlan had made it outside the walls, she had lost all chance of finding them.

Twenty-five feet of distance. A bow she had never used with a string that looked badly cared for. Four Qatlanis on lookout at the pool, flinching at every sound. Three arrows.

With forefinger and thumb she traced and plucked at the string. Nothing could be done. She set the first arrow gently, letting out a long, slow breath. Then she aimed fast and let fly.

She saw it strike. It hit low. She made the adjustment. The first man's scream did not register to her ear until the second arrow hit its mark. Still a bit low.

The last arrow never went anywhere. The string snapped. The bow jolted in her hand and she dropped it like a live coal. Sagam to the right hand, knife to the left, she ran at them.

The soldiers were still bewildered. Slow and clumsy with their hands. But they were fresh, and she was not. She struck a blow and she took one, but hers went deep and theirs barely made a mark. Swords clattered into the limestone rim. All of them stumbled over the lip and into the shallow water steps. They lost their balance, Tzal kept hers. She sent a head cracking against the tunnel rock—that one did not rise again—and her right shoulder scraped a long way down the rough wall before she gutted the last man.

The water reddened deeply where the light fell. A few feet into the tunnel, however, and the water looked black as tar. The roof of the tunnel touched the top of her head so she had to bend slightly. The floor was narrow and uneven, making the level of the water seem to fluctuate between her hips and her waist. She did not know when the darkness became complete, only that at some point she reached in front of her to feel her way and she could not see the least trace of her own hand.

She counted steps so that she would know how far she'd gone. Each time her shoulder or head hit the wall, she winced, both because it hurt and because she was convinced the tunnel was narrower than before. Was the water higher? Or was it just a brief depression in the tunnel floor?

Panic was not something Tzal often experienced. Fear, yes. Dread, certainly. No one could evade those. But she had learned at a hard hand how to extract, shadow, or numb the part of her that cared what happened to her. You just had to briefly give up hope, or pretend you had, while going on anyway. And that worked—up to a point.

But the sensation of being gradually swallowed, compressed inch by inch, threatened to disorient her. She stopped. Her breaths felt very fast and very loud. Her shoulder and the back of her head hurt, and she focused on the pain as she would have on a point of light. When she touched her left ear and the base of her skull, she felt the sticky wetness that was not water. Her hair was matted with it. It oozed, but not too much. She told herself it was not too bad, and she mostly believed herself.

A few more long exhales then she took her next step. Resumed counting.

A tomb of water. Perhaps that could be it. Perhaps not. She did not pretend to know exactly what it would look like when that bloody desert God turned to lay his vengeful claim on her once and for all. But she knew that she would know it was him. No matter who held the instrument of death in their hand, and whether it came by a sword or by a splinter, it would be as though she was face-to-face, eyes locked. She would *know*.

At the times when she lost hold of herself and began to reel—when she felt that the whole of her, bone and blood and soul, would soon go hurtling down an abyss far beyond recovery—she grasped this certain thing. Fastened herself to it. Wrapped it around her wrists, said it like a prayer, till she found her footing. She could die badly. Stupidly. Painfully. Failing whatever objective she had set for herself, or any objective at all. But it would come with an answer, so what did it matter if the answer shook her like a quake and swallowed her like the earth?

To be anything she chose, anything she could think of, anything she felt like—that dark, noisy, cavernous freedom—would be traded for a plain, brutal truth with no room for its bounds to broken or shifted out of shape.

But she hoped that was not going to happen today.

She didn't know when exactly, but she noticed that now she could almost make out the movement of her fingers in front of her face. As soon as she realized that, she heard deep voices carried over the water.

Tzal crouched low so that the water reached her face. Slowly, her knees scraping the rough tunnel floor, she closed in on the noise and—soon—the source of the light. Four men, if she saw right, pressed together, arguing in vicious whispers. Two torches between them, both guttering out the last of their life.

As slow and as silent as she had ever been in her life, she loosed the sandal from her foot and took the crimson strip that could have saved some Qatlani life but did not. She tied the cloth to the sandal and to her flint so that the leather rested lightly on the ground. It was the only thing she could think to use. Then she moved nearer to them, eyes only above the water.

She was as close as she could get without alerting them to her presence. It was only because of their argument—the tunnel split and narrowed dramatically—that she had succeeded so far.

Knife drawn to her right hand. Knuckles brushing the rough rock on one side. Left hand empty for now. Fingertips touched the other side. Slow. Slow. Deep breath. Then down all the way into the water. Half crawling, half swimming along the hard bed of the tunnel, Tzal slithered toward their legs in the dark water. Her lungs felt desperate and fiery. The voices rose and fell, garbled.

Then she found it. Grabbed a calf and ripped into it. She climbed up the man with the knife as her hook, into the thigh, ripping it out, then into the back.

The Qatlani Rokh thrashed and shouted and sank. The others, weighted by their robes and possessions, were slow to aid him. She took the second by the throat, hanging on his back while he tried to pry her off. Pulling him down under water, on top of her, his body shielded her, the blood from his neck changing the taste of the water on her tongue.

The first torch went down with him, which incited a panic. The last two men dug through the water with their swords, screaming at each other for failing to get her.

They did though. A bite on her leg. A much worse one on her left side. No knowing how deep they were, and no chance to find out.

She pulled one of them into the water. He slipped and his head cracked hard against the stone. The torch hit the water. Black swallowed them all. Tzal had to feel her way around his limp body to know where to put the knife. She felt the pulse stagger and fall.

The last one tried to live like prey do, by staying still, hoping to remain undetected.

But he was breathing so fast and loud.

It was a strange, confused grapple between them. The pain in her side flared bright. Her lungs burned. But she brought him back down into the water and did not let him up till she knew he was gone.

The darkness made her feel like she didn't know which way was up, and for a split second she thought she would drown in still, shallow water. She tore to the air and drank it in desperate swallows.

She went the wrong way first, dizzy and disoriented. She stumbled often. Turned. Leaned against the wall, for she could barely stand straight. Pain jumped from place to place on her body and she did not doubt she left a trail of blood in the water. But she had to be meticulous, and feel her way inch by inch along the floor of the tunnel in a widening circle,

After a few minutes—and an instant of sheer panic—her bare foot felt the frayed cloth from her sandal, fluttering like a reed in the gentle current, and she knew she had exactly six hundred and thirteen steps back to light.

27

Hidud was Azetla's before he even reached the wall.

The point of victory passed underfoot, and hardly a man of his noticed it, for the residue of the battle remained. But Azetla perceived it as if it had been spoken in his ear or handed to him in parchment. He saw the field. He saw the wall. He saw the movement of his men, and the dregs of Hidud's resistance. A surge of elation rippled across his skin, but soon succumbed to the thorny question of all that must be done *after*. By the time his men gave shouts of triumph, and the Janbari slave women of Hidud broke out in ululation, Azetla was already neck-deep in the troubles granted by victory.

As at Cozona, the most dangerous men were executed swiftly and silently. General Avinroe died with chin lifted and contempt on his tongue. He behaved precisely as James said he would and Azetla took note of this. He had no intention of giving the man a single look or word, though Avinroe spent every one of his last minutes of life trying to stir Azetla's ire. The man had pride enough to burn and he hurled it every which way.

Only at the last did Azetla give in and open his mouth.

"I don't know where you think you can go from here, jackal. My Emperor will see all of you, down to the least packing boy, put to the grave. He told me so himself."

"That may well be. But Riada did not write those words. I did."

Eyes wide. The horror of realization. Azetla could have sipped long on that, but he chose not to. He motioned to Sergeant Lachlan. A heavy sword. A quick death. And no time for foolishness.

Azetla's Hushai courier was found, unharmed, having played his part to perfection.

There were less than three hundred prisoners, for most of Hidud was dead. And there was only a small village's worth of women and children, for not many Qatlanis wintered at Hidud, but rather in their traditional tribal towns. That was a ferocious relief. There were certain tactical choices from which he was glad to be spared. Widows and orphans were pitiable and usually protected, but beyond a certain quantity they were anything but neutral.

He could afford to leave them in peace and he encouraged the soldiers to share rations as a sign of good will.

Plagued by the sense that he was missing something, Azetla pulled out his ledger for the comfort of it in his hand; he had nothing to write as of yet. The sky was more tan than gray now and his sense of the hour was faintly muddled. It took a long time to gather all his senior men together in the General's office, so that he could set them about their tasks. Not everyone was accounted for, but that was yet another matter to be addressed.

He had no desire to give a victory speech—he disliked the taste—but he knew he must encourage them and praise their valor. They had certainly earned that. He did his best. But then he took them and turned their faces abruptly to the mud, as it were, for what they had won for themselves was more danger and harder work.

Six hundred and thirty-two men lost. Hundreds more wounded. A whole outpost to manage in half-hostile territory on the border of Tus. Supplies. Rations. Preparation for the next move. And, at the last, one severe failure to be dealt with: by all accounts the most prominent Qatlani Rokhs, who were supposed to have been on hand, had escaped.

"No," Tzal's voice croaked, almost inaudible, from the back of the room, hidden behind his other officers. "They didn't."

Azetla had to look over heads to find her, drawn back from the others. He had not seen her come in. He noticed that she wore a thick over-robe that was not her own—it fit her badly—and leaned heavy against the doorway, arms hanging limp at her sides.

She cleared her throat, but her voice still came out dimmed and raspy.

"They were killed in flight."

"Where?" he said. His men had searched every home, every donkey stall, every storage room.

"In the water tunnel. The bodies are still there if you want them. Just over a quarter mile in."

Azetla gave a nod. He assigned the task. His army would not be accused of treating bodies as only the devils do. Questions arose in his mind, but he could ask her those later.

A few more matters of military housekeeping passed quickly through his mouth, then Azetla dismissed his officers to their meals and their work. He waited as the men dispersed, thinking that Tzal would stay to give her full report; the others had already given theirs. But she dropped out of the doorway and walked—very unevenly, he thought—in the direction of the east stables.

Grabbing his ledger and satchel, he left Avinroe's office. Soldiers approached him one after the other, but he gently deferred their questions. "Rest a while," he told them. "I have one more report to gather. You'll have work enough much sooner than you like."

Some time he stood at the far end of the stall, but she didn't even mark him. That told him most of what he needed to know. The way she shook out her hand and braced before pulling off the long outer robe told him the rest. The tunic and shirt beneath were both destroyed; they gaped from her, bloody. The side of her head was matted, crusted black. As best he could tell, it was the left foot she favored most.

"What on earth is *wrong* with you?" he barked.

He made no effort to temper his voice or pretend he meant those words in some kinder, more helpful way.

Tzal looked over at him and, for a moment, her expression was that of a thief caught in hiding. Then she slumped against the wall with resignation. She gave no answer.

"Do you know what I would do to Sarrez or Joseph if they crawled off into a hole to die like an animal? Without telling *any-one*?"

She narrowed her eyes at the ground.

"I don't think it's as bad as that," she said. She was having trouble pulling the scraps of her tunic away to see the wound proper. Her voice was low, her breathing jagged. "I thought I had it stopped earlier."

"That's what the damned physicians are for, Tzal. What an idiotic thing to do—what's the point of—"

He dropped the last of his words in sheer frustration. His anger made little impression on her. Indeed, it almost seemed as if she forgot he was there. She kept clenching her teeth, then biting against her lip, hissing out slow breaths. She shook out her hand again and, finally, he realized that she was attempting to lower herself down to sit.

"For God's sake..." he muttered in Mashevi, hurriedly covering the distance.

She flinched when he tried to help her. But she let him do it.

"By salt, *why* didn't you just go straight to the physicians at the square?"

She lolled her head a little to peer at him with a hazy look. "You have more than a hundred men wounded far worse than this. So go right ahead. Tell one of your physicians—who can't do a tenth of what any common Trekoan midwife can—tell him that he has to leave his own men to come help a Shihrayan devil. Go on."

There was a lilt to her words that he did not recognize. Almost a slurring.

He took his water skin and shoved it into her hand.

"Drink," he said coldly. "At least let me look at it."

"I thought you said you were bad at this sort of thing," she said.

"I am."

He only knew what any man who had been on a battlefield was forced to know. Cleanse. Dress. Pray to God.

Peeling back the cloth didn't help much. It was half dried, muddy, and sticking to his fingers. Tzal jolted when he tried to feel around the actual wound.

"Stop, *stop*. What are you doing?"

"I'm trying to get a good look at it."

"You use water to look, not your *hands*."

Azetla stood up abruptly. He flung a Mashevi gesture of exasperation toward her which she understood well enough. His mouth filled with a bad taste and he spat it out. "Wait here." Foolish thing to say; she couldn't very well do otherwise.

Rahummi was already outside the walls, meeting with nearby villagers. No good looking for him. And Azetla's physicians were up to the elbows in the dead and the dying.

Because Azetla was the one asking, he was able to get bits of all that he needed. Everything he had seen Tzal or the midwives use. He was aware that this was not how he should be using his time—neither resting nor working—but he was also aware that no one else was going to do it. And it had to be done.

The task cooled him. Set his anger in a revealing light. It was easy to be angry at someone when he knew he would incur no consequence from the lack of control. Easy to be angry at someone who might make him lose something—someone who *was* the thing he could not so easily afford to lose.

Easy to be angry in exhaustion when you crest the hill to face the mountain. Easiest of all to be angry when afraid; when the fear forces you to be honest about truths you would rather avoid.

The stall seemed dark to him when he stepped back into it.

"Wake up."

She did not open her eyes. "I'm not asleep."

"Tell me what to do and I'll do it."

With a faint nod she attempted to shift her body to a better angle.

"Pull all the cloth far away from the wound. Cut anything that's stuck. Start washing half a hand above the hipbone. I think that's where the worst of it is."

Slowly, meticulously, he followed her instructions. Flushed the wound in the manner she prescribed. Got more water. Flushed it again. Gritted his teeth at her insistence on a third wash when there was so little water to spare. She was as exacting about this as he was about nearly everything else, so it shouldn't have bothered him as much as it did. She insisted he do everything aggressively, precisely, and told him not to hesitate so much.

Mostly he knew he was doing a bad job of it. Her jaw was tight the whole time.

Finally he flushed the wound with arak. That was the worst part. Her whole body went rigid, her breathing grew labored, and she pushed her forehead into the wood beam of the wall till the pressure left marks.

Dried. Salted. Bandaged.

She didn't want to drink after that, but he made her do it. Feeling the pressure of time, he took what little water was left and set to cleaning the gash on her head.

With the same firmness she kept demanding of him, he put his fingers to Tzal's bloodied left ear. Abruptly, she knocked his hand away with far more force than she probably had to spare.

"Don't do that," she said through her teeth.

"Do what?"

"Clean the *cut*, don't touch the *ear*."

"What's wrong with it?"

"Nothing. Just don't do that. It's a...it's not..."

She failed to find the word, which he had never seen happen before. She seemed to have confused herself as much as she had him.

He had the gash rigorously cleaned in a matter of minutes. Much of her hair was still filthy and matted, but the needful work was done. He never could see anything visibly wrong with the ear and twice he could not help brushing the edge of it as he worked. She tensed both times, as if from a very unusual pain, but gestured for him to just hurry and be done with it.

Azetla spent the rest of the day with dried blood on the edges of his hands. He was hardly the only one. The only reason he noticed it in the midst of the relentless flood of work and the driving rain of fresh problems, was because he would not have left anyone else alone like that, in a dark stall, in that condition. But he didn't think he could wisely entrust her to anyone else until Rahummi got back.

That was yet another problem.

Dark was falling and several hours passed before he had a chance to take any pause. A thousand things he had yet to do, but the ones without which he could not afford sleep were ticked off the ledger.

He gave greetings as he went through for rations, satchel slung at his side. He clasped hands and met foreheads with Joseph. Sarrez. And Brody. Wordlessly he set his hand to Colonel Peterson's shoulder and the man seemed to tolerate it. Ishelor and Lachlan each offered a sip from their cups: a Juniper victory tradition. There was cheer and sorrow drifting softly through the cold night air, touching these men here, and resting on those men there. Azetla was careful to give firm, warm answers and start no conversations. Two portions in hand—scant stuff tonight—he worked his way back to the east stables.

"You look worse," he said, setting his water skin into Tzal's hand.

"I had to get up to the piss-pot once. It didn't go that well."

He held up the clean, woven tunic he'd brought.

"Think you can manage it?"

It immediately became clear that she could not. No matter how slow and stubborn she was, the moment she had to lift her arm beyond a certain point, it pulled on the wound and she recoiled.

Carefully, Azetla cut off the last shreds of the old garment so that she did not have to pull them over her head. Even so, there were still bloody bits of cloth half-dried to her skin which had to be peeled off before the whole thing could be discarded. The chill air seemed to strike her hard, tensing every bare muscle in her shoulders and back. It took some time and finesse to put on the rough tunic. Azetla scarcely felt embarrassed—such was his focus on the task—and she did not seem to care at all—such was her state.

In the matter of wounds, there was little dignity to be had for anyone. He did his best.

Inadvertently, he did get a clear look at the strange scars on her back. Across her shoulders. Down her spine. Faintly discolored lines with skin pleated and pinched at the edges. He had but a glimpse of them when the Black Wren took her prisoner, but now he saw them in full. Purposefully made, those scars, but to what purpose?

"Eat what you can of this," he said once she had settled back against the wall, and her shaking subsided.

She nodded, but seemed to forget about the food after one bite. He remembered being badly wounded once and that strange lack of appetite associated with the pain. He hated how Joseph forced him to swallow food that felt like sand in the mouth. Then made him drink. Then made him eat again. All he wanted to do was collapse and let the world fade to black.

He also remembered something Mali said about how she liked to ask questions when she was tending wounds because it "helps me focus my thoughts and helps distract theirs."

He told Tzal to *keep eating*. He couldn't seem to take the command-like sharpness out of his voice. She made the attempt. Now a sip of the sour barley wine, he said. She took one small swallow and then several more. With the barley wine, she kept going. He grimaced; that was, of course, the traditional way to soothe oneself.

"What's the matter with your ear?" he said bluntly.

"What?"

"Your ear bothered you. When I tried to clean it—"

She rolled her eyes at him, gnawing slowly on one crumb of a bite.

"It's not...it's nothing bad. Touching the ear like that is not an insult or anything. Just a little jarring." She paused. At his gesture, she forced another bite.

"You're telling me a lot of what it *isn't*."

She gave the faintest shrug, as if it was too tedious to explain. But she tore another bite, a better one, and spoke through her teeth. "It's a Shihrayan way of...well it's a gesture of sorts. A custom. Used very *sparingly*."

"And what about those decorations on your shoulders and your back. That's also a Shihrayan custom?"

She swallowed the bite and peered at him for a while.

"No. That's a Shihrayan obscenity." She tilted her head. "As am I."

She said it with neither sadness nor anger, but rather the same tone of shrugging indifference she used when talking of fate, death, or her own life. He hadn't the least idea what she meant by that anyway; this was strange and uncertain ground for him. Perhaps he ought to tread carefully. Or, better yet, he ought to leave her be.

But he was so tired. So frustrated with her and in so many different ways. Strangely bereft of his native restraint.

"You can explain it better than that, by salt."

She gave up on the food and leaned her head back against the wall. For a while she stared at the carved oak beam that stood decorative sentry over the next stall. Then she closed her eyes. Azetla couldn't tell if she was refusing to answer, distilling an answer, or inventing one.

"Those marks are for blasphemy...among other things," she said at last. "It's called Kakht. And it's why I was sold into the lowlands. It shows that you've been put out from among your people. Out of everything. Beyond the reach of the gods. Beyond the help of family. Beyond all. And you can't earn your way back."

She laughed a little and it was a bleak sound.

"Because I tried." She finished the barley wine in a few long swigs.

So that was what Rokh Imal meant when he tried to explain to Azetla that she was a "devil even to the devils." A spark flew from flint, kindling took, and Azetla began to see clear so many things that had been dark to him about Tzal.

"Well your gods are worthless if they can't get around some marks on the skin," he said.

She smiled at him and laughed again. She laughed so often, more than most. But with so little mirth.

"You see, that's what *I* thought. The Gods are free to take what they want, and leave what they want, right? They aren't beholden to us. Why should they be beholden to *anything*? The idea was, if only you can catch them by the elbow and bend their ears, then you can make your case." She clicked her tongue loudly and shook her head. "No. Oh no. They won't let me get within screaming distance. Not before Kakht. And certainly not after it."

She was slurrish and trying to use wide gestures, which she shouldn't do.

"Tzal, be careful," he said sharply.

"Be careful, little devil," she mimicked the high-blood way Everson talked and made a smirking face just as he did. Then her expression changed and she said the same thing in perfect Mashevi. That miserable laugh again. "My Gods won't look at me to either raise me or put me down. But after all these years, and for no good reason I'm still alive. And it's not because I was *careful*."

"Tzal..."

"It was your God that did it. Yours. Do you hear me? By the hand of some foolish midwife who thought she was doing a kindness, he traced a mark on me that no one can see." She touched her wrist where the slave band was. "Not to keep me—obviously!—but just to make sure that my own wouldn't touch me. So that no one would. Maybe he just likes to age the blood before he drinks it and—"

"*Stop* that, Tzal, God-save-you!" Azetla spat.

She grinned.

"Oh, you think he will? Regardless, if he only plays tricks, I'll still take that game. A God who fights back is better than one who does nothing at all." She lowered her voice so that he almost could not hear her. "Just *do* something. Anything. I don't care."

Azetla held a quiet anger, which cut through him at a terribly strange angle.

"You can't talk about my God the way you talk about yours. He will take vengeance when he must, but He doesn't act out of spite like those demons of yours. He is holy."

The grin drained from her face as if she simply didn't have the strength to manufacture it any longer.

"I never know what you mean by that, Mashevi. In Shihra, 'holy' means deadly and dangerous. That which can only be approached with blood upon blood. Aadin was never so angry as when he was afraid I might touch holy things and bring disaster. Afraid for me, his bloody shikk, or for himself, I don't know. For all us Illaris, maybe. All of Shihra. Peace with Dimash and his kind is the most fragile thing in the world."

Aadin. Now that was a name she had not spoken before. She had mentioned a brother once. Only once. *Illari.* Who knew? *Shikk.*

Dimash. Sounds he'd never heard were dripping out of her mouth, hitting his ears, sprouting small, quiet questions he didn't know how to ask.

Probably he should have cut the barley wine with water. Barefacedly, he was glad he had not.

Tzal tapped the bridge of her nose where the skin was pinched from an old scar which ran up to the eyebrow, cutting through it at the inner edge.

"Aadin did this when he was drunk one time. I taunted a statue of Dimash while the blood and incense were still surrounding it. I think he thought we were going to die."

"Did he do that too?" Azetla pointed to another scar he had often noticed on the left side of her collarbone.

Confusedly, Tzal felt the area with her fingers and shrugged. "Maybe."

She gave him a clear smile that Azetla was tempted, for half a moment, to think was genuine. "But he didn't do this one."

She pushed up her sleeve and showed him her forearm. It was not a bad scar, the one Azetla gave her. He remembered it being a very steady, clean cut. He also remembered dragging her across the rocks afterward like a carcass. Cracked, bleeding lips. Dead eyes. Stones thrown at her as she walked in seemingly dumb silence. Sopped in the muddy river, yanked about like a dog, his men laughing anytime she gasped or choked. The skin beneath the ropes chafed till it bled.

"Do you hold it against me?" he said.

She laughed. "This?"

"Any of it."

She tried to shift her position, but winced and gave up.

"I don't have to hold anything, Azetla. Why would I? None of it means anything. None of it matters. Where I go, or who grabs my shoulder, or whether I win. Because the things I want to be changed won't be changed."

She faced her last shred of chuvia-filled bread as if it meant her ill. She forced another bite.

"The real question is do you hold all of that against *me*?"

She said it through her bite. In Mashevi. So, so perfectly. If he closed his eyes, she was from Rinayim.

"Yes," he said firmly.

If it troubled her, she did not show it.

"But sometimes, when I can, I set it down." And that did trouble him. The truth was he set it down as often as he dared before guilt made him take it back up again.

She made no response to this beyond a tired, skeptical look.

"Anything else before I go?" he said.

Slowly, words dragging, she answered, "Shoulder me to the piss-pot and back. Kick out the pallet. That should do it."

28

Seven years passed from the day of Kakht. They should have been easy years, for Aadin was free. Free from his determination to keep her alive. Free from the guilt of doing so. Free from his fear for her and his fear of her. Free at last to make his name strong in Shihra now that the sound of her was sheared off so completely from him.

But violent fevers came year after year, eating holes in his family and his tribe.

And the rains failed, year after year.

Hunger spread, violence simmered, scarcely contained. Those who were weak in mind or body were put out of their villages and left for dead. Many newborn children went into the fires of Dimash.

Not Aadin's children, though.

As it turned out, he found in himself Birai's dangerous stubbornness, and Sa'ased's quiet savvy. He told no one. He hid his wife Nitzma and acted midwife both times. As soon as she was well, they roamed in and out of the lowlands, scraping what they could from the Zarajein below them, thieving their own children from the jaws of Dimash by trick and by evasion.

Aadin could not forget Nitzma's words the night Izelan was born. Tired she was. Blissful. Mesmerized by the little girl in her arms in a way that he was certain his own mother never once had been. Birai was often protective, rarely affectionate.

"It's because of that sister of yours. I know it. She bled into you and cut things out of you. You defy even the Gods because of that shikk."

He did not answer. It frightened him to put such words to his actions.

In a bare whisper, eyes fixed on Izelan, Nitzma spoke. "And it seems I will too."

Izelan was nothing like Aadin's sister. She was a gentle, tender thing, the likes of which Shihra did not tend to create nor let survive. Aadin did not know how he could have made her, nor did he know how not to destroy her. All his life he had spent his anger freely on Zare and never learned to do otherwise. He was terrified of himself.

It was a ruthlessly hot day in autumn toward the end of that seventh year. The air was haze, the dust hanging about with no interest in settling down. Aadin was near the lowlands hunting, not for animals to steal—there was so little of that left—but for anything that the wilderness between Shihra and the lowlands could provide of its own after the first good winter in so many years. His family would eat tonight, he swore it by blood.

When he saw the Trekoan in the distance, walking with a horse on the lead, he was elated. A gift from the Gods. He would strip that body bare. He would dress as a Makar and go on a lowland trade with that horse, though trade was so risky these days. Pulling his knife he said to himself, today, I become a rich man.

The wind went out of him and he buckled to the ground when he saw who that "Trekoan" was. He kept the knife in hand; he was terrified. She might as well have been a ghost, or a real demon of hell.

Like a wounded man, he stumbled down the rocks to her. She had come nearly as far into Shihra as a horse could be brought. The world was too rugged and harsh beyond there.

They stared at each other in silence for a very long time.

She was so unfamiliar to his eyes. Certainly she could be no taller than last he saw her, but she seemed it. Full and strong and hale she stood, with no hint of famine in her frame. No sunken cheeks like his own. No gnawing trouble in the skin and the teeth and the joints. No languid posture of mere survival.

He could have slit her throat in jealousy, or brushed his fingers over her ear in loving joy and relief.

Of course he did nothing. His hands hung at his side, the knife barely in his grip.

"You can't be here," he breathed.

She looked at him strangely. "I know."

"The Zarajein have indulged you, I see," he said. "Weakened you. Made you soft like them."

"Ask me how many Qatlanis I've killed, then tell me that again. Is that all you can think to say, Aadin?"

It was. He was like a man thrown suddenly off-balance, standing now very still to make sure he'd righted himself and had his footing once again.

"You cannot go up. Not to Yaqil. Not even to Kivaj. They'll kill you. Then me. No one can know you're here."

"I won't go up. I'll stay in the no man's land. But if you let me...I'll help you."

This incensed him. Was his desperation so obvious? He raised his hand to cuff her as he would have in the old days. But he was a starving man. And she was much faster than she used to be. He couldn't even get his hands on her.

She gave him and his failure a stone-cold smile.

"No need for your pride to be offended. Just say 'no, Zare, I don't require any help...there is no famine here...I have all I need. I want nothing from you.'"

From her satchel she pulled dates and bread. Real bread. Aadin could do nothing but succumb.

How long was it she kept his family fed? Nearly two years. Living in between Shihra, South Trekoa, and South Makaria. Beg, borrow, steal, or even work—he was not sure what she did. He rarely asked. Gone for weeks at a time, returning laden with the survival of his family.

How strange that she could still make him laugh. Still provoke. Still play. He brought Izelan with him sometimes when he went down. She was a little afraid of Zare, and did not know who she was, but the shikk did not mind.

"Ah, she looks like Dotiya!"

It was true. She was very like Dotiya. Especially when she smiled.

The day she brought a cut of linen and a small goat, she also had curious news in hand.

"In Golmouth they're saying Maurowan soldiers are coming to South Makaria."

"Why?"

She bit the inside of her cheek and shrugged. "The rumors vary. But some say they will come all the way to Shihra."

Aadin shook his head. "They never go past Golmouth. If ever they dared to come up, we'll be the devils they think we are. Easy enough for you to do."

"Oh! I'll just kill hundreds of men with a turn of the tongue, ah? Kill them with only a savvy word or two?" She laughed.

"I bet you get a dozen at most, then you're in the dust. I get to kill the rest."

She tisked her tongue and passed the skin of water.

"No, I get twice that many and turn them around before you even get a chance. No man's land is mine, see."

He smiled. Because, of course, neither of them for one moment believed they would have to prove their words. It was supposed to be a jest. Gods, it was a jest.

Zare relaxed into his good mood as into cool shade. He was beginning to realize that she also knew hunger, just a different kind. And like the starving, she took every carelessly thrown scrap with relish.

Why was he so glad of her? Rather he should resent her. How dare she be so well and whole when all of Shihra was staggering? How dare she roam so free, when he felt his every step was dogged by the vengeful eye of the Gods and of his fellow Illaris? Why was it that all the blows glanced off of her, all the hardship slid from her back like water from oil?

Yet this curse was his blessing. What does it matter whether she belonged to foreigners or even a foreign god? What does it matter that she was exiled body and soul? She was his sister. And he was glad of her.

He allowed himself that thought.

His thoughts, he imagined, were his own. The Gods couldn't have them. Could they?

Oh but they could, as it turned out. And they would punish him cruelly, coming at him from an angle he did not expect, striking at him where he had never even realized he was vulnerable.

He was a day too late when he walked back into the village of Yaqil.

They had killed Dotiya in a mob. The village men discarded her, mangled almost beyond recognition, at the lintel of Sa'ased's door. As a warning. A threat. "This house is a source of curses and blasphemy. This is what is done to those who speak against the Gods. We gave quarter to the last shikk and look what happened. We will never do that again."

Birai and Sa'ased told him how it had happened. What Dotiya had done and said.

Birai was a mask of stone, Sa'ased parched with weary acceptance. But Aadin burned.

He had not known he could burn like this. They gave her ashes to wind and her spirit to the judgment of the Gods. And when Aadin was ready, he trekked the long way down, down, down, back to the shikk.

She smiled when he neared and walked quickly to meet him.

Never in his life had he wanted to hurt someone in every possible way. Never had he wanted so desperately to make his pain her own.

"Dotiya knew you were here?" he said through his teeth.

He saw a flash of guilt.

"Yes. She knew."

"Well you've killed her, you bloody shikk."

He was strong and fast this time. His hand went straight to her throat, and he slammed her into the rockface. Strangely, she did not fight back. Not at first.

"I—Dotiya didn't—"

Aadin threw a fist into her mouth. He didn't want to hear anything she had to say.

"Dotiya told everyone that the desert god watched over you all this time. Took hold of you. She said that our Gods are ash and bone, dead where their stones stand. She took that damned red bit of string—I didn't know she still had it!—and tied it on her wrist for all to see. She spit on the black stones, because she saw you do it once. So they killed her, Zare. They tore her to shreds. Because of you."

He struck her again. And again. And again. So many times. It had been so long since he had loosed himself thus and he felt the satisfaction, the compulsion, and the horrifying frenzy of it all at once.

She almost stopped a blow, almost caught his wrist, almost tripped him, almost got away from him. Now she really tried. But he caught her hard and threw her to the ground.

Without question, he could have kept going. Without question, he could have done to her exactly what had been done to Dotiya. He wanted to. He felt the capacity for it in his chest, in his body, in his fast-beating heart and the miserable, blinding fury. Yet his mind was reeling and confused because the anger was against her and on her behalf at the same time. She was the one who had cared for Dotiya so fiercely. She would have killed for Dotiya. Died for her. There was no question about that either.

Instead she had contaminated her with blasphemy and tossed her to the wolves. And what if she had done the same to Izelan? To Nitzma? Gods, she had already tainted Aadin's mind, hadn't she? She blinded him over and over again.

The shikk got up to her hands and knees, but no further. She rested her forehead against the ground as she had done with Kakht. She made no sound. No sound at all. But he saw her shoulders shake violently, her chest heave, her hands curl helplessly against the rocky ground. And he felt grief like thin streaks through his anger. She was to blame. She deserved it. And he was so afraid. He wanted to see her collapse. He wanted to strike her with all his strength. And he wanted never to have done it at all.

The truth was, he ought to have finished the job. But as if someone had rested a hand on his shoulder and spoke calmly to him, the blurred high of his anger began to break and clear. Slowly, purposefully, he began to suffocate the frenzy in his blood. It did not die easily.

He knelt next to her. Still she did not lift her head.

"If I really wanted to hurt you, I would tell you how bad it was. No merciful knife to the neck," he said, his throat raw, a terrible ache around his eyes and nose. "I don't even know what all they did to her. And I don't want to. So long as you know that it's on your head."

For a long time she did not move but for the occasional silent shudder, the occasional furling spasm of her fingers against the dust. Aadin was certain that if he raised his fist again she would not care, and she would not even fight back.

The light had faded when Zare's voice came up from the dust, mangled and raw.

"I don't understand why. Why she would do that. I didn't say those things to her. I swear by blood. None of it is true. I don't belong to any god. Or anyone. Or anything. Why would she say that? Why would you do that, Dotiya, why? I never wanted you to do that."

Her shoulders shook again.

"She said it because she believed it, even if you don't. You're so bloody careless. You don't even realize how your words strike. They go to the bone. And nobody can get them out."

He gripped her shoulder hard, fingers digging with the vestiges of his anger, and gave a jerk.

"Look at me, Zaraje."

Slowly, slowly, she lifted her head. Swollen face. Bloodshot eyes. Wet streaks cutting through the dust and bruises and blood. She sat on her heels, her whole body sagging, his grip torquing her shoulders back.

"The Gods go round you with a wide berth, Zare. But they don't go round us. They go straight through. You burn on while everything else around you goes to cold ash at your touch. You are *a shikk. Worse than I ever believed. You don't have to want to destroy us, you just do. And I won't have you destroy me and mine." His words scraped out with a guttural mix of hatred and misery. "Don't come back this time. Don't you so much as touch my foothills. I swear by blood and by all the Gods of Shihra, I will kill you myself. I will strike. And I will not stop."*

He stood up and dropped the satchel of food she had given him just days ago. Depending on her would end in death.

Aadin turned.

Walked south, up into his native heights.

When he heard the real shout of grief behind him, that blood-curdling sound, he closed his ears to it.

Days later, the northern soldiers proved the rumor true, pushing through the lowlands. And when the fear in Shihra reached its peak, the shikk proved her words true as well.

Almost as soon as the foreigners came, they were gone, turned away. "The Gods have saved us!" the people said.

No. The one the Gods hate has saved you and you will never know it.

Aadin was hollow and bereft. This time, surely, it was the end. This time, she would not come back. He didn't want her to. For then he would have to prove his words true also.

Izelan dogged Aadin's steps as he started toward the craggy trail. He let her follow a ways, but eventually peeled her off and bid her back with a quick brush of his fingers over her ear. Aadin had become wildly frivolous in showing affection ever since his daughter had come through a bad illness. Izelan did not seem the worse for it. Namesh was too young to notice.

There was no telling what this journey would bring so he refused to regret his tenderness.

It was two long days to the village of the Usarin, the great man of Shihra. In years past the Usarin was a nominal position, imposed by the priests and shamans to give some muscle to their words, omens, and declarations. This Usarin was of a different strain. He was devoted to the Gods Dimash, Bosa, and Konak, and he honored the shamans greatly. But he was a crafty, savvy sort and managed to collect the loyalty of tribes and clans with or without the edge of a knife. He was as close to a king as the Shihrayans would ever tolerate.

Strangely, it was Shihra's weakness that built him his power. When heads were high and arms were strong, no Shihrayan ever suffered such authority.

Before the chill dawn, Aadin had burned incense. He had cut his hand and put blood on one of the local stones. He wore his sword and bow, uncertain if he would dare to use them. For he knew why he had been summoned. If even the inner villages of Shihra in the high rocks had heard the rumors, no outer villager such as himself could feign deafness.

He wished he lived in his grandfather's time, when a Yaqili villager would have scoffed at any other tribesman bidding him "come." But Aadin lived in a time where the whole way of the world seemed to be cracking and crumbling and disintegrating from every direction so that whenever you turned it seemed the path was falling out from under your feet.

He could blame her for it. And he would be right.

Yet he found a remarkable calm in acknowledging his own role in the matter. Something like power, but less dizzy than that. As his parents should have done, he also should have killed her. He *chose* not to. No one forced him to take her under his wing, to shelter her, to hone her, to teach her to survive. She was some strange sort of metal, no doubt, and surrounded by fires he did not make nor understand. Perhaps he was not exactly the hand that forged her, but he was the hammer, and he had allowed himself to be.

When he approached the Usarin's dwelling he stopped and stared. It was neither like the thick animal-hide tents of those in the west, nor like the fitted stone huts of Aadin's own village. There were wood beams and clay and woven doors and small fittings of marble alongside the native obsidian. So much of it must have come from the lowland, but how had it come? Not through Yaqil, that was for certain.

Gaudy and foreign, it was.

He armed himself with his contempt for the Usarin, so that he would not be afraid.

The Usarin brushed his fingers from his forehead to his chin. Aadin did the same. Some Kopkas had begun the practice of bowing, but no one expected a rough Illari from an outer village to do such a thing. The Usarin stood, weapon-laden, next to the fire-pit. His frame was powerful as if the famine had passed him over, and he gave not the least secret away through his cold, brown eyes or the mouth set beneath the curled black and gray beard.

No seat was offered. No food brought forth. No pleasantries exchanged. Shihrayans did not like to conduct their affairs through such superfluous mediums.

"You asked for me," Aadin said.

"I asked for you *and* your father."

"The climb grows hard for him. Besides, I am the one who is responsible. Not he."

"Your whole family is responsible, Son of Sa'ased. Don't deceive yourself. What your mother brought out, your father held, and you raised. No one is innocent."

"What do you wish to say?" Aadin filled his voice with hardness. Steadied himself with anger. He already knew all that the Usarin would say.

"Months ago we all heard rumors of a little Trekoan feud waft up from the lowlands, like a breeze. Nothing for us to dwell on or fear, no? But now the dust is rising and the wind screams two words: '*Sahr*' and 'jackal.'" The Usarin paused as if he hoped to see Aadin flinch. "You must be glad, ah? Perhaps you hope your shikk is still alive?"

"Not at all. Being alive has never proved to be much of an advantage to her."

The Usarin laughed; an ice-cold sound.

"You Illaris like to think you are clever when you talk. You think because you know the lowlander tongues that you are wise, but I say it dulls you. You have their words and their leavings but none of their power and craft."

The Usarin paused as if nearing a thought that offended him. He ran his hand against his beard and set his sharp eyes on Aadin once again, his smile vanishing as if it had never been.

"So it was your shikk who turned the northerners away last year."

"Yes. With a sword, a bow, and no help from you."

The words were delicious to say. They fell from his mouth in a slow, honey drip, but with a sharp vinegar taste.

So wise in your own eyes, Usarin, but she did what you could not do—would never do. She made the myth of the devils in the crags seem true. We pretend to be mercilessly strong, but we have become so, so weak. And if the northerners ever find that out, it is the end of us.

Aadin need say none of these thoughts. They were the Usarin's also, though no doubt far more bitter to him than to Aadin.

"And why shouldn't she have done? The Gods never wanted her in the first place. Not alive or dead. But even that shikk can't make war from the grave. For some reason they did not kill her."

"No one ever manages it." Aadin almost smiled. "Not even you."

"It was my *son* who insisted on Kakht instead of death! Cradling his wound and lamenting his scar. He is very devoted to the Gods and the old creeds," the Usarin said, his tone softened. "So let that be a lesson to you, son of Sa'ased, young father that you are. If you give your children even a moment of your weakness, the result is folly. Better to keep all things plain, and hard, and simple.

"And simplicity is what I look for now," he continued, the sandy growl returning to his voice. "Three things have always protected us from the people of the lower desert. Our land with its brutality. Our Gods with their ruthlessness. And the stories the lowlanders tell of demons and beasts, which we have so carefully upheld."

"But your sister will bring Maurow down on our heads. She offends the Gods, and the reward for her blasphemy is drought and fever covering the land. That desert god—"

Both Aadin and the Usarin spat at the mention of the foreign God.

"—Doesn't he hold her reins?"

Aadin spat again. "No one and nothing holds her."

"Not even the jackal warlord?"

"My Usarin, we have to be careful not to take every drifting rumor at face value. Northerners believe many foolish things. They think that when a bad thing happens, a jackal has done it. Much like your own tribesman, they like an easy culprit."

The Usarin drew himself up sharply. "You defend her without qualm?"

"I don't defend her at all. I merely speak of the way things are."

"So do I," the Usarin said. "There is no circumstance in which the lots will ever fall in her favor. Of that, our shamans have assured me. And she provokes foreigners and foreign Gods *toward* us. You may have cleverly held back all you could from Dimash—yes, many have seen—but you will give us your shikk."

A cold wind cut through Aadin's chest. "What?" Slowly he shook his head. "How can I do that? I don't know where she is or what she does. I know as much as you do."

"You know her. You know the tongues. You know the nearby villages—"

"I have never been beyond Kitzlat."

"You don't think you can do it?" The Usarin smiled again. "I thought it would take you less time than it would one of us from the inner villages, but I guess we'll see about that."

Never in Shihra had Aadin received so coy a warning. So much hesitation to say the thing out loud: *kill her or let your family be killed*.

"That one always was a true shikk. A violence against the Gods by her nature and—" the Usarin began.

"I know what she is."

"Then you know she built her death-pyre with her own mouth."

Aadin chewed and gnawed on the Usarin's words, as well as the words he had not said. Perhaps it was only a few breaths, but it seemed to take all the world's worth of time to pull words from his tongue.

"I am at your service, Usarin. You do not need to send anyone else."

"Is that so?"

"I'll deal with her."

"Young man, I want the body. I want to see it. And I want coals to burn her inside and out. Nothing less."

Aadin loosed his jaw and nodded.

"I swear it. I'll slit her throat myself."

The Usarin nodded. "I believe you. Not because you are trusted. But because I know you have much to lose which you never ought to have kept in the first place."

The journey home was so strange to him. Stretched out slow with an unusual weariness, as if it would never end. And yet too short. Much too short.

That night, he lay chilled in his blanket in a rocky village, halfway home. He drank to warm himself, and then to be drunk, for his thoughts battered him mercilessly. Nitzma, Izelan, and Namesh would have to go into hiding. He did not yet know where, but the dreaded answer was somewhere in the lowlands in Makaria. Safer, but by no means safe.

He himself would have to go into Trekoa, speak their language, and pretend to be one of them till he found her. It terrified him.

It was never as easy for him as for Zare. The southernmost Makarish and Trekoan villages were a wall he had feared to cross. It seemed impossible to go beyond them and still be Shihrayan. Impossible to go beyond them and ever come back.

By blood, Zare, why am I ever surprised at you being what you've always been? Why do I keep being turned over like a lamb on a spit? Why is this never over, you bloody shikk?

There was no point in cursing her with his breath. He could speak no worse over her than what had already been said to her face. Everything he thought about her was always being both fulfilled and turned on its head at the same time.

That desert god was a cruel and vicious trickster. What did he want with Shihra? What was the point of all this?

The old, blasphemous thought coursed through his mind yet again. The thought that even Zare herself did not believe. The thought that, spoken aloud, got Dotiya killed.

His sister belonged to that ruthless, enemy god. Whether as a cursed vessel to be used then cast off or a blessed one to be refined and taken up, he did not pretend to know. Somehow, both notions horrified him equally. The first consumed him with the image of a rag-doll, violently shaken in the teeth of a dog, pulled apart thread by thread. The latter was nothing but fire. Holy, fearsome fire. Burning all the way to the bone, and beyond.

It was almost like a vision. And it was, perhaps, a choice.

In the morning, clear-headed, Aadin bloodied his hands on the local stone, full of guilt, trying to scrape his shameful notion away on the sharp, shimmering obsidian. But he knew full well that no amount of blood and incense would ever wash it out of his mind.

29

"Wake up...wake *up!*"

Tzal didn't even remember going to sleep. She had been so uncomfortable, so hesitant to move or shift her position. Without opening her eyes, she could feel that it was still dark out. She could smell that she was near horses and pine, which disoriented her greatly. The voice, too, she knew well enough, but her mind would not produce the name or features for her.

"Do you hear me, Sahr? Get up. Let's go."

A hand fell hard on her shoulder. She braced to be shaken, but was not. The face that looked down, when at last she pried her eyes open, was Joseph Radabe's. She was in a stall. In Hidud. After victory. And she did not feel strong or steady at all.

She must have had a rather blank look because Joseph snapped twice at her face.

"Do you understand a word I'm saying?" He sounded angry, but that was his way with her. Her mouth was cotton dry and her tongue thick with a terrible taste. It was going to take her a minute to produce a single word.

"Listen, Sahr. Rokh Sadri Alremma of Numayr is here. *Right now.* All sorts of important Trekoans with him. They're being escorted to Azetla's headquarters. And Rahummi is still out west with Rokh Jumna."

The mist of her mind cleared suddenly, as if struck by the full sun. She had the sense not to bolt up from the pallet, but she got to work trying to get her arms beneath her to pry herself—slowly, gingerly—up from the ground.

"Alremma is the one you told us was so important, right?" Joseph said.

She could only nod.

Apparently she was not moving fast enough. Joseph reached down and pulled her firmly to her feet.

"Can you walk?" he said. "Can you stand on your own?"

She nodded again, though she wasn't entirely certain that was true. He had to help her with her sandals and her left foot wasn't particularly fond of taking weight. She half hobbled and was half dragged out of the stalls.

He peppered her with questions about the Numaryi Rokh, which she tried to answer in whispers and croaks. Finally she gestured toward his water skin, desperate to soften her tongue and soothe her throat. Joseph hesitated. He didn't make a point of it but he never broke his bread or shared his cup with her except through Azetla.

Yet, after a moment, Joseph grabbed his water skin and pushed it into her hand with aggravation, pulling it away when she'd had not half enough.

When they reached the lamplit headquarters room, Joseph whispered in her ear. "This is what you're good for. So don't you *dare* fail him."

Azetla seemed confused at her arrival. He gave Joseph such a look. But there was no time for her to understand it. Rokh Sadri Alremma came into the tent with all the pomp and circumstance of a little king who nevertheless knew his great value. He could make a historic peace that would lead to a historic war. He could hold a jackal in thrall. He could make the whole world part for him as the waters part for a boulder in the river.

The men began to exchange their greetings and their speeches. Tzal could not have told a soul what either of them said, despite every single one of their words passing directly through her mouth. Every muscle, and every bit of her mind that she could spare, was concentrated on the act of remaining upright on her own two feet. Indeed, her tongue seemed to work ahead of her mind, so that she approved of the correctness of her words only well after they had departed her mouth.

Weeks before, she had told Azetla how he should treat with the Numayri Rokhs in the event that they came to make peace. Numayri customs were different from Saqiran in ways both subtle and dramatic; they tended to bewilder most. Tzal always found them harder to please and harder to read. They had spent so many decades walking strange, erratic lines between the power of Qatlan and the power of Saqiran, between the service of tribal Gods and the service of the Mashevi God, between Maurowan influence and their own cherished independence.

They were the only tribe who held regular councils. Whatever Azetla achieved or failed to achieve with Rokh Alremma, the result would be carried out to the whole tribe of Numayr, the last and strongest ally of Qatlan.

Yet there Tzal stood, unable to discern if her words were even half as clear and strong and elegant as she needed them to be, or if she was like a mere drunk convinced that they spoke profundities while actually offering nothing but babble. No one in the room gave any indication that she was faltering. Her mouth felt and tasted like it was using a fine central Numayri lilt. Certain gentling or strengthening of phrases came naturally to her. So far so good. It had always been her favorite dialect.

As a soldier hopes that all his drilling will make his muscles do what his mind has missed, Tzal hoped her tongue worked for her through this fog.

The first indication of a problem was when she felt a sharp pressure against her back. Joseph and Sarrez had both drawn up behind her, she realized, to stop her from tottering. Her knees locked out and she had to try and loose them without going down. That was the first time she stumbled over her words. A fierce grip pinched her arm, both to hold her up and to jar her back to clarity. She blinked hard. Righted her legs and her mouth. On the meeting went.

On and on and on. Saying all their words felt like a feat of physical strength, as if she was shoulder to stone, pushing her voice forward with every muscle in her back.

Azetla did exactly what he was supposed to do both in what he said—he remembered all her advice, applying it in his own way—and in how he carried himself. He never looked back to perceive her expression or check his understanding against her. He behaved as though she was not there but for her voice.

Joseph and Sarrez stayed directly behind her, a wall that jabbed if you leaned on it too hard. How subtle they were, she did not know, but they kept the black from closing in on her vision, kept her focused, and she was pretty sure there would be bruises to show for it.

Dawn was edging through the cloth door when she began to notice the drumbeat in her ribcage, so painful and loud, it became almost the only thing she could hear. The delay of words from ear to mouth grew. She was sure it was noticeable now. Azetla quickly brought up the matter of horses—no Numayri pact was ever complete without an exchange of them—and gestured to the door. How he managed to so deftly move from mid-negotiation to final alliance, she barely understood. She doubted it was her finesse; it must be his own. The last words she remembered hearing were, "No, my Rokh.

Saqiran will not be Maurow's hand to you or anyone. It will be its own." She was not even sure she translated them.

All she knew was that Azetla left with the Rokh of Numayr. When the cloth door dropped behind them, her legs buckled and she dropped, too. Two firm pairs of hands caught and dragged her to the back wall. Someone put a water skin in her hand. There wasn't much and she gulped it so desperately, she choked on it. That hurt her whole chest like fire. The wound throbbed as if it was freshly made, but Tzal could not muster even the desire to check the bandaging. If it bled through, she couldn't do a thing about it.

She slept and didn't sleep. She heard everyone leave the room, and heard shoutings and work going on outside. She felt the sharp, cold wind come in through the doors and windows, whipping the cloth around. The light increased bit by bit. But never once did she open her eyes. Everything happened at an unreachable distance.

The pain in her side ebbed, but never left entirely. There was hunger, after a while, but no strength or will to do anything about it.

Perhaps hours had passed when she became aware of whispering voices in the room, and then she understood that the voices had been there for quite some time, hovering over her like a canopy.

"I know you like to think you have a handle on everything, that you know everything—"

"That's not—"

"But don't for one *second* tell me you think you could have done that on your own."

"I never said I could do it on my own, I only said she was not fit to stand. And I wasn't wrong."

There was a brief pause. Their voices, which had been increasing in volume, quieted.

"First of all Azetla, you *were* wrong. The Sahr lasted long enough to hand the man over to you, properly handled. Alremma was so eager to be offended by you, desperate to take your words the wrong way. The Sahr just didn't let him. No chance it ended like this without that devil's tongue. And you know it."

"Yes." A heavy breath. "I know it."

The conversation seemed to fade from her a little, or she from it. Many other matters seemed to be folded in, but they did talk on, and it was not always peaceful talk. She felt the tension of it in her bruised body. They seemed to have sat down after a time—their voices rested low to the ground—and they ate their meal between terse responses. The smell of the food drew her more and more toward consciousness. Some of it was for her, she hoped, and soon she would muster the effort, lift her head and take it.

"...But do you even remember how it was?"

Azetla's voice came very low. "Of course I remember."

"I don't think you really do. I used to get so angry with him. Thought he was being too hard on you. Too ruthless."

A tired, breathy laugh from Azetla. "It's difficult to imagine *you* thinking anyone could be too hard on me."

"That's kind of my point. The unfairness of it was hard to watch. I went to him about it."

"You did?"

"Azetla, you were still so young at the time. He was asking so much of you. Also, now that I think about it, Eyinda was still alive then. Maybe I was a gentler creature in those days."

There was another silence which Tzal did not comprehend until she heard whispered Maurowan and Mashevi words speaking peace over those passed away.

"I told him he was running you ragged. Showing no mercy. I was afraid he would embitter you, drive you mad, or that you would just...break in two."

"I nearly did. But I never knew you *saw* that." The bewilderment in Azetla's voice made him sound something like a boy, talking to someone like a father.

"Of course I did, but I couldn't *tell* you. I supported the Captain in all ways, especially to your face. But it seemed unsustainable to me. At the time, he would not even defend you or protect you, which meant that, for the most part, no one else could. In the end, he convinced me that it was all for the best and that he did it for your sake."

Tzal was truly awake now, and the words no longer floated above her, half-caught, half-lost. She put every one of them between her teeth to taste. And kept her eyes closed.

"He said that if he showed even the least bit of mercy or favoritism, then it would make the others hate you all the more. They'd find an excuse to slit your throat. So he gave you more responsibility, more work, more weight, enough to make you stumble. All so that no one would envy your position. No one could possibly say 'look how that crafty jackal has manipulated himself into power and privilege. Look how he lives off the fat of the battalion.' The Captain never let up until your place was firm, and *everyone* had seen you suffer for it. He made his right hand a harsh, painful place to be so that it was a place you were allowed to be."

There was more silence. Shuffling about. Someone stood.

"My point is—"

"I understand your point, Joseph."

"Do you?"

"From every angle."

There was a weary, head-bowed sound to his voice.

"Look, Azetla, I'm only trying to hold you to your own standards."

Azetla scoffed lightly.

She heard more movement. The clapping of shoulders which she knew accompanied the touching of foreheads. One left the room, and she knew it was Joseph. Azetla's movements and breathing were too familiar to her to be mistaken.

Tzal opened her eyes. Azetla was quick to notice. He had a ledger resting in his right hand. With his left, he gestured to the food that had been set beside her. Carefully, one inch at a time, she brought herself to a nearly comfortable seated position. She was able to see now that she had not, in fact, bled through her bandage. The air was cold, and she felt it, but she did not shake, nor did she feel feverish. Her thoughts were far clearer than they had been during the negotiations.

Looking at the light from beyond the cloth door she realized she had lain in the back of the room for several hours. While some of her sleep had been fitful, much of it had been true and deep, and she simply had not known it.

All good signs.

She ate slow to make it last and was not entirely satisfied. She knew that rations would be like this for some time. Azetla kept his eyes on his ledger till she was finished, his brow knitted tight all the while.

"Alremma took peace with him?" she said.

"Peace and six horses."

Tzal chewed on that.

"None of them were Sanchi horses, were they?"

"No."

She tilted her head back and forth.

"Well..." he said.

"He took you a little. But not a lot. It'll hold for now."

"For now?"

"Numayris are fickle."

And that was as many words as she had just then. She emptied her water skin, then gestured toward the privy alcove. Azetla nodded tiredly. He shouldered her there, turned away, shouldered her back, then helped her turn the lump of saddle blankets she had been resting on into something like a pallet.

His jaw was tight and working, as if he had any number of things to say, but none of them rose above the threshold of his tongue. Tzal recognized herself as one of his many problems. An inconvenience. More or less useless just now. So she too had nothing to say.

Azetla knelt down and gathered up his things, putting his reed paper and his ledgers in order, then placed them carefully in his satchel. He took his empty water skin and hers, standing to leave. He looked for all the world like the quiet scribe of no one in particular; the blood of yesterday was replaced with ink, his satchel was the kind only scholars and scribes ever wore, and he, like all who followed him, had no finer clothes now than before all this began.

He handed her a few sketch maps. "See if these need improvements. I'll have Durad draw up new ones if so."

She looked up at him, eyes narrowed. It was almost an insult. A pittance. A profoundly needless task.

"When should the dressing be changed again?" he said briskly.

"First thing in the morning."

He nodded and left. She brushed her fingers over the reed paper, then lay her head back with a deep sigh. *What good is a devil that can't give you anything?* All curse, and no reward for tolerating it. All she could do was rest, and it was the one thing she could not afford to do. She would have to find some way to assert her utility. In the morning, though. The stone-heavy weariness took her as soon as she lay her head down.

She might have heard Azetla when he came back, but just barely. The scuffle of boots, a whisper of prayers, then nothing else but night.

30

James Sivolne stared at the map on the table long after all the others had been dismissed, till all the lines and darts and troop markers blurred in his vision. Like a man caught up in a river, hurtling toward some great falls, he was always passing some fresh point of no return, each time convinced it was the true and last one.

The courier arrived with news of Hidud only yesterday. A year ago he couldn't have found Hidud on a map, now he was being told it was the key to holding the whole southern desert. And it seemed true enough. He knew that Molton and Pardish West would soon follow, succumbing like brush to a wildfire, and then the army would climb its way north, to the very door of Maurow: Wadi Kilsayn was the final road, Darton outpost the final gate.

The Mashevi certainly knew how to use his momentum, how to run roughshod over the worries and fears of others. The cunning ones always knew to ask forgiveness rather than permission.

In truth, the jackal did neither of these things.

Among the high-bloods and to his face, the soldiers were "the Corra's army" executing "the Corra's rebellion." But James was not as naïve and removed as others believed him to be. Among the common people and all the Trekoans, it was "the southern rebellion" and—perhaps more cautiously—"the jackal's army."

And who could dispute it? Qatlan shattered. Cozona and Hidud consumed. The tribes gathering in droves.

Azetla was doing things James could never have done, nor ever imagined doing.

To each according to his ability. James would not say he had no fear of the situation—he had a great deal—but he no longer felt like a man in the hull of a boat trembling at the wind and waves. He'd grabbed an oar as best he could. Come time, he might even take his turn at the rudder.

Because without James Sivolne, Corra of Maurow, none of it could have begun, nor could it continue. That was what Verris liked to say, anyhow. James wavered in the degree to which he believed it. How slow he had been to realize it was less a matter of believing it was true and more a matter of making it so.

Ten thousand more Maurowan troops were inbound from the Makarish coast. That would be the last such contribution from James' days of court and connection. Then it was using the tools at hand, for there would be no more to come.

What he was supposed to be doing, at this precise moment, was preparing a neutrality agreement for negotiations with Tus and Nurica. This was why he stared at that feverishly overactive map with such a spirit of procrastination. The negotiations were to be his alone; the Mashevi would have no part in them. That was a good thing, Everson said. Wise to have ropes tied to something other than the Mashevi.

Everson minced words about this part, but James understood it perfectly well.

When the likeliest thing happened, and all turned to failure, the jackal would be put forth as the villain and James would catch that hidden rope and slip quietly down to Tus for a life of comfortable exile. James began to understand, however, that the mental comfort of having a net should he fall was part of the problem. In some vague way, he had always known this about himself.

Probably the Mashevi was the way he was because he had no escape. The only way out for him was through, shoulder to stone, without rest. In their few conversations, James saw this clearly and marveled at it. Surely the Mashevi didn't want to die, but he was willing to regard himself as dead already, so that he might be free to act. Death would not be the astonishing thing. Life would be.

James had seen this before. In some of the jackals that had their throats slit on the Red River day. And in a few of the high court Mashevis who used to come to Piarago. They had that same manner, that same look in the eye. The look that said, "*kill me if you want, but you will not have taken from me what I really value.*"

James, on the other hand, had spent most of his life avoiding minor discomforts, and had never once felt like a free man. In fact, the freest he'd ever felt was when he made a wild leap and put Azetla at the head of the Black Wren battalion. That had earned him such high reward coupled with such tremendous risk, he scarcely knew how to judge the matter.

Shoving the map aside, James set down to form the terms of the negotiations with Tus. It was the thing that had to be done, so he might as well just do it. He was equal parts relieved and irritated by the knock at the door, breaking his concentration just as he was thinking of getting into the meat of things.

"What?" he said with a sigh.

Colonel Everson pushed through the door with a faint smile, eyebrows raised.

"Well. You sent for me, I suppose," he said in that perpetually sly tone of his.

"Oh." James had completely forgotten about that. "What took you so long?"

"I only just returned from Ustiral."

Everson gave a full, formal bow, then proceeded to make himself comfortable. His eyes scanned the map, askew on its surface, and all James' half-finished work. Since James was not interested in Everson's type of conversation, and he was very tired at the moment, he decided to head all words off at the pass.

"Do you trust the Mashevi?"

Everson blinked and laughed a little as if a five-year-old had asked him the question.

"What do you mean by that?"

"Exactly what I say. It's a simple question."

"Forgive me, Your Highness, I disagree. It is a very complicated question indeed. Do I trust his military tactics, his strategies? Do I trust his assessments and logistical decisions? Do I trust his prowess in a battle? Do I trust that he knows how to wield soldiers and peoples and devils? Yes. Without a doubt. But...do I trust that he is ours to keep?"

Everson smiled. "Of course not."

"How can you say that so calmly?" James burst out. "It is a matter of life and death!"

"I am calm about it because we are still a long way off from the point of separation. We need him. He needs us. The key is to relinquish our need ahead of him...to slip off the horse while it is still running, as soon as we have reached our destination."

James regarded this and grasped the truth of it. But Everson made it sound simple as a snap of the fingers when, in fact, it would require insight and agility and precision and any number of things James had always believed—and always been told—he held in short supply.

"Your Highness, you keep forgetting that you hold his life in the palm of your hand. However important his place, however much the soldiers look to him for now, it all remains precarious. We have many excellent officers who would gladly replace him, and even a small cadre of soldiers who still resent him and would not miss an opportunity to undermine him. He knows this. You must make yourself know it too. Let it give you confidence in your dealings with him, and a high head."

"I can't afford to undermine him."

A look of exasperation flashed across Everson's face, but he cooled it quickly with a languid smile. "Of course not. Not yet. You miss my meaning."

"No, I don't Everson. You want to say that I have a knife in my boot, ready to draw, and that I should remember that, even though we both know I can't use it yet. You think yourself coy, but that's all plain as day to me, and to him. No one is fooling anyone. I just think no good can come of it; everyone trusts him—all right, Everson, *nearly* everyone—while I'm nothing but a name to them. And he can never trust me, for all the reasons you just said. Wouldn't it be more...solid if, well...if..."

The words would not come. *If I were actually trustworthy? If I could actually keep my word?*

Everson adopted his most wry and patronizing tone, which James loathed, but which he also knew signaled something worth hearing. Everson always spoke lightly, but thought deeply, and always meant a great deal more than he said. Crafty as a jackal, he was.

"Your Highness, do you actually think Azetla is telling *you* the whole truth, so that you owe him some form of honesty?"

James did not like to admit his thoughts, so he bit on them. It was hard. Whenever he spoke to Azetla, he always felt that the man was speaking the truth from his bones. But only a fool would think that.

"Azetla Rinayimi, he calls himself. So he obscures his name by covering it with his place of birth."

James knew that, but...

"He obscures his birth by pretending to be a commoner, which is clearly nonsense."

"He never claimed to be common, he only—"

"Lies of omission are still lies, Your Highness."

"Well what good would it have done him to claim his scholarly background, or priestly family, or whatever it is, if he was bound by a twenty year debt of service? It's not as though it would have helped him."

"No, it would not."

Everson looked at James for a moment and when he spoke again, the timbre of his voice was different than James had ever heard from him.

"I think he is something much more dangerous than a liar, Your Highness. But I also think the very thing that makes him dangerous makes him invaluable. I think he wants Riada dead far more than you do. Let him reach that mark."

James shuddered at this one thought he always avoided and shucked it to the side. With a wave of his hand, he dismissed the Colonel.

He swirled Everson's words around in his mouth, like a tonic, and swallowed them. He wondered if Verris had the same thoughts. Would he give the same advice?

And if James confronted him and spoke to him like a man, what would Azetla say? "*Let us shake hands until we must draw swords*"? The Mashevi was always so bloody convincing in the moment. One wanted to trust him.

What a strange thing for *all* these to have pinned their fates to him. It was madness. They each meant to use him to their respective advantages, he knew, but then *why* ply him with speeches on strength and courage, when it was his weakness that they all found so damned useful thus far? It was beyond him.

Long after Everson left, James remained slumped in his chair. He put his head in his hands and wished by all the Gods that the pelting, pummeling thoughts that exhausted him were *his own*. He wished that he knew how to sift, until all that was left was fact and sense and right.

For he was soon to start shearing men off like limbs. This was how emperors were made.

31

Lord Artur Noben trudged to the Imperial training fields like a man going to the gallows. He did not know why the Emperor had summoned him there—there were a thousand likely reasons in such dire times—but it meant a weary, painful morning, and weeks to recover from it. He was a young man no longer.

Emperor Riada was already in full kit, with light armor and wooden swords. His eyes were feverishly bright as they were when he was either exultant or angry. Today it was anger; Artur knew that much. The events in the southern desert left Riada greatly disturbed, and all Piarago with him. In some circles of nobility, thriving solely on rumors, the talk was practically apocalyptic.

Artur stood at a distance from all this. Of course the rebellion should be swiftly destroyed. But the idea that anyone—least of all the Corra James and a few tribal fighters—could even so much as lightly bruise the great Empire of Maurow? Well, it was absurd. Only a child and a fool would allow themselves to be frenzied by such things.

Now, Emperor Riada was not exactly frenzied, and he certainly wasn't a fool. But he had ascended to his throne as a youth and, in some ways, he was a young man yet. Artur had reached beyond his sixtieth year of life and found that, after three decades of advising emperors, he was growing tired and detached.

Yet one does not dismiss oneself from the divine Emperor's service of one's own volition. And Artur was a loyal Maurowan. He would serve until he was dead. How many times had he said that to himself as a young man with such bravado? Now he only thought it, and that with weary bitterness.

"Good morning, Your Highness," Artur said with a bow. He took his time donning the kit and tried to feel out the circumstance gently. "What news from this morning's council?"

Perhaps that was the reason for this punishment disguised as play. Artur spent the morning smoothing away some trouble for his eldest son, who had been in South City. The boy had grown unsatisfied with the sorts of pleasures that could quietly be brought to his door, so he began to cast a wider net. It was not Maurowan custom to begrudge an important young man expansive or even unusual desires, but one had to be careful not to anger the wrong people; southerners, for instance, were extremely particular about such matters. Peace must be kept, as well as appearances.

All very trivial and tedious, but Artur had missed the impromptu council thereby. He did not often do that.

"Pardish West has succumbed," Riada said. "Hurry up, Noben."

Artur made a motion of hurry, but was ready no faster than he meant to be. "Well we knew it would as soon as we heard about Hidud. Molton and the Oavi grove can be assumed. They are only picking up the carcasses that are already on the ground, and calling each one a kill."

"You make so light of it," Riada said. He gestured impatiently for Artur to come near. The Emperor always liked to begin with light, classic sequences, so that he could have his say first. Pine and Hare to warm up. Then Flame and Fox to really get the blood going.

"You already have twenty thousand men en route from Isvatya and Kouris to join the thirty thousand in Darton. Your brother's rebellion will wash out as with a flood and no one will even remember it happened.”

“You’re glad.”

Riada rapped Artur’s shield to begin the sequence.

“Your Highness?”

“You think this proves that you were right. That I should have poured our efforts into soldiers rather than ships. Strengthening what we have rather than trying to add to it.”

Watch your words. Artur swung for the shoulder, retreated to take his blow, then moved forward again. Slow and lax.

“No, Your Highness. This proves that your concerns about the Trekoan Rokhs were wisely placed. I think the shock of it all is James.”

Sword strike, shield strike. Parry. Push. Riada wasn’t hitting too hard yet. Still warming up.

“It’s only a shock if you actually think James did this himself. It makes perfect sense if he has fallen into the hands of someone who knows exactly what they’re doing,” Riada said. “Stop with those limp strikes. I can’t do the sequence properly if you don’t.”

Artur threw a bit more muscle into his next blow, but he knew to conserve his energy for later. Downward strike, parry, upward strike. Retreat. All at a rhythm that used to be so easy for him. His knees and his back no longer enjoyed this.

“I only meant I’m surprised James went along with it. Of course it is Lord Verris who yanks him about.”

“Callan said otherwise this morning.” Riada changed to the Fox sequence without calling it. Light on his feet, more aggressive now in his movement. “He said the early rumors grow more and more consistent. It really *is* a jackal who has James by the neck. A jackal who has gathered all Trekoa into his hand. And the sword he draws to do so? *Our* Sahr devil.”

After a long advance, Raida took the retreating posture. “Move faster this time, Artur.”

Artur was warm now, and felt stronger. He repeated the advance three times. He had heard that rumor about the jackal and held it at a distance like everything else. Jackals were an exhausting topic for Artur, for ever so many reasons. He did not like it when Riada's eyes turned upon Masheva. He became dangerously fixated.

"James has to dig his allies out of the rubbish heap, Your Highness. But, yes, it is a hard thing that we lost that bloody Sahr to him."

Riada bit back with sharp, unexpected blows. Artur defended and returned; his shoulder began to ache through the shield.

"Do you know what *issar-na* means, Artur?"

"No, Your Highness."

"Left-handed." A hard downward strike. "In Makarish." Harder. "An insult." Another fierce blow, with no place in the Flame pattern. The Emperor's voice was calm, but his movement was relentless and violent. "And it is what the South Makars call this Mashevi." Riada struck again and again, finally driving his shield at Artur and knocking him to the ground.

Riada bent over Artur, wooden sword aimed at his throat.

"We've cracked open South City's mouth well enough by now. And how long was this rumored jackal in the Black Wren? Oh, a dozen or fourteen years, they say. From Rinayim. A scribe, or raised by scribes."

Worry skittered through Artur's chest, but he made no answer. He clambered painfully to his feet, knowing that Riada would not tolerate withdrawal until he was satisfied. Artur tried to return the same sequence in kind—that was what Riada always claimed he wanted—but there was no real exchange now. Riada parried everything, and struck to bruise and jar till at last Artur stumbled to a knee.

Again the wooden sword jabbed into his neck.

"So, old man, is he alive?"

Artur's arm suddenly lost all its strength. Sword and shield hung limp in his hands.

"What?" Artur said breathlessly.

Riada struck down so that Artur was forced to block.

"*Is he alive?*"

Gods. Why was this bloody mess being brought back *now*? Artur thought he had it all cleaned up, no trace left. Tread carefully.

"You mean Aver?"

"Don't play coy, Artur."

"Your Highness, as far as the public is concerned, Samuel Aver *is* alive. So he haunts us from the grave, flickering in shadows everywhere. That's the price we pay for letting the Mashevis hold onto that husk."

"Get up," Riada said, his voice low, his brow deeply knitted. "Pine."

Once again, Artur rose.

"Go ahead. Burn the husk, Your Highness. No need for us to be duped by our own lie," he said, raising his arm wearily, hoping he had salvaged things. He tried to set a measured pace, to bring Riada back down, to calm him, to sate him. Strike, step, parry, side-step.

"I will burn it," Riada said. "But strange to have to kill him twice. Once in private, then again in public. And strange that this Black Wren jackal should cast such a familiar 'shadow' as you put it."

"Not strange at all, Your Highness. There are jackals out there—all different factions—trying to use the name of Samuel Aver to gain power for themselves. If it sounds like him, they certainly *mean* for it to sound like him. I'm not the least bit surprised."

A mask of thought fell over Riada's face as they worked, at a strong pace, through Hare and Willow. Though growing weary in body, Artur began to let his mind relax. He had answered wisely. The Emperor focused on his stance and his strokes, remaining silent.

He would not lose another emperor to this obsession. Riada's father had flinched at the name Samuel Aver, and for no good reason. Writhing under the fear of that jackal long after the boy was killed, frenzying his mind with conspiracies, seeing omens everywhere, sealing his fate with drink and worse poisons. How many times did the old Emperor send for prophets and seers and mediums of every stripe, seeking from them some bit of comfort—and those damned charlatans set him off instead. Vague they sometimes were, but always they left room for his suspicion that a jackal would be his ruin.

Artur should have slit every last one of their throats.

How fiercely he hated this whole subject. It should have stayed dead and buried. Whoever this jackal soldier was, if he tried to stitch that old name onto his arm thinking it would gain him power, he was sorely mistaken. Riada would raze Masheva to the ground if that name rose from the grave and took on flesh, no matter who carried it.

This jackal was not Aver. He simply was not. *Tell yourself again, Artur. Tell yourself a thousand times if you have to. It isn't him. Riada will not believe it if you don't.*

Artur adjusted his grip on the wooden weapon; his hand was growing tired, his wrist locking up. He nearly dropped the sword twice.

For a moment, it seemed his Emperor had pity on him. He paused. Tossed the wooden sword casually to the ground. Looked at Artur a while. Then spoke in a hard, heartless voice.

"Flame, now. Fast and proper," he said, drawing his real sword from its sheath. "And you will answer every question I ask. In full. On your life."

Grief more than fear washed over Artur. *I would have spared you this, my Emperor.*

Artur dropped the wooden sword and pulsed his grip to revive the taut muscles. Drew his sword. And braced.

"Did my father tell me the truth? Did he call for Samuel Aver's execution that day?"

A high feint. Artur moved toward it, as he was meant to.

"Yes, Your Highness. He did."

A blow toward the ribs, greeted by the shield. Calm and measured.

"And that night, did King Keved Aver hand the boy over freely?"

"Yes. He barely even hesitated. It was framed as a test of loyalty, but the truth is the boy—and the name—were causing him real trouble by then. I almost wonder if he was relieved to have the excuse to get rid of him."

Riada nodded. He ran swiftly through the next four strokes of the sequence, saying nothing. He was steadier now, less ferocious.

"And how was it done, Artur?"

"It was meant to be just as on the Red River festival, clean and quick, blood to Serivash. In secret though, not on the dais, obviously."

"Meant to be?" The blow came toward the neck, clean and quick. Artur's block was sluggish and Riada did not like that—he pushed Artur back and made him do it again.

"It did not go to plan, Your Highness."

"By Serivash, spit it out, man."

"One of Keved's men betrayed him. The boy escaped, soldiers on his heel. You may not remember, but that was the night of the great west district fire. Aver ran straight into it. All the soldiers who pursued him were caught in the flames and died."

Riada suddenly stopped the sequence and lowered his sword. He stepped forward, his gaze all hunger, all fire, ready to consume every word and likely scorch the speaker.

"Was there a body?"

Artur almost flinched.

"Yes, Your Highness. Only—"

"Only *what*?"

"It was badly burned."

"You mean to say it was unrecognizable," Riada said coldly.

"Yes, Your Highness. But the right size, the right build, and all the right accouterments—bits of copper from that little wooden lion's head he wore. A salvaged shred of Naftali and Areshi weave. The gold crest from a Mashevi long-knife…"

Riada looked down, staring fixedly at his own sword.

"Sagam. Why would a scavenger take the sagam and leave the crest?"

Artur bit his lip. *That was what your father said. By Serivash and Shouma, don't do this.*

"I think we got there quickly, before the bodies were stripped. And I think the boy probably pried the crest off to prove himself, and discarded the long-knife as likely to attract problems. I tell you, Your Highness, with all my strength and soul, I believe that the body we returned to Keved was the body of Samuel Aver."

"Did my father believe it?"

Artur gritted his teeth "No. He wanted to prove the unprovable. We fed so many jackals to Serivash in pursuit of your father's mad fear—forgive me, Your Highness, it *was* madness. I hold to that. We scourged them to no gain. Truly I served your father with all my will, but he was spitting curses into the wind which only fell back on his own head, Your Highness. I—"

Riada gestured for silence with a low cut of his sword and a jerk of his head.

"The purge in the Mashevi assembly the year before he passed away: My father said there was a conspiracy on his life."

"He meant the young Aver. He was still looking for him. And how can you find what is already ash?"

Riada was still half in a trance, tapping the ground with the tip of his sword, examining the blade intensely.

"I spent two years after my father's death raking all of Masheva over the coals to find would-be conspirators…who never existed."

"I wouldn't go so far as that, Your Highness. There are, at all times, two or three jackal factions either fantasizing about or plotting your death. You did your father justice, and you did very well to keep those who have any hint of teeth from ever having a chance to show them."

Looking up sharply, Riada frowned.

"Noben. You are neither uncle nor father. And sometimes you forget that I am not a child needing to be pacified or puffed up. This is a grave error. Stop trying to step around it."

"I only wish that—"

"Do you honestly think I would have dealt with Masheva as I have done if I knew he might be alive? Who else knows of this?"

Artur, aching body and soul, sighed deeply.

"No one, if I followed your father's orders aright. And I daresay I did. Those who believe Samuel Aver is alive never knew he was sent to death. Those few who believe he is dead—such as myself and King Aver—have no good reason to doubt it."

"If he were alive, this…this is exactly what I would expect of him," Riada said in a low, far-off voice.

"Forgive me, but you are inventing a man in your own head. He was an arrogant boy, and difficult, but many children are those things. Don't draw down the sun just to lengthen the shadows."

Artur lifted his head and held his breath. He was the only person who dared speak to Riada thus and the avenue for him to do so was narrowing rapidly year by year. The Emperor was so swift of mind and decision that few even tried to keep up with him. He knew his strength. To be caught not knowing something like this was to be bruised by the blow of that knowledge. And to be thus bruised, Artur's long years taught him, was to lash out at whoever was near.

The look on Riada's face was distant, hard, and pensive. Artur knew well to wait out the silence. After a while, the Emperor firmed his grip. He righted the shield arm. Squared his shoulders. Faced Artur with tremendous calm.

There was no comfort in this. He was at his most terrifying when he was most calm.

"Set your stance. Flame sequence, ten times. Then Eagle. Serpent. Maybe we'll make all twelve forms, if the rain holds off."

Already stiff and sore, Artur did as he was told. He was not to escape his punishment. And he was not to escape the matter of Samuel Aver.

Sweat trickled down Riada's back and, at a brisk walk, he remained warm from exertion. But when he reached his hall, he felt the cold air hitting his damp clothes. What satisfaction he had sought in the exercise—in seeing Noben's strength fade and fade as Riada's loomed greater and greater by comparison—was already dissipating.

One word and his slaves attended him. A hot bath. Oils. Fresh clothes. A plate of olives, cheese, bread, and wine.

Riada sat perfectly still, but in his thoughts he was like a fish on a hook, writhing to free himself from a conclusion he did not wish to reach. Flatterers said he had no flaw in him, and detractors muttered that he could see no flaw in himself. But that was simply how it had to be. He saw how James was so keenly aware of his weaknesses that he became mired in them, unable to escape them. It disgusted Riada. So he chose to breathe in his strengths, suffusing his thoughts with them, letting his will be his shelter and refuge. Let others doubt and totter and fall. He was his own staff by which to walk, he and the Gods that chose him for this place. All others splintered beneath his hand.

Would Samuel Aver have splintered? Aver would never have let himself be grasped in the first place. If he was dead, it was better for him and his stupid pride. If he was alive...

Riada composed himself. He would not give this jackal, whoever he was, such power over him. Noben was right about that.

Had he known, would he have tripled his Navy on the Mashevi coastline, centering all his work on their fine harbors where even the prevailing winds seemed to favor Masheva as a blessed land? Would he have given the administrative offices and shipping contracts to wealthy, pandering jackals, tying them to his will by means of gold? Would he have let them become the port chiefs, ship-builders, rope-makers, bow-carvers on whom he so relied, for no one could be forced to do it as cheaply as they? They worked as if for pardon from a prison sentence. They were meticulous, they excelled, and none of the money went amiss.

Shipping flourished, filling Imperial coffers. The Navy grew in power and prowess, striking fear into the islands and nations across the Bigharan ocean. His father had begun this work forty years ago, and Riada had surpassed all his highest hopes. And all because of the tender joints of the Mashevi nobility, twisted till they had to yield.

Well-born Mashevis succumbed to delicious opportunity. Lulled with money and favor, Riada wound the strongest of them tighter and tighter around his finger. They ruled over their tiny domains of ships' payroll, trade-route bids, and manifests, and practically lolled their tongues at him like dogs to receive any token praise. The once restless noble classes now slept a deep, drugged, pampered sleep. Most of Masheva was trussed up by silk thread and silver cord, and they *loved* it.

So would he have done it if he had known?

Perhaps. To see the horror and humiliation on his old rival's face. To see Samuel realize that his people had so utterly melted at the feet of Maurow that they were nothing more than a puddle to be lightly stepped over. To see how quickly they turned their backs on god or traditions if it gained them Maurowan clout. To know that Samuel might beckon with all his pride and all his knowledge, and none of them would ever answer. All their vigor, sedated. All their strength, poured into Riada's hand. All their great learning, extracted to Riada's purposes.

And you thought you could rally them, did you Samuel? They are cowards, all, just like your father.

Riada dwelled on this thought. Fed on it as though it were meat. He pictured how it would be if the two were once again face-to-face. There was a flicker of difficulty in this. In his mind's eye, Samuel was indeed still a boy so that in Riada's imagination, he too kept shrinking to his youth. And there both of them remained. Two boys with the burden of hundreds of thousands resting on their shoulders, though Riada had not understood the heaviness of it at that time.

Samuel, he suspected, already had.

The strange thing was the faint sense of loss woven throughout Riada's vision of triumph. Riada had hated Samuel Aver out of practical purpose, and craved his enmity. But Aver would not rise to it. He was indifferent to Riada, and that was a far worse thing to feel than contempt. Never had he been so glad and proud as he had been when he finally got through that jackal's armor, and the boy rounded on him with quiet, relentless, unmistakable hatred.

Riada had looked forward to their conflict; he felt it would prove him. He liked looking Aver in the eye, knowing that he wouldn't balk. Without the least mote of kindness, Riada imagined a sort of harsh solidarity with Aver. Everyone feared and fawned over Riada. Everyone hated and shunned Aver. Thus they both stood apart from others. Both were preparing every day to fight for their lives. Both had names that pressed down upon them with the weight of generations. Both held whole nations in their hands, entire histories on their backs.

32

"We leave behind us no gaps, my brothers. The whole desert is at our shoulder."

Rahummi said this after the negotiations with the Dinsar tribe of South Makaria, his voice full of pride. The words struck Azetla at a strange, sharp angle. The time of preparation was coming to a close. Only one narrow pathway remained and it led to a wall he was not certain could possibly be scaled.

It was not often fear came over Azetla like a fever. He usually kept it deep in his pocket, or slung over his shoulder. Acknowledged, managed, and off to the side. But that night Azetla wrestled with a visceral fear that was skinned open, raw to the touch. He could not comfort himself with certainties—they were nowhere to be found—nor shore himself up with his own strength—he saw his weaknesses scattered about, both small and great, too many to gather up or even fully know.

What if he failed? *Completely*. Tens of thousands of lives. The whole desert scourged as Masheva had been.

It was enough to make a man ill.

Silent prayers poured out of his mouth that night. Pleas and laments and imprecations. Anything and everything he could think of. Words of prophets and words of priests, put in their mouths by

God. God who was more to be feared than death, more to be loved than life, and who never lied. The words felt like mere rhythm at first, something to tune your breathing to. Then they felt like jibberish, something that was supposed to sound holy and strong, but seemed meaningless in the face of circumstances.

Then, only at the last, did the words begin to flicker to life on his tongue.

Suddenly a memory came to him, almost as if it was given by hand.

The first time he had felt this kind of fear was when he was seven years old, the day his sister Talya was born. He was still of an age to be among women more than men and he did not like to leave his mother in her distress. He realized now that the atmosphere of the birthing room was a calm, joyful one, not the dark, dangerous terror that he had thought. The girls among his cousins and among the servants were all about, excited to see the new baby.

His mother, after a deep groan, told him to play Kufs-Arratul with Shirel, who was being a sheer nuisance. Playing with Shirel meant having no business with strategy but merely letting his little sister stack the pieces and knock them over, while he collected them for her repeatedly. It was easy to lose patience with Shirel, and she thought the loss of his patience was hilarious, the best game of all.

The younger midwife, who was used to high-born households, did not like all the talk and bustle, the eating and playing that happened. Why were all the children allowed in here? The women she attended were delicate, preferring quiet for their labor. But Azetla's mother was of Naftal. She had grown up in South Trekoa. She still did things, as some of the servants whispered, "like a village girl."

But the older midwife, who was also from the tribe of Naftal, was very happy. Naftalis loved a boisterous birthing room as a good omen. She told the older cousins to make themselves busy and helpful. Sing a few songs from the holy words, if they liked. Bring fresh water. Take turns holding the damp, steaming cloth over the small of his mother's back.

Shirel fell asleep on Azetla's lap. After a while, Azetla grew antsy. He carried his sister to the rug, tucked her carefully then left to retrieve his writing implements. He did that when he was uneasy. He liked to write things down as long as they let him use his left hand.

His mother, who had thus far labored calmly and steadily, gave a sharp gasp when he returned. She had been walking about, leaning on the midwives as needed, but now she went to the floor, hands and knees. The midwives encouraged her to crouch instead, but she cried out that she could not, and her voice broke and cracked. She gasped again. The midwives admonished her to breathe more deeply.

Azetla knew now what he did not know then. Had he been a little younger, like Shirel, he would have gleaned the perfect calm from the midwives and had not a care in the world. But the fear was sloshing already at his feet. His mother cried out. She gasped again, saying she could not possibly bear it. She gave low, deep yells. There was a great shout then, and a gush of water with a bloody look to it. Azetla sat still, barely breathing.

Everything inside him trembled. Mothers were lost this way, he knew that much. Many of them. Even the smallest child understood that in some sense, but now the dread of it, the grief and terror of the possibility came over him with suffocating force. The attention of the room was far from him, so no one saw his dead quiet tears.

He would lose his mother, he thought. Her shelter. Her songs. Her prayers. The way she shielded him from the unholy things that were done in his holy city. She was about to die before his eyes.

This fear was painfully articulate within him, as real as if it had already happened. But he understood now what a seven-year-old could never have explained. The fear had depth as well as breadth. It hid a second layer.

Soon, no matter what happened, he would have to go out from under his mother's shelter. Later, perhaps, than a fisherman's boy, but sooner than most of his ilk, he must move from the world of women to the world of men. His days of study would grow longer. His presence would be required in circumstances he did not yet understand. Much would be expected of him. The life of an innocent child would end with death-like finality.

This was the way of the world. To be given from the gentle, caring hands of the mother into the firm, instructive hands of the father. But he did not think that it would be like that for him. Muddled as he was between ignorance, intuition, and observation, he dreaded going into his father's hands. Even then, he knew that they were not firm. In some unseen way, those hands trembled. They left their works misshapen, either by purpose or sheer accident. They were aimless and careless.

That fear, which he could never then have put his finger on, did soon come to pass.

But the first fear did not. His mother cried out a second time that she could not go on.

"What must be done?" he'd asked the elder midwife, in a determined voice.

"Nothing, dear. All that can be done, has been done. Now she must simply go on in strength down the one and only road there is. She only feels that she cannot do it because she is almost finished doing it."

Mere minutes after the peak of his panic, Talya came into the light, her fist curled tightly by her head—the cause of all the sharp, unexpected pains. Blood there was aplenty, but no danger. His mother lived. To this very day, she lived. As did Talya. She was a grown woman now with a child of her own, last he heard.

All that could be done had been done. He must not waver just because the pain and hardship would soon increase rapidly. He must go on in strength down the only road that was left.

First thing in the morning, Azetla felt the dry cold in his bones. He traversed briskly through the south edge of camp to warm himself and was gratified by all the stomping, folding, clicking, readying sounds.

Breakfast was meager. Water was sufficient, but only just. He stared briefly at his empty bowl, then stood up to find Tzal. She was already with Nashuv, checking his hooves, adjusting his tack, and talking to him in what he assumed was Shihrayan. She did that sometimes.

He readied and mounted, then watched carefully as Tzal did the same. She did not pause to brace before pulling herself onto Nashuv; she did not wince when she came to the seat. For the first time since Hidud, the natural, lissome quality had returned to her movement. He counted in his head, marking the days by movement and battles. It had only been three weeks. Considering how short her time of actual rest, and how little he had spared her since, it was a wonder she could ride at all.

Tzal had not allowed herself to be spared, in fact.

In a manner both mutual and silent, they agreed to use her as much as she could reasonably be used and, once in a while, a bit more than that. When her sentences began to fray and fragment and she needed someone's shoulder to walk a simple distance, he knew he had drained the well dry. But they usually did the same thing again the next day.

The men found themselves dealing with her in a new way. Twice, Sergeant Lachlan took rations to her. If Azetla was not mistaken, he even joked with her. Once Nuss shared his water. This ruthless, unrelenting use of a strained vessel pleased Joseph, Sarrez, and all the others immensely. If it were possible, it even softened their contempt for her.

Joseph had been right about that.

But it all troubled Azetla. In more ways than one. The least that could be done for her, had been done; the problem was he had wanted to do much more, but had been afraid to.

Now here was a strange, contemptible sort of cowardice. He had always considered himself inured to the opinions and accusations of others, able to take abuse in stride, able to suffer scorn to do as he thought was best.

But one whisper of Captain Hodge's name and he would fold his arms and stand at a distance, when he would far rather have sat with or walked alongside her. In the very beginning, this was all purposeful and honest. He hardened himself by his own sense of justice, his own remembrance of grief. But for some time now, he merely wanted to be *seen* doing so for his own sake.

Once he understood himself, he was appalled.

Few had been the hours lately in which a man could sit and take stock of himself, even if it was in his nature to do so. But that cold morning, going at the lumbering pace that fourteen thousand men can achieve at once, he reviewed the lists and ledgers and discrepancies of himself. He drew a razor-sharp pen and, in his mind's eye, marked the necessary changes. Fierce and troubling they were, but it did him no good to deny them.

One cannot sift thoughts if one will not admit to having them.

⁓ ⚶ ⁓

Just before dusk, they reached the open plain with Acolomey Rock rising to the east. Azetla gave the signal and men hurried to the tasks—food and fires. Tzal slipped off Nashuv in a smooth motion. There was no uncertainty or pause, but she did bring her feet to the ground very gently, and she did stand still a while, like a sailor who had just laid first foot on the dock and wanted to be very sure of his feet.

Duties pulled and overtook all stray thoughts. Azetla received reports. Sent a contingent with Rahummi to try and purchase a few dozen goats to add to the lean barley pots. Went among the fires. Greeted all the men along the northeast watch, where his tent was pitched. Visited the men who still nursed injuries, but had been well enough to leave Hidud.

It was almost second watch by the time he washed his hands to the rhythm of his prayer, and sat down with his own ration. The camp had grown still, by and large. He listened to the gentle orchestra of coughs, shuffles, crackles, and wind. He was halfway peaceful with exhaustion, and besides there were two small and savory bites of meat in his bowl and a bit of bone to gnaw on. He left no marrow in it whatsoever.

Tzal came and sat without a word, as was her habit, and no bit of gristle was wasted from her bowl either.

"Did you go up Acolomey?" he said in Mashevi. The thing that seemed to bother her most about the wound now was how it inhibited that ibex impulse of hers. She wanted the heights.

"Not far up. I'll try it again in the early morning, when I'm fresh."

"Save your strength."

Tzal nodded half-heartedly. "For Wadi Kilsayn."

Well. Yes.

"And for your own sake," he said stiffly. He shrugged his hands and stood up. "Have you tried out any sequences or forms just to see? Flame and Pine are good for that."

She laughed. Not bitterly. "I don't know those little northern dances."

"Yes, you do. You used to mimic them behind the storage house after the training fields were empty. You had trouble with Fox and Hare, but the others you memorized."

She bristled. Azetla smiled. She really had thought herself unobserved.

"Well I don't know all their names," she muttered.

He doubted that as well. He reached down.

"The forms are good for strengthening and limbering. We used them for recovery from wounds all the time."

She grabbed his hand and pulled herself carefully to her feet. "*We?*"

He shrugged. "I'm not Maurowan, but I am a soldier, and I use what's useful. The point is to go slowly and note which movements give you trouble. If it's only faint discomfort, keep going. If sharpness or tearing, do the motion just shy of that. Pain is fine, as long as it remains dull."

She gave him a weary, wry look. "Azetla, it's not my first time dealing with this."

"Up to you."

But she had already drawn the sagam. She rolled her shoulders a little, testing. Some liked to use sticks just to enact the movements and have something in hand. But Captain Hodge always said that if the purpose was to find out whether or not you were ready to draw a sword in battle, then you had better *draw a sword*. The weight, the way it met the air, and the set of the mind—it was all too particular.

She came to a natural stance. Set thus, her look and her posture became very serious. They parried slowly, not letting the blades touch at all, just to see if she could move her body as she needed to.

"Again?"

She nodded. They moved a little faster. Let the blades tap gently. The fourth time was about half speed and Tzal almost dropped out of sequence, doing what was natural for her to do rather than what the choreographed back-and-forth dictated. She shook it off, and tried again.

"So far?" Azetla said.

"Not bad. Pinches a little when I turn quickly. And then pulls when I come out of the duck. Do it with more weight and pressure this time. A couple firm, controlled strikes."

Azetla nodded. He still moved with precision and care but, when he parried, he did it with enough force to make her stumble and when she did the duck-through he almost lost his balance.

She never faltered, but Azetla saw her face tighten in a sharp wince more than once.

"Still all right?" he said. He was warm, sweat on his neck, and taking quick breaths.

"Sure," she said, wiping the edge of her hand across her forehead. "Let's do the other one the same way. Gradual increase."

They never got even to half strength or speed with the Flame sequence. It was far more dynamic than Pine, and rather less likely a thing to occur in real battle. Azetla had never seen its like for training fluidity and speed, however, and when he was young it had been so difficult for him to make the movement feel natural. It had four variations, all dependent on the whim of whoever assumed the initiating position.

It was more like Tzal's style of movement, with her nimble, evasive bent. But the constant twisting of the torso, the high swing of the arm—it gave her trouble. He could see her brace, her mouth pinch, her movements grow more stilted rather than less.

Azetla put his hand up.

"I think that's enough."

She shook her head. "I'm fine."

"No." He put his sword away and sat down. "The point isn't to exhaust yourself. It's a week to Areo. There's time."

It became such an easy, refreshing habit those nights. Like stepping out of a hot, over-crowded room into a place of cool, open silence. If they ever talked, it was only in Mashevi. They went through the sequences slowly, methodically. He taught her the ones she did not know. It was a deeply pleasant routine.

He was alarmed by the sharpness of his disappointment the one time she did not come. But really, he shouldn't have been. He knew himself now, for better or worse. Ragged with exhaustion the following morning, she smiled wide with bruisy shadows beneath her eyes.

"I climbed the tower of Oyesh-dir-min-yazha."

He glanced at the rocky rise to their immediate west, which he knew required careful footing always, and occasionally the use of both hands.

"And?" he said.

"I feel like I could have done it with my eyes closed."

She was like someone who had abruptly lost hearing but was now gaining it back. The sequences grew swifter and harder after that, for she began to trust her own movement again. Her wound had the healing look to it still—slightly reddish, but firm and raised, cool to the touch. Likely she was still doing more than she ought to, but she did it with sheer gladness and relief.

"I won't have any trouble at Kilsayn or in the Ghallaz," she said when they reached the gate of Areo. "So put any doubt out of your mind."

And so he did. From that moment, for every last one of his purposes, he regarded her as whole.

33

Tzal circled the grounds of Areo like a hawk, searching, searching for the signs of trouble. The cold wind beat at her face and pummeled her back. It herded the soldiers into stamping and talkative huddles, which she swooped lightly through. She knew how to move in and about the crowds without making a point of herself; you only had to look as if you were going purposefully elsewhere.

Yet she inhaled the scent of every possible conversation, catching tones and manners, gauging the weather of all the many new faces at Areo. Most of these would march to Wadi Kilsayn, though they were untried.

Already she knew from Naima that many of them were suspicious of this Azetla they had never seen until now. The Makars among them were especially scornful. It was easy to find the flow of such words and follow it to the sources. But, rap her knife handle as she might, there was little she could do about it. It had taken months for him to win the others over. Now he had scant days.

Tzal eased herself into a long stride. The wound at her hip did not trouble her so terribly now, but the bitter air seemed to cut through her clothes and burn it. She always ached by the end of a long day, and even though it was only noon, it had already been a very long day.

First there had been the Janbari boy, found with several coils of Everson's personal papers and logs, as well as a purse with unstamped gold coins. The coins could have come from anywhere in the Empire, but the papers came directly from Everson's quarters and were full of all sorts of damning information. Numbers of troops. Points of contention. States of rations and wells. Vulnerabilities of all sorts.

And this, just as they were about to leave for Wadi Kilsayn, their riskiest endeavor yet.

There was more in the papers even than that, things that Tzal could tell Everson would not wish Azetla to know. The panic in his eye, for one moment, was like nothing she'd ever seen in him.

The boy was being held. He could not read and did not know what it was he had.

Everson wanted to hang him. Not because the boy intended treason—it became painfully clear that the boy, even on threat of death, did not fully grasp what had happened . He could name no name and offer no source. He insisted he never took either coin or paper, but had spent the entire day hawking goathides, water skins, cheeses, and dried gut-strings in a market almost too thick to walk through. Anyone could have put those things in his baggage.

Everson was concerned not with blame, but with results. It must never happen again, and there could be no such thing as innocence without vigilance. Istamo, Azetla, and Everson worked the matter over and over in the small hours of the morning.

As of yet, they had reached no conclusion.

Then, for two hours, Rahummi sat with the leaders of tens and fifties and hundreds of all the new Trekoan soldiers from across seven different tribes. Tzal's sole purpose was to translate for Azetla, who gave great honors to all the leaders, but deferred to Rahummi to give the speeches and explanations.

Rahummi excelled at this. He had a surprising finesse—such a firm yet delicate way of drawing his people to confidence and unity. He gave the impression of being much older than he was. Tzal wondered at it, pricked in the chest with something like the pride of an elder sister. Her voice was raw, but the work was good. When she glanced at Azetla, she saw that he too looked at Rahummi with warm pride.

As they left, Azetla turned a vivid smile of satisfaction on her. She had vouched for Rahummi from the beginning. He was the finest proof of her.

They passed through the Saav River festival gatherings; she was tempted by the smells and sounds. Today they would eat. Really eat. For the first and last time in a long while.

But not until the work was done.

Azetla cut into the alley, toward the Maurowan barber.

"So you *are* going?" she said.

He nodded with a grimace.

"Why? You do know that Everson just likes to get a reaction out of everyone. He wants to see his high-bloods gasp and jump. At your expense."

"I know."

Azetla rinsed his face.

"Everson will get what he wants," he said. "But so will I. Can't keep avoiding them."

Tzal shook her head and dropped the matter. "Sidara and the Taya."

Azetla rolled his jaw. He still didn't like it. But he confirmed, "Sidara and Mali."

He set about his work carefully and she stepped around him, leaving the whole procedure with a disdainful glance. She never understood why northern men shaved their faces, nor why Azetla himself still kept up the practice. She derided him about it once or twice, just to see if there was a tender point under the skin. He only paused, blinked, and carried on with it.

Tzal was far longer in the Trekoan quarter than she would have liked. She felt the day trickling out like water from a cracked vessel with each question and argument Sidara brought forth. Those certain corners of time that she hoarded for comfortable routines were not likely to remain when she finally reached them.

But Sidara, the Taya, and the other midwives must be made ready. Azetla had agreed at last. They would go with the army to Wadi Kilsayn. They would live among the Hushai. And when the day came—the day that might even meet them even as they arrived—they would raise the tent cloth in hopes of salvaging some of the dying.

Sidara was quick to agree—"my children are grown and established, I am not afraid to die"—but she was set in her ways and had to be coaxed into a great many compromises. She had lived all her life between the nearby village of her birth and Areo. She did not like Hushai people as a rule, Naima excepted, and there was a clear hierarchy of tribes in her mind.

Sidara gave her customary spit of contempt when Tzal first entered the room, and a few times throughout, whenever Tzal contradicted her in any way. The Taya gentled things with little assurances, given in hobbling but effective Trekoan. Otherwise Mali listened with a keenness, a leaning-forward, a readiness to be already on the way.

After Sidara left in some degree of contentment, Tzal gestured that the Taya remain.

"I need you to understand something, Taya, and you will not like it. You are to be the one in charge. Of Sidara. Of the other midwives who have agreed to come. And of the dozen field physicians who will be assigned to the rear tents."

The Taya paled and shook her head.

"Sidara has been doing this for thirty-five years. She has delivered hundreds of children and reset dozens of bones. What she knows about local herbs and creature venoms takes half a lifetime to learn! She is my *elder*."

Tzal smiled tiredly.

"It's nothing to do with your expertise, Taya. You know enough Trekoan now to get by. And even a little Makarish, am I right?"

Mali nodded slowly.

"You are, insofar as such a thing is possible, a neutral hand. Sidara doesn't speak a word of Maurowan. She has a list two hands long of tribes she hates. And as you saw from our conversation, she has no interest in understanding Azetla's protocols or systems or anything that would be needed for everything to run smoothly. There is no one better for curing than her—" Tzal paused with emphasis. It was clear that Mali needed Sidara's superiority to be acknowledged. "And if you are taking command, you free her to do what she does best."

"She will not like it," Mali said in a whisper. "And I don't know if I'm suited to—"

"You will have to use some finesse," Tzal said, rising to her feet. "You did that when the wounded were brought in from Zoqra and it turned out well."

"That was no small thing," Mali said sharply. "You are putting me in a difficult position."

Tzal smiled down at this northerner who used to be terrified if Tzal so much as raised an eyebrow.

"Then welcome, Mali. Because that is where most of us reside."

Naima marveled at her situation, sometimes with pleasure, sometimes with great suspicion. Why should she, only just come to the age of twenty, from a humble family of Hushai weavers, suddenly be a woman who commands attention and instructs her superiors? For many hours over the last five days, men of battle and of twice her years had come to hear her teach the customs of her people so that they might know how to behave—how to tell their men to behave—when they went among them in the Ghallaz.

The Mashevi Commander, Azetla, had been the first to come and set the example for all the others; he sat on the ground, just as she did, lowering his head to her as though she were a great lady of Maurow or the Rokha of a tribe as powerful as Saqiran. He listened intently to Tzal's translation but kept his eyes fixed on Naima. He asked excellent questions. He smiled at the baby's wonderful, ridiculous, disruptive sounds and gave another tassel for her shawl. A Shayali woman of Hidud had given it to him. He asked the infant's name, but for luck, Naima did not answer it out loud. *Inaya*. A name with the rare quality of being used by both Saqiran *and* Hushai.

Naima relished the chance to talk about her home and people. It filled her with both longing and spiteful satisfaction. All those Janbari and Saqirani women saying that her people were wild and wanton; she could speak the truth over their slander, showing everyone all the best of what she was and where she came from.

The Shihrayan noticed this. She noticed everything.

"Careful, Naima," she said quietly after the second of these "lessons." "The point isn't to give a painting. It's to craft a map. The good and the bad. People's lives depend on it."

Naima bristled; she knew it was true. She did her best to strike a balance. If her map had affectionate flourishes, she did not conceal the hard trails and the sheer drops. Maybe her people would not be fully accepted, but they would be respected, for they were the road to victory and everyone knew it.

Naima no longer worried about whether the servant girls sneered behind their hands.

The whole festival day, however, had been strange for her. Good, but strange. Rahummi celebrated in short stints but was often summoned away by Azetla. Rokha Ayla was well and had arrived at last, bearing blankets and tassels and scarlet thread. There was some stiffness between them at first, but Rokha Ayla fell upon Inaya as if she were her own grandchild and laughter burst about the room. Even now, Rokha Ayla was out at the market to find something fine for the girl on her first Saav's day. Naima knew—truly she did know—she had no reason to be discontented.

She was surprised to see the Shihrayan come in, and a little wary. With Tzal usually came work and questions and tasks and—often as not—the Mashevi Commander himself. But he was not with her now.

"Rokha Ayla is out, if you came to see her," Naima said uncertainly.

The Shihrayan gave a nod of acknowledgment.

"I saw her there." Kneeling and sitting on her heels in the taut posture of one who is not sure they are really invited, Tzal handed a bit of cloth to Naima. "Life and death are in the Saav, she comes and goes, thanks be."

Naima smiled at the distinctly Hushai version of the festival greeting, which she had not heard all the day long. She unwrapped the threadbare bit of cloth. Inside was a small, cold barley-raisin cake. It smelled of cinnamon.

"What's this?" Naima said, confused.

"Sidara made some for her clan and for the Taya. They had a few left and I was remembering how it is done in the Ghallaz. I mean, you don't have to actually eat it." Tzal looked wryly at the festal spread of cheeses, dates, breads, olives, honeys, vinegars, and wines. "It's just symbolic."

Hurriedly Naima waved her open hand at the cloth-spread of food. She felt a sting in her eyes and hoped that, since Tzal fell swiftly to the meal, she did not notice.

In the Ghallaz, during the two high festivals, half of each household remained in their crag—their house or tent—and the other half took to the hard trails to practice anqthashur. Sweetening the home. The host provided music and drink and savory food. The travelers brought all that was sweet. Cakes and dried fruits and every honey-soaked thing. Gifts were often exchanged. Then the travelers moved to another home, as many as four throughout the night, until dawn broke.

It could become a complicated matter—a home not visited perceived a slight, gifts could turn into debts and power-plays, and of course everything had to be planned quite carefully, for offended families and Ghallaz trails alike were extremely dangerous. But Naima remembered the sheer joy of walking in out of the wild dark, handing her sweets to the host, and drowning in warmth and light and music.

Naima ate the crushed barley cake slowly. This pittance. Mere scraps from another's poor plate. Barely sweet. Hearty. It was all the Shihrayan had to give.

"How is the festival among your people?"

Naima felt wild and bold asking the Shihrayan about her home. Rahummi always told her not to do it. He said she would get answers she did not like and wished she had not heard.

"Our river is the Limila, not the Saav. It is—" Tzal glanced from Naima to Inaya to the food. "Suffice to say our festivals are not like this. But I always liked anqthashur."

"Even though you were never allowed inside."

"I heard the music. And Rahummi set aside food for me."

Naima smiled. Of course he did.

"Take the rest of the wine please—Everson's finest," she said with warmth. "This little one will fuss all night if I have more than three sips."

After a brief hesitation, Tzal took the skin and poured a cup. Savored it. Sat down all the way, cross-legged.

"I don't suppose you have anything new for me. Any stray words?" Tzal said.

"I already told you all the best worry and gossip that came my way."

All gossip except for that which regards you, Shihrayan, Naima thought. She had sense enough to hold her tongue on that score. Who could know what was true when it came to her? Anything could be true.

Inaya had been stirring a while. Now she was well awake, hungry, and contrary, determined to make herself known.

"And the Commander? Does he celebrate the Saav?" Naima asked with careful lightness.

"He does. In his own way. But he says the story is different in Masheva."

"Different how?"

"Well for one thing, it is not Godri the soothsayer who is running away. It's some prophet from Rinayim and the enemies chasing him were not foreigners, but powerful people from his own city who didn't like what he had to say of their corruption. Then, instead of cutting the river with a black bone-knife, the desert God summoned a shake of the earth and a ferocious rain, flooding what was only a small gully. Either way, it ends the same. The enemies were washed away and the Saav became what it is now."

"Strange to omit Godri. Every tribe agrees he was the most powerful soothsayer in a century."

"He actually is in some of their stories but..." Tzal tilted her head slightly. "Not in a very good light."

"And I suppose the Mashevis claim their version is the true version," Naima said, mildly irritated. Oh, Rahummi thought Azetla so wonderful, so righteous, but even Naima could see from her distance that Azetla was not without the arrogance and rigidity for which his people were specially known.

"Well, yes, of course they do," the Shihrayan said with half a smile. But with another sip of wine she started to explain the stories with unusual detail, winding between the versions that Naima had grown up with, and their harsh, hearty Mashevi parallels. She elaborated the history of one particular Mashevi prophet and quoted his writings. Quoted *holy writ* word for word, in that driving, crafting voice of hers that could tap the blood like wine. These were songs sung in the Mashevi temple long before its destruction. These were words, so the Mashevis claimed, from the very mouth of God.

Naima listened, entranced. She had never heard any of these things.

Yet a Shihrayan had. A devil.

"The Commander *tells* you all this?"

Tzal glanced up at the scandalized tone in Naima's voice.

"It's not like in the Ghallaz, Naima. They give the words to everyone there, not just a shaman or a priest. A fisherman can read or be read to. They put holy script on the walls and doorways. Some things are sacred and separate, but never *secret*. Holy words just gush through the streets there so that the people are used to it and forget even to notice."

Naima hesitated to speak her thoughts.

"But doesn't he profane those words by...by..."

"By putting them in my mouth?" the Shihrayan said calmly.

Naima fixed her eyes on Inaya's face to avoid Tzal's.

"You think less of him for doing that?"

I don't know, Naima thought. But she brought no words to her lips. Her thoughts were too thick to tread through properly.

"Naima, he is generally alone here too, you know. Far from home. And sometimes he wants to talk of such things. People usually take what ear they can get, even if it's one like mine." The Shihrayan's voice was soft and wry, and it made Naima wince. "Anyway, I wouldn't worry so much. If those words are so holy, they'll scorch me and live to tell the tale, not the other way around."

Naima was bewildered. Such a great and important woman she had been all this week, but now she was only a young wife of plain birth who followed a desert God that she did not know or understand, with whom she had not been raised, and whose words she had never been taught. So little was expected of her in that way. And here before her was this Shihrayan devil who *understood* things—too many things—and who, with a few deft words, could put Naima's mind to work. Or to ease. Or to dread. Whatever the Shihrayan wanted.

Always Tzal came like a desert mirage, flickering in sight from gentle to brutal, from foreign to familiar, an unholy blur that might bear up into something holy by a mere shift in the searing light.

With slow, gentle hands, Naima placed Inaya back in her basket. Once again, Tzal was sitting up on her heels as if bound at any moment to depart. When Azetla bowed his head through the cloth door, she drew instantly to her feet.

Azetla offered Naima the proper Hushai greeting—for he surely took as many words from Tzal as ever he gave her—and he did a fair job of it. He was often difficult for Naima to understand, his accent hanging heavy on the Trekoan words, but he usually *tried* to speak to her in Trekoan. Today, after the greeting, he did not. He went straight to Tzal and to his own tongue. His hand numbered things off, and the Shihrayan answered, countered, or shrugged in turn.

Naima understood not a word of it. But she was not uncomfortable with her exclusion. She simply watched the faces and heard the tones with keen interest. She didn't know exactly what she was looking for. The rumors were scant and muddled. And, after all, what was the significance of a flicker in the mirage? It was all guesswork.

The conversation was over almost as quickly as it had begun.

Azetla bid Naima a formal goodbye. Then he lifted his scribe's satchel and placed it over Tzal's head; she tucked her fingers at the shoulder and gripped it firmly. He said one last thing in his own language. Tzal gave a nod and a faint smile. Then off he went to be scrutinized by northern high-bloods who hated him but needed him.

Perhaps Naima would have eventually been brazen enough to say the sly remark that came to mind as Tzal smoothly adjusted Azetla's satchel to the opposite shoulder. Perhaps not. But Rahummi came back, tipsy and amorous, lacking all of his usual propriety, causing Tzal to slip out with an amused expression on her face.

Naima chastised Rahummi. Then kissed him and drew him close. They finished the festival in a warm, pleasant, and proper way. Life was in the Saav, thanks be.

34

Orde Everson fingered the gaps in his books where the pages had been stolen. He had feared that they might contain a few things beyond military and conspiratorial matters. Personal things. His relief was far greater than it should have been considering he still had the matter of a traitor to deal with and only the one idiotic boy to hang for it.

By the fading light from the high curved window of his library, Orde could see that it would soon be time for him to go to the festival and greet his guests. Tonight may be the last night they dared pretend their necks were not on the block. The last night to indulge in wine and fill one's belly to the full.

He had very high expectations of amusement tonight. Lady Kathryn was always an interesting challenge. There were many new faces, eager with curiosity and fear, all looking to Orde for comfort and understanding.

Then the Mashevi would arrive.

Orde hadn't the faintest idea what would come of that, good or bad. Most of the northern high-bloods did not know "the jackal Commander" would be there, and most of them were still of a contemptuous mindset. That was what would make it interesting.

He began to ready himself at a relaxed pace, pausing every so often to assess himself in the silver mirror or take a sip of wine. He didn't like to feel rushed. He washed his face one last time then rubbed his dry knuckles with rosemary-scented tallow.

His hands—and his face—were darker than he usually allowed them to get; so much time spent walking about the training fields. He had always dressed in a mixture of Maurowan and southern styles and, if he grew a beard, some might suppose his blood was a mixture as well, which was precisely why he never did such a thing. He dabbed lavender and vetiver oils on his fresh-shaven chin, and at his neckline. Donned his blue-and-gold sash.

He glanced up from the mirror when the door guard let the Shihrayan in.

"What do *you* want?"

"A blessed Saav day to you too. Vellum, reed paper, the two new maps Durad supposedly finished yesterday. And ink."

"How the blazes does he go through it so quickly? He's going to bleed me dry."

"I doubt that," she said coolly, rifling through his writing supplies in a leisurely manner. She put three small, sealed bottles of ink into the satchel, then turned to the box where Orde kept his reed papers and such. She glanced briefly at the silver mirror as she walked past but made no move to right the loose braid of her hair or fix her threadbare sash.

As she ran her fingers gently along the satchel's seam, Orde realized whose it was. He straightened.

"Wait. Has he already gone into the peristyle?"

The Shihrayan shrugged. "I don't know. He was going to give Saav greetings to Istamo and his family and then go in. That was just a few minutes ago."

That should hold him a short while. Istamo's children would jump on him and make him play a game. But now Orde must hurry, which he did not like.

"At his rank he should be one of the *last* people to arrive," Orde said.

The Shihrayan smiled in a childish way. "What rank?"

"By blood, even he knows he can't play that angle anymore."

"If he wanted to go in early, drink one cup of wine, and walk back out before anyone noticed, he'd had every right to do so. But he keeps his word, so he'll do it your way and I'm sure it will all be very entertaining for you. Where are the maps?"

"Third shelf. Top left coils with the braided strands."

Orde placed his outer cloak carefully askew in accordance with the newest Piaragoan fashion. Once she had the maps in hand, the Shihrayan stood a moment, one arm akimbo, and watched with open amusement as he labored briefly over the elaborate belt of a ceremonial sword he rarely wore. For the Gods' sake, what business did she have to be so spry and free and untroubled just now? She did not even like the Saav's day.

"You're starting to cause him problems," he said, straightening and smoothing himself.

"Oh, is that so?" she said cheerfully.

"Some of the new officers won't go near him because of you."

"The Makarish ones, you mean? Good."

"Is that really what you want? That they're afraid of you rather than trusting him."

"No," she said, unperturbed. "That they're wary of me until they have a chance to trust him. After that, what they think of me doesn't really matter."

He adjusted the sash again, not satisfied. "You're very confident in the outcome."

"I've good reason to be."

He raised his eyebrows. Her posture was wholly relaxed, her voice warm, but there was a steel-hard look in her eye.

"It's not like you to take such a strong side," he said.

"Nor you. But you'll have to in the end."

He did not like the depth her voice cut with those words. He tisked his tongue, brushed his silk, and made light.

"Now see this is the trouble. I don't know if you expect me to take you seriously or not. It's all a matter of ownership. You were a Saqirani slave, a tool on loan, a Black Wren prisoner, and now you're—"

With a bright and unbothered smile, she cut him off. "Now I'm nothing and no one's. This is all by choice, Everson. I told you before you wouldn't like the look of it. No bit. No reins. I know you would rather I have gone straight from Imal's hand to yours and expected me to regard it as a great privilege—"

"I told you a thousand times, it would not have been like that—"

"No, Everson, it would have been much, much worse. More freedom perhaps, but less dignity."

The words came out with solid bite. *Finally*. Orde laughed. "It always amuses me when you pretend that notions like dignity, honor, or virtue matter to you in the least. They're things you neither have nor understand. Anyway, you're a safer bet when you're indifferent. But the moment you try to put your whole blood into something, you *sully* it. Everything disintegrates, just like last time." He smiled and handed her his half-finished skin of wine. He would not be accused of being miserly. Not on the Saav's day. "You'll eventually run him aground, you know."

That was the closest to a flinch he got out of her, there and gone like a spark.

"This is nothing like before and you know it," she said, taking the skin without hesitation.

Orde shrugged. "It's only different insofar as the risk and scale is greater. And, whether you like it or not, even Azetla is not so different from me—"

She breathed out a scornful laugh.

"—*Not* in the ways that matter, believe me. He'll get what he wants from you and discard the rest, never mind how many holy rituals he wraps around his wrist while he does it. In the end, little devil, he's still made of the same raw material as any other man."

She pulled the stopper on the wine and took a gentle whiff. "Someone who believes that vice is the secret behind all virtue would certainly say that."

"You don't know what the word virtue *means*, Shihrayan."

"Maybe, maybe not." She shrugged. "But I know what *you* mean by it. It's a thing you hold in contempt but can't be seen to lack. Something you laugh at, but still desire the shade and shield of. Did you ever consider that not everyone is pretending like you?"

"And *you*."

She tisked her tongue and waved her finger. "I don't have to act like I have something no one thinks me capable of having. Aren't I the lucky one?" She took a small sip from the skin and nodded. "It's good. Thank you."

Ever quick on her feet and deft in taking the last word, she turned and was gone.

Orde walked down the hall at a brisk pace, smoothing his clothes, curating his demeanor. He ought to be satisfied. Usually the Shihrayan was so opaque, muddy river that she was, constantly shifting and obscuring what she really thought. But once in a while she made herself clear as the pool in a mosaic fountain, showing the color of every single stone and indeed the whole image. It wasn't like her to tell the truth for its own sake, so there had to be another reason. He just didn't know what it was.

Anyhow, why did she pretend to hold him to some standard?

That little devil cornered innocents and slit their throats. She carried wars in her pocket to draw out at her leisure. She could tease and mock and drink contempt with as much vigor as ever he could. It was absurd that he should have to remind himself of this.

Azetla, Rahummi, and Imal provided guilt enough for anyone, always subjecting him to their strict veneers of southern morality. He chafed under their silent judgment, their rigid beliefs, their self-righteous way of talking. That devil had no right to add to it.

His northern high-bloods were far easier to deal with. Their façades came off at the lightest touch, kohl smeared by a brush of fingers. The cocktail of their fears and sins and lusts and needs were so plainly laid bare for him to take and store for later use. He never felt small or defensive in *their* presence.

Ah, maybe it was a mistake to make Azetla come tonight after all.

But, no. It had to be done. Orde must show his fellow high-bloods a bit of the truth so that, when all hell broke loose, they would be able to put a face to that name.

Azetla arrived not long after Orde did; he caused only a mild stir at first, because he entered and moved so calmly. His threadbare clothes were clean. His face was clean. The faded battalion cord was neatly laid and the worn baldric refreshed with cedar oil. Sword at the right hip, jackal band on the left arm. He looked even more soldierly than usual, having handed off his scribe's satchel to the Shihrayan, and scrubbed the ink from his hands.

Well, he knew what he was doing, didn't he?

He spoke much like he looked. Firm, plain, unadorned, and unaffected by the more flamboyant dress and speech of those around him. But he was not, as Orde had expected, stiff and grim. He held a cup of wine in his hand. He did not hide at the edge of the room. He always looked everyone in the eye. He took no notice of those who were offended at his presence; snide words slid off him, and he answered every question that was put to him in a satisfactory way.

At one point he made a map on one of the tables with cho nuts, dates, and a bit of thread to explain something or other, and the more military-minded high-bloods watched the map with fascination as its scale and location shifted in accordance with his words.

He did not banter, per se, and he certainly did not participate in the more lurid conversations that arose with the increase of wine. But he was at ease. He let the people go to or from him like water, he let them think what they would, and let them take from him what they thought they must have.

They asked him about his men. About his battles. The tribes. Kilsayn. Hushai. The Ghallaz.

After a short while, wine and music began to haze the atmosphere. Clusters of conversation formed and dispersed. The ebb and flow gave Azetla the opportunity to extract himself from the center of attention, and find a quieter place in the room next to the desert rivers tapestry. It seemed the crowd had done with the novelty of him all they saw fit to do.

All except Lady Kathryn, who kept something of a distance. Through the hour, she had watched Azetla out of the corner of her eye. It was difficult to tell what she thought of him. Without a doubt she took in every word he said, though she never spoke to him. She was not the sort to raise her hand like a child in an audience, or heckle from a crowd.

She liked to have the subject of value all to herself.

When Orde stepped toward Azetla and the tapestry, she came deftly to his elbow as if *he* was her point of interest, not the jackal at the mouth of the Dirra River who held a cup of wine he never seemed to taste. Lady Kathryn cast all her warmth and allure upon Orde; he did not mind one bit. Crimson-lipped, kohl-eyed, and golden-sashed, she smiled and put her cup to her lips with a sidelong glance.

He looked at her as long and as ravenously as he wanted to and, because she was not like the southern women he usually dealt with, she received it with gratification instead of shame. It was the Saav's day after all, and the wine was unmixed.

But her true intent was on that jackal. Slow and languid, she made her way to lounge on one of the low, Makarish-style couches. She propped up on her elbow and looked at Azetla with a cool smile, as if she were about to hear a recitation of him. She managed to give the impression of snapping her fingers and beckoning without actually doing so.

Azetla slowly peeled his eyes away from the shimmering indigo threads of the Dirra and the Saav and set them on the wealthiest and most powerful woman Maurow. He seemed to begrudge the task. So did she, Orde realized.

"So now that we have you for once, jackal, I have to know: did Lord Everson bring you tonight by a jerk of the reins, or did you decide to grace us with your presence for your own private reasons?"

Even Orde was surprised at the sheer contempt that coiled within her soft, sensual voice. But he should have foreseen it. Everything about Areo was a reduced state for her. A humiliation. No one's blood equaled hers and so little of her power came with her. Most of it sat in Piarago, broad and deep and unreachable, lying in wait. And to then have to seek the eye and word and favor of a jackal? To have to take *him* into account?

"I came as a duty and with purpose," Azetla answered in a curt voice as if, indeed, he was quite done for the night and she was precisely the last thing he had time for.

"You give me both answers knowing I like neither. If you are simply cowed and driven by the stick, then you cannot be trusted. You will someday want to bite the hand that feeds you. Or find a new hand by which to be held. But if you are independent with ambitions of your own, you will swallow your master whole. I know your kind."

A strange look passed over Azetla's face and he took a slow, deep breath before opening his mouth.

"My kind, hm? And I know yours. A worse bargain for me than for you, I think. Because regardless of the threats that brought me here and the fact that my life is worth as little to you as it is to Riada, I've put my hand to the tiller. I've brought my own men on board. And I have no intention of running aground."

Never had an assurance sounded so like a threat. Azetla had doffed what gentility he'd worn for the night, discarding all honorifics, and tossing the Emperor's name down as if he was merely a man one might regard and then look past. The Lady's deep blue eyes shimmered with fierce emotion and Orde waited with curiosity.

"The word of a jackal, as I've ever encountered it, is a knot of double-speak. There is nothing you can say that I will trust."

"Then you will have to walk always afraid, and I pity you for it."

She was given no chance to answer, for several lords and ladies came over to the tapestry in a sloshing manner, filled with tawdry gossip and teasing questions about how—"in this prudish, barren place"—one goes about acquiring a fine body for the Saav's day. They were laughing and jesting and shameless in their talk, for they were among their own kind. Orde indulged their jokes and sent them back for more wine, but gave them no knowledge of the local whores of any variety for he felt Azetla's contempt without even looking at his face.

"You were rather coy, Lord Everson," Lady Kathryn said after the group lurched their way back to the table. "I had never pictured you as having southern sensibilities about such things."

"I've certainly never been accused of it," he said with a forced smile.

"But the slaves tell me there *is* a red corridor here like any other in Piarago...or Rinayim," she added pointedly. "Or any city in the world. Only the goods are said to be of very poor quality."

Orde raised his eyebrows, but it was Azetla's calm voice that answered.

"If by 'poor quality' you mean girls and boys that have lost all their relations or been cast off by them, and slaves who are sent to earn money for their masters' hands, then I suppose so. But it seems unjust for buyers to complain of 'damage' for which they are the chief cause."

Orde felt Azetla's words like a crisp slap. Orde never made the least attempt to curb any particular trade in flesh on Areo. Why would he? It was perfectly mundane. People would want what they would want and take what they could get. Sometimes Orde wanted and took. So too did trusted soldiers like Ishelor, Brody, and Sarrez.

Lady Kathryn merely gave a soft laugh.

"You southerners are such peacocks. Flashing bright feathers. Searching out little matters that you might take offense. So much fuss over pride and perception, over honor and shame. I find it all ridiculous to begin with, but ten times more so for you, jackal. What claims of purity or honor can you possibly have, when you keep an actual jinn-devil as your hunting dog?

"There's the real shame, jackal. By now, you could have thrown it away, if you really wanted to," she added with a gesture of her soft, elegant hand. "Burned it alive or something."

Azetla rolled his jaw slightly, chewing on his words before he brought them out.

"The Shihrayan is by no means an innocent. Nor am I. Yet we have you, Lady Kathryn. With the whole world beneath your feet, you still could not bear the one remaining inch you were not allowed to climb. Now you would count ten thousand lives lost as nothing for the chance to gain that last step." Azetla cast a cold glance at Orde. "And you who spent an hour this morning trying to convince me we should kill a foolish boy who did not even know the charges against him. Hang him, you said. Out on the training field. For a show. A warning. Yet we both know the whole audience for such a warning is actually right here in this room."

"There are no clean hands here," he said softly. "So yes, Lady Kathryn, I've many reasons to be ashamed. But the Shihrayan is not one of them. Next time, when you send your slaves out to gather gossip among the sheaves, have them ask about Hidud. Molton. Pardish West. *Cozona*. See if they get tired of counting how many lives she saved and at what cost."

He tilted his cup in a mockery of a toast and set it down, untasted.

Orde did not even look at Kathryn to see her expression. He watched Azetla walk toward the southern door. Maybe the wine was fooling with him, and maybe the unease would rinse off later, but the damned Mashevi moved across the room like he was the only one truly walking perpendicular to the floor.

35

Azetla took a deep breath when he stepped out of the stifling warmth of the hall and into the cold night air. He was not the least bit surprised to see Tzal sitting on the bench next to the balcony's pit-fire. With the sense of a man who has finished a long march and can finally toss his pack to the ground, he walked over and sat down next to her. Less and less did Tzal require precision, precaution, or proofs of any sort from him.

Restraint was still needed, perhaps, but that of a very different kind.

"I told you I could get out quickly if I wanted," he said, smiling. "But I also told you to get some rest."

"This is rest," she said, gesturing at the woven cushion and the lively fire, then tapping the wineskin in her hand with the tip of her finger.

"Joseph and Nimer told you to stay, didn't they?"

"It's more of a look they give than something they say."

"I was never in any danger."

She shrugged. Tucked a foot beneath her. Watched the fire. So did he, content. She took a swig of wine, then handed it to him. She didn't say "life is in the Saav" like everyone else had, but she did regard him solemnly as he spoke the Mashevi blessing of the day for the first time.

"Holy and honored is the Lord and creator of the Great Dirra and the Saav. King of mountain and desert, of rainy season and dry, thank you for the water that flows, the life it brings."

He had been offered a cup many times today but this was the first one he accepted to drink. He savored it and let his shoulders fall. Passing the wine back to Tzal, he allowed the quiet night to rest on him for a moment.

Glad as he was of it, warm and rich as it was, the silence carried a faint edge.

Tzal would leave for Wadi Kilsayn in two days. Azetla in five. That knowledge surrounded them like the brisk air, which dried throats and chapped lips at each breath. It was thick as smoke about the eyes. And all the while Azetla's own thoughts crackled and burned like the pit-fire, which Tzal fed thoughtlessly, one scrap of date-wood at a time.

Whenever he glanced at Tzal to hand her the wineskin—or merely glanced at her because he wanted to—he saw her fiddling with the leather slave band on her wrist. She would catch herself quickly and still her fingers. Always trying to give as little evidence of herself as possible. After a still moment, her fingers would crawl back to the wrist, and scrape the band as if she meant to go to the bone.

After a long day, and two hours of carefully curated words and demeanor before Maurow's nobility, Azetla had no interest in doing anything sidelong. When Tzal handed the wine back to him, he grabbed her wrist firmly and held it up between them.

"I know it's your habit to pretend that nothing either does or ever could bother you, but if you got rid of this stupid thing, you'd get rid of your tell."

She did not stiffen or pull away, but simply gave a wry glance to the wooden lion's head on his chest. "I'm sure I'd just find another one."

"Then you should," he said. He brought her wrist down toward him, slowly studying the Saqirani designs limned in the leather as if he'd never seen them before. But he'd looked at them a hundred times. The patterns on the neck band were different than the ones on the wrist. More angular. "Because they're a falsehood. After all this time, why have you never taken them off?"

"They're useful."

"Lots of lies are."

"You would know."

"Stop doing that. I don't even think these *are* useful to you anymore. If anyone knows who you are, they know you don't belong to Rokh Imal. And, by now, everyone knows who you are."

"Azetla, if you drew your knife and cut them off right now—no, no, no...*stop*, I didn't say to do it—but *if* you did, I still wouldn't be able to go home. Little good to be redeemed in the eyes of foreigners, if my own blood won't take me."

Azetla put the knife back with his right hand; Tzal's upturned palm rested lightly in his left. He gave her a sober smile as he pressed the slave band back and forth across her wrist with the edge of his thumb, much as she had been doing herself, though slower, softer.

"That, I understand." *More than you can imagine.*

She watched the gentle rhythm of his fingers for a moment. And then a few moments more. Long enough that he felt it rather belied the sudden curling of her fingers to a fist and the silent look of reproach. He dropped his hands away from the band immediately, but kept his eyes fixed on her.

"Cut them off," he said. "Even if you can't go home, you're not going back to that."

"It bothers you more than it should," she said, reaching out for the wineskin, and switching abruptly from Mashevi to Maurowan.

He took a sip then handed it to her. "I think you're forgetting how I came to be in the Maurowan army. It bothers me precisely the right amount."

She conceded that with a tilt of her head. "Well, I suspect you were someone before, and that you lost much. It wasn't the same for me. Everything I thought I lost, I never really had to begin with."

"Like your name?"

Tzal stiffened. "What?"

"*Tzal* isn't your name."

"No, but—"

"I asked Rahummi months ago what your real name was and he said you always refused to tell him. Rokha Ayla said the same. You left it behind, and claimed you never had it."

Suddenly, Tzal laughed. Without joy, without humor, putting her head in her hands. She muttered something in what he assumed was Shihrayan and laughed again, shaking her head.

Azetla was bewildered.

"I'm not trying to take what isn't mine to know," he said. "I just wanted to be able to call you by name."

He was such a hypocrite, saying that out loud. Wanting from her what he absolutely could not give in return.

Tzal leaned forward to the fire, resting her elbows on her knees, closing her eyes against the sudden drift of smoke.

"Azetla, if I had a name to give you, I'd have done so. A long time ago."

She laughed again. A bleak sound.

"Poor Rahummi, always convincing himself certain things about me *can't* be true. But that's my fault. I sheltered him from the worst. Lied through my teeth all the time. So, of course, he doesn't believe me when I *do* tell the truth."

"You're not making any sense," Azetla said. "All I want to know is: what did your mother and father call you?"

"Nothing, Azetla. Very carefully, and on purpose, *nothing*. Others called me deela, shikk, or zaraje. I'd translate them to Mashevi for you, but you've refused to teach me any curses or slurs so…" She shrugged. Then she lifted her head as with a sudden strong memory.

"Now, Aadin would sometimes call me—" She paused thoughtfully, staring into the fire. When she started again, her voice was tight around the words "—he came up with his own nicknames. But they never meant anything. More like a tease, than a name. A slip of the tongue. That sort of thing."

She almost twisted the slave band again, but reverted to tapping the table lightly instead.

"Aadin is your brother."

"My oldest brother."

"Who used to get drunk and split your face open," he said.

She instinctively touched the faded, pinched scar across her eyebrow and nose. "So I did tell you that…"

"You had lost a lot of blood. And drank a lot of barley wine."

"Did I say that I'm of the Illari tribe?" she said. He shook his head, struck dumb by the sheer pride in her voice. "My mother's name is Birai of the Ghoshri line. My father is Sa'ased of Haddar. They are from Yaqil, but you already know I wasn't born there."

She gave him a stiff-jawed smile. "There. That's all I've got. Now you can call me whatever you like."

"Daughter-of-Sa'ased-and-Birai is a bit cumbersome," he said.

She tisked softly, still bent toward the fire. "Yes, I suppose it is."

"But I still don't understand the reason."

"I've told you the reason." A hardness crept into her voice. "*That* I remember."

"You blame my God, somehow."

"Then you would prefer I blame the thoughtless midwife, who swore me over to your God with nothing but a bit of red string on the wrist and salt on the skin? She couldn't possibly know or understand the consequences. But she put a sign on me that never washes off, that bleeds into everything I touch, and which neither my Gods nor my people will tolerate."

"As far as I'm concerned, she did a holy thing and died a martyr," he said coolly.

The look of contempt Tzal turned on him in that moment would have made anyone less certain, less determined than Azetla flinch back and recant. He stayed close, and held her disdainful gaze as long as she offered it.

"Better both of us had died and the whole thing stopped there," she said with forced lightness, turning back to the fire. "That would have been a mercy on my people and my family."

She began to twist her mouth into that mirthless smile of hers; the armor she donned when she wished all his words, and all that lay beneath them, to glance off of her. "I don't know what that nameless, formless God of yours wants with me but he's certainly more devious than you give him credit for. Whatever joke he made the day I was born, it has yet to land, but I promise to laugh in his face as soon as it does."

"Tzal, stop it," he said quietly. "Why do you call curses down on yourself?"

"Habit, as best I can tell." Her smile flickered. "Besides I can't really fall farther in the eyes of the Gods, so what is there to lose by inciting them? In any but the useful ways, I really am jinn."

"You are not jinn," he said in Mashevi.

"You don't know that. *I* don't even know that." She still spoke in Maurowan. "I mean, there's luck. And then there's devil-luck."

"I'll say it every time: you're no more a devil than I."

She laughed tiredly.

"I didn't say you were good or kind or innocent, Tzal. But even the cruelest man is just a man. And those who have turned to devils can turn from them."

"I believe that you believe that," she said.

Her voice was weary. She turned her hands about before the fire, looking at her palms. They were dry and calloused, like Azetla's. The firelight didn't tell it, but there were faint scars tracing across the natural lines. It took close attention and patience to mark them enough to ask why they were there. In Shihra, Tzal had explained, it was customary to cut the palms for certain forms of supplication. The most desperate forms.

So, like a prey wounding itself to better draw its predator, she gashed her hands. Let them come down with fire, she'd said, and devour her.

But, again and again, her Gods ignored her every plea and provocation. They surrounded her only with the silence of the dead. And that silence followed her. No voice telling her to turn to the right or to the left. To do this or not to do that, to come or go or stay or to know who or what she was.

Every step and every rail of his own life was built out of holy writ, holy prayers, teachings of the prophets and the sages, stories of the forefathers, and a fierce affection for the least syllable from the mouth of God. And still he often fell, lost his way, and had to grope about to find those rails and right himself.

And if all this were taken from him? He too would not know who or what he was. He would not know heaven from earth from hell. He too would thrash about in hopes of finding a boundary against which to break himself. Better to stumble on a firm stone, than run unhindered straight off a cliff.

He began to understand. An understanding that brought very little comfort or assurance. She really did think his God as cruel as her own. And her people really did sound like demons to him, if only because it was demons that they worshipped and feared and bled for.

"I did try. Sort of," Tzal said gruffly. "For a little while. To serve my Gods. To submit to their whims. To put blood on the stone in earnest, rather than in mockery. I thought it would protect my family. But blasphemy came so much more naturally than reverence did, and it never made any difference. Perhaps I would have followed my Gods if they had just let me."

"Then what you're saying is you would have been their slave unless my God kept you from them."

"Well I'm not his either," Tzal said in a cold voice.

"No. You would have to choose that. You wouldn't get to be 'a devil' anymore. But you garner a great deal from that reputation, don't you?"

"I don't care what anyone thinks I am," she said.

"I believe that you believe that," he said with a faint smile. He kept on speaking in Mashevi, hoping to draw her back to it. But she held to Maurowan, easier for her and less vulnerable because she never stumbled in it.

"Azetla, you talk so easily about something you don't understand. The favor of the desert God is your birthright. Use it or waste it. It doesn't even matter what you do, it's always yours."

Azetla raised his eyebrows, both at what she said and at what she could not realize she said. "Is that what you really think? That because I'm Mashevi, nothing I do can bring consequences? That if my people turn their backs on God, as they often have, heaven simply shrugs and does nothing, while you'll be baited for a mere jest? Look at the state of my people and tell me we're spared our falling away."

"That makes you a disciplined child, not a forsaken one, Azetla."

Azetla bit his tongue at the irony of it. What she said was exactly what he was supposed to believe. That he was not abandoned, in spite of everything. That his "birthright"—such a troubling choice of word—was still with him.

Easy to tell Tzal his certainties about *her*. They leapt from his mouth at the sight of her. Much harder to hew to the ones he needed to hear in his own ear. He knew himself too well for easy mercy.

"Perhaps," he said, almost under his breath. "But for as much of a liar and a hypocrite as I am, it's a far worse shame for me than for some outsider who never knew any different."

For the first time in a while, Tzal turned her face from the fire and looked at Azetla, lips parted in surprise. For once, he had let all the real bitterness seep into his voice.

"It's easy to misuse a birthright and make yourself unworthy of it, you know," he said. "I am forever ceding ground and forever trying to recover it. Truth told, I'm just as desperately far from home as you. And, possibly, just as unwelcome."

Tzal gently took the wineskin from his hand where it had been hanging untouched for some time. She thumbed the rim for a moment. The fire was dying and they were losing its warmth.

"But you still bow and scrape and pray to that God of yours." Her voice had a hint of mockery, but she spoke in Mashevi this time. That was all he wanted.

"Even if nothing I do ever comes to fruition, and I am wrong about even more things than I ever imagined, I will still do that." And it was true. It was the only thing that was always true. "And you? You'll go on provoking and grappling with God, will you?"

"I honestly don't know how to do anything else," she said with a warm, tired smile.

"Tzal, what is the point of battling something you *know* you cannot rout?"

"Because fighting with what is holy may be as close to it as I can possibly get."

There was a bruised sound in the words. An awful turn to her mouth. What he would have liked to say then, she would not have been able to hear. So he said nothing.

A sharp breeze cut through the balcony, telling them of the lateness of the hour. Wordlessly, they stood.

Azetla slowly drew his fingers under the band of his satchel, lifted it from Tzal's shoulder, and placed it on his own. As they walked back from the balcony and through the outer corridor the music from the soiree passed over them, distant and distorted. When they came out into the open night, sounds of revelry came from the training fields, and from the Trekoan village. Drums and oud. Shouts and song. But the wind, picking up, was the closest and loudest. Azetla and Tzal added only their footfalls.

What could be heard had been said. What could be known was known. They did not walk a fast pace and they did not take the short way.

36

The saddlebags were packed and tucked by her pallet. A lean amount of food for Nashuv, and an even leaner amount for her. Just enough to reach Kilsayn and not a grain more. She had begged, borrowed, or stolen all that could keep her warm in this coldest month of the year. A woolen overshirt with goatskin to keep out the rain. A thick headdress. Leather handguards like those the Hushai used to protect their palms going up and down the rocky trails.

Tzal ran her fingers over the thread on the Kitaire—the sleek, strapped pack all the Hushai runners wore. Naima had commissioned that two be made; one for Tzal and one for Rahummi. No one else was fit to wear them, she said. No one else knew the Ghallaz. It was not merely a pack. It was tradition and honor and belonging. It had to be worn just so, the threads and straps carefully adjusted so that nothing trailed, scraped, or left a mark. The brass loops and the meticulous embroidery made it the costliest thing Tzal had ever worn; probably Naima did not mean for her to keep it.

She set the pack down next to the saddlebags.

Everything was as ready as it could be. She was only stalling, and she knew it. She stood, shook her shoulders back, and brushed her hands off against her clothes. She glanced briefly at her wrist, then walked out toward the south wing of Everson's villa.

She was a while waiting at the door for the young Saqirani woman to return and let her in. She heard their voices inside. The muffled, argumentative tones.

"The master wishes to know your business," the Saqirani woman, Uli, said at last, peering through the cloth.

"I'm here to borrow a knife," Tzal said.

Uli raised her eyebrows, confused. But after a few moments, Tzal was allowed in.

Ayla was circling the room, gently jostling little Inaya, whose name Tzal wasn't supposed to know yet. Ayla hummed and sang Trekoan songs that would have made Azetla wince, so mixed were they with the things he liked to call pagan superstition. Rokh Imal sat on the floor, drinking a cinnamon and anise-scented tea, glowering at Tzal.

"What do you want?"

Tzal dropped to the ground, sitting on her heels.

"I want you to take these off," she said, touching her neck, her wrist, and then her ankle.

Imal let out an exasperated noise.

"You can do that yourself any time you like. They're not made of iron."

"That's what you told me then too. But I want you to do it."

"Since when do you care for symbolic gestures?" Imal said.

He made no motion to draw his knife or to do anything except wait out her presence.

"Oh for God's sake, the sheer stubbornness of you two..." Rokha Ayla muttered.

"I don't know how you forgive so easily, Ayla. Haani was your son same as mine," Imal said. His voice was so cold. And so weary.

A shadow of pain passed over Rokha Ayla's face.

"She didn't kill him, love." Ayla kept her eyes on Inaya.

"She left him for dead."

"I did *exactly* what you asked," Tzal said.

"In what world could you think I would ever trade my firstborn son for some paltry victory?"

Tzal wanted to say there was nothing paltry about it. It was the crowning achievement from years of driving Qatlan out of Saqirani territory. It was all the power Saqiran still held to this day.

But she had said that last time, and little good it did her. It only threw salt in the gaping wound. And there was no other defense. She had not meant for their son Haani to die. But nor had she taken care to keep him alive. When she saw her chance to catch that most powerful Rokh of Qatlan unawares, she left Haani to fend for himself. If he was wounded, he would mend, and if he was captured, he could escape or survive till he was retrieved.

That was what *she* always did.

All these things could be easily accomplished from the seat of such a great victory. Surely, she thought, the value she gave would one day outweigh the shame Imal felt in using a "devil." Wouldn't it? Surely, it had to prove her once and for all.

Instead, she obliterated her hopes and Imal's future in the very moment she handed him everything he said he wanted. The memory made her chafe with frustration. But at least she held her tongue this time.

"Enough of this," Ayla said with a sigh.

With a gentle but firm hand, she set little Inaya in the Rokh's arms. His eyes widened as he stared first at his wife and then at the little girl who was not his grandchild, but was certainly as dear as one and of his blood.

Ayla took the common knife from its sheath at Imal's belt and he did not offer a protest. She knelt next to Tzal and gestured for the ankle first. Tzal sat back and slid her foot forward.

"You didn't know what you were doing," Ayla whispered as she slid the knife between the skin and the worn, cracked leather.

"Yes, I did," Tzal said.

Four hard jerks and the strip of leather dropped onto the stone floor.

"No. No, you didn't."

Ayla was stubborn, in her way. Blind, if she wanted to be. Merciful, always.

She took Tzal's hand and, somewhat clumsily, cut through the leather. Tzal ran her fingers over the bare wrist, the strip of lighter brown skin left behind, the coarseness of the skin where the leather hardened or chafed. But then Ayla was tilting her head and Tzal braced for the neck band, which was thicker than the other two. She sucked her breath in when Ayla nicked her under the jaw.

"You'd better do it, my-love," she turned to Imal.

With a look of resignation, Imal traded Inaya for the knife which—by Tzal's estimation—was not as sharp as it should be for such a task. Tzal tilted her head once again as the thin drop of blood tickled her throat and stained her collar. Imal grunted with the ache of bones and joints as he rose and then knelt next to Tzal, but his hands were swift and deft, and the collar dropped to her shoulder, catching on her shirt.

Before Tzal could pick up the leather strips and trace her fingers over the last ten years of her life, Ayla snatched them up and threw them into the pit-fire. "There, that's done now."

The pieces did not burn all that quickly. They coiled, resistant, for what seemed too long a time. But they were going. And soon they would be gone.

Feeling strangely naked and bereft, Tzal came to her feet.

"Thank you," she said stiffly. They were words she did not often use. They tasted strange in her mouth.

Rokh Imal followed her to the lintel of the door, but said nothing. It aggravated her.

"What?" she said, the cloth of the door resting on her shoulder.

"Shihrayan, you—"

"I'm sorry," she cut him off with a harsh tone. Another pair of words she never said, full of thick, bitter flavor.

A thousand caveats strained at the bit in her mouth. *I'm sorry, but you knew who and what I was. You knew what I would do because it was what I always did. You wanted that victory so badly and were willing to do all sorts of devilish things to get it. Always so fiercely ashamed of me no matter what I did, yet always quick to put me to a task. I'm sorry, but how much of this is your own guilt, buried deep, seeking absolution through my wrongdoing?*

By some miracle, she said none of these things. Not this time.

"I'm sorry," she repeated.

Imal looked down at her, his face a grave and impenetrable wall.

"I only meant to say," he began slowly, "that I know you watch over the Mashevi. No one will touch him because of you. But don't betray his convictions in pursuit of his success. He will grieve it. And so will you."

Tzal turned to him with stone-hard contempt. She all but hated him right then. Even now, he conceded *nothing* to her. Took no blame from her. Offered no answer to her. Not the least succor.

"Don't look at me like that. You can't see it, but I'm trying to help you," he said. "One truly wonders at it, Shihrayan. I've seen souls far kinder and gentler than you receive much less mercy, as it seems. And all that you take from it is scorn."

She shrugged her shoulders sharply at him and walked away, the last of his words trailing her.

She did not sleep well. Rose at third watch. Spent an inordinate amount of time fiddling with the Kitaire: Hushai runners usually went in pairs and helped each other with their packs, but she was doing it by herself. She would only be a couple hours ahead of Rahummi and his contingent; she would mark out tonight's camp for them and they would catch up. Only she wanted to ride alone for a little while.

The only people awake to see her depart were the north night-watch and the gate guard. She inadvertently touched her throat as she rode out, then her wrist. But the watchmen did not seem to notice at all.

Mali listed off the contents of the supply wagon one last time and Lieutenant Jotha Karem made careful marks on his ledger. She had packed the wagon herself, as well as the one ahead of her, which was already accounted for and set to position.

Now it was Mali's turn to take her place in the marching line. She and the younger women would go on foot. The two elder women on donkeys, if they chose. At quite the last minute, and to Mali's shock, Azetla had agreed that Khala could come to assist in the medical tents.

"Just for the asking, he did that?" she said to Joseph the day before. "It took the Sahr jinn a month to convince him to let me and the others come."

"Just for guilt, he did that." Joseph grinned. "Sometimes Khala knows how to twist a joint and drive a bargain. 'How dare he put someone else's real sister in danger, but hold back one who was not even his own blood?' You should have seen his face."

"You do know the danger is very great, don't you, Mali?" he added softly.

"I do."

There had been no time to feel nervous. Even now she only felt slightly dazed. A bit out of her skin. She was a cupful of water put into a dammed river. When the gates opened, the river would flow, and without the need of any particular thought or wisdom, she would pick up her feet and follow its steady course.

She would be told where to put her pallet and when to take her rations. She would be told when to rise and where to stand. She would be told if and when someone needed the help of her little platoon. She had twenty-seven souls in her contingent: fifteen army physicians, eleven Trekoan healers or midwives, and Khala, who knew a bit of this and bit of that, yet was resilient and stubborn in her silky way. "It seems to me armies should have seamstresses wherever they go," she said.

Each night Mali would report to Lord Karem, and he would report to Azetla.

It was almost like being at the inn, she realized. She was both snugly inside and easily outside of all that flowed around her. A lord captain was her vast superior and she would bow and honor him, but he should have no commands for her. If he suffered injury, she would have commands for *him*. She was not detached from status, but must go around it. She was not expected to behave like a soldier, but she must keep up and keep track.

And this whole thing was the Sahr devil's idea.

Well, she supposed it was a little like this for the Sahr too. Part and not part. Ever a strange category. Ever an exception to the rules.

The first time she explained to her papa what she was doing, he understood. He worried and argued. He was scared and he was proud. When the matter came up again, it was fresh, as if he never heard it. She decided to bring it up no more and rest on the worried blessing she received when he was most himself. The Trekoan servants looked out for him, and Anna too. He was in good hands.

She tried not to be ashamed of her choice. Tried to be sure that the seemingly brave thing was not actually cowardice. There was no denying it was easier to dress wounds and wear blood on your sleeves than to gnaw the bone of the same tedious conversations and suffer the slow daily loss of someone still very much alive.

Mali put it all out of her mind as the soldiers half a mile ahead of her began to worm their way out of the great gate. The women around her started to shuffle their feet in anticipation, but Mali held still.

"Mali-le! Mali-le!"

Anna tackled Mali from the side in a crushing and uncomfortable hug.

"What are you doing here, Anna? You need to get out of the way or you'll be trampled. Why aren't you with Niri?"

"I have something for you!" Anna said, unslinging a small woven bag.

Mali opened it and a fine, warm smell emanated from the handful of sachets inside: cinnamon, clove, pepper, cardamom, juniper.

"From Niri?" That woman had never given her a second look except to chide her on Anna's behalf.

"She said that the Sahr left it for you."

Mali opened her mouth in surprise. But she recalled how the Sahr had come to Sidara's house once to get a palmful of the tea that many women found soothing at a monthly time. And while Mali had gathered it for her, the Sahr quietly smelled each and every herb and tincture that hung from the ceiling or sat in the baskets.

"Much better in here compared to the training fields and wounded tents," the Sahr said. "Always good to have something to draw you out of that death smell, ah?"

And it was true.

Mali took the bag and gave Anna a kiss on the forehead. Her sister seemed taller all of a sudden.

"Anna-le, you need to get back to Papa. Tell him I love him and I'll be back as soon as possible."

Anna gave a more sober and obedient nod than Mali was used to. She ran off toward the villa, dirty heels kicking up, her favorite little knife looped on the sash of her Trekoan-style dress. She had outgrown all her old clothes.

But Mali could not watch her more than a moment. Now they were actually moving. First at an uneven, mincing pace, but then at a steady march after they came through the gate to the open plain.

The uneasiness in the pit of Mali's stomach reached its height as she passed out of the walls; she almost felt dizzy. But then the hours wore on, the monotony set in. The land rose and cut jagged in the distance, but under her feet it was flats and biting scrub. The sky was a cold pale blue and the desert had never looked so bland and bleak to her as it did that first day marching toward Kilsayn.

She barely remembered rolling out her pallet; she slept like a stone. The cold did not even trouble her. All the women lay tightly packed together, Khala's back to hers, their blanket shared. The next night was the same. She was always on the verge of hunger, satisfied in a bare way at each meal.

Some days there was chatter and laughter among the women, filling and speeding the hours. They admired the lovely Makarish totem Khala had, asking where she had got it; she was delightfully coy. Only Mali knew from whom it came.

Other times there was weary silence, which no one thought to break. Once in a while Mali saw Azetla riding southward from the head of the army, circling round it seemed, like a sheepdog corralling his sheep, making sure not one is lost.

Mali watched the dust pass beneath her feet and the al-most-beauty of the northern desert rise up and surround her.

On the seventh day the ground began to grow harder and more rugged. The pace, which Mali had found very difficult, abated a little.

On the eleventh day they slowed almost to a halt. The proper road disintegrated beneath them. The sky was painfully clear and the sun burned her cheeks even as the wind cut icily through her clothes. Each hour saw stranger and stranger cuts of rock jutting up onto the horizon and dropping below. The stone was a deep brown, with gray and black streaks. Soon there were formations of dark red rock looming above her head. It was the outer edge of the Ghallaz, Lord Karem told her, but they could not go through it. The trails were too difficult to navigate, especially for so many. They would have to enter by the wadi.

On the thirteenth day the marching formation began to parallel a small riverbed and, as the land rose gradually, the slit in the ground deepened and widened into an imposing ravine. There was a shelf chiseled into the eastern wall, like a walkway on a rampart. The western ridge was flush with juniper and desert pine and dotted with sharp man-made towers. With the cold sun hanging at the very top of the sky, Azetla's army poured into Wadi Kilsayn like a winter flood.

37

It was a two hour hike from Azetla's command tent to the high point where the eastern ridge and the undulations of the Ghallaz joined together. Rahummi said that a good Hushai runner could do it in less than half an hour.

When Azetla reached the tiny stretch of flat ground, with the whole ravine to his left, and the jagged land to his right, he paused in awe. The sun was low on the horizon, sending shadow and color across the whole broken land. The reds and blacks and browns in the rock seemed unnatural in their hues, as if ink had spilled. He felt like he was in another world.

No small wonder that this patch of land was unconquered. Who could take it? And what would they do with it once they had it? It caught the foot at every step. It would tolerate only those who gave their entire life to knowing it.

And no small wonder it reminded Tzal of home. So different in color and vastness—so much more vivid and open than Shihra—yet it was a place whose beauty was in its sharp edges, and whose value was in its impassibility.

It seemed that a people could keep only what no one else would want.

From a strategic standpoint, it was troublesome. A labyrinth of rock. His encampments were spread out like an archipelago in an ocean of unmoving waves. Tzal had explained it to him but only now, from this vantage point, could he see why the Hushai runners were the great fame of the Ghallaz. You could not walk a straight line from one village to another. You could scarcely do so from one home to another.

If it weren't for Naima, Rahummi, and Tzal, it would have been mad to attempt this. The Ghallaz and the wadi would suck them in like mud, and wear them away like water on rock. But because of them—because of the Hushai—this brutal place would be their fortress.

He had still not seen Tzal. For seventeen days now. He'd gone rapidly from one task to the next, and Rahummi had been the first to find and guide him as they made their many, scattered encampments and marked the main trails.

"We should head back," Rahummi said. "The Hushai elders have invited you into their place of meeting. There will be ceremonies and such."

Azetla nodded and followed his step. The sun was low against the rocks, tipping them with red, but by the time they reached the great chiseled flat, all was shrouded in deep blue, black swallowing the edges bit by bit.

The meeting hall was natural rock at each far end, chiseled stone between, carved beams of desert pine, and animal-hide awnings. But even though it was made of many disparate things, it was pieced together like a mosaic, rife with symmetry, artful in every detail. The glow of fire blazed warmly from within.

Azetla paused.

"You will go in with me, and translate?" he said, furrowing his brow.

"Of course," Rahummi said. "And you don't have to stay long. These things can last all night and the elders come and go as they please."

Azetla ran the edge of his thumb over his wooden lion's head and tapped it lightly.

"And where is—"

"She's been on the west side of the wadi for two days, preparing the Makars for Lord Sarrez to woo. If she got the runner I sent this morning, she'll be back later tonight." Rahummi gave a slight smile. "Don't worry, Commander. In most other ways the Shihrayan bests me, but I assure you my fluency in Hushai dialect is at least as good as hers. Maybe better. Naima would vouch for it."

Azetla returned the faint smile, nodded, and in they went.

The music and the heat rushed over him, and the elders bid him join the meal.

He did everything Naima had taught him to do, said everything Naima had taught him to say. He struck his palm to the center of his chest with each greeting, a gesture of deep respect. He gave the formal greetings, omitting only the parts about their gods and spirits. They were taken aback by this, but not yet offended. They observed his hand-washing and prayers as if he were a creature found in the wild, doing its inexplicable creaturely things.

The Hushai elders were loud and humorous—so different from the ever-dignified Saqiranis—and they seemed to find Azetla's gravity extremely amusing. Food and repartee passed around at such a rate that Azetla could not keep up.

"You're leaving out a lot," he said aside to Rahummi.

"They like to talk fast and all at once...and the jokes are bawdier than I like in my own dialect," Rahummi said with an embarrassed glance. "I'm doing my best."

Azetla tried to be grateful to Rahummi, but the disparity in experience was marked. Tzal had a deft way of handling these situations where it was impossible to hand over each and every individual word. She chose one trail of conversation to follow like a central river, thoughtfully aggregating the little tributaries into it as needed. And she never left out the bawdy things, because his own disdain for them amused her immensely.

The Hushai asked Azetla many questions, but almost none about strategy and battle. It bewildered him. If someone came to his home to make it a battleground, there would have been nothing else to do or talk about but that. There was some nod to religious ceremony here and there, but all done with a strange humor and nonchalance. Surely they understood the gravity of what they had agreed to?

Azetla was left briefly to himself, as Rahummi was beckoned across the room to give honors to Naima's grandfather.

Feeling fully welcomed yet fully out of place, Azetla waited for an opportunity to quietly take his leave. There was so much left to do.

He was taken aback when the dancers came in. A drumbeat flared, men clapped, and the four women moved at first in unison, then in pairs, and then one at a time around the room. They were, by southern standards, barely dressed. There was almost as much copper and beading on their bodies as there was cloth.

The style of dance was wild, sensuous, and entirely overpowering. It was difficult to avert the eyes, and he had little success for the trying. So instead, he stood, glanced at Rahummi across the room—Rahummi gave an approving nod—and stepped out into the brilliant black and cold of the night. The heat lingered a while in his face, as did the image of the dance in his mind's eye.

⁕

Tzal sat back on the ground, leaning into the little cut of rock. The Kitaire shielded her back from the jagged surface. Her legs ached from the swift journey down the northwest shelf and up the east.

389

Gado, the Hushai runner who had been with her, smiled when they reached the fire outside the beams of the great gathering hall.

"I suppose you don't shame the Kitaire as badly as you might," he said. "But the Inze are devils so devils must be Inze."

Tzal swallowed the compliment whole, without a word. Inze were the smaller, wild breed of ibex that lived in the wadi. They were known for being dangerous if approached, bullies to the domestic goats, and quick to scale unreachable places. Among the Hushai they need not always represent evil, but they certainly stood for mischief and waywardness. Stubborn three-year-olds were called Inze. People whose eyes turned the wrong way.

Anyone who unnerved, confused, or exasperated, as it were.

Now that they had fire and food, the runners were full of banter. Tzal enjoyed listening to their ruthless jokes at one another's expense, but felt no need to insert herself. She was too tired to be clever, and too content with the fire and the stars.

Each time Tzal heard someone leave or enter the meeting hall, she listened carefully. The drums began, which meant the dancers had gone in. Tzal let the beat swirl around her like a high wind, and watched the runners tap their feet or rap their thighs to the rhythm. They soon got into a lewd chant that evoked the moves of the Hushai dancers inside.

She smiled in the dark when she saw Azetla walk out of the meeting hall and come to the fire. It took his eyes a moment to find her in the shadows, but when he did, she put her hand up. Azetla gripped it firmly and pulled her to her feet.

"Got a little too warm in there for you, ah?" she said with a grin.

He set his jaw, shook his head faintly, and said nothing.

"I told you the Hushai have a very different sense of propriety than other Trekoans. Grab that torch, will you? Parts of this trail are tricky at night."

She led him on the trail toward the place where the rock was hewn flat for a quarter-mile in each direction. The hewing had been done centuries ago, by a Makarish lord who tried desperately to make the Ghallaz profitable to himself. The man's plans came to nothing, but now Azetla's command tent and fifty others were pitched on that great plain of rock, a central node to all the other encampments.

"You decided to allow yourself a southern face at last," she said in Mashevi.

He ran his hand over his scant beard, a mere fortnight's worth.

"It seemed advisable," he said. "And I'd had enough of your mocking me about it."

"Suits you better."

Watching her footing closely, she wondered if he thought she was mocking now too.

"How was it on the west rim?" he said after a time.

"I've been having more trouble with the Makars than I'd hoped," she said. "But Sarrez is Zawishi on his mother's side, and Baradi on his father's side, so I think he'll be able to finish in a few hours what I couldn't quite accomplish in two days. Rahummi can take him over to the west rim tomorrow."

"Can he do it? Will they listen to him?"

Oh Azetla, don't ask me for certainties. I have fewer of those every day.

"I think so. He's from a powerful lineage. They know his name. And they can see the army with their own eyes." She held up her hand. "Stop. We have to go single file here. Keep close."

Tzal took the torch and the lead, while Azetla followed with trustful steps.

"Hopefully I'll have better luck with the scout. The Hushai say it will take us two or three days, but that's just covering ground. If I'm going to be thorough, it'll take a little more than that." She scrambled down a sheer spot and turned the light to him so he could see how to get down. "First light. I'm assuming that's still the plan?"

He cleared the drop.

"That's still the plan," he said gravely.

They soon came into the glowing brightness of cookfires and torches, and the ground was flat and lit at their feet all the way to the command tent. When they stepped inside Azetla took a dry reed stick and lit the hanging lamps. In the orange-yellow light, he turned and gave Tzal a long, scrutinizing look, his eyes moving from head to foot, from Kitaire to Sagam, as though he was doing inventory to make sure she was indeed all there.

She was aware of her dry, cracked hands, chapped skin, and the streaks of dust dried in sweat on her face. And she was exhausted. But she didn't think it showed too much. If she stood square, and kept her gaze firm, with the sleek Kitaire fitted to her like a glove, she could make someone think she was as lithe and tireless as any Hushai runner. Even Azetla.

"Where are you pitched?" he asked.

"Most nights on the jut next to Naima's family, just outside their home. Twenty minutes of trail from here."

Azetla shook his head.

"That's no good. You pitch here. It's shoulder-to-shoulder in all the tents, even this one, but put your pallet where you can fit it. It'll clear out somewhat once we're finished setting up the Gul and Banti camps. I'm not sending a runner each time I need you."

Tzal gave a nod of agreement and began the slightly tedious process of unstrapping the Kitaire. Her fingers were getting used to doing it without tangling the threads or pulling out the loops, but it still required concentration.

"The runners treat you in like one of their own, don't they?" Azetla said, watching the movement of her hands carefully.

"Almost." *Always, always almost.*

She slid the pack gently to the ground. Tacking up her sleeves—an old habit from her years as a Saqirani slave, but this time very consciously done—Tzal began to tuck all the loose straps into their threads and pouches. She unrolled her pallet, drew out her outer cloak, and set the Kitaire at the head, a sturdy pillow, though none too soft.

A bright, keen look entered Azetla's eye. He raised his eyebrows and knelt down next to her. Tzal was not the least bit surprised when he reached out and took firm hold of her wrist.

"I see you decided to finally tell the truth," he said.

He ran his fingers over the strip of skin that was a different shade of brown than the rest. She had started to feel accustomed to the bare skin of her own wrist, but he made the strangeness of it fresh and palpable to her. Azetla drew aside the Hushai scarf she wore around her neck until he could see that, yes, she had cut that one off too. He traced the line where it had been as if to be very certain. Gently and thoroughly certain. She held still. Offered no expression. With all her might, she made no show of his effect on her.

Then he sat back on his heels.

"I'll leave your boot wrappings alone, but I take it that one's gone too?" he said.

"Like you said. They were used up."

A smile flickered across Azetla's face, but he said nothing. He brought water for them to drink and for washing too. It was cold and sharp on her chapped skin. The cleanness burned her raw. Azetla rolled his pallet to the rhythm of his prayers and soldiers trickled into the command tent. One by one, they collapsed onto the hard ground. And Tzal did the same.

Exhaustion could be such a stalwart friend. It sedated thoughts, smothering words and worries as with a blanket. The thin pallet seemed a luxury. With the stink and sweat and crowded heavy breaths came warmth. She did not even remember the lamps being snuffed out.

The call of the fourth watch dragged Tzal out of sleep and she begrudged it. The dark in the tent was still absolute, not a shadow could she see, scarcely her own hand in front of her face. Blindly, she extracted herself from those around her and packed her Kitaire. It was more luck than sense that she reached the flap without kicking someone in the head.

Bowing through the cloth she stepped into a shockingly dark night.

The clouds had come. The rain would follow. She began donning the Kitaire—a tedious affair even in daylight with warm fingers—with nothing but the dull orange flicker of the dying watchfire.

"Let me help you."

Azetla came behind her, his voice husky with morning and cold. She told him how to secure the straps on the back and tighten them so that the Kitaire gave a lean profile for narrow passages, and so that no bit of cloth or metal would catch on any jagged rock or acacia thorn. He was quick and surprisingly adept at the task, but then he had always been one for tedious details.

"Hopefully I come back with a good report," she said, turning to him.

"I rather doubt it," he said grimly. "Tzal…"

"Yes?"

"Don't go too far. And don't play games."

"Azetla, I'm going to do the same thing I always do."

"I know. That's the problem. You always walk on the cliff's edge and dangle your feet for fun. Or taunt a captor just to measure his anger and see how he strikes. You like to tempt fate. To tempt God, if such a thing were possible." He lowered his voice. "You aren't careful. You've said it yourself."

Faint was the gray light coming. But it was enough to see the quiet frustration on his face.

"I've only ever been caught when I meant to be, Azetla," she said in Mashevi. "And, by the way, when I provoked you that time, I knew you wouldn't kill me."

"No, you didn't."

She smiled at him. "Yes, I did."

It wasn't the least bit true. All he needed was permission and he would have gutted her in a second. She knew that. It was easy to say, after the fact, that what happened was precisely what you meant to happen. But most of the time Tzal was just ramming her shoulder against whatever came till all that could break, broke. And wherever there is left to go, you go.

He wasn't wrong. It just wasn't supposed to matter.

"Azetla, you've no right to ask me to do one mote less than what I'm good for."

"I've no right to ask you to do anything at all, remember?"

That was true enough.

"Don't forget to have Sarrez keep a sharp eye on the new Makarish officers," she said. "He needs to pay attention to their talk."

"I've got it in hand."

She shook her head. He really was such a hypocrite sometimes; he walked the edge of cliffs same as she did. He dared his God to answer him with life or death, same as she did. Would he take his own admonishment? Would he be careful just for the asking, regardless of what needed to be done?

No. Not to her satisfaction.

So she would not hold back for his. Tzal had set her copper on the wager table. She would give Azetla all she could muster, blood and sweat and everything else besides. She had some real use left before the time would come for him to slip the knife through, cut her off like a strip of limned leather, and cast her aside. Because that time *would* come. Azetla didn't know he was going to do that—he obviously didn't think he ever would—and Tzal didn't know when.

But it was good to be ready for the rope to break and brace for the fall.

No one could say she had not tried.

38

"Lieutenant Haqir, look up."

Maadun Haqir lifted his head from his meager meal to look the jackal in the face.

"Yes, Commander?"

"Gather your things. I need you to accompany Captain Sarrez to the west rim of the wadi."

Maadun gritted his teeth.

"Captain Elyas was supposed..."

"Elyas is taken ill like so many others. You are the one I chose to replace him. Lieutenant Sarrez leaves in one hour and so do you. Your runners will meet you at Uqarti rally point and I'll brief you on your role."

"Of course, Commander."

Haqir had made himself outwardly amenable for the last several months and he knew he must continue to do so. He disparaged the jackal Commander only so much as he could reasonably get away with. Sometimes in earnest. Sometimes in a more perfunctory manner, to prove to his fellow Makars that, no, he was not under the spell and, no, he would not ever kiss that filthy jackal's boot the way Nimer Sarrez and the others did.

But he did as he was told. And those beneath him did as they were told. He did not shirk. The lieutenant's commission had cost his family dear. He was supposed to make something of it; to the best of his ability, he did not shame the rank panel he wore.

But the question he could never easily answer was, did he shame *himself*?

He was beginning to think he had. His hatred and disdain for the jackal Commander often cooled to a scant ember, so that it took a great wind and much kindling to rouse it. At the battle of Hidud, Maadun Haqir found himself on a strange precipice. He stood strong in the battle. His men fought beautifully. The battle was swift. The Commander was victorious; so Maadun was victorious.

He was caught up in it. He was gravely tempted. For one disorienting day, it was as if he held the torch of the world in his hand and whichever way he turned, it cast a wildly different shadow.

Was the jackal a great General and warrior, who would unshackle Trekoa and Makaria? Would they become what they once had been? Was he as pious as he pretended to be, walking in faithful duty to his strange god and his hard people? Was he honorable, after all? Straight and bright as a king's sword, though fierce as a devil?

Ah, *the devil*. At that, the grand shadow flickered and formed anew.

Was the jackal a mere demon perfectly content to ally with demons? A cynical opportunist, riving Maurow apart for no purpose but his own? Was he spending tens of thousands of men like stolen coins for which he must make no account? Was he a liar of all kinds, a thief of pride and place, a snake in the grass?

Thus the precipice.

Either walk back down the path up which he came, remind himself once again never to trust this Azetla, and to hold fast to what he had known all along about the greedy cunning of jackals.

Or fall, knowing not where he would land nor how it would undo him.

He had not imagined how terrifying it could be to consider not hating a man. It felt like he was about to let a murderer go free. To invite a robber into his home. To hand his sister over to a scoundrel who would dishonor her. Who would do such a thing?

All these long months, Maadun had braced for the jackal's retaliation, imagining how honorably he, a Makar of good blood, would bear up under the coming mistreatment. How clearly cruel and vindictive the jackal would seem to all.

But the Commander never spoke of the day that Maadun, Sable, and the others had beat him down into the muck of the privy trench. He certainly knew that they had intended to shame, abuse, and then kill him. They almost managed it before Sarrez showed up. It was a plain matter of honor.

No formal punishment had ever been demanded; lawfully, they had done nothing wrong and, practically, Azetla had not the sanction and support then that he did now. No one had thought their actions unreasonable.

But now? Such an attack would be unthinkable. Treason. Officers from all over the Empire would stand in Azetla's defense. And, no doubt, the devil would get to your throat first.

How could things change so quickly? How did jackals do that? And how could Maadun right his own mind?

Relief from the question came when the army had returned to Areo and to all the thousands of new soldiers that had arrived. Dozens of Makarish officers from good families all throughout North Makaria were settling in. Some were old friends or distant relatives. People of power and influence and rich history. Their contempt for a jackal was mercifully fresh and untarnished. They welcomed Maadun and made much of him; he gladly scrubbed away his doubts.

He had to scrub again sometimes. Mostly when the jackal was standing in front of him, looking him in the eye.

Maadun ate and gathered himself quickly for the long trek to the Makarish side of the wadi. The Hushai runners could show them the best paths, but they could not make them easy or smooth. They could not keep the rocks from rolling under Maadun's feet, nor stretch his lungs to better fill with air as they descended, then rose, well over a thousand feet. It would have helped if the Hushai did not so obviously mock Maadun and the others behind their hands in that jibberish dialect of theirs. The only words Maadun understood were "slow as mud" and "like children."

Lord Sarrez took the insults with laughs. He had the role of a captain now, for the jackal required much of him. Sarrez gave no special attention, either good or bad, to Maadun until they reached the first rim village. The other Makarish soldiers were given relatively free rein to speak with the villagers as they wished, to secure their support for this movement or that requirement over stewed goat and a cup of wine.

But Maadun was required to be Captain Sarrez's shadow and, after a day of this, he realized he had never been allowed to speak without Captain Sarrez present. This humiliated him. Maadun, an officer, a grown man, a son of the Zawish tribe and of Maurowan nobility, was trusted less than Dani, a Baradi boy of nineteen years. A friendly, stupid tackman of no birth whatsoever, who just happened to think better of the jackal than he ought.

Against his better judgment, Maadun let slip a sideways remark of complaint as the men rolled out their pallets.

"What was that, Lieutenant Haqir?" Sarrez said coolly, lifting his head.

"Nothing, Captain. Only seems a waste I'm here if I'm no use to you." He was not able to drain the bitterness from his voice.

Sarrez, whose looks, lineage, and position might make any man at least a bit envious, did not answer right away. Yet there was soft scorn in his eyes. *This man*, Maadun reminded himself, *trades away his blood for fleeting power; remember that. Don't let him make you ashamed with a mere glance. He hasn't the right.*

"Your presence here is of tremendous use," Sarrez said in a measured voice.

Here, not there. Maadun began to understand. With the bloody Sahr devil gone north, the Commander might be seen as more vulnerable. So divide the troublemakers. Spread them far and wide. Let not their hands be idle lest they be treacherous.

"I have failed no task ever put to me," Maadun said in a low voice. "Yet you still do not trust me."

"You tried to have him killed once, Haqir, and when that failed, you tried to do it yourself. You should have had your commission stripped and been put to debt-work. He didn't do that to you." Sarrez's voice grew gritty and thick. "*I* sure as hell would have. But he stayed his hand and I thought maybe he was right. Maybe mercy would win out. It did for Brighton and Sable. But I see you, Haqir. You sniff out anyone who says an ill word against him, cling to them, begging for their approval, *encouraging them*! By blood, man, why would you do that? If not for honor, at least for your own sake! We live here or die here together."

Maadun stood, the stew of fury and frustration within him reaching its full, rolling boil.

"I have not shirked. Nor will I, till the Corra's way is won. I promise you that. But I'll not spit on my own blood, and I'll not have that jackal's mercy turn me into his slave as it has done to you, Captain."

He could not believe he dared say that out loud. The words came from the depths of himself, almost unknown to him until they poured out with their heat and grief. How dare that jackal put Maadun in his debt. How much easier this all would be if the man had just taken his revenge the moment he had the power to do so.

An eye for an eye. Then Maadun would feel he had a weapon in his hand. But the jackal refused to do it, twisting mercy into power.

It scorched the skin and smoked the mind. Ever it was in his thoughts, plaguing him.

"I was the one who had mercy on *him*, Maadun," Captain Sarrez said coolly. "And only after that was it the other way around. We've scrapped the books by now, and stopped keeping record. You'd be a freer man if you did the same."

Maadun kept a few choice words firmly behind his teeth. He had arguments left but they were best kept inside his own head, told to his own self, or those who would approve them. Sarrez's words itched across him like lice.

It was a long night and day of clawing at the itch. Each time he thought he purged it, bloody Nimer Sarrez would stoop down, retrieve it, and set it right back on his skin.

How much trust and value among his own would he lose if he trusted and valued the jackal? It was beyond imagining. One might as well say, "*how much blood would you lose if you cut open your veins?*"

Everything. The answer was, absolutely everything you had.

⚬⎯⎯ ₩ ⎯⎯⚬

The Mashevi did not tell James to follow. But he did. It was the only sensible thing to do if no one remembered to tell you what to do.

He was self-conscious of the way he walked over the rough ground, the way he wore his armor, the way his sword moved uncomfortably at his side. It seemed that any common desert goatherd must see how unused to all of it he was. A special rank panel had been sewn for him, which marked him as something like a general and something like an emperor. As of yet, he was neither.

Yet that bright little panel was the only thing about which he did not feel self-conscious. He felt it as a command. A duty. It was what he was supposed to do and be. Wearing that was just about the only thing assigned to him, so he better make the most of it.

It was exhausting to keep in step with the Mashevi. The man was raggedly busy. He didn't show it much, but when you shadow a man day in and day out, you begin to see the signs of fatigue. Eyes blinking and carefully rhythmed breathing just to tenuously hold focus on what was being said. Bruised under the eyes. And a glazed, distant look in those few brief moments that he was let be.

Well. That was how James saw it because that was how he felt. Blistered feet. Fiery chafing in the shoulder and left side of his armor—it was fitted just for him, so he didn't know what he was doing wrong there—and his first experience of truly limited rations.

When, as it happened sometimes, the Mashevi was surrounded by an ongoing whirlwind of officers, being struck with so many questions of so many wildly disparate kinds that he could scarcely take a breath or a piss between them, James stood by fascinated. At first, he was in awe of how deftly Azetla seemed to manage it all, when James was sure that his own mind would fray to bits with such an inundation. But, by their fourth day in the Ghallaz—James' fourth day of silently accepting his role as one of apprenticeship and taking it very seriously—he saw something new. Something that gave him hope.

There was no question that Azetla had certain giftings that made him well suited to this role of commander. Giftings James had never possessed and likely never would. But none of that was the actual coal that kept this forge alight. Watching the man day and night in the intensity of battle preparation, James saw all the cracks. All the imperfections. Impatience. Weariness. Doubts. Even, he thought, a little fear.

The Mashevi was just a common man, after all.

It was only discipline that kept the Mashevi on his feet. Discipline that made him tap his little lion's head, take a deep breath, and find the answer for one man and then the next. Discipline that made him work over the plans with a fine-tooth comb when they seemed done enough to James. Discipline that made him rein in his impatience when the Hushai leaders shrugged off his questions or his protocols, and start over with them again, ever trying to reach across the cultural canyon.

Discipline was something that came over time.

And discipline was something that any common fool could have, if he was willing.

James was willing, by blood.

Already in the last months, he had gained muscles of decision and reason beyond anything he had known in his former life. Less and less was he afraid to have thoughts that others did not give him. By now he had come to regard his own life both more gravely and more lightly. What he said and did truly mattered; many souls were tied to his hands and he must honor that. But his life was, in some sense, already forfeit. If he died, it would not be obscurely in battle, but rather in the aftermath, after failure upon failure. Publicly, he supposed. Indeed he had given some thought to the manner of his execution and decided that he didn't want hanging or poison. He wanted it just like they did to the jackals on the Red River festival. Very quick. Blood to the Gods.

Morbid as this thought was, there was a haziness to it. It affected nothing. It did not change his step or direction or the fact that he was going to carry on as if he would survive or at least escape. He was going to prepare. He was going to put his shoulder to stone. Just in case he lived.

Shadowing and learning from the Mashevi was the first part.

Undermining and overtaking him were the second and third, respectively.

Not yet, of course. Not until after the thing was done. If indeed it could be done.

James had to discover how to—as Verris had put it—find the exact point of divergence where it lay ahead, and stand in vigorous wait for it. To use the Mashevi's own momentum to eventually shuck him off, so that James could come out free and clear and unstained.

Wesley's preferred solution was of the final variety. Everson hedged, but did not deny the simple efficacy of the idea. James was still gnawing on the question. Death, or prison, or debt, or what? He didn't like any of the answers. But at least James was no longer afraid to disagree with strong minds and strong wills. They may know more than him, but they didn't know everything, and sometimes he could see that they were nothing more and nothing less than simply terrified.

James toyed with the idea of merely taking Azetla's legs out from under him, so to speak, but trying to leave the head on. If it were possible. Wesley would redden in the face and tell him this was blasphemous and ruinous and would sully James' rule at the outset. Masheva would instantly revolt. Colonel Everson would offer a sly grin and say, "Come now, Your Highness, don't be so naïve."

And Riada's voice was clear as day in his head.

Mercy to that man is mercy to a viper, James. You release him and he will instantly turn to bite your hand.

And that was probably true.

But Riada, the whole reason for all of this is the hope that I might do things differently than you, isn't it? Have you quieted the jackals, or have you riled them up?

In any case, James did not plan to leave himself entirely defenseless. He was gathering the Mashevi's weaknesses even as he observed and tried to practice his strengths. And he had sense enough to be friendly to the Makarish officers in particular. To sit at their fires. To let them know they were seen. To hear their talk.

Of course they were too wise to speak badly of Azetla in front of him. But once in a while he perceived gentle insinuations and he made certain they were warmly received, never reprimanded.

He sought those certain Makarish and Maurowan officers out until they began to seek *him* out in return. He would surely need them when the time came.

39

They had gone as far as they dared go and seen what they dreaded to see.

All of them wanted to leave immediately before the threat of rain came to pass and washed out the narrower trails.

Tzal refused. The Hushai muttered anxiously among themselves, while Iraal—the only Saqirani with her—tried to coax her. He was shaken by the report they must bring back and, indeed, had been uneasy the whole time. Tzal made them go further than any of them wanted and then she herself had gone further still, making them wait cold and still in the dark, at the outer edge of the Ghallaz, till she had proof of her concern.

"What else can we expect to see, Shihrayan?" Iraal said pleadingly. "Shouldn't we hurry?"

"Yes, we'll hurry," Tzal said in a brusque, distracted voice. "As soon as I'm done."

"Done with *what*, for God's sake?"

She would have answered him, but she saw the distant flicker of a torch and shadows proceeding from it till they fell into darkness, visible no more. Dawn was at least half an hour away.

"Gado!" Tzal whispered sharply.

The Hushai runner jogged over to her.

"Guide us to the outer Fahoun trail, right where it meets the Inze-na rock."

"But that's the—"

"I know. Don't worry about it. Leave it to me."

She fell in step behind Gado who had to feel his way slowly, for even the most skilled runner in all the Ghallaz must move like a blind man on a night with clouds so full of rain, waiting to burst over their heads. The miracle of it was that he could move at all. Tzal kept her hand on the leather strap at his waistline, Rejaw behind her, Iraal behind him. Gado used different pitches of clicks and tisks to indicate a sudden drop, a sudden rise, or an overhanging rock. *Duck your head here.*

Dawn began to stagger in with faintest gray. When they turned onto the high end of Fahoun trail, crouched, the others saw what she needed them to see. Now they understood. At Tzal's gesture, they all remained silent as the dead.

Tzal signed to Gado and Rejaw, telling them what to do. Gado grasped it instantly and nodded. She waved for Iraal to follow them. She crawled, scrambled, slid, and scraped down the back side of Fahoun by the Inze rock.

Lying flat against the rock in the dark morning, she tried to breathe quietly and she did not move. It was not long before she heard the enemy scouts pass below her. The purchased Hushai guides first, whispering back and forth in their northeast dialect. Then the Maurowans, loud and heavy with their feet. If her eyes had seen aright, two Hushai, three Maurowans.

The moment their sounds struck her from the correct position—it was still so hard to see—she slid from her perch, and jumped the rest of the way down. Landing on the first scout in a jarring tumble, Tzal cracked his head into the rock and drove the knife hard. The second swung for her but hit stone, the narrow path hemming him in.

She had to fight him plain and head-on. Something she never willingly chose to do. There was no advantage of strength or sword-skill, and the surprise was already spent.

Only her footing saved her. And that bloody stupid Flame–Pine sequence Azetla had her do a hundred times. Drop to a kneel, twist up to the back, knife in the ribs. It wasn't clean, she gashed her knees, but it got her where she needed to be. He stumbled. She finished him.

Gado, Rejaw, and Iraal blocked the passage from the north and killed one of those that fled. They captured the last Maurowan and the limping Hushai who had dared hire himself out for the enemy. Tzal questioned them, softly at first. Once she was reasonably certain she had taken from them all they had to give, she and Gado killed them. Disgusted that one of his own had chosen coin over clan, Gado spat twice on the bodies in contempt.

Suddenly, as if in response, the sky broke out in strong rain. Gado's shoulders sank. Iraal's too.

Tzal shook her head and began to drag one of the bodies off the path.

"The longer we wait, the worse it gets. Let's go."

She let the Hushai decide what covering to give or not give their brethren and the men who hired them. Contempt was one thing, sacrilege was another. *But for blood's sake, hurry!*

Never were bodies covered so quickly or haphazardly. Gado did not even kneel beside the corpses to speak their final words, nor did he take their Kitaire. Mud was already churning under their boots, and each time they criss-crossed the outer paths, water filled the low points reaching up to their ankles with swirling stones and silt. Several hours later, when the dull gray began to fade to black and they reached the main path where the rocks were too hard to scale, they had it up to their knees.

The rain lightened then, but it did not stop. Not when the water gave a sudden gush and they had to clamber and cling to the sides;

Iraal was almost swept away, but Rejaw caught his arm. And not when they missed the outclimb and had to go back, Gado cursing himself for having passed it.

Only when dawn broke again and they reached the high path did the sky begin to clear a little.

But by then it was obvious that something was wrong with Iraal. He stumbled often. He burned with fever.

Tzal and the Hushai runners took turns shouldering him up and down the trail of mud and rock.

⚜

Azetla jogged down the steep Iom trail toward the medical tents, pausing briefly at the lookout. He tapped his wooden lion's head through his outer cloak and made the same calculation he'd been making for the last two days. They should have been back by now. Little good it did him staring out; the return trails were scarcely visible from here. What he could see, however, was all the rubble and washout from the rain, the pooling in the lower trails.

The Corra James caught up to him and paused also, imitating Azetla's line of sight, down the jagged tiers of carved wadi shelf to the north where dark blue sky was cutting its way through the clouds.

Without a word, Azetla resumed his pace. So did James, following at his heels as he so often had these last several days. Azetla should not begrudge him this attempt to fulfill his role. But he did. He was not used to being clung to like this. At first it made him feel like he had no room for the use of his elbows, no rest for the thoughts of his mind. Through mere will, Azetla kept his routine of work and prayers. To the best of his ability he changed no word of his mouth, no expression of his jaw. He answered every question as plainly as possible. He endeavored to both give James nothing and withhold nothing from him.

Quite simply, James must affect him nowise. He must be talked to as an emperor, utilized like a corporal, and remembered as a future threat. He seemed to understand this well enough and made no trouble about it.

They wound through the soldiers, all sitting on the ground at their rations. Azetla no longer needed to give the gesture of omission—omit salutes, omit honorifics, omit all signs of an important man walking by—because it had become known policy. James certainly did not want the ruckus, and Azetla did not want his officers wearing targets on their backs.

"Well, Nuss?" Azetla paused next to a large cluster of Juniper and Black Wren soldiers.

Corporal Nuss looked up.

"A dozen more for the medical tents last I checked."

Azetla nodded. An illness was going about. Mali said it was nothing serious, but it knocked the men down for a day or two and bled out rations; the sick men must receive an extra portion of water, goat broth, and salt. Coughs and scratched throats, mild fevers, and weak stomachs abounded. The rain and cold were sapping the life out of Azetla's army.

"Mostly Juniper still?"

Nuss shook his head.

"Afraid not, Commander. Three were from Blue Rock. And one was that Saqirani fellow, just got back from scouting. Don't know his name..."

"Iraal?" Azetla said, lifting his head and squaring his shoulders. "When did they get back?"

"Sahr devil was dragging him in just as I left. He looked a good bit worse than the others, I'd say."

Azetla clapped the young man on the shoulder. "Good man, Nuss. Give the day's final tally to Lieutenant Karem so he can make the ration adjustments."

A few of the soldiers in hearing let out faint groans, knowing what that meant.

"Yes, I know, I know," Azetla said toward the groans. "As soon as the resupply from South Makaria is confirmed we can return to full rations."

Quickly, Azetla turned toward his headquarters tent, assuming that's where Tzal would go first. When James stepped to follow, a mild irritation flared.

"Your Highness, I recommend you go take your rations and make your rounds with the soldiers. I'll call for the final brief of the day after I have the scouting report."

Then he turned to the dusky west without waiting for James to argue or acknowledge.

He was anxious to hear the report alone, without prying eyes, without denial or pretense. There must be a full, clear moment where he was not tempted to whitewash either dangers or fears for the sake of seeming in control or keeping up morale.

He remembered when he was new to the Black Wren, how bewildered he had been by Captain Hodge. When dire news was given him, he would force a grin and say, "*that sounds like a devilish good party.*" Eventually Azetla learned to read the false cheer, and his heart would race; he knew that all was not well. Losses and hardships and failure were about to pour down upon them.

Azetla always wished Hodge had just plainly stated what they were about to face. But he understood why he didn't. You don't want to knock the men's feet out from under them when they needed every last inch of their footing and balance to stay alive. A confident man can do things that a terrified man simply cannot.

Tzal was not in the headquarters tent, but her Kitaire was, covered in half-dried mud, tucked in his corner. It was not torn, however. Nor bloody. He took a deep breath. Uncovered the smoke hole in the tent. Kicked the fire back to life, feeding it a few dry scraps.

Lit two lamps. Welcomed the day of rest in prayer, though surely no rest would be had by anyone.

The words of an ancient king—of dire, holy songs—were still on his lips when Tzal slipped in. Almost perfectly silent, with the bowl of meager rations in her hand.

She nearly collapsed to a cross-legged seat. Damp and muddy as the Kitaire, from head to foot. The food was gone in seconds, though she swallowed each bit with a slight wince. Azetla walked over and saw that even her overshirt was soaked through and now that she sat still, she shook, teeth chattering violently inside an ill-shaped smile. Her fingers, curled and trembling, were a dark, unsavory bluish-gray color. She thrust them toward the fire, as close as she could without burning them.

"Iraal fell ill," she said. Her voice was raw and cracked, her jaw jittering. The words barely came out.

"I heard."

"We just had to keep moving." She took a sip of water and coughed. Her voice did not improve. "But they'll warm up quick enough. And so will I." She tried to cough her dry throat clear again, but it was useless. "We went on the Gori trail first—"

Azetla held his hand up and shook his head.

"Take off the overshirt and tunic, right now."

He pulled out the only spare bit of clothing he had—a thick woven Hushai tunic Naima had gifted him just before they left. For all he knew, it was the only clean and dry thing in the whole camp, so fierce had been the rain. He tossed it to her and turned. He heard the shudder and gasp when the frigid air hit her bare skin; she clenched down on clacking teeth.

He turned back as she pulled her head through the collar, handing her his blanket and anything else he could find that was even half dry. Tzal unknotted her hair with clumsy fingers so that it would dry more quickly, and she stiffened as the wet strands stuck against her face and neck.

Azetla turned to leave.

"You don't want to hear it?" Tzal rasped.

"Just thaw a moment. Get your voice back. I can barely catch your words."

"Delaying won't make it any easier, Azetla."

Azetla rolled his jaw and left the tent.

He gathered all he could take in good conscience. It wasn't much. A few more scraps of wood. A warm, Hushai-style head covering, and a small jar of tea. He was not dishonest. He told Mali it was for the Shihrayan; she assumed it was for a womanly malady and used the herbs set aside for such things as well as the boiled water she kept on hand for her patients.

Whatever else he requested, from Mali or anyone else, he would certainly have been given. He knew that. Azetla was the commander. This thought occurred to him more than once and pulled particularly hard at him as he walked past the cookfires. But he set his gait and walked through the wafting temptation. He had never in his life broken rations and it was no credit to Tzal if he did so on her behalf. There were already too many behind-the-hand jests about her influence over him. Some dishonorable to mention. None without a vein of truth.

"Drink this. Then tell me what you saw."

Azetla handed her the small jar. She smelled it and gave him a strange look, which he ignored. He tried to give the fire some life with the scraps he had, but the night's ration of fuel had to be reserved till second watch. The Hushai said the next few nights would be unusually sharp with cold, for now the clouds had been swept away, and the north wind would cut in like a knife.

Tzal's tea was down to the dregs almost instantly.

"It's not good, Azetla," she said. Her voice was still hoarse and faint, so Azetla had to lean just to hear her. "By now they're probably holding one or two days from the north outlet of the wadi. They're moving very slow because...there's forty thousand of them."

"Forty thousand," Azetla repeated heavily.

"Or more. It wasn't as though I could ask for a census. I tried to be thorough." Tzal bit her lip and furrowed her brow. "And you say more are coming?"

"Undoubtedly."

Azetla closed his eyes and pressed his knuckle into the lion's head where it was caught in his clothes, digging it into his collarbone. Then he righted the bit of wood, forcing it to lay straight. It hung there like a cold, hard knot on his chest.

"Azetla..." Tzal hesitated. It was not like her to do that. She tried to clear her throat, to no avail. "We have to consider the possibility that they'll wait until they outnumber us to an extent that no genius of terrain or tactics will make any difference."

"Yes, I know." He watched Tzal massage her fingers, then curl and uncurl her fists as the life and color came slowly back into her hands. "But I don't think he's going to do that."

"He?"

"Riada. His generals will tell him, wait till mid-spring. Till the weather clears and the waters run off. But I don't think he's going to listen. Not at first anyway. He thinks he'll catch a jackal rebel in the act of treachery. He thinks of the south as weak. He thinks of Trekoans and Makars as goatherds with sticks. Pride will make him quick to act. It is one of his few weaknesses."

Tzal narrowed her eyes. She touched the red lines of chafing from the Kitaire on her collarbone.

"I've never been in your position, Azetla. But I have to say what you certainly already know; there is nothing more dangerous than crafting a plan around an assumed weakness. It's wishful thinking. It's expecting a gate to give way. When you find it's barred, what then?"

Azetla smiled at the ground and then at Tzal. She was, of course, right. And he was not ready to explain why he expected Riada to do this or do that, nor could he explain even what he himself was prepared to do when the time came. Not yet.

But for once, Tzal did not put up a front of apathy. She did not see the need to harden herself in front of him and pretend that her life and the lives of those around her were worthless, so easily shrugged off.

No. It was he who had to harden himself to the brutality of his task. Of grimly using up lives. Of picking up all those that were most valuable to him, like stones from the river, admiring their strength and shape, then hurling them at the head of a giant.

"Don't worry, Tzal. I do not think Riada is weak or foolish. If I were in his position I would want to extinguish this as quickly as possible. *I* would make the choice *I* want him to make. He knows the books of history. He knows what can happen." Azetla stopped Tzal from trying to open her Kitaire with numb, clumsy fingers, and unbuckled it himself.

"Let's have the rest of it, then," he said.

By salt, nothing in her Kitaire was dry.

"They sent a scouting party with hired Hushai. Five scouts."

Azetla nodded, pressing her pallet over the ground.

"Did any get away?"

She clicked her tongue at him with a look of irritation.

"Don't be offended, it's my job to ask. Did you get anything out of them beforehand?"

Tzal nodded.

"One of the generals is called Lord Pall. The other is called Lord Warwick, and a third in an advisory capacity: a Lord Munroe. The brigades are Red Pine, High Cedar, Gray Wolf, Brown Wolf, Blue Dome and...others the man didn't know to name. They were just scouts so they only knew so much. Nearly a third of the northern infantry has full armor. They did mention that. And we should expect more attempts at scouting into the Ghallaz before they try anything."

Azetla nodded soberly.

"What about the terrain?"

"The Sol riverbed was still nearly empty, but then the rain started. It'll be up to the knees for the next few days, I'd say. The crossings are rugged, but manageable. There's only a few places where you can stow archers to harass them during an advance, but if you do that, you have to know that the climbs are rough. I coerced a few informants for us in a southern Maurowan town, though I don't think they realized exactly what they were agreeing to. I might be able to get the rest of the pitch I need from them. Maybe even more than that. Not allies, exactly, but...I had to be cautious. That's all I have."

"It's enough. I'm going to grab the others for our final brief."

It would not be easy for them to stomach what he had to say and Tzal's report was the least of it. Far worse would be all the things he would not say, all the explanations they would ask for that he could not yet give.

Tzal collapsed on her pallet. "Wake me when it starts."

<h1 style="text-align:center">40</h1>

For the first time, Tzal felt a terrible sort of solidarity with Joseph and Sarrez and even the northerners: James, Verris, Peterson, Truillon, Brody, and Ishelor. She stood next to them, staring at Azetla with them, bewildered alongside them.

Never had Azetla given such bizarre orders, and never had he given them with so little room for discussion. His word always reigned in the end, but usually after a sharp honing which he himself readily invited.

Not this time.

Tzal folded her arms and held her tongue. She scarcely knew what to say and her voice counted less amid the others than it did to Azetla alone. She would wait.

Joseph felt no such restriction.

"Why on earth would we even accept a cessation if they offered it? Our whole advantage right now is hellish weather on hellish terrain and the fact that northern winter is slowing down his reinforcements." Joseph seemed to be trying to speak with a modicum of respect, but the look on his face was the same as the one he often wore; that of an exasperated older brother. "If we draw them into the Ghallaz, as we drew them out of Hidud, there is at least a chance. But if we push them hard enough that they send a negotiating party, we'll break ourselves. There will be nothing remaining behind the threat."

Joseph was the only one who dared speak like that. Sarrez and Peterson looked uneasy. Ishelor's face was a silent mask.

"That's true," Azetla said in his calm yet authoritative voice. His hackles were not raised. Indeed, there was a slow and lumbering quality to his voice, as if every syllable was under the most careful discipline. "The threat will come from elsewhere."

He raised his hand to gesture for silence before Joseph—or anyone else—could say a word and start a clamor. So the room was silent but for bated breath.

"If we can push them hard enough, jar them badly enough, that they wish to negotiate a cessation till the rains end, it *will* seem all to their advantage. It must, otherwise they would never give it to us."

Azetla briefly clenched his teeth, but loosed his jaw and, at last, the next words came.

"Given a cessation, I will go to Masheva." His voice held steady, but only just. "The rebels of North Sarrama will break their contract with Riada and fulfill their old vow to my people. That will be ten thousand men, some of which are already prepared and waiting for word."

"We will close all of Riada's Mashevi ports, arrest all incoming cargo, which—as of two years ago—has become the chief source of his entire treasury, though most of his advisors do not know this. It will cripple him at a scale impossible to ignore. We are at half rations. His soldiers will be living off stones and dust."

Tzal was as amazed at the subtle vehemence riding under Azetla's words as she was at the words themselves.

"What makes you think you can accomplish such a thing?" the Corra James said, his confusion plain for all to see.

"Your Highness, it is already half done."

Comprehension began to seep through the room and sting the eyes like smoke. The soldiers blinked and winced. Only James seemed to resist the obvious conclusion.

"How and by whom is this being done?"

Azetla's expression was as dark and hard as flint.

"Your Highness, do you think I am so cold-hearted that I would tell you that? That I would risk the lives and causes of those far more worthy and honorable than I?"

The horror that filled James Sivolne's countenance fascinated Tzal. His hatred of Mashevis had always seemed to her to be of such a casual and second-hand nature. Adopted for the purposes of looking and feeling the same as those around him.

But here was real contempt. And real shame.

"We will not come alongside jackal traitors," James spat, eyes wide.

"It is a late hour for you to worry about your coup being sullied by Mashevi hands, Your Highness." The Corra took those words like a slap, shrinking back and pressing his mouth shut. "Do you really hate my people so much that you would choose gallows over throne?"

There was a crackling silence in the room and Tzal could almost feel each man's thoughts and realizations rising up like tongues of flame. Azetla had led them here, knowing that the means of victory was one none of them could stomach, and would never have approved. Yet how could they be surprised? Did they really think they could remake the Empire without feeding a few of its enemies, without letting them climb up those same steps of chaos?

They had chosen him. They knew all along what he was. He had promised nothing more nor less than this. He was going to give them everything they asked for and no matter how bitter it was to them, they could only blame themselves for having trusted him. And having needed him.

Tzal watched flickers of all this pass over their faces in the lamplight. Her own thoughts she held at bay with a firm grip. Her own tongue she kept silent.

Azetla knew what he had done to them. He was wise to wait. Wise to mount no defense, but to simply let his words stand or fall before them.

Sarrez spoke first.

"So we raise our hackles and fight as if we are larger than we are. As if we have men to spare, when we do not. We astonish them. They balk. They do what the Emperor's generals would probably prefer in the first place: they agree to hold. A month or two. The mud dries. And you," he looked at Azetla in an almost sad way, "you go light a fire in the east to draw their eyes away. The Emperor hesitates or turns—it only takes a moment—and we pull Darton and Piarago out from under his feet."

Azetla gave the barest of nods. "That's the only way I see it is even possible."

Sarrez narrowed his eyes thoughtfully. "If we make your people into a diversion, it will put them in grave danger."

"Yes. It will."

"What are you going to do about that?"

Tzal saw the muscles in Azetla's jaw tighten ever so slightly, and the heavy swallow of his throat.

"That is another matter on which I must remain silent."

There was a flinch of confusion from Sarrez. Yet the Makar remained calm, and Tzal marveled at him. Always she expected Azetla to have met the last of the man's good will and trust. Always she watched out of the corner of her eye to see his mind change, his contempt bubble to the surface. He would have been a hard man to defeat, so she had given the "how" of it a great deal of thought.

Yet always Nimer Sarrez surprised her. He looked at the Corra.

"Your Highness. This is the way through. We must take it. If he can garner aid from those violent factions, bitter though it is, we should not refuse."

From the mouth of a Makar, the words had unmatchable potency. The one who ought to have been the most resistant, the most horrified, was the first to say, *"yes, Commander."* The others swiftly did the same—even Verris—until the Corra was left with no one to join in his fears, though his grudging acquiescence had more spit and fire in it than Tzal had ever witnessed from him.

The outworking of tactics took them deep into first watch. Then the men dispersed to other tents. Only Joseph stayed back. It was clear he wanted a word, and he wanted it alone. Against the will of every muscle in her body and her now throbbing head, Tzal scraped herself off the ground. She had to hike down to the privy and the washpool anyway. Better to do it now.

But she walked slowly and with care, so she managed to hear the first words fall behind her as she left.

"All this time, you kept your finger dipped in the rebel pots—" Joseph's voice was a low growl.

"You knew, Joseph. You damn well knew."

And he certainly had.

The wind stung the dry, cracked skin of Tzal's hands, and her palms felt bruised each time she steadied herself against the rock edge. She let her own thoughts skitter and sputter now so that they would spend their strength and quiet down. Then she would hike back up to the tent, drop to her pallet, and say not a single word to him. There was simply nothing to say.

He would go on keeping himself to himself as he had done from the very beginning.

He would go on having his own separate plans.

He would go on not telling her. What he admitted tonight was still not the whole. She knew that. It would never, ever be more than he could afford to part with.

She knew well enough how to don her indifference, as tight against the body as a Kitaire: meticulously fastened, well-set, and so perfectly fitted that she could almost forget it was not part of her. After that, all she had to do was keep moving and never rest.

By blood, this was all so much harder than it used to be.

She saw Joseph on her way back up. Walking down from the headquarters tent, taking in deep breaths of the cold air, eyes fixed upward on the clear, clear sky. Without either one breaking stride, they exchanged a glance as they passed. A rare look from Joseph, lacking the usual dart of contempt. She read in his eyes the same silent charge that she had gleaned from him before: "*It's down to you and me. He's our responsibility. You have to hold his feet to the fire. Challenge him. And watch his back, because this is fresh trouble.*"

It was not merely her imagination. Joseph and Sarrez had made it clear that if she saw any acute danger arise, she should deal with it quietly behind everyone's back before there was a chance to question the how or the why. Because she was allowed to do things in the dark. She was allowed to have dirty hands. And eventually, she was allowed to be sloughed off.

She walked in and shifted her pallet back toward the fire. The tent was oddly empty. The sea of pallets had dried up while she scouted north, and only four were left, two of which were rolled up for second watch. It wouldn't be as warm without the press of bodies, but she cared about nothing now in all the world except that she should meet the ground and not rise till daybreak.

Shuddering out the chill that still lingered in her bones and muscles, she made the most of her nearly dry pallet and blanket, swaddling herself, wasting no corner of wool. Then she pulled the worn-out canvas which she pitched as shelter whenever she was out on the rocks of the Ghallaz.

Azetla walked over. He sat cross-legged beside her and—stone-faced—waited for her to speak. But Tzal wanted none of it. She barely even wanted an explanation. The value of knowing things others did not know was in using it above and around and against them. There was no chance of that here, and she wasn't even sure that was what bothered her.

"I'm not going to ask you any questions, Azetla. Do as you like. Makes no difference to me."

Her voice was pretty well gone now, which frustrated her. The strongest thing she had, obliterated by a common cold. Azetla strained to hear her, his head bent low.

"I'm sorry, Tzal." Those were his only words, gentle and calm. She did not think he could have said anything more infuriating.

"I think we have it well established that you don't owe me any-thing," she said. "Especially not anything you wouldn't even tell Joseph or Sarrez."

"That's not entirely true. Not this time. I owe you more because I'll be asking much more of you than I will of them." He paused, pressing his lips into a flat line.

"What's that supposed to mean?"

"It means I need you to come back from this without a gaping hole in your side. I need you on your feet, because there's very specific and very thankless work for you to do."

She laughed—an empty air sound turned into a cough.

"Just as well tell me I'm not allowed to be hungry or tired. I'll tell Rahummi he's on his own, I can't so much as scrape my knuckles, is that it?"

"That's the opposite of what I mean. Rahummi always takes his cues from *you*. He'll use his men strong and wisely, if you let him. He'll squander them if you go your own way, trying to see how far you can lean over the cliff before falling. Not everyone has your footing, you know. What leaves you limping might leave others dead."

Tzal furrowed her brow. She wondered if Imal had told Azetla about his oldest son, Haani.

"I know we're going to have to pay a high price for this," he continued. "But don't you dare give the Maurowans one more drop of blood than you have to, understand? And don't let Rahummi do it either." One of the lieutenants came into the tent and stumbled toward his pallet. Azetla spoke in Mashevi, putting a firm hand to her shoulder. "I'll need you after this."

"If there is an after," she replied in his tongue. *You can't tell me not to fight as I fight. I don't know how else to do it.*

He gave a grave nod. Stood. Snuffed out the lamps. Said his prayers under his breath in the dark.

Tzal knew them all by now. She could have mouthed every syllable.

If she wanted.

⁕

"Are you going to hang me, my lord?"

The boy's voice cracked only a little when he said it, and even that might have just been because he was the age for it. Thirteen or thereabouts. He was a bold child and far less stupid now than he had been a month ago.

Orde was always a bit charmed by the brazen ones. This Salil Yammunad did not take his eyes off Orde. Every nervous swallow of his throat could be seen. But he did not waver.

Never quite convinced that the boy was innocent, still less was Orde Everson convinced of his guilt. His family of Janbaris from a village two days north came to plead for him. Orde had given them gentle words, but no assurances, and sent them to wait with prayers on their lips. And after twenty-nine days in a dusty cell—well-treated but with full knowledge of the sentence looming over him—the boy had not changed a single word of his story.

Many nobles and the servants of nobles had wandered through the market that day, he said. Salil had been inattentive, making jests with his friends, teasing one of the younger market girls. Till she cried, Salil admitted. He felt badly about it but didn't want to look soft in front of the other boys. He waited till they had gone before he went to her stall to make amends. Anyone could have put those papers in his saddlebags, tucked under his blanket and clothes. Anyone. He'd scarcely glanced at them.

Perhaps Orde had agreed with Azetla from the beginning, only he had not liked to admit it. Easier to do so now, out from under that judgmental Mashevi gaze. Besides, the flutter and gossip of the matter had died down, and most of his fellow high-bloods seemed to neither know nor care about what had become of that desert boy who was accused of treachery.

Little Anna Colha had not forgotten Salil, however. Every day she asked Orde—respectfully—and every day, he gave her no answer.

Buried in his inner pocket was an indecipherable wooden carving that the little Colha girl had made and begged be given to Salil. But Orde was here to be stern, not to give the boy more hope than he ought to have.

"You were shamefully careless, Salil. *At best*. You almost put all of us and your own people in grave danger just so you could kick rocks about and neglect your work."

Salil nodded deeply and, this time, his eyes stayed on the ground.

"I have a task by which you might—*might*—redeem yourself and prove you are telling the truth. But you will be under closest scrutiny and you will not be allowed to return to Siy-Yammuna until you have served your time."

For now, Salil's task was merely this: to remain stitched to Orde's elbow at all times, and to do everything he was told whether it was to scrub or run or pour wine or whittle with a knife. Orde made a point over the next few days to see every last one of his fellow high-bloods and watch them carefully. Most took no notice whatsoever of Salil.

What was a Trekoan house-slave to them? Most couldn't have said who or what Salil was if offered all the gold in the world.

Only a few gave Salil a second glance. Lord Thearaty, who always had a sharp eye, spoke plainly.

"I thought you hanged that boy."

"On the contrary, Lord Thearaty. I am trying to find out who it is I ought to hang."

Thearaty was satisfied with this, or at least he pretended to be.

Lord Yitamar of North Makaria noticed Salil with a flicker on his face and a furrow on his brow, but he kept his thoughts to himself. Orde left it at that; let the worry simmer and encourage a bit of rash behavior.

Captain Istamo was instructed to keep watch over Yitamar.

Lady Kathryn recognized Salil too, but Orde struggled to read her eyes and even her words. The more she spoke, the less sure he became of his own perception.

"That's the boy that wanted my earring," she said softly when Orde sent Salil to wait outside the door with Tackman Shavi.

She gestured that Orde sit down at her private table and drink her wine.

"Yes, my lady. It's also the boy that was framed for treason."

She nodded thoughtfully. "I don't think I realized till now that they were one and the same."

Her girl poured the wine then disappeared with the quiet precision that the Lady no doubt demanded of all who belonged to her. Orde leaned in his chair, relaxing into himself. He didn't actually think Lady Kathryn was stupid enough to attempt such a clumsy treachery—or any treachery, really—but he did believe she was clever enough to have plans and actions he could not easily understand. She was above him in more ways than one. And *other* than him as well. Even she did not realize how much so.

"You took the jackal's advice," she said. "I'm surprised."

"Well he's right often as not."

She smiled warmly and he smiled back, but he honestly had no idea what they were smiling about.

"It's good you came, Colonel. I was going to ask for you," she said with a queenly air.

"Wanting to loot for information, I suppose?"

Her lips tightened, but she did not take as much offense as he had intended.

"One can hardly loot for what is already properly one's own." Her voice was cool and soft, like mist.

Orde gave a laugh. "True enough. I'm only the steward of all that is yours, my lady. Your humble servant. What would you ask of me?"

"It is *you* I wish to ask about, Colonel Everson."

"Me?"

"Yes. You. In all the time I've been here, I've not been able to make head nor tail of you. I'm sure it thrills you to hear that, since you like to keep people guessing. But I am tired of walking blind; my neck is on the block, quite the same as yours. So first, answer me this: why are you here, with wine and cheese and bread, sitting on that soft cushion, while Lord Verris—who is no real colonel and has neither your experience nor your finesse—is at the Corra James' side on the battlefield?"

Well. She wrapped her compliments elegantly in insults; he was clever and a coward, was he? He pursed his lips and began to carefully order his words.

"It would not have taken much maneuvering on your part to replace Verris as James' chief advisor," she added. The look in her eye was as sharp as a dagger.

What did she want out of this?

"Lord Verris is precisely where he should be," Orde said. "And so am I. I've no interest in being the Corra's side-arm."

"You don't worry at all that Lord Verris could be turned against the Corra?" she said.

"He is the one I worry least about of anyone."

"Then what about you?"

"My lady?" Orde caught himself a moment too late, and real surprise leaped through his voice.

"Well, given your nature, I would have marked you more as the Emperor's man. Not the Corra's."

Orde tisked his tongue. "My nature, hm?"

"No need to take offense. None is meant. You like to fall on your feet. And you don't like to tie yourself to those who will take you down to the grave."

"Are you sure it's not a mirror you're looking at?" he said, amused.

The truth was, he liked that she should think him so brilliantly duplicitous. It was more intriguing, more playful, more attractive than the truth. Without any particular conviction or any real valor, he knew he was fixed on his course. He knew it more in this very moment than he had ever known it before.

Always, he had meant to remain on the periphery of all this. A fine, light hand, and a clean one too. Always, he had planned to keep safely distant from all the real dangers and treacheries. And, if it were possible, he would jump out and claim innocence at the last moment.

He certainly could not do that now.

He could prick the moment of change with a pin. It was allowing Azetla to live—and being forced to justify that choice—which had put him in this position. That damned Shihrayan. That sly, bloody devil's tongue. She roped him in and he had barely sensed it at the time. Hadn't he known better than to listen to a word she said?

She really was jinn, he thought. Her words really did reach in like a hook and drag you her way till you wondered how you got there.

"Again I must say, our necks are on the block, Orde. I just need to know that your hands are steady," Lady Kathryn said.

"Steadier than I ever wished them to be," he answered, shaking his head.

He could not read the look on her face just then, except that there were many thoughts whirling behind her eyes. With a sense of purpose, she put her fingers to her cup of wine as if she needed her hand to be somewhere, to do something.

"Good," she said. "Because so many of our allies are likely to turn enemy on us already."

"You mean the jackal."

"Of course. I cannot fathom why you trust him."

"My lady, I trust him just enough to do all he has done for us and then to take all the blame."

She smiled at that. It was both sufficiently contriving and condemning for her. Well thank the Gods, because that was the only thing he could think to say to please her.

Lady Kathryn did not look at Salil when he came back in to carry Orde's things. She pretended to have forgotten about him. And perhaps she had. Orde took her hand as he took his leave and kissed it in the Kourisian fashion. She received this tribute warmly, though Orde was sure he did not have anything like the effect on her that she did on him.

Back in his room, he surveyed his words, assuring himself that he had given her nothing with which he did not wish to part. He sent Salil away to Tackman Shavi.

Orde walked briskly to the furthest room in his quarters where he kept all his personal parchments, maps, and family heirlooms. From within a chest, wrapped in a goatskin, he took out a small cedar box which had the crest of the Everson line limned into the reddish rough-sanded wood. He brushed his fingers briefly over the limning and slid the top panel out through its grooves.

There wasn't much in the box. A silk sash that he kept from one of his Trekoan lovers of years ago. Risha. He had been far more careless with his desires in those days and the woman had suffered for it. Beaten badly. And she would have been killed, had the man in question been anyone but himself. On account of his position, and with a great deal of blood money to the family and the new husband, the matter was quieted.

It was not the only time, but it was the worst one. He took better care after that. Whatever guilt he felt was well-dimmed by now, kept perfectly hidden away with that faded bit of cloth. Yet here he was retrieving it, like a fool.

The rest of the items in the box were remnants of the day when the family of Everson had been stronger, savvier, and more in favor. Except one small trinket, which had nothing to do with any of that. Orde fingered through the seals, rings of billet, military cords, and the old family rank panels until he grasped it. It felt heavier than he remembered.

In design, it looked exactly like Azetla's. But Azetla's was made of red cedar, with worn grooves that might once have held rivulets of copper. Orde's was made of Kourisian gold with hammered silver accents. The eyes of the lion's head were sunstone crystal, and they glinted back at him as though the bloody thing was wide awake.

His mother never should have kept this. She never should have told him.

41

It was like a hunt to Tzal. Precise and patient. For satisfaction and survival. And so strangely quiet. Since dawn she had trekked back and forth across her ragged prowling grounds in the north edge of the Ghallaz. Every few hours she met with Rahummi. The Hushai were stationed at the crucial nodes of the labyrinthine trails, to guide and run at a moment's notice. The Saqiranis, Janbaris, and Lahashet under Rahummi's command were dispersed on high trails and hidden lookouts, waiting to take any prey by the throat.

But the air kept silent and the dust laid low.

Tzal did not like that she had to leave Nashuv with the runners at Qahiru flat—more than an hour away at the furthest point of her patrol route. The Hushai were no horsemen. They didn't know how to properly deal with a strong plains horse like Nashuv. They had only dour mules for heavy goods. They rarely rode them; the Ghallaz was a place made to break the feet of men and horse alike.

Thus far, there was only one kill to speak of. A stray scout on a Lahashet horse. Separated from a patrol that was nowhere in earshot or signal-sight. Tzal happened to be the nearest and have the best angle. Plain target. One arrow. A clean shot to a broad chest.

Tzal scrambled across the ridge. Ran down to the wide trail, hand to the rock. With a butcher's focused efficiency, she cut the last of the life out of him. Led the horse the long way to the Lahashet to make use of as they liked. She found a dagger, a cloak, a headcloth, and a fair amount of food. Not too bad. A few extra mouthfuls for the meal that night.

Jogging back to Qahiru, Tzal unlashed Nashuv.

"I'm going to do one last run on the Yapo. Catch a different line of sight," she told Rahummi after they briefly exchanged what amounted to no real information.

"The horse trail is exposed as it cuts southwest. Stay in range of sound-signal at least."

Tzal pulled herself onto Nashuv with a vague nod. She meant to go as far as the only proper horse trail could take her, and then farther still. Until she found them.

It was slow moving on the Yapo, even though the horse trail was wider and flatter than most. Tzal dismounted every so often when the rocks cut away, and the view into the wadi basin was too clear. If she could see everything, everything could see her. When she reached the part of the trail where the Yapo cut down into the wadi itself, she stopped. Lashed Nashuv at a sheltered node post. Continued on a foot trail.

She didn't know the name of this path—the Ghallaz had dozens and dozens of them—but the etchings on the rock told her it was a difficult one. There were special markings for dead ends, for family and cargo trails, hunter trails, passes, pinnacles, shelter, and water. And many more besides. It was almost an entire written language, though Tzal knew only the bits of it Gado had taught her.

Every footfall had to be taken with care. Twice the path required a rough climb. The sky was a translucent yellow-gray, offering little thought of rain. Tzal shielded her eyes from the sun-haze as she slid across the dark brown crest of the rock face.

Faint, very faint, something reached her ear. She stilled. Slunk low to the ground and crouched over to where she could see into the wadi. At first there was nothing in view. But the sound was distinct.

Horse hooves, slipping rough across the rocky banks. People trying to be quiet, but failing.

She moved a little further, staying low, knees just off the ground. Now she could see them.

Twelve. Four on horseback. Eight on foot. Mostly Maurowan. Three Trekoan guides. Janbari by the look of them.

There were two Hushai posted somewhere near this trail, but Tzal could not see them. Perhaps she had gone too far beyond them; it was easy to lose the sense of distance in the winding trails of the Ghallaz.

As best she could tell, the group of enemy scouts were either looking for their lost companion, or looking for the horse trail and its potential shelter. More than once they attempted upward trails and then abandoned them when the way grew too steep. Naturally they did not want to remain in the basin, exposed to all the heights from every direction.

She shadowed them southward, hoping they would abandon the horses and split up. Make things easier for her. But they clung together. Soon they would spot the wide, gentle slope of the Yapo and make their way up from the wadi into the rock walls of the Ghallaz.

Where Tzal must be waiting for them.

Pulse quickened, she was swift and light on her feet, running till she found her perch.

While she waited, Tzal closed her eyes and tried to picture where, exactly, she was within the maze of the Ghallaz. How far from Nashuv. From Rahummi. The Janbari patrols. The Hushai lookouts. How long it would take. How steep the next trail break was.

The map in her mind had many gaps and hazy areas, but it would have to do.

She set her bow in one hand. It was already strung but, out of habit, she ran her finger from the base loop to the top, ticking it gently. She did a similar thing with the arrow before she laid it, running her thumb against the arrowhead, and shaping the nock feather between two fingers while letting out a long breath.

She heard them a long time before she saw them. Then she waited so, so many deep breaths till they breached a steep climb and turned west. Finally they came into view, their backs to her, a pebble's throw away.

Tzal licked her cracked, dry lips. Put her fingers in her mouth and gave the piercing Hushai whistle.

The enemy froze. Tzal's fingers dropped from her lips to the nocked arrow and pulled. Just like she had done in Shihra when Azetla's battalion came, she took only one breath to sight. Base of the skull. One breath to draw and lay the next. Second arrow to the thigh. Breath to draw, breath to sight. Horse's neck. Breath, breath. Through the ribs.

For those brief moments, they were like fish caught in a barrel, their horses wheeling, running their riders against the juts of rock, stumbling precariously, the men not sure what to do—flee instinctively from the overhead attack and into the maze of the Ghallaz, or retreat back through the arrow-fire, down the Yapo trail, into the dreadful exposure of the basin.

Instinct won, though Tzal barely glimpsed it.

She slid down the far rocks, out of sight on the far-side trail. And she *ran*. Ran like a flood. Like only a seasoned Hushai ever should. She thought she heard a shrill whistle, but it might have been a horse scream or a man's death. Either way, she did not stop.

She knew where she was now. And she knew that if she moved up and down these rocks like the Inze that Gado said she was, she would get to Nashuv before they did.

Only once did she slow down. She questioned her sense of direction, thinking she should have reached the trail node by now. A shout came, close by, to her west. Then a streak of blood-red flew up into the air, trailing an arrow.

The sight-signal. The Hushai had seen the enemy. The signal oriented her.

Squeezing through a passage that barely admitted her except by scraped arms, Tzal came through to the sheltered flat. She saw her buckskin gelding tossing his head and stamping anxiously. He did not like to be lashed when there was action.

As she pulled herself onto him, she had a moment of feeling dizzyingly tall and exposed high upon his back. She shifted her weight backward so that he wouldn't bolt.

Knees gripped, whispering in Shihrayan—"It's all right Nashuv, keep your feet. Keep your feet"—she drew. And held the draw. She could hear everything, everything. And though she barely comprehended it all, her mind sorted the sounds into her muscles and skin. She could almost see where they were beyond the rockface.

Still, she held the draw.

The quick, dark flash of a horse's head jolted round the bend; she let go.

The arrow went through the rider's throat, tip coming out the other side. Tzal dropped the bow and drew her sagam.

She barely had to raise it. The Hushai ran up from the north trail. The Janbaris and Saqiranis down from the southeast, swarming in, wrapping round the remaining scouts like rope.

"Leave two alive! One of each!" she shouted. Tried to shout. Her voice was still broken, coming from her mouth like sand scraping over stone. Barely a sound.

Tzal grabbed the senior Janbari soldier and made him shout the order for her.

So quick was the slaughter, they barely managed to salvage two live scouts for Tzal's purposes. One Maurowan. One Trekoan.

She sent most of the soldiers back to their posts, keeping only two with her, while she waited for Rahummi. As soon as he arrived, they divided the scouts; he took the Trekoan soldier, she took the Maurowan one.

Tzal spoke genially to the Maurowan scout. Gave him a sip of her water and chobi leaf to chew. She used her warmest manner, her mildest posture, and her best work-a-day, slangish Maurowan. The effect was entirely calming. After a little coaxing, the man spoke freely. He confirmed many things that Azetla surmised, and others that Tzal already knew. Bits of bread, but not much meat. Likely it was all he had to give. Either way, time was of the essence.

The soldier so clearly thought he was being taken prisoner. He had resigned himself to it. He gave her no trouble. So she gave him as quick a death as she possibly could. He barely had time to widen his eyes.

Rahummi had more difficulty with his captive. The only thing the Janbari man told Rahummi was the incredible payment and terrible threats Maurow offered in order to purchase North Trekoan spies.

"His mother is Lahashet of Pardish. His father a Yazha Janbari. I know that family," Rahummi said miserably.

"Doesn't matter," Tzal said.

"He said that he was forced to spy for the Maurowans on pain of death. That his family was threatened—"

"If you can't do it, I will." Her voice was barely a rasp.

Rahummi always had trouble with these situations. What mild ruthlessness he possessed, Tzal had taught him. But so often, he refused to learn. She did not begrudge him that, but neither could she indulge him.

He gave the faintest of nods, his eyes fixed far off in the distance, at nothing in particular.

The Janbari man saw the knife come, still bloody from the man before him.

"You think I had a choice!" the Janbari shouted, eyes skittering for a flight that he knew was impossible. "I was forced! I am Trekoan to my heart's blood, I swear. I swear by the desert God, and by the Saav, and by—"

Tzal gripped him, his back to her chest, and pulled the knife hard across the throat.

"Mercy," she muttered in Shihrayan. That's what this was called where she came from. Strong, cold mercy. Drink it down.

"Rahummi, they're all going to claim they had no choice," Tzal said. "But it's not true."

"I know," he said. He straightened himself, focused his eyes. "I know."

Trekoans knew better than any alive how to evade Maurowan service, even when the cost was brutally high. Whatever flowed out from the Maurowans and into the Ghallaz could not be permitted to live. This was no time or place for prisoners. Azetla had made that clear.

Rahummi's patrols found another small scouting party before the day began to dwindle. Tzal did not have to remind him again of what must be done. However, he did prefer to have her question them before they were killed, because she was able to make them feel comfortable, and extract so much more. "Like a butcher," Rahummi said with a grimace, "soothing the lamb before slaughter so that the meat keeps its taste and tenderness."

Well if they had to die, why should they die afraid? She didn't see the need.

"Let them face it like men," he answered. "Not like animals."

They never did resolve that argument; they worked their routes, then lost the light. All the Trekoan soldiers trekked in precise silence back to their rally points.

They were now deep within the Ghallaz and well-shielded; they could have a small fire. They could talk softly. They could eat their little portions in a leisurely way so that it seemed like more. One pinch of stale flatbread at a time. One thin scrape of goat's cheese to those who got there first, which Tzal did not. The wishful talk among the Janbaris and Lir-Ruhhalans was chiefly of olives and honey and thick, meaty stew. Date-cakes, of course. And good wine.

The things their mothers and wives made, God bless them. Oh how a drizzle of good oil was taken for granted, and how a bit of salt would satisfy the soul.

But there were at least hot cups of bishi tea for everyone. Usually Tzal did not like it, but the strong smell gave one the feeling of more substance than was really there. The steam warmed her when she dipped her face down to drink, the spice burned and soothed her raw throat.

She sat a little outside the circle and Rahummi sat beside her.

"I'm losing track of the days. Is it the eighth or the ninth of the month?" he said.

"Ninth."

"Then it's Inaya's name day."

"That was the compromise? Only three months?" She tisked.

"A year is too long a time to wait to call a daughter by her name."

Tzal wrapped her fingers tightly around the cup of bishi and pressed her lips hard together.

"I try to honor Hushai traditions," he added. "But that one is beyond me."

"So you're not too disappointed," Tzal said.

He pondered this briefly.

"No. I don't think so. But really, I wasn't surprised. Naima went to the prophetess Beyadri at Pardish several months ago. She said the baby would be a girl. And so she was."

"Bold prediction. A one in two chance she's right. I never put much stock in that woman."

Rahummi's smile flickered in the firelight.

"That's because you didn't like what she had to say about *you*."

"She never gave a single word of sight to me. She wouldn't let me in the tent. She said I was a demon."

"She said you *had* a demon, and asked kindly if you would please leave it at the threshold." He raised his finger in correction. "And she certainly did say something about you, remember? She told my uncle that—"

He paused. Tzal's face had betrayed her shock. And her foolishness. Why feel a sudden ravenous hunger for something she was sure would never have filled her stomach. Not then. Not now.

"He didn't tell you?"

"Rahummi, just spit it out."

"But you don't even believe Beyadri, so what difference does it make?"

He was enjoying himself now. Rare was it that he knew something she did not. She had always been the one to explain things to him, to hold things over his head, not the other way around. She, the older sister and he, the younger brother, sometimes coddled and sometimes bullied by her, but always trailing just behind.

That was true no longer.

Don't fool yourself, Tzal. It was never true to begin with. You were never really any such thing to him. Never. Why do you keep believing your own lies?

She sipped the pungent tea and bit her tongue.

"Always too proud to ask," Rahummi said, his voice calm and needling.

She took another sip.

What of it?

"It did make Uncle Imal very irritable."

"Goodnight, Rahummi." She put her hand to the ground and came to a crouch.

"Stop, stop, *stop*. I can never be as stubborn as you. Honestly, it was nothing so shocking. Nothing dramatic. She just laughed and said it was good you were deaf and blind."

"What?" Tzal sat back down, bewildered.

"Deaf and blind. Can't possibly see where you're going, can't even hear the plain answer to the questions you ask. Yet look at all you managed to do while running around like a chicken with your head cut off. 'One day she'll actually hear and see,' Beyadri said, 'and God only knows what will happen when she does.'"

Rahummi grabbed Tzal's cup and stood, looking far happier and more wakeful than he ought to be. He dipped their cups in the bishi pot.

"That's not a word of sight," she said as he handed the cup back to her. "That was just her opinion of me."

Rahummi pinched a small bishi leaf off his tongue and shrugged. "All right. The point is, she was right about Inaya. And I'll tell you this: if I have daughters only all my life, but they do not live under Qatlan and Maurow, then I will still die content."

"If we succeed—"

"It's not a matter of *if*," Rahummi said quietly, looking off into the pitch-black night. "We will do it. Azetla will do it."

Azetla does tend to make one feel that way. It's a tremendous skill of his. But not a fact.

She decided not to dishearten Rahummi. All she said was, "It's a long road yet, but he's brought you this far."

"I'm a little surprised he didn't keep you with him in the main army," Rahummi said.

"Why? What good would I be there?"

"I'm sure he'd have found plenty of use for you. Spying on the Makars. Interpreting with the Hushai. And generally just being...nearby."

The muscles in Tzal's neck and shoulders tightened. She was several feet from the fire, but the heat of it seemed to lick across her face. Her eyes fixed on the cup in her hand, as she tipped the dark water back and forth.

"That's not a wise jest, Rahummi," she said. She spoke in Maurowan. She did not want the others to understand.

"It's really not a jest."

Tzal closed her eyes and felt the night press over her.

"Is that what everyone thinks?" she whispered.

"It's what Naima thought—"

"Then keep that nonsense to yourself. It's not like you to indulge in malicious gossip," she said. Her voice had gone almost too rough to hear again.

"Malicious, is it?"

Tzal scoffed and looked at him with plain scorn.

"It's all that piety and holy-talk your people love about him, no? They'll forgive him for making practical use of me. They won't forgive him for anything more than that."

"*Is* there anything more to forgive?"

It took careful footing to answer with neither defensive speed, nor doubtful slowness.

"Of course not, Rahummi."

"No?"

"No."

"Tzal—"

She smiled sadly. He hadn't called her that in a very long time.

"Yes?"

"I meant no harm by it. I just worry. Your words always seep through everything like water. And that's when you're barely trying. If you wanted something—or someone—I can't imagine they'd have any hope of escape."

Tzal breathed out sharply.

"I would never do that to him."

"I'm not sure you'd even know you were doing it. Do you realize—"

"Rahummi, you assume he's in some danger of me. What makes you so sure it's not the other way around?"

Rahummi's eyes narrowed. He said nothing.

"This is a waste of time," Tzal said tiredly. She stood up. "It doesn't matter anyway. No one is going to make a fool of themselves, rest assured. We've only a couple hours to sleep before the signal goes out."

"Tzal, I didn't—"

She put up her hand and shook her head softly. "Goodnight, Rahummi."

42

T zal bit down on a chobi leaf. The bitter aftertaste filled her mouth as she ground her back teeth. She didn't expect much effect, but with only three hours of sleep and winds howling overhead the whole time, it was better than nothing. Nothing was just about all they'd have after today.

In the dark, she took stock of herself. Sagam fixed aright. Knife opposite. Bow and quiver slung over the Kitaire which held all her water and rations. Tzal traced her wrist and, moments later, her neck, her fingers searching out of habit to feel the limned markings and turn the slave bands round and round. *Stop doing that.* She set her hand to the rock, and her feet to the uneven path.

Over the next two hours, Trekoans from six different tribes trickled up through the Ghallaz, joining in a pool at its northern edge. Saqiranis, Janbaris, Lir Ruhhalans, Lahashet, Shayalis, and Hushai.

From here, the enemy could be seen. An awesome sight, even in the dark.

The whole swath of black ground below Tzal was thickly flecked with enemy campfires. They stretched across the end of the Ghallaz, packed tightly over the outlet of the wadi, and beyond Tzal's sight to the north, lining the Sol riverbed the whole way.

Rahummi was in chief command over all the tribes. Tzal was in something that was not command, but looked a great deal like it. She was the one on whom Rahummi must stand to be known, heard, and understood by all. The interpreter and enforcer of his word. The invisible seam in a patchwork garment.

It would be a thankless task. Maybe an impossible one. The tribes did not know how to come alongside each other for more than one skirmish at a time. Up until now, Azetla had employed the Trekoans carefully, purposefully—and *separately*. But now they were called upon to do what they were most famous for failing to do: fight the common enemy rather than each other.

Why Azetla thought they could do this, she did not know. Even Rahummi couldn't please everyone. Even she could not wear three mannerisms at once, or dance between four dialects without the illusion she projected being instantly shattered.

But Azetla put them to the task without flinching and without looking back.

She could perceive respect out of that. Or ruthlessness. With him, there was always a bit of both.

The susurration of battle prayers met her ears as she walked through the gathered Trekoan troops. She heard the names of Makarish, Maurowan, and Trekoan Gods. The names of ancestors and of celestial bodies. But over and around and through them all, there was that one whose name was not spoken, yet still rose louder than all the others. The God of the desert and of all, as Azetla liked to say.

When Azetla spoke in Mashevi, he usually just said "the name." This irritated her.

How many of them truly believed in this God of Azetla's, she did not know. Rahummi certainly did. But most would bow to anything they thought would give them comfort or power or safety. She heard some Janbaris pray mercy for going into battle with a Sahr devil.

"Dear God, let the evil of the Sahr be turned for good."

This, she shrugged off. It was mere noise and rustling to her. She routed her mind to the task ahead.

Quietly, with soft signals, the Trekoans formed their staggered ranks.

Tzal gave a patterned click of her tongue. Through several mouths, Rahummi's confirmation echoed back through the dark. They carried no light with them. The moon was a sliver, sometimes hidden and sometimes revealed by thin, rainless clouds. The razor-sharp crags cradled them as they made their careful way toward the outer watch of the Maurowan encampment.

Those with Kitaire led the way, and those behind them held to the gripping strap. Everyone beyond that kept a hand on the shoulder in front of them. The Hushai never moved in groups this large, especially at night, so this was a strange method even for them. Tzal looked up at the sky and would have laughed if not for the silence needed; never had there been an advance so slow and strange, with all the soldiers toddling like children first learning to walk.

By the time they came to the clearer ground—so close to the encampment now—the moon shone its thin light again. Now they had to crouch close to the ground, leaning into the shadows and crawling around the light. It came so naturally to Tzal, she had to slow herself to keep position.

A soft sound, like that of a mother hushing her child, carried down the line of Trekoans from Rahummi to Tzal. She repeated the sound as she crouched low, fingertips against the ground. They moved a little further forward, some of them almost on hands and knees.

Here. Tzal halted and tapped the Janbari next to her on his shoulder. He sent the halt down by touch and gentle tongue signal.

Tzal unslung her bow and laid an arrow.

Far from soundless, yet so much quieter than the danger they carried, two hundred arrows flew a low arch into the Maurowan encampment.

Who in all the desert knew if a single one of them hit anything alive. But the arrows tore the camp awake. Shouts erupted from within the watch. Rousing and warning. Clamor and disarray. Before Tzal could make anything out of the sounds, there was flint striking all around her. Tzal drew her prepared arrow, marked on the shaft so that she could know it by feel alone. She took the waxen bag off the tip. Just below the shaft, it was wrapped in pitch-soaked cloth.

Little fires blazed from one shrouded arrow tip to the next, until Tzal received her fire.

Two hundred streaks of flame dove into the Maurowan tents. Aim was irrelevant. Anywhere was a good place to land.

Now the Maurowans were desperately trying to make sense of themselves. Trying to form something. Anything. Some defense against that which came out of the darkness.

The Trekoans fired a third volley. Those who knew how to aim, aimed. Those who did not know the tricks of the trade simply let another arrow fly, then immediately turned heel and ran.

Tzal and all the Trekoans rushed back into the impossible black terrain, like goats over crags. The Maurowans would not—*could not*—follow. Not unless they wanted to stumble in the dark to a certain death.

The brief probing attack—if it could even be called that—had two purposeful lies to plant in the Maurowan camp. First, that *this* was the avenue of approach which they should fear and, second, that this was the type of assault they should expect: the fleeting and skittish efforts of the very, very few. Only two hundred Trekoans attacked. But thousands more awaited their turn.

Back into the rough, winding trails of the Ghallaz, the Trekoans moved further west toward the mouth of the wadi. Tzal crawled to the lookout and watched. Waited. Two dead-quiet hours of the frigid night. The effect of their attack made the camp more alert at first, but this was fifty tents down; already they were settling back into usual routines and patterns.

Rahummi clicked the signal.

This time, they left their bows behind. And this time, they crawled much closer.

And as soon as there was a chance the enemy could see them, the Trekoans rose up and ran at them. Two crashing waves, attacking the outer guard, Tzal with the first, Rahummi with the second.

Tzal struck her sagam into the first Maurowan she encountered, pushing through the outer watch toward the camp. Two more men bloodied her sword before she caught herself. *Don't go too far. Not yet.* She sprinted back into the night with the rest of the Trekoans, barking the Hushai battle-cry as it rose, scattershot, from all the mouths nearby.

Her blood was quick in the veins now. The firm grip on her hand and the muscles in her arms went limp, not from hard use but from the tension of bracing and the sudden rush of doing. She would shake them out and they would recover. The whole assault had lasted less than three minutes.

Tzal felt a little giddy with the ease of it. This sort of attack was pure harassment, suited to her nature, satisfying at so little cost. Only a handful of Trekoans were wounded. Two killed. A third died as night wore on and crept slowly toward dawn.

She knew they had taken far more than that from the Maurowans, in less than ten strokes of each man's sword. Rahummi had no excuse to wear his losses on his face, to carry them in his voice, to show them in his posture.

"That was victory, understand? Don't take that away from your soldiers. Get your head up," she whispered, gripping him roughly by the arm as they reached the rally point.

Azetla ate losses bitterly too, but he hid it much better. He let the men rowdy themselves and get the strength from it. He had to.

"It's your responsibility," she told Rahummi. "We're very far from done."

"That may well be," Rahummi said calmly. He washed his face with cold water and did, indeed, raise his head high and shake his shoulders back. "But *you* could stand to mourn once in a while, Tzal."

She slipped past those words.

"Why are you calling me 'Tzal' again, all of a sudden?"

"What, only *he's* allowed to do it?" Rahummi answered in a wry voice.

"It's just that you haven't used it since before."

Since before Haani was killed.

"You made everything so much worse than it needed to be, you know. You made it so hard to stay in your corner," he said. "And I *tried*."

Maybe he had tried, little good it did him. Those who favored her usually found ample reason to regret it.

There was no more talk. They slept, a few hours each, trading watch command with the other tribal leaders, sheltering in the rough of the Ghallaz as daylight invaded the wadi. In the late afternoon, Tzal scouted along the ridges, perusing the enemy encampments down below like market stalls. She wanted to buy a heartier and more satisfying harassment come nightfall. There should be a savory number of enemy dead, with few losses to embitter the taste.

Because, after tonight, their whole objective would shift, and so would Tzal's role. This was the easy part and she wanted to get the most out of it.

She returned to the main Hushai rally point an hour before dusk. She kept clenching and rolling her jaw in anticipation, as if her very will would speed the sun's course—or stop it. Let the fight come quick or let it not come at all, but the wait was like an invisible drumbeat, driving at the back of your skull, making the mind flare and the muscles go taut.

Under the orange dusk, Tzal and Gado led the others through so they could see the assault point. There was a slight groove in the otherwise even terrain north of the Ghallaz. The riverbed was almost empty around it, the rains having drained to a shallow pool, then run on westward. The Maurowan encampment was spaced around the dip in the ground. The watch patrols had to walk out further there than elsewhere; the pitched tents and watch-lines bulged with the shape of the land.

Get the timing right, and it was a beautiful target. The camp was most lax halfway through third watch; the vigilance waned and they burned their watchfires low to save supplies. Still better, rainless clouds blew in and shut out the glow of night. This time the Trekoans crept even closer, for here the land gave them cover until almost the last moment.

As soon as they reached the mark of sight, Rahummi broke the rustling quiet with a war-shout. Hundreds of voices echoed it in a heart-pounding roar. All the tribes together burst forth like a flame, scorching the edge of the enemy watch-line.

Amid the Janbaris near the center of the assault, Tzal broke into the outer watch. She cut her sagam upward into a soldier's chin, riving the skin of his throat apart. He dropped straight to the ground, sputtering. Another watchman hacked at her and she feinted retreat. He followed. Stumbled on the rocks. And Tzal ran him through.

Let's gouge them deep tonight. Deeper than they could ever expect. Dig hard, so that when we finally pull back, we are practically daring the enemy to chase us out into the jagged dark, out to their deaths. Shake them to their bones, so they're rattling when Azetla finally gets to them.

The fourth soldier she struck was visibly terrified. He barely looked old enough to wear armor. Practically a child. But he tried. And tried again. Brave in his last moments. Took three strokes to get him down.

Her final swing left him face to the ground, trying to move, bleeding profusely from the thick vein of his thigh. Tzal didn't have time to do him the kindness of one more blow. The enemy was rousing now. And swarming. It was getting harder to slip through the thick of it, to move along the shadows' edge.

But I'm not done yet.

With a driving need to make the assault count, to make it tell the story it was supposed to tell, Tzal cut past the watch-line. Just a little further in. One Maurowan fell easily, blind to her. The next nearly caught her before she wounded him. Less light on her feet and a mere scrape would have been a laming blow.

If a mere five hundred of us can leave this great army limping, let them imagine what the rest of us can do. When they begin to see we are thousands, let their knees turn to water.

The thought had been pounding in the back of her head like a prayer, over and over, as if she alone could make it so. By blood, Azetla was so sure. She *had* to make it so.

With the intensity of the assault, and the weak light of the watch-fires against the all-consuming blackness of night, it almost felt like she could. Even though she fought headlong, with others beside her, she moved in something like her usual way, at her own evasive rhythm, taking every scrap she could get.

She did all that came natural to her, determined to make this worth her while.

A fragment of a thought passed through her mind; *shouldn't the withdrawal have been called by now?*

She heard Trekoan shouts, unclear. Panicked. Confused. One split second she had to cast her eyes east and west, and she saw her mistake. She wasn't where she was supposed to be. The Janbaris with her were fighting ferociously but...they were *alone*. Separated from the other tribes, collapsing inward from both directions, fighting on three sides. Soon it would be all four sides; they were about to be swallowed into the Maurowans. The enemy was fully alive now, voracious, and endless.

She had gone too far. She was using too much blood on too small a task. To her left and to her right, Janbaris fell. Most did not rise. And no call of retreat ever came to her ear.

It was almost too late.

She clamped down on a panic and shouted the retreat in Janbari dialect with what little voice she had. Turning and scrambling out of the wide-open jaws of the Maurowan enemy, she shouted again. Did they not hear? Her voice disintegrated across the words, till her raw throat was spent and would give no more sound for all the furious effort of her lungs.

The attack was far past any purpose—only now as she scraped and cut and clawed her way out could she see *how* far past. It had broken like a wave, crashed hard, and lost all its strength.

At last, one of the Janbari leaders took up her call. A firm shout rang out. A second call cut off in the throat. A third echoed clear. But the whole retreat was mired as if in mud.

Tzal cut her sagam across the stomach of a too-eager enemy before she escaped back into the night. Arrows skidded behind her. Something nicked her heel and she barely caught her footing. Where was Rahummi? Where were the Saqiranis and Lahashet?

She could see no one. She could only hear, and what she heard was the chaos of a rough and desperate retreat. For, this time, the Maurowans did pursue them. They wanted deaths. They wanted prisoners. They wanted whatever they could get before the night and the Ghallaz consumed them.

It put the retreat to shards, the Trekoan soldiers scattering every which way into the dark, unable to find or follow their Hushai guides. Vocal signals were cast, missed, and muddled.

Tzal tried to herd them—truly, she tried—but they were too scattered and paid no heed. There was no room left for slowness. She coursed across the rocks like the river in high winter, bashing into or stumbling over obstacles, trying to discern the pathway. Each time her ears were struck by a certain too-familiar sound, she would stop, catch a Maurowan feeling his way around a rock, and gut him. Then she sprinted again.

Two more she killed like this. Quick and quiet, one at a time; this she knew how to do.

Not until she was deep in the Ghallaz, and the Maurowans finally gave up their quarry, did she stop to find her bearings. There were cuts and bruises on her arms and knees from two instances of lost footing over the rough rock and up the narrow crevices.

She slowed. Whistled the signal, waiting to hear an echo. It did not come the first time. Or the second. She lost count. The Trekoans had been as one in the attack; yet they had fled by tribes, by clans. Even one by one. And Janbar had fled last, and fewest. They had followed her. Imitated her. And paid the price.

"*Not one drop more than you have to,*" he'd said. She had not meant to go so far.

She scrubbed the words out and shook her shoulders back. Nothing to be done. There was no question that they had met the objective, and met it well. These things are never so simple and clear-cut as one wants.

It was more than an hour of tediously slow steps and out-stretched arms—sometimes crawling, often feeling with fingertips against a rock wall—before she reached the rendezvous point. Others gathered in streams and trickled into the camp with her. There were several wounded already laid up near the fires. No doubt there were still more, lying somewhere along the trails in the dark, hoping to be found. If they hadn't been discovered by now, they probably wouldn't be till morning.

The moment firelight struck Tzal's face, a Saqirani soldier named Saji ran up to her.

"What took you so long? He's over here."

"Who is?" Tzal said.

But Saji simply gave her a look of profound scorn and turned to be followed. He led Tzal to Rahummi. Laid upon on the ground, tended by a Hushai woman.

"By blood," Tzal breathed in Shihrayan.

She dropped to her knees and ran her hands purposefully over his chest, lifting and hovering her fingers when she reached the main wound. The dark sheen of blood on him and all over the ground told plainly what would happen in the next hour. His chest was uneven—plainly deformed—and his breath came as a thick, wet scraping sound.

"We need to take him back to the Taya," she said. "To Sidara. Now."

Saji gave her a strange look, and she could not read it or understand it at all.

The Hushai woman slowly shook her head at Tzal.

"Inze-Sahr, it is much, much too late for that."

"No it isn't," Tzal said, but the voice did not come with her words.

Tzal began to do what she knew to do, till her hands were slick with blood. She saw the wound, she saw the truth, but she steadfastly refused to acknowledge it. She defied Gods and death all the time. Rahummi could too.

No one stopped her desperate, stupid efforts. But she knew it wasn't because they hoped. It was because they pitied.

When Tzal heard the Hushai woman begin praying to Uza, the God of suffering, and Mahar, the God of death, anger seeped into her lungs. Tzal stood and jerked the woman's hands out of the ritual gestures and twisted her arm till the woman cried out.

"He does not need your damned spirits, woman," she rasped. "He follows the Mashevi one, God of the desert."

The Hushai woman shrank as Tzal released her grip, muttering shaky curses against "that *Inze*, that foul *Sahr-jinn*."

"Saji. You know the words. You know the prayers. You know what to say. Don't you?"

With a dazed and uneasy face, Saji began to say the common prayers for the wounded and the dying, the ones said by all Trekoan followers of the Mashevi God. He fumbled over them, not knowing them well; he served the desert God in some rituals, the Trekoan Gods in others. He was not like Rahummi: so soft, yet so single-minded. How could he be like that? How had he endured Tzal so unscathed?

A devout Janbari soldier joined Saji's words, bolstering them.

Tzal put her hand under Rahummi's neck and then—a thing she had never once done—grasped his hand. She lowered her forehead to his shoulder. She didn't dare sully the prayers by joining them out loud. She would not blaspheme over him. She would not. He would not want that.

But it was hard not to mouth the words in Mashevi which, because of Azetla, she now knew so very well. Her lips would move till she bit them still. And then they would move again.

Rahummi's breaths shortened. Tzal could feel against her skin his desperate and failing fight for air. It took so many minutes, and yet so few, for his breaths to shallow and heave into nothingness. Then Rahummi Bin-Deghan was just a body.

She kept her grip on him. Tight and desperate.

When at last Tzal lifted her head, her face was wet with his blood. It stung in her eyes. She could taste it in her mouth.

"Sahr," Saji's voice came tentatively.

Tzal turned.

"I...I need to perform the final rites. And you—"

Tzal stood immediately and backed away from the body. They would not let her partake in holy death rites. Nor did she wish to. She called for two other Saqirani soldiers who had known Rahummi well and who were in their beliefs as he had been. It took some minutes to find them, but they quickly accepted their duty.

Tzal stepped away from the circle of mourners, just beyond the touch of firelight. Several more bodies were brought to rest beside Rahummi's. She listened from her distance. Heard their shamelessly grief-ridden and God-filled repetitions. Their fervent ritual mourning. Their humble acceptance. The words seemed cruel in their trustfulness, in their strange grasping at comfort.

So unlike how it was done in Shihra.

She should have walked away and left them to it. Separated herself completely. That's what she usually did. But no matter how far back into the shadows she crept, she did not wish to go beyond the sound of those awful, gutting words. Or beyond the reach of that awful, gutting God whom Azetla would swear by salt heard every last syllable. What did that God do with all those words they gave him? If they did not fall to the ground, where did they go? What did they accomplish?

Nothing, she thought. *Nothing*.

Yet she could not extract herself. She could still see Rahummi. Just the edge of his face. He looked nothing like himself.

They sang. The sound made Tzal's jaw ache, made the bones of her nose ache, and she hated it and wished they would stop and just be done with it.

She closed her eyes against it all.

Immediately an image flooded her mind that she vaguely recognized—as dream or memory, she was not sure. A boy that looked like Rahummi when she first met him, although only a little like. Less well-fed, but cheerful like him, naïve like he once was.

The boy sang with the cracking voice of one whose manhood is on the horizon, but still a little ways off. He walked about, simple and content. Maybe a little neglectful of his flock of goats.

Then the boy's throat was cut open and his blood pooled thickly on the rocks. A shocking amount of blood. It did not seem possible anyone could have that much blood.

Flint struck sudden in Tzal's mind, lighting a fire in a dark, dark room.

She *remembered* this. It wasn't a dream. She was the one who did it.

And that was why there was so much blood. Her hand had been so shaky and hesitant. It had taken her three or four tries to cut deep enough.

Tzal lowered herself to her knees in her quiet shadow, the songs still drifting softly overhead. She hadn't forgotten that day. Not in the normal way of forgetting. She hadn't thought about it for so, so long. Carefully, and on purpose. She'd dimmed and blurred it, till it took on the shade of something merely imagined, lacking all color and detail. She'd made the path in her mind to that day too far and too obscure to walk.

Now it came back with the force of a closed fist. The disgust in her stomach as the boy writhed under her knife and then, abruptly, stilled. The ache in her shoulder from where Aadin had gripped and pulled her, furious with her hesitation.

She could remember it all viscerally. She could feel in her hands the doing of it.

The truth was she had done many such things ever since. Worse and crueler things too. Yet this one had bothered her. Not only because it was the first time she'd killed in plain, cold blood, but because it had been so stunningly needless.

And it was the most cowardly she had ever been.

She was afraid of Aadin. But likely he would have hurt her no worse that time than he had done a dozen times before or after.

She was afraid of being cut off and cast out. But that had happened anyway.

She was afraid of being less Shihrayan, less of what she wanted to be.

And never had she been more unlike her people than she was now.

She had lost herself by every means she used to keep herself.

And now she had lost much, much more.

Tzal could not make her mind walk clearly through the night to see how much blame she owed herself. Had he been struck as any man might be struck, through no fault of anyone's? Had Rahummi gouged too deep, as she had? Had he waited too long, trying to bring the Janbaris out of the mire she put them in?

She did not know. And she did not see the point in trying to know. Those kinds of questions were rarely answerable and she wouldn't trust her own answers anyway. She knew she could lie to herself just as well as she could to anybody.

Tzal touched her wrist, trying to turn and scrape the slave band that was no longer there. Her fingers dug into the skin instead. With two hard flicks against the bone of her wrist, she stood up. The death rites were ended. Tzal stepped back into the firelight.

"I'll take Rahummi's task," she said blankly. "Iraal, Saji, Jarash, Imron, and Gado…meet me at Rijhaq-i-saar pass in one hour. We've still got work to do."

She walked toward the patrol path which led—by winding ways—to the wadi pass; the Trekoans would have to secure and guard it at dawn.

"Why did it pretend to mourn?" she heard one Hushai say in a hushed voice.

"I don't know—" Saji answered.

He said something else, but she was beyond the hearing of it.

The bits of scrub under Tzal's feet were already crackling dry again after four days without rain. The desert air extracted moisture from earth, lips, skin, and tongue. That was good. The drier the better for her task. She wanted a good north wind too.

The hollowed-out, cut-off-breath feeling came twice, like a jab to the ribs. Rahummi's voice in her mind telling her all the things she usually ignored, smiling at her sadly, knowing she would do only as she pleased.

And Naima beaming brilliantly down at that little girl, three months old, just named.

But Tzal was adept at stopping this sort of thing. At skirting it. Turning it dim.

Snuffing it out.

And walking away till it was all but forgotten.

43

Joseph saw the messenger as soon as the watch did. He threw the weak coffee down his throat and flagged the soldier down, who followed Joseph dutifully. Azetla stepped outside the tent to hear the report. He was already in full battle attire, though it was still dark and the watch had yet to rouse the camp.

"Are they in position?" Azetla asked Sergeant Lachlan.

"The runner said they were ready to start the raids when he left. Probably started a while ago by now. Saji and Rahummi had three well-hidden camps for retreat. The Shihrayan reported that the Rijhaq-i-sirr pass was clear and walkable, so that won't be a problem when the time comes for them to go through and secure it. They killed quite a few scouts as well."

Azetla glanced at Joseph with a lively eye.

"Well?" he said.

"Do you even need to ask? Can't line them up fast enough for me. Let's move."

Azetla walked up to the ridge and sent them out, all the watchers, the wakers, and the runners. He moved like a runner himself, going from ground to ground, officer to officer, setting all to rights, bolstering their spirits. He even smiled and laughed with them, his spirits strangely and infectiously high.

Never having tried too hard to cut a commander's figure, he looked it now more than ever. Until these last months, Azetla had never had anything for armor but a badly worn leather chest-piece. Now he had plain pauldrons, bracers, and greaves. Like a real officer, if not a wealthy one.

Across the face of this grown and ever more dangerous man, Joseph could not stop seeing flashes of that rail-thin, stone-silent, self-righteous boy. The one who had been startled by every scrap of kindness Joseph threw his way. The one who scoured the armor of a certain wealthy Makarish Lord till he claimed to loathe all those gorgeous, hammered-bronze scales.

"So needlessly elaborate," said that starved little jackal. "Can't fight in that. Can't even move."

"Well, you learn to, jackal. You learn to," Joseph had said, smiling at the boy's bald envy. "But I wouldn't worry about it; we don't see armor like this in the Black Wren very often."

Who was that boy? He had given up trying to answer that question years ago.

Who was this man? Joseph was pretty sure he didn't want to know.

Joseph circled round his own contingent and took words of readiness from each of his officers. When all was certain he took his mount and rode over to Azetla, who sat astride that dark and lovely Sanchi beast.

"Mine are set. Gods be with us," Joseph said with a steady breath in and a steady breath out. "And tell that desert god of yours not to neglect me either."

Azetla smiled vividly at the dark horizon. "By salt, Joseph, I will pray just that."

Joseph rounded his mount to the small flat leading to the outer Ghallaz trail. He gave a hearty shout of greeting to warm and liven his men. But only a portion of them could hear him, no matter how he stretched his lungs. For Joseph Radabe—Nagonan by blood, though he had never seen the land nor had his parents, the son of a common jeweler, Sergeant in Maurowan records, but Captain in Azetla's more meticulous ones—would lead sixteen thousand men to the battlefield. To him belonged the vast majority of all the southern troops clustered at the head of Wadi Kilsayn.

If Joseph had heard of some General attempting what he was to attempt now, or if he had read it in a scroll of history, he would have scoffed and said, "*that's madness! What fools!*"

And, of course, when Azetla first told him his plan, he said it out loud with his own mouth. Azetla's dogged confidence might overrun some people's common sense, but not Joseph's. Yet as Azetla drew the details down on the map and told him what the Sahr and Rahummi would do, what Sarrez would do, and where Azetla would be, he began to see it in his mind's eye, like a hidden path through the wilderness, which must practically be stood upon before it could be seen.

So the nervousness in Joseph's body was not a sickening thing, as it might have been with the same order said by a different tongue. It was invigorating. Waking the heart and the muscles, heightening the senses, and straightening the shoulders till Joseph sat like a giant among men on the back of his horse. And his men looked at him like that. Whether it was truthful or not, it was probably for the best.

One must find some deep grit and traction in the ground to start a wild path like this.

The men lumbered at first, though. So many compressed into those narrow corridors. Up and down and up again, as far to the soft eastern edge of the Ghallaz as they could go without reaching the Maurowan road and exposing themselves.

"The widest, easiest path here," the Hushai said blithely. "Like being carried by a current."

It was not remotely true. Joseph would have deemed this a shattered ground had he not known how much more difficult the inner routes were. The cavalry had to dismount more often than ride in order to guide their poor mounts step-by-step through the hard straights. No matter what the Hushai claimed, the going was slow and they rested only a little at night. Joseph received runners, telling him the positions of Azetla, Sarrez, and the Trekoans. But each report was hours from fact and he felt time toying with him.

He must show his face at the battle-line neither too late, nor too soon. Even the Ghallaz cannot hide sixteen thousand men all the way to the last moment.

On the third day a runner confirmed that the pass was secure. Azetla and Sarrez were ready. All rested on him.

Two hours before dawn on the fourth day, the advance scouts spotted the thousands and tens of thousands of Riada's soldiers encamped along the Sol riverbed. And if they moved any further, the tens of thousands would spot *them*. They halted within the last edge of the Ghallaz's brutal shade.

"What are we supposed to do if we actually *take* the town of Lisah?" Lieutenant Ishelor asked.

"I doubt we make it that far, but we'd occupy that gentle ridge north of it and act like we intend to hold it."

"Act like? We'd *have* to hold it. There'd be nowhere else to go."

Joseph smiled and slapped Ishelor on the shoulder.

"What did the bloody Sahr say that one time? If you want to deceive someone, your best bet is to do it with the truth."

Ishelor laughed and shook his head, saying, "by blood, by blood" under his breath. Joseph didn't know which sort of amazement overcame Ishelor just then. Was it because he was serving under a Mashevi commander and was not ashamed of it? Was proud, in fact? Was it because of the still grander, more terrifying purpose underlying the whole thing: the toppling of an emperor?

Or was it simply the here and now of this one battle? A battle in which Joseph and Ishelor were to lead nearly the whole army like bait—a bait so robust as to be indistinguishable from the real thing. Joseph's assault was to seem the main assault. And so it would be. It was to seem as though the market town of Lisah was the objective. And so it must be. They were to fight as if this was the only way and the only chance. And so it was.

The only way to make the appearance of the assault believable was simply for it all to be true, risk and cost included. As far as Joseph and his men were concerned, the town of Lisah was all that mattered, and the entire hope of this day rested on Joseph and Ishelor's shoulders.

And truly, it did.

Joseph looked up at the sky and the stars to gather the hour of night.

"About time, I think. If I break cover with Red Dome and Blue Rock, they should be formed on this side of the riverbed by first light. Just make sure your lookouts have every angle for the signals."

Ishelor nodded and called over to Colonel Peterson.

"Ready?"

"Ready."

So we all keep saying, Joseph thought. But the truth was, it didn't matter if they were ready. The hour had come.

For a brief, breath-held moment, the night pressed a strange breed of quiet just above the jangling, crunching, scraping sound of four thousand men shuffling their way out of the rough roads of the Ghallaz. Onto smooth ground, under a scant dawn, and straight into the enemy's view.

Joseph did not wait to see what the enemy camp did. It didn't much matter yet.

He gave the signal. Then the war-shout. Used all the breath in his body.

The sound rose through the ranks like a flash-flood through the wadi. The march burst into a run as soon as they hit the scrub flats. They took a slight northeastern bearing to the Sol riverbed.

The signal-bearer galloped close within Joseph's shadow, stopping when he pulled up to take the command view. Joseph's most important duty was to see and be seen. Near enough to join the fight if he saw fit, far enough to stay out of it until the end could be known.

The Maurowan lines were forming fast. But it was to their decided advantage to keep their ground and wait for this rebel army to come to them. Anyhow, they had men enough to lose, didn't they? Not like Joseph.

"Cavalry forward!" Joseph barked.

The signal-bearer gripped his pike. The long red-and-blue flag cut through the sky. Once. Twice. Three times.

Each flag down the ranks answered, those strips of cloth snapping into the skyline and back down.

The nine hundred horsemen broke away from the main army, cutting a hard eastern bearing before wheeling north and picking up speed. It had been a long time since the horses had been on ground that would let them truly *run* and they seemed to relish it.

Immediately there were signs of the enemy's bewilderment. They had prepared their defensive lines facing south at the most sensible and obvious avenue of approach. But now Joseph's cavalry was skirting far around, bypassing them entirely. From the perspective of Riada's army, it must seem like nonsense.

"Where are you going, rebels? To a little market town where we shall surround you like a noose? You could have attacked us and run back to your rocks like before, but now you mean to give yourselves entirely into our hands."

I damn well hope it looks that way to you, Joseph thought. The breaking and reforming of lines on their front and flank was a good sign. They were ready, and content to wait and see what these strange, desert-mad fighters would do.

Joseph shouted the second command. Signals swirled down.

As Riada's army stared at the thunderous cavalry running far afield of the assumed objective, Joseph's first battalions crossed the cracked mud of the Sol riverbed and formed a fighting line along the eastern flank of the enemy. It wasn't a strong line, and it had far too little depth. But it was the beginning, and it was all Joseph could yet afford.

Five hundred archers and three thousand men faced toward what, from this vantage point, seemed an infinite army.

The flag. The signal. The shout.

The southern army rushed into the enemy's thick and ready flank.

Already Joseph's next wave flowed behind that protective line on the flank, further and further north toward that meaningless little market town. The wall of Joseph's men trembled, but did not give way. It stood as a violent shield for the next wave, which ran north behind their backs.

But now Maurow was inclined to be livelier. There was a distinct ripple and lift. More were coming to the aid of their eastern flank. Coming from the wadi's mouth and, if Joseph's eyes did not deceive him, turning and marching from their western positions.

Triumph and blood-rush filled his lungs.

Come. Every last one of you. Here we are. Ripe for the taking. Our lines are paper to your steel. Try to run us through.

Joseph gave a new order to his signal-bearer. They rode in with the outer edge of the third wave. At the thin flash of cloth, sent up and down the ranks, the first line purposefully collapsed and drew back.

It was a rough game, and required constant attention, constant signaling. Form a line. Pull north. Break the line and form another. Drag the enemy north. It gave a man the feeling of betting on bones or horses. How many wins could you get before you lost one, then two, then all? Break the line. Pull north. Again and again.

Joseph watched the dark and deadly relay. One contingent of men took up the torch of being the battered front line, then handed it off to the next, just as they got there, only to drag themselves north. All this while, Joseph kept the signals running, so that more and more men flowed out of the jagged Ghallaz and across the Sol riverbed. Joseph hoped the sight tricked their eyes as it nearly did his. *"They are still coming? There's still more? The southern rebels are more than we thought."*

The truth was, all but three thousand of Joseph's men were in view now, so the illusion would be shattered very soon indeed. The flood would end, and Riada's army would quickly see that they had by no means been drowned in it.

No, it was the enemy that went on and on and on, hurling men with abandon at Joseph's lines, spearing them and collapsing them, giving some chase as new lines reformed further north, but not as much as Joseph wanted. The enemy ranks thickened and compressed with reinforcements from west of the Ghallaz.

He was directly behind the fighting now, the din roiling in his ears. No shout of his could possibly be heard. But the signal-bearer never took his eyes off Joseph, and the flags swooped and curved and struck up just as they should. Joseph raised his arm.

The last three thousand men came out of the Ghallaz rocks at a sprint, filled with the shouts they had been holding off. They were ready and fierce and wonderful, and they were all the coins Joseph had, slammed desperately onto the table in a final bet.

The last men crossed the riverbed, and flew past the shambles of the first battle-line. It barely shielded them. When they were past, it disintegrated completely.

They ran past the second line, which had some strength in it yet. When they got beyond them, they formed a third line. So close now to the market town of Lisah, that on a day of peace and quiet, one might have heard a goat bleat from that meager distance.

For a few glorious minutes—seconds?—everything was clear as mountain water, and exactly as Joseph wanted it to be. He could not see all, but he could see most. This rough-hewn, cobbled-together army held fast like a weapon made by a master craftsman. Joseph did not realize until that strange moment that he had not fully believed it possible. Azetla had made this. *Joseph* had made this. This was a child, grown taller and stronger than the father could have ever believed.

One for one, they were superior to Riada's men. No sheen of pride could have told him that as truly as the bodies on the ground, or the stunning speed and maneuverability of men with far less armor and far more to lose. Joseph's men thrust their swords into every inch of unarmored flesh and held their form long, long, long after he thought they could. He had to *force* them to collapse their lines and trace them northward. They wanted to hold to that last man. They were that strong and that sure.

Riada's army had at first been tepid in response, unsure of what Joseph's men were really trying to do; so they had been content merely to react rather than initiate. It wasn't as though *their* lines were going to collapse. They were not going to lose the power of retreat, as Joseph's men might. They could afford to be patient.

But something shifted in their ranks, hard to notice, like a distant, foretelling thunder. More and more reinforcements marched in from beyond the wadi's mouth. They covered the land like flies, like locusts. The din of a coming swarm came to Joseph's ears too late.

The beast decided to wake in full. And Joseph's beautiful lines were instantly shattered.

"Bring your men back. Pull them back to the riverbed!" Joseph shouted at the top of his lungs, while his arm gestured fiercely to his signal-bearer. His bearer cast the signal, whipping the colored cloth, but few responded.

The Maurowans had come against them like a sea swell, where the riptide stole away footing and dragged a man deep into the churning waters. Signal and ride and shout as he might, Joseph could hardly pull his men into the southeastern retreat. Signal flags fell to the ground, swallowed up.

Then, from the corner of his eye, Joseph saw his signal-bearer switch the pike to his left hand and draw his sword. Joseph had waited too long. The battle was lapping against his feet, swelling to his knees, and eddying all around him.

He was a different man from the first stroke of his sword. The instinct of a common soldier moved his arms and pulsed in his grip. He knocked an enemy off his horse and under the many hooves with the corner of his shield. One clean, solid blow cut halfway through a footsoldier's neck. Joseph no longer had time or breath to re-order his men; only time for his sword to find the gaps and drive deep.

The blood of others grew cold on his neck. Near misses left a bruise here and cut there on his body.

He thought he saw an opening. Once again, he tried to pull his men out of this typhoon. He had to get to where he could signal and command, but no matter how hard he tried, he could only fight just to keep his seat and his throat.

One chance arose to swing his arm for the signal instead of for a body. But it was no good. Horror flashed through him and out again; his signal-bearer was down. Lost. Sunk to the bottom of this bloody mire. Trampled. If he wasn't dead when he fell, then he soon would be. One of Joseph's line commanders fell before his eyes, gored through by a Maurowan spear. Joseph cracked the edge of his sword down on the Maurowan enemy's head; the man dropped to the dust, lifeless.

At last, Joseph came into the line of sight of a senior line commander; it was Lieutenant Ishelor. Joseph raised his arm and voice to signal. His eyes played tricks on him. Did Ishelor see? Did he acknowledge? Did his signal-bearer—

Without warning, a lightning pain seared through Joseph's thigh. An instant later, an unseen blow across his head threw him from his horse. Without fully understanding how, he found himself lying in the rocks and the blood-red mud. Immovable. His vision was strange, and so were his thoughts. Did Ishelor acknowledge? Was Sarrez still on the far line? No. Sarrez wasn't here. He was...somewhere else.

Oh, Azetla, what becomes of all this?

Why does the whole bloody world smell of tar and smoke?

That was the important thing.

Good. Yes. Smoke.

Everything blurred and darkened. Sound and sensation seemed to alternately overwhelm and evade him...and then it all came to a halt.

44

Azetla and his six thousand men had made it through the wadi pass, taking their time, picking their way over the rugged trail. They were not in a rush. Their time had not yet come. And, thus far, all was as it should be. At each marker along the trail, up the wadi shelf, and out onto the western rim, he calculated where the others would be.

When he had reached the basin of the wadi, Joseph would have been halfway through the outer edge of the Ghallaz. Under the cover of darkness, Tzal would be soaking the scrub fields in pitch.

When Azetla had camped a night on the gently undulating tableland of the west, Joseph would have reached the Sol riverbed on the eastern side of the wadi; Tzal would be waiting for the signal.

Strange to be so still and quiet when battle was upon them. It may already have begun.

Daylight breached as Azetla approached the western end of the Sol riverbed. The water was pooled and sluggish here, the downward flow barely discernable. The bed was saturated, unable to bear one drop more of this rain to which it was ever unaccustomed. Tzal had told him that, despite the looks of it, it would go no higher than the knee of a man.

Four or five thousand men held a standard battle-line just beyond the shallow waters. They were stock still, not making one motion to attack. Their signal-flags resting horizontal to the ground: a neutral posture.

"They've no higher orders," Azetla said to Sarrez, alarmed.

"But they can't have left so few over here to defend the rear flank," Sarrez said. A sick dread crept into his voice. "If they have they've sent *all* the rest..."

Over to Joseph.

The realization struck them both over the head. Their gambit had worked far too well. Joseph had posed too perfect a threat. He had drawn all but the rear guard to him. And he would drown.

"Send the messenger to General Pall *now*. With the precise words. Every syllable."

And pray he gets there before the Maurowan General sees the truth.

Sarrez obeyed the order; the carrier flag rose up, and the rider circled out eastward.

"What about the Sahr devil? If we can't get someone through, how will she know when—?"

"She'll do it either way."

Azetla said it to soothe Sarrez. But it was no lie. Azetla believed it with the heady strength of conviction. Maybe he shouldn't. But he did. For Tzal was apt to do troublingly more than what was asked of her. Never, ever less. She did not walk underneath the words of a command, but the intent of it. As interpreted by her.

Sometimes Azetla had attempted to guide her with a light hand. Other times he had gripped her hard and reined her in. Only days ago he warned her to take care. But that had been a mixed matter in his own self: half duty, half fear.

Fear for her, of that strange and certain kind. And duty from him not to let one of his own risk beyond all reason and boundaries and purpose. She made herself seem invulnerable. But seeming was her strength. Always seeming.

All this his mind could cut away with a firm stroke. Right now it was utterly simple. He wanted her to do anything and everything she could think of. He wanted her to risk and risk and risk, to the very height of her seeming *or* being. Later there might be guilt, but now it was practically a command, silent in his mouth, woven like thread through his battle prayers.

"How long do we wait to hear back?"

Azetla looked across the river. Closer to five thousand than four, he realized. Well-formed and well-armed. They watched Azetla's eastbound messenger like wolves watch a lamb.

He drew his sword.

"We don't wait at all." The horse, Barra, gave a quick shiver and prance, knowing now what was coming. He looked at Sarrez. "To a man, you hear me."

"Yes, Commander," Sarrez said, his voice hoarse and fervent. "And then straight through from behind?"

"Right into the spine."

Sarrez nodded.

Azetla called to his signal-bearer and shouted as the flag flung the battle order into the sky. "Crag Eagle!"

The sound of his own voice rang loud through the still, quiet air. The Maurowan line rustled with uncertainty at the sound. Had they thought that messenger bore terms of surrender? Had they felt secure? Had they thought that these tribes and traitors would hesitate?

The Crag Eagle took form and surged forward. *Here is your answer, Maurow. No matter your size, we will get our talons into you and hold tight until you say you will tolerate no more.*

Across the shallows of the Sol riverbed, the Crag Eagle formation swooped, alighting onto the Maurowan line. They tore into their prey.

The Maurowans braced hard against the initial attack, as Azetla's wing of the assault curved around and broke into their western flank. This time, he led. His sword gave bite after bite, claw after claw, gouge after gouge. The blows he took or evaded his mind knew nothing about, only to drive in further and further, to force collapse. At first, the Maurowans stood stalwart and hardy, determined to guard the rear and Darton, few thousand though they were.

But Riada's men did not know—they could not know—what kind of men they were facing. Azetla's soldiers had fought in crags and scrub hills, and against the mountainous Maurowan outposts of the south. Azetla's men had lived on little and on nothing. Azetla's men knew that it would be better to die today than to fail.

The small and bedraggled can astonish the great. The fly can make the horse flinch and skitter. The desert could make the Imperial city of Piarago dizzy, even from this distance.

Within minutes the Maurowan flank was foundering to the rear, retreating into itself, stumbling over the comparatively mild terrain. Azetla reared himself out of the fight, pulling back to a command line so that he could see. His whole body was wildly awake with blood-rush; he watched briefly and was overcome with a coarse and savory joy at the precision of his line commanders. They knew what they were about.

He waited until he knew he saw all, though it was a hard thing to hold back for even so short a time. But it was good he did; he saw the opening he needed. And he knew how to get at it.

Azetla barked a command at his signal-bearer, whose spear-flag was thoroughly blood-stained. The signal flew through the ranks. Three of his battalions on the west broke away and flocked around to Azetla's lead, while the rest continued to press on the front line, battering them headlong. Already there were signs of flagging, the body of the enemy ranks growing lean with fear and death.

His men followed, swift and beautifully formed; the final dive of the Crag Eagle. The battalions plunged deep into the ribs of that emaciated body, scraping out the innards. Azetla could sense the winded, buckling jolt almost as a last breath. This only made him fight all the harder, take all the more risk. His left arm—the fighting arm—never ceased to strike and drive; his shield arm throbbed and then went half numb from the deflected blows. He did not bother to number his kills. His shouts initiated every signal, every shift, every break, every new angle.

His voice broke at last, disappearing from his mouth. But the signal-bearer caught the end of it and then pressed east, and east, swallowing up the stragglers as they went. Many of Riada's men tried to flee, for there was no one left to offer surrender, and no one left who would take it.

How brief. How brutal and brief. Then, so bewilderingly quiet in the sudden moment of absolute victory; the plains between the Sol riverbed and Darton were scraped clean of all Riada's soldiers, yet foul with bodies and blood. Azetla's eye could not yet discern how many were his own. He had no doubt it would be a number to cut him to the quick, much later, on a quiet night, in the midst of the prayers of a man who sometimes foolishly thought he was wise and righteous, yet always somehow managed to do just as he pleased.

It was good not to know yet. Good to keep clear, sighted aim. Good that he should not stop and wonder for more than the space of a breath. Because this moment of victory was not victory. Joseph and Peterson and Ishelor needed him and whatever was left of his men.

But before Azetla's soldiers drew themselves back together, before they covered any ground eastward, he noticed the thick, hot pine-pitch smell in the air. The wind was driving steadily out of the north, filling their nostrils with the acrid odor and their lungs with a smoke that must have been billowing long since. It was a wonder they had not been choking and collapsing from it; until now they had not stopped to think of the burning in their throats or the stinging in their eyes. They had thought it the toll of battle.

The men lowered their heads and began to cough on every drawn breath as the pale blue sky was veiled with heavy, black smoke.

Azetla hesitated before raising his arm to start movement. Sarrez came alongside him, battered, but alive.

"You don't think she actually got into Darton, do you?" Sarrez said, through amazement and coughing.

Azetla shook his head. But he was not at all certain she couldn't have done it.

Sarrez's eyes snapped to the east. Azetla turned. Lifted his head to the figure riding toward them.

From the distance, their messenger gave a wide, clear signal.

Hostilities must cease.

General Pall will negotiate.

45

General Caridon Pall maintained a stone visage for his commanders and signal-bearer. But he was shaken. When the Corra's army first began to pour out of that craggy wasteland, he was sure he had the measure of them. Nine or ten thousand at most, though they were trying to seem like more. Of course, they had killed all his scouts and their pesky little raids had taken deeper bites than he would have liked. But, out in the open, these desert creatures would be burned up by true battle, and scattered like ash.

He hoped to keep most of his men in the rear guard, directly outside of Darton.

The idea was to finish this quickly, to please his Emperor, and at little cost, to please himself. The desert liked to rise now and again, thick like dust in the wind, but it always, always fell back to the ground. Caridon would let them try what they might, but he would not let his men follow them into their wadi or their rocky pathways until he had whittled them down a good bit.

Then he would send his men in with their bribed Hushai. He would kill the soldiers, capture their commander, and deliver him to his Emperor.

Caridon did not understand why, but this particular order was especially important to the Emperor. He wanted to see this jackal commander face-to-face. Caridon did not say as much, but he rather thought the Emperor cared too much about the damned jackal and too little about the condition of the soldiers who had marched swiftly in the season of illness and fever, and had too little rest. Caridon also would have liked to wait for another ten or twenty thousand men, just to be absolutely sure.

But the Emperor had his ways. Wiser and higher than mine, Caridon told himself with bitter resignation. At the very least, there was no cause for worry. The coterie of court men and women who accompanied him were, at this very moment, having music and playing Arratul in Darton. They would carry on until he finished his business and could join their revelry. His wife had picked the precise vintage of wine with which they planned to celebrate. From her hometown, in Lariton.

The southern rebels confused him at first. Where were they going? What on earth were they doing? Did they want nothing more than to terrorize the market town of Lisah and then retreat into the Ghallaz? These little pinpricks would do them no good.

The desert rebels made their attack; they tried so very hard. A pitiable attempt, it seemed, since their lines strained almost from the moment they were formed.

Strained, yet did not break. Kept not breaking. For some minutes, Caridon tried to understand what kept them on their feet. He felt as though he was watching a single thread of rope remain attached when nature surely dictated it should have long since snapped, dropped its cargo, and come to nothing.

Irritating, only because he had hoped not to throw too many men at this.

He began to order more and more men from the rear guard. And he had to make them come double-time so that his main force would not weary and lose their overwhelming advantage.

More ragged rebel soldiers trickled out of the Ghallaz. So few, yet water can wear away at a mere drip. So, at last, he commanded that all but the last full brigade come to reinforce the lines. He saw no need for this to drag on.

And it worked beautifully. Even just with the first wave of reinforcements, the enemy instantly staggered.

Their commanders began to fall. Their lines snapped, shuddering back again and again, trying to reform, but losing structural integrity with each desperate attempt.

"We can end this here and now," he told his Colonel, who sat with him on high watch. "Grind them to a powder and do not let a single one scamper back to the rocks. I want to give the Emperor a definitive end to this nonsense."

He liked the look of the battlefield at that moment, and reveled in it. Yet a sour taste began to stir under his satisfaction. Already he could see that he was taking far more losses than he had expected. More than he would deem an acceptable amount against such a scrawny enemy. Though they were near flight and on the cusp of defeat, the desert rebels continued to show resistance and even some fluttering signs of command, for now and again a section of them evaded or flocked or attacked in a unified and effective manner.

He didn't like seeing that. But the last of the reinforcements had nearly arrived from the western line; it would be very quick now.

That was when the messenger arrived, offering to negotiate a temporary cessation of hostilities, if the General should so choose.

"Don't you mean surrender?" Colonel Montare barked in disgust.

"By no means, Lord Colonel. If you do not wish to negotiate a cessation, I will return with those words," the messenger said, cool as a north wind. The man had a North City sound to his voice; Caridon would have rather he had been incomprehensible. He was a Makar of no rank or blood, with black hair, brown skin, and a shocking lack of fear in the face of men so much greater than he and who held his very life in their hands.

Something within Caridon wavered, as if he heard a sound from very far off and though he could not discern its meaning, it beat through his eardrum and into the base of his skull.

Perhaps the Gods had been warning him.

As he ordered the rebel messenger be held hostage—still the man was infuriatingly calm—pitch-smoke began to fill the sky behind them. Caridon and his Colonel turned to see what loomed.

Before Caridon could even perceive the source or nature of the fires, he saw his rear guard. What remained of them. Even across the distance, and the undulation of the land, flags could be seen swirling in the smoke. Caridon's men were being swallowed before his very eyes, like a prey going whole into the mouth of a snake scarcely bigger than itself.

Soon the view of Darton and half the riverbed-line was obscured by unwholesome black smoke. Caridon could not tell if it was coming from within Darton or if the wind out of the north simply made it look that way. But he could not take the chance. By Serivash herself, he would not be the man who was routed by a jackal. He would rather die.

"Rescind the last order!" he growled to his Colonel. "Throw the cease-flag and withdraw the men immediately."

Caridon flicked his hand at the soldiers who held the southern messenger hostage. They released him.

"And you," Caridon said coldly to the blank-faced Makar. "Tell your bloody jackal that he'll have his negotiations, by the Gods. And I damn well don't think he'll be glad of them by the end."

Did that bedeviled southerner *smile* at him? No. A flicker of the mouth. He wouldn't dare. Lightly, the Makar swung onto his horse; calmly, he settled his seat. Then he plunged west into the thick, low-lying smoke that filled the basin of the wadi and the riverbed across its mouth.

Half an hour later, as the tackmen collected the dead and the dying, General Caridon Pall sat high on his white horse at the mouth of the wadi. Shoulders square, armor polished, his gray hair brushed clean of soot and ash.

I am here to grant a cessation that gives me the greater advantage. A cessation. Over and over he told himself this as he waited for the southern army's delegation. A month from now, with all the troops from Kouris, Aruque, and Berdan, Caridon would be able to put every last one of these desert bastards to the sword. The lowest of his officers would scarcely need to break a sweat.

So why did it feel more like surrender than cessation?

At last the Corra's southerners came round the rocky bend. Their Commander had a dozen men with him, no more, no less, as per the agreement. His army was beyond the rock, just as Caridon's was beyond the riverbed. All bows rested on the ground. This was how negotiations must be done.

Smoke still hung low, stinging the eyes. Even now, Caridon did not entirely know what had happened within Darton outpost; none of the five messengers he sent had come back. He had finally sent a whole battalion and the answer they gave him was only more confusion: "*Darton burns, but no enemy in sight. Messengers killed, but we know not by whom. Somewhere there is something lurking in the smoke. No one sees anything. But there are dead littering the path to the gates. And Darton is braced like a city under siege.*"

Worry tapped at his skull, but he must focus. All signal-bearers held their flags low to the ground, cloth trailing to each man's right.

Caridon knew immediately which one was the jackal Commander, though he could not quite have said by what marker: his bearing, his Sanchi horse, or his features. Nevertheless, it was clear as day which of these bedraggled, quarry-slave-looking men bore the responsibility for all words and all commands and all deaths today.

It was an unmistakable look, for Caridon knew it well and had worn it himself.

The jackal was younger than Caridon had expected. Thirty years, maybe, but not much more. He had blood aplenty on his shoulders and hands; this also showed his youth. He could not help but take the lead into battle. Young men can't bear to remain in the Commander's perch, even when they ought to.

Again, a thing Caridon knew all too well. Those days were far behind him, and yet they rested taut in the muscles of his right hand.

Gods' damn this jackal. A mere boy to Caridon's years. *Why is my Emperor so afraid of you? Even if you are the worst of what the rumors say, I still do not understand it.*

The jackal's horse shifted back and forth with its dark, bloody flanks. But the man remained like a buoy in the sea over a wave, his position changed not a whit, his gaze fixed.

"Do you agree to a month, Lord General? Or will you require more than that?" he said.

No protocol. No niceties. No refinement. No *name*. Here was a mathematician interested only in arriving at the sum. And why should this surprise Caridon? What use have those who defy the Emperor for all that which surrounds and upholds him.

"I do you an honor you do not deserve by even granting these negotiations, jackal," Caridon said evenly.

The jackal made no answer.

And Caridon was glad of it. There would be no play here. No dances. What dignity must be lost had already been taken on both sides. This was the magnanimity of the jackal's offer. *Let us do this quickly and quietly*, he said without saying it, *and be finished.*

"Let your men and mine stand aside," Caridon said.

The jackal nodded in agreement.

The two of them withdrew to the bank; in full sight of all, in earshot of none.

"What is your name, boy?"

The jackal accepted no offense from Caridon's words or tone.

"Azetla of Rinayim."

"I know *that* name. We've all heard it. That isn't what I meant."

The jackal offered no additional explanation but looked patiently at Caridon.

"There are tales in Piarago," Caridon said quietly. If the man wanted to be calm, Caridon could meet him there. "Of con-men who wish to pull the name of your King's son over their face like a mask and wear it for power."

Still the jackal was silent. Caridon smiled. "Are you hoping to wield the name Samuel Aver?"

If there was a flinch or flicker in the man's face, Caridon could not detect it. He was so stone-still, so precisely controlled in every breath that the very wind against his face seemed more expressive than he. Perhaps—for Caridon must bring some word to his Emperor—those knuckles grew tighter about the reins.

"Is it very important to you, Lord General, that I be something other or more than what you see before you?" The jackal's eyebrows lowered faintly. "Do you need me to be of blood or rank or power? Does it really save that much face?"

The man's words had swift aim and the shaft struck Caridon's chest. Of course this whole thing was an insult. To face these starveling rebels and tribesman and traitors with a jackal at their head.

But the jackal had given no true answer, and Caridon was wise enough to slip that trinket in his pouch for safekeeping. Caridon could laugh, then. At this jackal. This *boy* who imagined he was doing some heroic thing.

"Even if you were Samuel Aver himself, I have had to lower myself to the very ground just to look you in the eye and strike hands. But I can bear it...for my pride will be recovered when the cessation ends. Yours will never again lift its head."

Strangely, the jackal gave a faint smile. "Well thank God for that. I've been in grave danger from my pride of late."

Caridon narrowed his eyes. He did not understand these southerners, their gods, or their idioms. Devils take them.

"We strike hands on thirty-five days, jackal," Caridon said.

The jackal raised his eyebrows. "Thirty-*five*, Lord General?"

"I retain the right to name the number," Caridon said.

Petty it may seem, but it felt like having the last word. And it meant a surer guarantee of getting much-needed supplies from the Mashevi coast for his men.

"You withdraw your troops from Lisah and from Darton. Cross back over the Sol. It is the inviolable line." Caridon gestured to the Sol riverbed.

"For us. And for you, Lord General. We will spare none who cross it."

"Don't worry, jackal." Caridon smiled stiffly. "We'll leave you to your barren wasteland. Swear it and so shall I."

"Lord General Caridon Pall, I swear by salt and I swear before the God of the desert and of all, whose name is holy: not one of mine shall cross this line for thirty-five days."

Caridon had never heard a jackal swear by anything. He had never dealt with them before. He marveled a moment with neither anger nor contempt nor any particular feeling at all. This no one and nothing before him, young enough to be his son, sword at left-hand position, dirty with battle, and probably very afraid, though quite good at seeming like he wasn't. With a little concentrated effort, Caridon could despise this man. That was easy enough.

But he did not know what he would say about him to the Emperor. He could not satisfy his master when he himself was not satisfied. In any case, he was not to be outdone by this man.

"I swear by my Emperor, by Shouma of war, and by Serivash of blood."

The jackal didn't like that. Tightened his jaw. But swallowed his distaste without a word.

Thus it was sworn.

All Caridon needed to do to win was wait.

When the fields of blood and the smoke of the air had cleared, Caridon was told the day's truth. He had lost thirteen thousand men. Far more than he had anticipated.

And the fires? No enemy was ever seen inside the walls of Darton, they said. No one knew how the fires had started. No one knew anything. But there were dead everywhere just outside the walls; messengers, patrols, officers, and tackmen. Anyone who dared trek through that lung-searing smoke.

The wine went bitter through Caridon's teeth that night. There was no music. No revelry. The whole of Darton outpost cowered like one struck by an unseen blow.

46

Mild insults leaped back and forth at the Sol riverbed while Azetla and the Lord General held their private negotiations. Sarrez was in a frame of mind to be amused by it. Men who would have died today had been granted a reprieve. They could live a few weeks more. Might as well be forever, to hear the jocular tones of both his men and their enemies across the riverbed.

Sarrez felt the vigor of the reprieve himself. They had done it. By the skin of their teeth and with losses not yet counted or understood. *We have done it.* This desert army, crafted and led by Sarrez's own battalion, had made an army beyond twice its size flinch, cast up its hands and say, *"we can take no more of this today."*

And thirty-five days of life were purchased for all.

He could have laughed at the insults Riada's army hurled. Laughed because he didn't care, or laughed because some of them were truly amusing. Only one line of jest stuck in him like a wedge and, as the day wore on, the wedge was driven deep till he wondered whether he might be split down the middle.

"You know who that jackal of yours is, don't you," they liked to shout. "Leader of all their rebels, he is. They call him the goatherd. But surely you know this. He'll lie to anyone, pretend to be anything: commoner, general, or king...until he has Maurow on its knees. How does it feel to know you're helping the jackals destroy Maurow? To destroy everything you love? How does it feel to be tricked?"

Most of the men took no notice of this. Those who wanted to retaliate were silenced with one swift gesture of Sarrez's hand. They reverted to common banter.

"What food do you have over there. Anything other than worms and dust?"

"We have all we need, northerner; and how is your Emperor feeding you these days? Hopefully half as well the dogs under his table."

Two starving armies mocking each other's hunger. Another good jest, but Sarrez's humor was knocked out of him and, anyhow, the matter was done with quickly.

Sarrez and Azetla rode side by side the long way round west through the plains rather than take the rougher wadi pass. They had to camp at night and would have another long day before they reached the southern edge of Kilsayn.

All the needful, practical things were discussed. And then there was deep, quiet warmth between Azetla and Sarrez, with little needed but a look. Sarrez could see the weight on Azetla's shoulders and he tried to bear it with him. And when Azetla saw that Sarrez was beleaguered by his own thoughts, he attempted to do the same in turn.

But this time, Azetla could not help Sarrez. For he did not know which thought knotted Sarrez's face with worry. And if he did know, he could offer no balm for it.

Two or three times in those long, otherwise comforting silences, Sarrez nearly asked.

Are you what they say you are? Will you do what they say you'll do? Am I a traitor twice over because of you?

The words swirled on his tongue. And Azetla would have answered them. Sarrez knew he would. With no varnish, and without blinking.

And that was why Sarrez said nothing.

He wasn't ready to lose his commander. Or be lost to him. Not yet.

Azetla did not notice it at first, but he had slowed down. He could not be more than an hour or two from the south end of the wadi; he moved like a man coated in lead, dismounting Barra and walking the rocks.

Ever keen and ever gentle in his approach, Sarrez came beside him.

"I think we'd better get it over with. We already know it's going to be a brutal number."

Azetla nodded.

They had received a rushed messenger with an incomplete report of the battle on the eastern side of the wadi. Certainly no less than four thousand killed, many of them leaders and officers. But the report was over a day old now; how much higher had that number climbed? It was probably double that. Azetla breathed away the constriction in his chest and walked on at a steady pace.

He had hoped Tzal would have caught up with them by now. He wanted just that one simple assurance against the many he knew he would not have. Long before Hidud, there were many and sundry thoughts that ran toward her, but none of them had ever been named "worry" or "dread." Hidud laid those fresh across his shoulders and he simply had to carry them now.

An hour later, when the rear guard called out that one of their own had joined them from the pass trail, he did not turn back to verify. He just signaled confirmation. Felt his shoulders relax. His lungs released breaths more freely and took them in more deeply. And he waited. He did not look back once. But when he heard a man behind him mutter, "Oh, there's that devil of ours, looking like it's come back from hell," he smiled faintly to himself. He slowed Barra down.

Not until she reached his periphery did he turn his head to look at her.

She *did* look like she'd come back from hell, or somewhere like it.

Her face was streaked with blood and pitch. Her arms too. The knuckles were cracked from sere air, bled out, and then dried black with dirt caked in. It was hard to tell bruises from smears of smoky residue. Her hair was half unraveled from its plait, her lips chapped crimson, and her eyes burned with a strange look that Azetla could neither read nor recognize. There was not the least smirk or relish of triumph on her face. She looked as if she returned from a battle that was lost rather than won.

"Are you—"

"I'm not wounded," she said in a cold, raspy voice. "You told me not to be injured, so there you go." She said she was not wounded, but she moved as if every joint was on the cusp of giving out, as if her whole body protested being upheld; she barely even looked at Azetla, just walked on in a determined, plodding way. He matched her pace.

"Did you actually go inside Darton?" he said.

She shook her head. "I got others to go in for me."

When she did not elaborate, Azetla walked into her line of sight and stopped her in her tracks.

"Tzal, I need you to give me a proper report."

Azetla did not understand why that elicited such a look of contempt from her. She stepped around him, clicking her tongue at Barra.

"There are women in the village of Lisah who sell themselves to the Darton soldiers. But the soldiers were not using them very kindly, to say the least, and then they were beginning to make trouble among the women who were not for sale as well. Lucky stroke for us." Azetla narrowed his eyes at the flat indifference in her voice. "So it wasn't as hard as I initially thought it would be to convince them to set the fires. Once they saw the pitch burning on the scrub fields, they lit them all over Darton.

"After that, I kept the fields clean. It took them a while to realize they shouldn't send any more people out of the gates. To the best of my ability, no one who went into the smoke got out."

She cleared her throat as if trying to put sound and strength back into her voice.

"What about the raids at the beginning? How many did you and Rahummi lose then?"

She winced. Her step faltered oddly for a moment, but she recovered it. Her mouth chewed a while over her next words, so that Azetla was surprised when all she said was, "eighty-nine." She paused in an odd way. "Most of them Janbari."

Azetla nodded, faintly relieved. By the look of her—and by the scant reports he'd received—he had imagined a much worse number. It was said that their raids bit the enemy deep, shook them hard; the Imperial soldiers were still collecting their dead when the next attack came.

But Tzal would not look at him. Her teeth were grinding over some bitter taste.

"Tzal, finish the report," he said firmly.

"Rahummi was among the dead."

With a heavy step and a deep sigh, Azetla came to a halt. They had crested the gentle hill and could see their camp across the way, on the shelf at the southern head of the wadi. Tzal stopped too. She levered a miserable smile onto her face. The one he hated most.

"But you said that would happen. You said I would go too far." Her voice was barely audible and her eyes were fixed on the rocky trail ahead. "Didn't want to. But I still did."

Instinctively Azetla snapped his fingers at her face, like he did with any inattentive tackman, so that she finally *looked* at him.

"Listen to me," he said harshly. "If there is a lesson to learn, learn it to the bone. But don't you dare wallow in it. You can't afford that. *I* can't afford for you to do that. Just tell me what happened, and keep it plain."

"Last raid. I was near the center with Janbar. Cut a bit too deep without looking. Just wasn't looking. Had trouble getting them out. And I never heard Rahummi call the retreat. He was dragged off the ground by one of the Saqiranis. I...I don't actually know what happened to him. Or how."

"And you can't know, most likely," he said in a distant, command voice. "Even if you had done everything right, that's still no guarantee. You and I both know that."

His words did not seem to reach her. He tilted his head, indicating that they must keep walking. In an attempt to sand down the gruff edge in his voice, he turned his words gently to Mashevi.

"I'm sorry, Tzal." Then he lowered his voice further still. "Holy and Blessed is the God of Masheva and of all, the true judge."

She shied at the death benediction like horse at fire, pulling her shoulders up, gritting her teeth. She shook her head. Then walked down the trail.

Azetla had deeply admired Rahummi. He called him friend with no trace of hesitation. But there was a focused numbness after battle; the loss of Rahummi was still distant, and it could not reach him. But the loss to Tzal was very near, and *she* could.

Thus the grief he felt first and strongest was not even his own. It was hers. Sharp, bitter, and hopelessly guilt-ridden.

They walked side by side saying nothing else, carrying that needful silence slung over their shoulders. The smells of roasting goat, bishi tea, and many fires rose with the wind, teasing them, drawing them in toward camp. The sun set behind them and the sky turned a deep sapphire blue, with just enough light left to step by.

As they walked across the lower western plateau inside the wadi entrance, the mixture of victory and grief was everywhere palpable. Azetla collected reports as they worked their way through toward the eastern camp and his headquarters. It took a long time. So many men wanted him to share one bite, one sip, one lowered head, one prayer. He did his best to give everyone as much of himself as he could; each time he thought he emptied the well, it turned out there was a little more left.

Tzal and Sarrez helped him here. They asked the questions and gathered the smaller reports from individual men, sifting and distilling them for Azetla, while he gave either the joy or the mourning that was asked of him.

He had not yet received the full and most crucial report: Joseph's. Only bits and pieces of what happened on that battlefield had reached him.

But the tallies of the dead thus far were like those Tzal had given him: less than he had thought. He did not take this with relief. Not yet.

Even now, if he drew each of the deaths he knew about as a single tick mark on a scroll, it would take the better part of an hour to complete all of them. He knew, because his mother had made him do this once. Had been reading an account of an ancient battle and, after six thousand of his men were slaughtered, the King withdrew. Being young and stupid, he had exclaimed in scorn: "Why does he give up? He should not have!"

"Perhaps not," his mother had said. "The story shows that over and over again, he refused to call upon God, refused to listen to the prophets. But you count them, my son, one by one, a single stroke at a time and tell me how easy it would be to bear that weight. Then you'll see that pity would be better than scorn here."

The rough estimates already brought Azetla to nearly five thousand lost in total. He had no doubt that, before the night was through, he would have far surpassed that ancient King's tally. In the story, the King repented, listened to the prophets, and won his next battle handily. But in the wake of victory, he promptly succumbed to the temptations of prostitutes and idolatry. He died of a wasting disease. Reading the story as a direct guide was not exactly helpful.

Azetla was braced for the blow. To hear the number climb and climb and climb.

But he had not braced hard enough for the single tick mark that met him.

"He's here!" someone shouted as they passed the central camp. "The Commander is back!"

Lieutenant Colonel Truillon jogged briskly over to Azetla.

"You should come to the Taya's tent, before it's too late. It's Lead Sergeant Radabe, sir..."

Blank-minded, Azetla felt Tzal pull Barra's reins slowly, gently out of his hands. Then the words coalesced within him. He flew to the tent. And why, why was his hand so tightly gripping his hilt? Was there some enemy in that tent he might defeat? What on earth did he think he could possibly do?

Mali let Azetla in, but he was the only one, for the tent was overflowing with men whose chances were little to none. Tzal and Sarrez were told to remain outside. The tent seethed with too much warmth from too many bodies, boiling water, and canopied fires. Blood, anise, urine, filth; the scent was sickening. Soon the rancid smell of infection would be added to it.

A weary, red-eyed Mali silently pointed to the pallet where Joseph lay looking like death itself. Though it was clearly no help to her or to anyone, Mali permitted Azetla to kneel down in the scant space between Joseph and another dying man.

Azetla stared at Joseph in complete silence, his fingers clenched tightly against himself, his mind searching for an option. A reparation.

Joseph still breathed. But one glance at the signs of cracked ribs, and the wound in his leg as Mali replaced the bandage—these told Azetla all he needed to know. Men did not often survive such things. Mali washed the wounds with water and arak a third time, but Azetla could see in her eyes that it was only to prove to him that she had done everything in her meager power. She expected nothing, and it would be wise for Azetla to expect nothing as well.

Joseph's forehead and jaw were bruised, horrifically swollen, his lips dark gray. He scarcely looked like the man Azetla knew—the man who had taken him roughly, but kindly, by the collar, tolerated him when no one else would, treated him like family in ways both good and bad, calling him jackal for a cruel tease but never letting the others call him that if it was in his power to stop them.

He stayed next to Joseph much longer than he ought to have. Mali graciously ignored his useless presence inside the chaotic, blood-filled tent.

God of Masheva, don't let his death be on my hands, he mouthed in Mashevi. *Don't let his death be at all.*

There was no one to snap at his face and tell him not to carry the blame. Nor would he have listened if they had. His was the final responsibility for every single death. Today. Tomorrow. And until it was ended.

47

Tzal left the tented hut that belonged to Naima's family with an odd, bruised feeling all over her face, as if she'd been beaten to a pulp by a steady fist. She kept palpating her nose and jaw and cheeks, searching for the explanation, the source of the bruise, the taut feeling that went from skin to bone. She desperately needed sleep.

Naima's family had surprised and confused her.

After stepping away, leaving Azetla to his hopeless vigil, Tzal had sluggishly climbed up to Naima's village—those several little huts clustered on a shot of flat ground in one of the eastern shelves—and given the news.

It was all done properly. She did not cross the threshold of their door—she was not allowed to—but merely put knees and forehead to the ground, speaking the formal words preparing one for a message of grief. Then she lifted her head and told them that their daughter's husband, the honored nephew of the great Rokh Imal Bin-Zari, had been killed in battle.

Naima's father looked up at the night sky, breathing out a ragged sigh. He had always seemed to feel two ways about his daughter's marriage. A grave disappointment for her to marry outside the tribe.

An honor for her to marry into so powerful a family. What he truly thought of Rahummi, Tzal did not know.

Naima's mother, on the other hand, looked down at Tzal, who remained on her knees, waiting for acknowledgment and dismissal. The woman's eyes glazed with tears, but they held fast to Tzal's face for a long time. Tzal wondered, at first, if Naima's mother blamed her and was angry.

But she said, "Come in, Shihrayan."

"In?"

"Yes. In. Wash the blood and tar. Tell us how it was. And then," Naima's mother drew Tzal upward with a jarringly gentle hand, "tell us how it will be."

Tzal began by telling them of Rahummi's excellence and bravery and leadership. She assumed these were the sorts of things they wanted to hear. They gave her bread to eat and wine to drink as she worked, worked, worked the tar out of her hair and skin. Naima's mother nudged her with a word here and a word there, but for the most part, she merely listened. The children played a tossing game, which frequently resulted in errant red balls of cloth bouncing lightly off Tzal's back or arms. When they were chastened, Tzal said, "No, let them play. I don't mind."

Why did she talk on so long? About Rahummi and Naima. About Inaya. About her first months at Bir Herash, both she and Rahummi so young and so far from home. Tzal had pretended to know everything and made herself his guide. And it worked. He followed her everywhere. Took her side. Until he didn't, of course. Until he couldn't possibly.

She never did tell them what was to come, though.

Because she did not truly know.

All she could think as she walked down the path in the deepening night was that they must have cherished Rahummi more than she thought in order to let a Shihrayan pass over their threshold like that.

Something he would have been glad to know, but of which he had never been quite sure.

The bruised feeling pounded through her jaw and eyes. And the wine feeling was mucking up her head. She had to step very carefully.

When the headquarters tent came into view she stopped. Hesitated.

Around Azetla, everything was as plain as anything ever came for her. Exquisitely unvarnished. The weight of careful curation was removed from nearly all her words. So many mannerisms and postures simply slid off like ragged clothing, and she had grown to like that bare feeling. But she wasn't sure how she would like it tonight.

And she doubted whether she had the least capacity for his grief. She would not even know what to do.

She ran her fingers over her bare wrist with agitation. Then walked into the tent.

He was bent over his makeshift desk, reed pen lodged in his left hand, hovering aimlessly over a ledger. She crossed the tent and looked over his shoulder, but the cutting of reed paper was blank.

"What are you doing?" she said.

He looked up at her, staring a while as if she was not entirely in focus.

"I'm not even sure," he said quietly. "I've always made a record after a battle."

She didn't want to say anything. But she thought it best to get it over with.

"Did Joseph—"

"No." Azetla stood up. "Not yet."

He clapped his hand on her shoulder like he might have to any of his tackmen, somewhat thoughtlessly. But then he did a decidedly Black Wren gesture. He cupped the back of her neck and brought her forehead to his in the same warm, rough way that she had seen him do to Sarrez after sparring, or Joseph after a skirmish. Only he left his head there, resting, as if it was too heavy a thing to hold up.

This too seemed to be done thoughtlessly. But that was what made it almost unbearable to her. The casual depth of it smarted against her skin. It made the bruised feeling infinitely worse. She had already endured too much of being handled this way tonight. Call it pity. Or warmth. Or something else. This vessel of hers was not made for it, could not carry it; it was going to crack at even one more drop.

She could by no means bring herself to lift her hand and mirror the gesture the way his brothers-in-arms did, though he didn't seem to care much about that. He simply lingered there, taking from her a comfort she didn't know how to give. Then he lifted his head, looking at her with steady, solemn eyes.

"Mali says it will take longer than she initially thought. Maybe another day or two," he said.

Tzal sighed. "That always makes it harder."

His hand still rested firm at the back of her neck, like the grip that an old man keeps on his staff—he was still trying to draw succor from this bone-dry well. She ought to remind him that he was liable to gash his hand and fall if he leaned too hard on her. Ask Imal. Ask Everson. Ask anyone.

No one is supposed to take the whole brick of salt, you know. Just a scraping. Otherwise all is ruined. Impossible to swallow. Parching the throat. Desecrating the soil. *Don't you know that, Azetla?*

"Tzal, I leave for Masheva in the morning," he said.

"I know."

"I mean for you to come with me."

Tzal narrowed her eyes and shook her head.

"Why? I can only guide you as far as the hill country and it's not as though you'll need my tongue for anything."

Azetla pressed his lips together and took his time drawing out the next words.

"I will, actually. In Masheva, it won't be..." He closed his eyes in seeming frustration. "It is not safe for me there. There's a good chance I'm in danger the moment I enter Rinayim and I can't turn my back to anyone, or anything. You speak Mashevi. Enough to listen, keep watch, move around, and—" He paused with a grimace.

"Pretend to be things that I'm not?" She gave a bleak smile.

That made him flinch a little, but he nodded firmly. He looked like a beaten man all of a sudden. As if some blow had landed against him—one that made him think he just might not get up this time. Was it Joseph that made him sink like this? Or was it Masheva itself?

Tzal looked at the wooden lion's head hanging against Azetla's chest. It had a smear of dried blood on it. Maybe Joseph's. Maybe an enemy's. She slipped her fingers softly beneath the leather cord along his neck and drew down till the rough bit of carving sat in her hand.

"Azetla, I—"

"My name is not Azetla."

The words fell out of his mouth as if they'd been shoved. Then he swallowed hard.

Tzal pressed her thumb over the cedar mouth of the lion, letting the words slide lightly off her back. It certainly wasn't the sort of thing that could surprise or deter her.

"I don't really care," she said, concentrating on the eyes of the lion, barely detectable for all the wear of years and Azetla's worrying hand.

"Tzal, look at me."

She set her jaw with nameless frustration and looked up at him.

"My name is Samuel Aver."

Tzal narrowed her eyes. She knew what that name was. He had talked about it before. With considerable disdain, in fact. "That's the infamous name your King gave to his son? I thought you said it causes too much trouble. Why wouldn't you use something else?"

"I can't," he said. His voice was rough. Then it cracked. "It's all I have."

The understanding she didn't want coursed inexorably across her skin and lodged in her chest. She dropped the lion's head. Stepped back. And with a cold, careful eye, she began to examine the man in front of her. Examine everything around him. His maps and ledgers. His satchel and inks.

The sagam at her side.

She had to draw a new map. Right now. Almost from scratch.

"Tzal—"

She made his Mashevi gesture for silence with her right hand. He pressed his lips closed.

"It's not just a tactic," she said slowly.

"It's my given name, Tzal," he said with slow emphasis on each Mashevi word. "And the only reason I'll be able to do all I've said I would do."

"But also the reason you need someone to watch your back."

"Yes."

Tzal squared herself to the task of seeing the terrain in front of her.

"So." She gestured eastward. "This was always the end, never just the means."

"It's both, and I'm sure you can see why."

She laughed and shook her head. "Well good job, Mashevi. You're a better liar than I ever was."

The muscles in his jaw went taut. He did not like that. But he took it.

"Have you told—"

"You're the only one I've told. I'll speak to Sarrez in the morning. God only knows what he'll say, but I'd rather him hear it from me. And Joseph..." He shook his head.

Tzal folded her arms. She needed to get her head around this quickly, lest she lose her footing.

"So your people are...the bait," she said thoughtfully. A cold wind shot through her. "*You* are the bait."

Each word from her seemed to reach him like a lash, which he endured in stiff silence.

"Yes. And no. It's more complicated than that. It's more complicated than I ever wanted it to be. But I will do what I said I would do. For them—" he gestured over the camp, his voice grim and steady—"and for them—" he looked eastward. "If I fail one, I fail both. Utterly."

The night watch called out the hour. The movement and rustle of camp filled the strange, strange silence in the headquarters tent. The truth was, Tzal simply could not see the terrain in front of her clearly. But she was going to walk it, even if she had to feel her way by hand in the pitch dark. She doubted whether she was capable of being anything other than the enemy of an enemy on Azetla's behalf. She had never once succeeded in it for anyone, try as she might.

But he kept taking the risk of her. So she would keep taking the risk of him.

"Samuel Aver," she said, tasting the name, raising it up to measure it against him.

The look on Azetla's face when the name came out of her mouth was something to behold. Like she'd struck him with an open hand, and then, after, like he was pretty well drunk.

"I'm not going to call you that, Azetla," she added.

He almost smiled.

"Tzal, I don't care what you call me," he said. "Just now Samuel Aver is nothing but the absent son of a useless king—some lofty, imagined thing, conjured to control the people. Some think I'm dead, others think I've gone mad, and the rest hope I'm some holy symbol I have tried and failed to be. But to you, I'm still Azetla. Alive, real, and in my right mind. You're not obliged to me in any way—"

"No, I'm not," she said coolly.

"—but I mean for us to leave at sunrise."

EPILOGUE

All Aadin needed to do to find her was follow the trail of blood. Follow the stories of a jackal and a jinn. To flock, like any local Trekoan or Makar, to this army that was riving the world apart.

And all he needed to do was go beyond the tiny village of Kitzlat.

His feet dreaded those fatal steps. Not only because he had never taken them, but because he knew he was being followed. By his own kind. The Usarin's men. He felt the shadows behind him. He knew their ways and movement.

Aadin was the scent. She was the prey. And they would track him to her.

They wanted to leave no chance. They were willing to risk their souls to destroy hers. Because, with this next stride, Aadin led them out where no Shihrayan who still belonged to their people had ever, ever been.

He would certainly get to her first. But there was no comfort in that.

ACKNOWLEDGEMENTS

Thank you Lottie for your sharp editor's eye and your encouraging words.

I can never say thank you too many times to Laura who has strengthened and elevated this story with her wise critiques and heartfelt enthusiasm. Everyone should be so lucky as to have a friend like her.

I am forever grateful to my husband who has invested so much time and effort into the publication process, using his strengths in areas where I am weak, and supporting me without fail.

An enormous thanks to all my friends and family who gave their support, who encouraged me, who read a book they wouldn't usually read, or who simply celebrated the book's existence. You brought me such joy.

Lastly, I want to thank all the readers who took a chance on a debut indie author. Thank you. Thank you so much.

J.L. Odom hails from Oklahoma. After a five year stint in the Marine Corps as an Arabic linguist, she graduated from George Washington University with a degree in International Affairs with an emphasis on Conflict and Security. She lives with her husband and five children wherever it is that the U.S. Army happens to send them. Her hobbies include running, jiu jitsu, and cooking to feed a crowd. She can be found online at jlodomauthor.com.

www.ingramcontent.com/pod-product-compliance
Lightning Source LLC
Chambersburg PA
CBHW022013300726
48970CB00003B/865